By Aline Templeton

Evil for Evil

Bad Blood

EVIL FOR EVIL

ALINE TEMPLETON

Allison & Busby Limited
12 Fitzroy Mews
London W1T 6DW
www.allisonandbusby.com

First published in Great Britain by Allison & Busby in 2012.
This paperback edition published by Allison & Busby in 2013.

A CIP catalogue record for this book is available from
the British Library.

10 9 8 7 6 5 4 3 2 1

ISBN 978-0-7490-1470-4

Typeset in 10/15 pt Sabon by
Allison & Busby Ltd.

The paper used for this Allison & Busby publication
has been produced from trees that have been legally sourced
from well-managed and credibly certified forests.

Printed and bound by
CPI Group (UK) Ltd, Croydon, CR0 4YY

For Xander with fondest love

'So we beat on, boats against the current, borne back ceaselessly into the past.'

– F. Scott Fitzgerald

I think I'll go mad if I can't confess my guilt. But whenever I've tried to speak about it, the terrible pain from the acid that rises in my throat takes away the breath to form the words. My hand's cramping now just thinking about writing it down, but for my sanity I have to try, one agonising page at a time. If I'm only writing it for me, not to show to anyone, perhaps I can do it – but even so I'm scared, knowing what it'll cost me to live through it again. I've got to get it out of my head, tip it out into written words. Then burn the paper, destroy the memory? I wish – oh, I wish! But could it give me any relief, when there's no chance of forgiveness? I can only try . . .

He came from the sea, and in my nightmares he's dripping wet, draped in fronds of seaweed and with shells crunching under his feet. His eyes, glinting in the dark, are fish eyes, glassy and blank, and the hand he's holding over my sister's mouth – or my own mouth, sometimes, since in my dreams I am often both of us at once – has glittering scales. I'm paralysed; I can't do anything, even scream as he carries her – me – across the room to the door and opens it on unimaginable horror.

Then I wake up in a sweat of terror. And I always wonder: how much of that is dream, and how much memory?

CHAPTER ONE

The island. He stood at the window in the half-dark, looking out to where it lay in the bay, no more than a shape in the early mists.

The landscape was all grey: dark-grey land below his window, then smooth pale-grey sea and sky which had just a hint of silver there in the east where light was dawning.

It was so near! Only five hundred yards away in distance, but in reality . . . He chewed his lip in frustration. It might be all grey, but what he was seeing was gold, gold, among the cold, ancient stones.

The island. She turned in her sleep, crying out, but only a muttered groan emerged. She started awake when his hand touched her shoulder.

'All right?' he said, half asleep himself.

'Fine. Sorry.'

She waited for his breathing to become regular then slipped out of bed in the darkened room. She dared not risk going back to sleep again.

The island. She watched the light strengthen as she lay in bed, looking out at it through the window whose curtains were never closed.

Its outline was becoming clearer as the early mist lifted to hang in the tops of the trees at the blunt seaward end; from there it sloped down to a tail of rocks, covered by the incoming tide. Its image was etched in her mind and she could see it even when her eyes were shut.

Tears gathered, gathered and silently spilt over. She made no attempt to wipe them away as they trickled down the side of her face and soaked the pillow. It was always hardest in the morning when she woke from sleep and remembered with a fresh shock of despair the tiny grave that lay over there across the water.

The island. He glanced at it as he passed in his boat, on his way out to check the pots for crab and lobster. Just another of the Isles of Fleet – Ardwall, Murray, Barlocco and this one, Lovatt, though the locals knew it by its old name, Tascadan. He didn't like thinking about it, and mostly he succeeded. But recently . . .

He grimaced slightly, then headed out into the bay.

The island. She was there, in her dreams, the peace weaving magic around her, the only sounds whispering waves and the soft rustle of a gentle breeze shivering the leaves on the trees. She walked on soft turf, her feet barely touching its surface, and as she went towards the wood a dappled fawn stepped out of the shadows, unafraid, and walked beside her. She stroked its soft ears and smiled in her sleep.

The island. The swelling tide rose into the little cave on the seaward side, the waves sweeping round in the confined space, scouring away at its walls, breaking below one of the rocky shelves up at the back. Only at the highest tides could the spray reach it, to continue the cleansing work on the skeleton that lay there, leg and arm bones still shackled to the rock.

* * *

It was a milk-opal morning now: the sea still, pearly, shot with sparks of fire from the sunrise; the sky palest blue, with low clouds tinged pink and apricot. The bulk of the island was still shadowy in the dawn light.

The man swimming from there to the shore in an arrowhead of spreading ripples, his dark head sleek as a seal's, powered his way across the shallow channel to the sandy bay. Above, on the springy turf beside a tangle of bracken and briars, his dog watched him.

Beside the little jetty where a couple of boats and a flat barge were moored he waded ashore naked, brushing water from his shoulders and arms and shivering in the morning chill. His last swim of the year, he decided. Though the forecast was for a few more days of this golden September, there had been a vicious hint of autumn in the water temperature this morning.

The dog bounded to his side and he fondled its thick ruff, then picked up a towelling robe from the jetty, rubbing his dark hair with it and wiping his face before he shrugged it on. The smooth, plastic feel of the burn tissue under his right eye gave him the usual tiny shock of distaste. He tied the belt round him then stood looking towards Lovatt Island. His island.

The air seemed full of memories today. It had been a morning just like this three years ago when Matt Lovatt had taken his first swim across the narrow strip of water that isolated Lovatt Island except at low tides. Then, though, it had been late spring, the perfect weather an early promise of summer; today the trees in the wood on the island were showing red and russet, the bracken was brown and dying and the later sunrise spoke of the journey into long, dark nights, of endings not beginnings.

Melissa had been sitting on the jetty like a mermaid on a rock with her long brown wavy hair. She was singing, and as he came out of the water he saw the round heads of two or three seals bobbing about in the bay.

11

She smiled over her shoulder but didn't stop singing: '*I am a man upon the land, I am a silkie in the sea . . .*'

The seals turned their great mild eyes on her, then when she finished the plaintive ballad submerged again with breathy sighs and a whirl of bubbles.

Lissa's own eyes were lit with happiness. 'I didn't believe it, you know. I thought it was just a pretty myth, that they liked music. Oh Matt, this is an enchanted place! It's paradise – I could be happy here.'

He had agreed, laughing at her shining face. It was all he had hoped for, but even then he had misgivings. Lissa was so volatile, so fragile! He had seen that unhealthy excitement before, that enthusiasm so quickly quenched by cold reality. Happiness wasn't a natural state for either of them.

And it didn't take long for the serpent to show itself in Paradise: a crude daubing in whitewash on a wall saying, 'White settlers go home'. They had shrunk into themselves, like snails at a sprinkling of salt; they were oversensitive, perhaps, seeing general hostility in places where there might only be shyness or indifference, but the petty persecutions left them with little will to struggle for local acceptance.

Paradise turned to purgatory. The tragedy of a stillborn child, now in his little grave on the island, might have brought them together but instead drove them into separate grief. When they did talk, the words seemed weighted with too much significance, and the mourning silence spread and spread until there was nothing between them any more but echoing space. Matt could see the destructive darkness drawing closer and closer around her once more, and this time he could only watch, powerless.

Kerr Brodie's arrival had been a relief. There were, to quote, three people in their marriage now, but if it hadn't been for him there would have been no marriage at all. For all that stresses were inevitable in any relationship involving three people, they could have conversation and even laughter over the kitchen table, before they went to their separate rooms to wrestle with their individual demons.

The dog, digging aimlessly in the sand, grew bored and loped over to its master, looking up at him expectantly.

'Yes, I want breakfast too,' Matt said, shoving his feet into broken-backed deck shoes and heading off up the hill.

He wasn't looking forward to the day. In fact, he decided, he'd take off somewhere till it was all over, go for a long walk. He'd agreed to the TV interview after they'd somehow heard about his rehab idea but he wasn't going to appear himself, like some sort of freak show. He was unconsciously fingering the disfigured side of his face as he let himself in through the gate to Lovatt's Farm.

The woman talking to camera was standing in front of a backdrop that looked as if it had come straight out of the VisitScotland Galloway tourist brochure. The sky was blue with dinky fluffy clouds, just like it should be, the grass was implausibly green and out in Wigtown Bay the Isles of Fleet looked as if they were auditioning for the precious-jewels-set-in-a-silver-sea cameo part.

A stocky grey-haired man, with soldierly bearing but an awkward, limping gait walked beside the reporter, saying, 'So Major Matt and I discussed it and felt that what this place had done for me, it could do for others.' He had a strong Glasgow accent.

The camera swung to a square-faced young woman with tousled light-brown hair, smiling as she stroked a red deer hind that was nuzzling her with what came across to the viewers as affection rather than greed for the carrot she was holding out of shot. Then it closed in again on the reporter.

'So here on the deer farm, amid all this tranquil beauty, courtesy of Major Matt Lovatt – and with Dancer's help, of course,' she smiled as the camera panned back to the deer, nudging impatiently now, 'troubled former soldiers like Christie here can find peace, and healing for the wounds, visible or invisible, which have poisoned their lives.

'Carla Brewer, *News at Six*, Innellan, Galloway, south-west Scotland.'

Eddie Tindall was studying his wife, under cover of reading his evening paper. Even after eight years, she still seemed a marvel to him and when they were in the same room his eyes were irresistibly drawn to her. He knew she hated being watched, though, so he had developed a range of subterfuges: a mannerism of putting his hand to his forehead to shade his eyes, looking up under his brows with his head bent over paperwork or, as now, pretending to read a newspaper.

The Six O'Clock News was showing on a huge plasma screen above the marble fireplace of their Salford Exchange Quay penthouse. The polished floor was honey-gold, the soft leather sofas were biscuit colour and the most expensive interior designer around had used a palette of warm, creamy shades for the paintwork with a feature wall of glowing bronze and gold wallpaper. Even Eddie had blinked at the cost of that wall.

He had bought the flat for Elena three years ago. They had been living until then in the house where he and his ex-wife had brought up their family, still unchanged from the day Debra and his son and daughter had left, hurt and angry, for a new life in London. Naturally, he'd told Elena she could gut the place if she liked, but she hadn't liked – nor even, apparently, cared that nothing in it was her choice.

Her indifference began to bother him. Eddie had no confidence in his hold on her heart and without material things she cherished to anchor her, she might just walk out of his life as randomly as she had come into it. Choice, too, was personality given concrete form and he had offered her the Exchange Quay flat as a blank canvas, in hope if not expectation that her decisions would give him an insight into the mystery that was Elena, even after all these years. If he understood her better, he might obsess about her less.

Elena's one decision had been the designer, picking him, Eddie guessed sadly, purely on the basis of his reputation among the Salford ladies who lunched – you couldn't call them Elena's friends – and giving him a completely free hand. Looking round the room, Eddie could not see a single object she had chosen herself.

She was sitting watching the news. Elena never fidgeted; she had a quality of stillness which to Eddie seemed to permeate the room, so that coming back from a bruising day he felt his cares slipping away as he stepped into the pool of tranquillity she created. Just at this moment, though, he noticed tension.

Not that it was obvious. Her slate-blue eyes didn't blink, her manicured hands lay folded in her lap, her long, slim legs in the well-tailored black trousers were crossed, just as they had been five minutes before. But there was a tiny pulse flicking just at the corner of her eye and now she put up her hand to try to quieten it.

She turned her head, as if she had felt his eyes upon her. Eddie leant forward hastily to pick up the remote control as the music for the end of the news came on, switched it off and stood up.

'Drink, doll?'

'Please.' Elena smiled up at him and he smiled back, his heart as always skipping a beat at her loveliness.

He had bought it all, of course – the neat, tip-tilted nose, the shining caramel bob with its subtle highlights, the white, perfectly aligned teeth. But those had been her decision, not his; he had seen beauty in the Elena he had first met as one of her clients, when the hair was peroxide and stringy and those eyes had looked too big for her pinched face and had bruised-looking shadows beneath.

She had been suspicious as some little feral cat, happier in the familiar gutter than with the promise of a silk cushion and a saucer of cream, because in her experience any change was a threat. Eddie had bought hours and hours of her time, taking

15

her out to feed her, to talk to her, to amuse her, until at last she trusted him – as much as she ever would trust anyone.

He would never know just what had at last brought her to agree to marry him – the ugly death of another prostitute, perhaps. In a rare, treasured moment of closeness, she had quoted a favourite story from her childhood, the childhood she would never discuss: '*I am the cat who walks by himself and all places are alike to me.*' She was that way still.

The thirties drinks cabinet had a mirrored interior and as Eddie got out the triangular glasses to make vodka Martinis he caught sight of himself: a balding middle-aged man with a roll of fat forming round his neck and a face like Les Dawson on an off day. How could someone like Elena love that?

She never said she did, and he never asked her. It was enough that she was there, that she was his. She had cost him his marriage and his children, who had not spoken to him for ten years. But if her smiles were bought, they were sweet even at that price.

He brought Elena a glass. She was pressing her cheek again, and he felt a sense of disquiet. He needn't bother asking her what was upsetting her; she would laugh and say it was nothing. But he would be watching nervously to see if the wide cuff bangles that covered her wrists would appear again.

The Smugglers Inn was quiet this early on a Friday evening. Most of the visitors had gone, though the belated apology of a mellow September after a disappointing summer was drawing back some owners of the many chalets and caravans tucked into the rising ground above Fleet Bay for the weekend. The sun was warm enough during the day, but the evenings had a chill which was already bringing autumn livery to the trees, and lengthening nights were a reminder that the decline into the long dark winter had begun.

The inn, once the Innellan Arms, had been rechristened by a

romantic previous owner to reflect the time when excisemen like Robert Burns – that champion of freedom and whisky – policed the Solway Firth where the free traders brought in goods from the Isle of Man.

The little village of Innellan, looking out over Fleet Bay towards the islands, was at the end of a narrow road: no more than a couple of dozen houses, some outlying farms and cottages, an abandoned church and a graveyard. Georgia Stanley, the licensee, claimed the Smugglers was a local where the dead outnumbered the living by ten to one.

She was here because she'd fallen in love. She and Harry both had, seduced by Innellan's beauty. Each year after their fortnight in a caravan it became harder to go back to Walsall until they started asking themselves why they should. Then the Smugglers came up for sale with a price that made them burst out laughing, and they couldn't wait to begin the adventure.

Then Harry had died. Who dies, without warning, at forty? It was hardly his fault, but in some complicated way Georgia sort of blamed him that here she was, alone, five years older and in an unsaleable property, with the shadows lengthening towards another long winter. They'd never seen winter here, from their caravan.

Not that she'd go back to Walsall – never! But Kirkcudbright, now – with its pretty houses and the bustle of its shops and friendly folk who smiled and said hello; unlike this weird, secretive little place with its mysterious alliances and feuds going back generations, so as an incomer you kept putting your foot in it because no one would tell you who was on speaking terms and who wasn't. She'd learnt tact the hard way, and she was tolerated now – though of course you couldn't expect to be accepted until you'd had your own fifty-year feud.

Not that it would be hard to start one. It would be a luxury not to have to be pleasant to some people, but luxuries had no place in Georgia's life now. She sometimes thought her tongue must be scarred from keeping it between her teeth, but she always managed to smile. As long as the pub was a going concern, there might be a bedazzled summer visitor who was as naive as they had been, and then she'd be out of here. That dream kept her going when each night she came through from the adjoining house to open up.

Georgia took a pride in polishing the mahogany bar counter and brass fittings and the wooden floor, hollowed with the traffic of years. She kept a fire burning in the cast-iron fireplace, even in summer, since the white building with thick walls and small windows was always cool. Soon she'd be drawing the red curtains and switching on red-shaded lamps; the pub looked at its cosy best during the dreary winter months, though six customers then was a busy evening. Once the nights drew in and everyone retreated into their houses, she barely saw her neighbours. It was, well, creepy.

Tonight, though, it was cheerful enough, with low sun streaming in and the back door open to the view and the soft sea air. Georgia was polishing glasses and watching *The Six O'Clock News* on the TV at the end of the bar. They'd all been agog when the film team arrived at Lovatt's Farm and she was expecting a gossiping influx later. At the moment, though, there were only two regulars sitting up at the bar and a couple wearing shorts and hiking boots drinking lager at a table.

Derek Sorley made small, explosive noises all through the item, like a kettle that might blow its lid off once it built up steam. He was one of Georgia's leading feud candidates: rat-faced, bald at the front with straggling grey hair at the back caught into a ponytail, an unfortunate style suggesting the whole lot was gradually sliding off backwards.

Sometimes she could almost see a miasma of spite and envy around him. He had a grudge against anyone with 'advantages', which seemed to mean anyone who hadn't lost several jobs through rudeness and idleness as he had, to her certain knowledge. Still, he was good for a couple of pints every evening, and Georgia couldn't afford to be choosy.

When the report finished, Sorley burst out, 'Oh, great! And how did St Matt arrange that little piece of PR? Our wounded hero, healing "our boys" – and girls too, you notice. Could be on to a good thing there! Wonder how Mrs Matt feels about his brave little soldier?' He gave an unpleasant snigger. 'And what chance now of an enforcement order for access to the island? He's only to say they need peace and quiet to recover and he'll have everyone sobbing. Oh, I never said he was stupid!

'Right to Roam – that's a joke! Bloody government promises access all over Scotland, but they just roll over for the landlords.'

Georgia had no special brief for Matt Lovatt. Bit of a moody sod, and she could count the number of times he'd come in here on one hand – but then, the locals had hardly made him welcome after he'd refused Steve Donaldson a tenancy agreement so he could farm himself. Pub etiquette meant a non-committal response, but she heard herself saying, 'Well – he's got fallow deer there. They're shyer than the red deer – maybe they'd panic if tourists went tramping around.'

The man at the other end of the bar had watched without comment. Cal Findlay had a prawn boat working out of Kirkcudbright, but lived here with his mother in an isolated croft house on the hill behind the village. He came in most evenings, but sat mainly in silence, his eyes – so dark that they looked almost black – watching with what looked like a cynical contempt for more sociable beings. She rather fancied him, actually, but he'd never shown any interest.

Now Findlay said coldly, 'You've got it in for him because he caught you with a metal detector and threw you off his island.'

Sorley bridled, his face turning red. 'You're a liar!'

Findlay, infuriatingly, did not answer, only raising one eyebrow and taking another sip of his whisky.

Sorley began to swear at him, but Georgia cut in crisply.

'I don't have language like that in my pub, Derek. There's the lifeboat box – that'll be two pounds.'

He opened his mouth to argue, but a steely look from her changed his mind. He put the money in the box with a bad grace, getting to his feet and downing the rest of his pint.

'You could ask *him*,' Sorley pointed a shaking finger, 'who tipped Lovatt off when I was just taking a wee walk on land that by rights belongs to every Scot?'

Findlay didn't respond. He went back to watching the news impassively as Sorley stormed out, though Georgia could swear he wasn't hearing a word of it.

The small TV in the corner of the Mains of Craigie kitchen was tuned to the news, but neither Janet Laird nor Catriona Fleming was watching it.

Janet was making skirlie, gently cooking onions and oatmeal to go with the chicken already roasting in the Aga – one of their own plump birds. In her basket beside it, Meg the collie was giving small sighing whines, tormented by the delicious smell.

Cat was peeling potatoes. She was eighteen now, strikingly attractive with fair hair and blue eyes like her father and her mother's long, slim legs. She looked dubiously at what she had prepared.

'Do you think that'll be enough, Gran?'

Janet Laird was in her seventies, but she was still active and cheerful even if her brown eyes were a little faded and her shoulders more stooped. She was as busy as ever with her good causes, one of which was ensuring her daughter Marjory's culinary inadequacies did not deprive her family of good Scots home cooking. Together with Karolina, the wife of Rafael who worked the farm with Bill, she saw to it that household chores didn't add more stress to her daughter's already stressful job.

Janet assessed the pile of potatoes. 'You'd better do a few

more, pet. You know Cammie's just a wee terror when it comes to roast tatties.'

'Only you could describe Cammie as a "wee" anything,' Cat protested. Her brother Cameron, at sixteen, had reached six foot two and showed no signs of stopping. 'He's just a greedy pig.'

'Och, he needs to keep his strength up with all that rugby training. What time's he back tonight?'

'About seven. And Mum said she wouldn't be late – if you can believe her.'

Going back to her task Cat sighed. It was somehow terribly important that all the family should be together tonight. She'd chosen her favourite supper – creamy cauliflower soup, roast chicken and Gran's special lemon meringue pie – because tomorrow she was leaving home. Her stomach gave a nervous jump at the thought.

Oh, she was up for it, excited about her place at Glasgow Uni to read veterinary science, and her boyfriend Will Irvine was there already in his second year studying medicine. They'd be together in the same place at last – she'd hardly seen him this summer, when he'd been working as a hospital porter in Glasgow.

Oh, it would be great! Living in the big city instead of a boring backwater would be brilliant.

But this evening Cat felt shaky. She couldn't imagine opening her eyes in the morning in a room without any of the evidence of her life so far – stuffed animals she couldn't quite bear to give to the church jumble sale, children's books she still reread sometimes, the wall of photos of everything from her thirteenth birthday party to the school prom in June. Without her past, among strangers, she could become someone totally, excitingly different – or be utterly overwhelmed and lost. Tonight she was favouring lost.

The phone rang and was answered before Cat could dry her hands to pick it up. Her voice was flat as she said, 'I bet you anything that's Mum, saying she's held up.'

'Not necessarily, dear,' Janet said, but without conviction, and a couple of minutes later Bill Fleming appeared.

He was a big, solidly built man, fresh-complexioned, with fair hair imperceptibly going grey and thinning as his waistline expanded, but his eyes were still as blue as his daughter's.

As the women turned questioning looks on him, he pulled a face. 'Yeah, I'm afraid so. That was Mum.'

'Oh, don't tell me. She's delayed. As usual.'

'She's really upset, Cat,' Bill defended his wife. 'She says just to go ahead without her.'

Cat looked at him sharply. 'Go ahead without her? You mean she won't be back for supper?'

'Seems unlikely, apparently. You know how it is, love – she's no option. It's just the job.'

'Oh, I know all right! The rotten job – the rotten, rotten job!' Cat felt humiliating tears springing to her eyes. 'I'm . . . I'm just going to do some more packing.'

She hurried out and up the stairs. Big Ted, her comfort in childhood miseries, still sat on a chair beside her bed; she grabbed him, burying her face in his worn pile, and flung herself down to sob.

The bar, in one of Glasgow's seedier backstreets, was run-down and unappealing. The paintwork bore the scars of pub brawls and the frosted glass of the dirty windows still had the name of a long-forgotten brewer etched into it. Smoke wafted in from banished drinkers clustered round the open door and its clientele was almost entirely male. It was doing good business this evening and already there were pools of spilt beer on the floor.

The TV on the wall, ignored except for football, was showing the news, barely audible above the raucous voices. The only person looking at it even idly was a gaunt young man on his own, ill-shaven and in scruffy clothes that looked as if he might have slept in them. He was taking sips of the cheapest lager on the slate as if seeing how long he could spin it out.

When the item from Galloway came on he suddenly sat up, stared, then got off his stool and pushed through to the end of the bar where he could hear. He listened with painful attention and when it finished turned to the barman.

'Hey, pal! Got a pen?'

The barman glanced round, then found one by the till. 'There you are, mate. OK?'

'Cheers.'

The young man drained his glass in two gulps, wrote something on the palm of his hand, put the pen back and hurried out.

The sun was going down now, meeting the golden path it had made across the still waters of Wigtown Bay. As the little boat with its outboard motor chugged across on the seaward side of the Isles of Fleet, ripples shivered the reflection into splinters of light, but the glories of the autumn sunset were wasted on its occupants.

The boy steering was a tow-headed lad of thirteen, his frame bulking up into adolescence already. The glow on his face came only partly from an afternoon of sun and sea; there was also satisfaction at the blue-silver mackerel in the bottom of the boat beside the fishing tackle. Reluctant to see the day end, he throttled back the engine and called to his companion.

'Here, Jamie! How about we check out the cave there? The tide's right.'

They were passing near the western shore of Lovatt Island and he was pointing towards a small sea cave, halfway down its length. There was warm light still on the cliff, just, but it was fading fast and the cave mouth looked black and forbidding.

Jamie, younger, slighter, dark and with a sensitive face, covered his shiver with a look at his watch. 'Naw,' he said. 'Dad said to be back at seven or he'd kill me. It's near enough eight already.'

'So he'll kill you anyway,' Craig pointed out with pitiless logic. 'It'll only take a minute. There were smugglers used these caves.' He leant forward to open the throttle.

Suddenly, the sun was gone. The cliffs were grey not gold and shadows were gathering in the rock clefts.

Jamie couldn't conceal a shudder this time. 'It's . . . it's too dark,' he muttered. 'We'd not see anything.'

Craig eyed him with contempt. 'There's a torch in the locker. You're just feart!'

'No, I'm not. Well . . . it's haunted. You shouldn't go on the island at night.'

Unimpressed, Craig said, 'Oh aye – ghosts! That'll be right. Oooooh!' He waved his hands, waggling his fingers.

But Jamie was stubborn. 'There is. My mum told me – crying and wailing. Heard it herself, years ago. She wouldn't go near it if you paid her.'

It suddenly seemed much colder. The boat rocked on a rippling wave, and Craig, unsettled by his friend's nervousness, glanced at the cave, a gaping darkness now.

'Trying to wind you up, that's all,' he said, but he sounded uncertain.

'But I heard it too. That's how I know. I was out one night a while ago, down on the shore, when it was like this, just getting dark, and I heard it – screams and groans and stuff. And you know there's a *dead baby* on the island.'

It was a telling detail. Craig gulped. 'What did you do?'

'Went back home. But I tell you, you'll not get me going there at night.'

Always the leader in their ploys, Craig was reluctant to give way. 'I still think it's bullshit. Probably just the deer. They make noises you could think were ghosts if you were daft enough. It'll only take a minute.' He headed for the opening.

'We're not supposed to go too close inshore where there's rocks. Dad'll go, like, mental,' Jamie said in a last desperate attempt. 'He won't let us have the boat again.'

'We're not going to tell him, are we?' As Jamie sat straining his ears for untoward noises, Craig steered in through the entrance.

It was almost dark now, but it was clear immediately that it was a very dull cave – just a shallow hollow worn in the cliff, with no tunnels leading off or anything. Disappointed, Craig shone his torch round as the boat bucked in the swell of the waves in the confined space.

'See? There's nothing here,' Jamie said with some relief. 'Come on, let's go before you cowp the boat and we're in real trouble.'

'Oh, all right,' Craig said sullenly, giving one last sweep of the torch round, then up across the roof. 'Here – what's that?'

A wide shelf, high above. Something white. Bones. A skull, gleaming in the light, gaunt and grinning, its blank eye sockets seeming to stare directly down at them. The gasp of horror from the two boys came as one breath, then as Jamie set up a terrified wail Craig found reverse and they shot back out into open water.

'What'll we do?' Jamie said, when he was able to speak. 'We'll need to tell someone.'

Craig was pale, shaking but more composed. 'They won't let us out in the boat again if we tell them. It's probably just some old smuggler or something, hundreds of years old – nothing to do with us.'

'Not say anything?' Jamie was torn. It seemed the sort of thing you ought to tell about – but his dad would really rip him up for going in there. And it was so gross, maybe if they didn't talk about it Jamie could just forget they'd ever seen it.

Neither of them spoke as they headed back to Innellan.

What can I clearly remember of that night? Being wakened by moonlight shining on to my face, certainly. One of the curtains, which had been closed at bedtime, had been roughly drawn back and as I opened my eyes, still half asleep, I could see a great white full moon against a black sky, and a man silhouetted against the darkness.

He was bending over the other bed, picking her up – my sister. He had his hand across her mouth and I could see her eyes, wide and terrified. He had, I think, a stocking over his face – or was it a mask? So much is still unclear, so much confused and dreamlike.

I know that he saw me watching. I know that he snarled under his breath, 'Keep quiet. Say nothing, or it'll be you tomorrow night – or the next, or the next . . .' The words are burnt into my brain.

He carried her out of the door, struggling, moaning – my sister, my twin – and shut it silently.

I didn't   My hand – I can't

CHAPTER TWO

The paramedics were kneeling in pools of blood on the kitchen floor of the council flat as they worked on the young woman, trying to staunch bleeding from stab wounds to her throat, chest and arms. She was battling against them drunkenly, flailing her arms and groaning obscenities.

'Oh God, she's going to be sick again,' one of them exclaimed. 'Pass me that bowl.'

DI Marjory Fleming left them to it and went through to the lounge, her stomach churning. The scene of crime team were standing by. The woman could die later – or even before they could get her out.

Just another domestic. Fleming realised with revulsion that the lounge carpet was so disgustingly filthy that the soles of her shoes were sticking to it. It was actually an effort to move them when DS Tam MacNee came in.

A hard-faced Glaswegian, MacNee was wearing his invariable uniform of jeans, white T-shirt, black leather jacket and trainers. His expression was grim.

'They've picked him up. He's about paralytic, blood everywhere, and it looks as if she chibbed him too. Didn't seem clear about what happened, but any decent brief will tell him to cop a plea.'

'Oh, I suppose so.' Fleming sighed. She was several inches taller than her sergeant, a fit-looking woman with a neat chestnut crop; clear bright hazel eyes were her most striking feature. In her smart trouser suit she looked out of place in these squalid surroundings.

She was breathing through her mouth, not her nose. The plastic trays bearing evidence of half-finished, rotting takeaways, the empty bottles, discarded clothes and battered toys were the least of it: there was also a pile of soiled nappies and what looked like dog messes on the floor. She didn't want to think what she was carrying on the soles of her shoes.

'The paramedics are trying to get her stabilised. It shouldn't be fatal, but she's so drunk they won't make predictions.'

MacNee shrugged. 'Frankly she'd not be much of a loss.'

Fleming's pent-up anger, which had been seething as she dealt with hysterical neighbours, organised an investigation, liaised with social workers about the two toddlers, the baby and the two Staffies and issued a press statement, burst out.

'Why the hell do we do this job, Tam?' she raged. 'Such a sodding waste of our time and the taxpayer's money! Two worthless people drink themselves stupid and belligerent, then think it's smart to involve a carving knife in the row they're having. They terrorise the neighbours and apparently she's worse than him. Sometimes I think we should leave them to get on with it.'

MacNee raised his eyebrows. 'That's not like you, boss.'

'Oh, I don't know,' Fleming said tiredly. 'It's this place that's getting to me.' She gestured at the rubbish-strewn room. 'They're living in a midden and it's not as if they had anything else to do – even ten minutes with a black plastic bag would help. And now there'll be three poor bloody kids who didn't ask to be born to parents like that – at least, she's presumably their mother, though how many he fathered is a whole other question. They're going into care, and we know what that means.'

'Aye. Not that they'd be better off left here. Just another generation of neds in the making.' MacNee paused. 'Only we're not to call them that now, are we?'

Fleming gave a faint smile. 'Glad the directive's had some effect. They're "youngsters in need of choice and chances", Tam.'

MacNee snorted. 'Or chancers, for short. Anyway, what more is there we can do tonight?'

Fleming grimaced. 'I'm waiting to see what happens with her, then I'll have to go back for the formal bit. Oh, it's the job, but this is so damn depressing! And I can't see any hope it'll improve.'

'Ah, you need what I heard some guy on the radio describe as Presbyterian optimism – we're all doomed, but we're not letting it get us down.'

MacNee grinned hopefully, exposing the gap between his front teeth. Fleming was surprised into a half-laugh.

'Sorry, Tam. I suppose I'm pissed off anyway because it's Cat's last night before she goes off to uni and we were to have a special supper.'

'You'll not be back in time, will you?'

'No. I told them to go ahead.' Fleming sighed. She'd been doing a lot of sighing this evening.

Christie Jack was feeling cheerful as she came down the drive from Lovatt's farmhouse on her way to the Smugglers. Today had been a good day, with the excitement of the news team, and seeing herself on the telly too. Matt was pleased, said they'd done really well. It gave her a warm glow, Matt's approval.

When she saw Melissa Lovatt sitting on a grassy knoll, staring out across Fleet Bay, she checked, pulling a face. She'd have to say something, but it would probably turn out to be the wrong something. Lissa was the sort of woman Christie despised – droopy, a bit weird, either sick as a parrot or over the moon, and if you didn't get the tone right, she'd a genius for making you feel uncomfortable. Poor Matt spent his life on tiptoe.

Christie liked to think she was tough. She'd had to be. The only way to get respect was to fight for it and she'd no truck with people who whinged. You needed to put it all behind you and get on with life, that was all. Which was perhaps why she'd been so totally poleaxed when everything fell apart.

It came out of a clear sky, a bleached sky with a blistering white sun and air that was shimmering with heat. Just an ordinary day, as ordinary as a day ever was when there were towelheads out there trying to kill you and you were in a Snatch Land Rover that offered about as much protection from roadside bombs as a frilly nightie. But you didn't let yourself think about that, any more than you worried about personal freshness when your whole body was permanently bathed in sweat.

Just an ordinary convoy, just the commute to work, except it never followed a regular route. Just an ordinary Afghan village they were driving through, with its street of ramshackle houses and the men standing talking in groups who turned their heads as the vehicles passed. No waves this morning. Sometimes they waved, sometimes they didn't.

Then a movement in a dark doorway, caught a fraction of a second before the grenade came arcing through the air, slowly, slowly, as if it were floating, and yet too quickly for the officer standing on recce in the hatch to duck, and the world exploded. A hell of gunfire, primitive yelling and whooping, then tearing groans – groans right at her side, and the smell of terror and hot blood as her comrade bled to death. Her own hands slippery as she tried futilely to staunch the flow. An animal scream, which she recognised as her own voice . . .

It was a sound that became familiar over the next weeks and months. The first flashback hit a week after – and again, and again and again. Without warning she would be right back there, and a quivering wreck wasn't much use as a soldier.

They'd given her treatment, but in the end she had been given a medical discharge, feeling an abject failure and impossible to live with. She was so angry – angry with herself, angry with everyone who crossed her path, angry with the whole world. She'd dumped her boyfriend before he could dump her; he hadn't protested and getting through the day took so much energy she barely noticed he'd gone. And all sorts of things had started crawling out of the woodwork, too, things Christie thought she'd banished long ago. Her coping strategies simply weren't working any more.

It didn't help that she was skint, going without proper food to pay rent for her lousy bedsit, living with the 'what-if' terror. She'd been homeless before, until the army took her in; they'd washed their hands of her now.

The chance encounter with her former CO was a sort of miracle. He'd served with Matt Lovatt in Bosnia and heard his plan of offering a bolt-hole for soldiers needing peaceful R and R.

'A working holiday for as long as you need it,' he had explained, 'though the work's meant to be therapeutic rather than a quid pro quo.'

Christie wasn't entirely certain what a quid pro quo was,

but she could understand all about a roof over her head and food she didn't have to pay for. She could hack it, whatever it was like.

Yet she'd actually considered leaving, the first couple of days. It was kind of a weird household, for a start, with odd relationships – a job lot of emotional cripples, though Kerr was the only one who actually had a missing leg. And it was so effing quiet! No music, except sometimes the classical stuff with no proper tune, no banter, no outlet for the aggression constantly bubbling below the surface as Christie was politely grateful and on her best behaviour. The nightmares were worse than ever.

That second night, sweating and trembling, she went down to the kitchen to escape them. It was July, one o'clock in the morning, and the darkness was lifting already. In the cool grey light she made tea and found a handful of Hobnobs; she was still perpetually hungry, craving the comfort of starch and sugar. When the door opened she jumped guiltily.

Kerr Brodie limped into the room. He was a thickset man with grizzled grey hair; he smiled a lot but Christie noticed the smile seldom reached his hard grey eyes. He was fully dressed; he obviously hadn't gone to bed yet. He grinned at her startled movement.

'At ease, soldier. Heard you moving about.' He sat down at the table. 'Got the heebie-jeebies, then?'

The silly term got her on the raw. Digging her nails into her palms, she said, 'I'm fine.'

'That'll be right,' he said sardonically, then took out some keys and threw them across. 'The major's orders. These are for the small motor boat. There's a shack on the island with bedding and blankets. Get across there and yell for a bit. He'll leave food till you're ready to come back.'

Being there alone might just push her over the edge, but she was past caring. She took the keys and went.

After three strange days when Christie spoke to no one, screamed, cried and hurled rocks into the sea, she felt spent and peaceful. The fourth night, she slept like a baby.

Back at the farmhouse, she still had bad days, but could believe now that eventually the horrors would recede. With hard physical work she slept more soundly and on bad days she could go to the island and let the murmur of wind and waves which was somehow part of a deep, deep silence wrap itself all about her.

She seriously owed Matt, and by extension Lissa too, though it was hard to see what she'd contributed. Christie pinned on a big smile now as she approached.

'Hi, Lissa!'

It was much colder now the sun was only a line of gold down on the horizon, but Lissa didn't seem to have noticed. She'd pulled her cotton print dress over her bent knees and was clasping them, her blue eyes dreamy. She was small, with a faded prettiness, brown curling hair and fine, pale skin, but her cheekbones were too sharply defined in her thin face.

She looked round. 'Isn't it a perfect evening? And look!' She reached down to delicate blue flowers growing by her feet, cupping one tenderly in her fingers. 'I love harebells. Witches' bells – that was the old name. Hares are witches' familiars, you know, and they were meant to ring to warn them if the fox was around.'

'Mmm.' Christie tried not to wince. 'I'm off to the pub. Fancy coming?'

Oh God, she'd done it again. 'You know what they're like,' Lissa said, blue eyes tragically reproachful.

'Mmm,' Christie murmured again. 'Well, see you later.'

Yes, she knew what they were like. A few poisonous characters holding a grudge, and the rest absorbed in their own lives and indifferent to strangers. But once you'd hung out for a bit the regulars were mostly friendly, and during the summer there were all the holidaymakers too. If she was still here come the winter, she couldn't quite see herself walking along to socialise with the bizarrely awful Derek, but towards the weekend even now there was usually quite a jolly crowd. Matt and Lissa were making a big mistake in cutting themselves off, even if neither of them was exactly sociable.

As Christie reached the Smugglers, a group of young men appeared from the opposite direction. They were in high spirits, one with a helium balloon tied to his wrist, wearing a T-shirt with messages scribbled on it, mostly obscene.

They arrived just as she did, but the one in front stepped back to usher her ahead of them. He was seriously fit – big and broad-shouldered, with close-cropped dark hair and brown eyes. Christie smiled a thank you.

The pub was quite full now and Georgia was being kept busy, but when she caught sight of Christie's new acquaintance she called, 'Andy! Didn't know you were around. Come and give us a kiss, then.'

Andy, grinning, obliged. 'I've borrowed the family caravan for a weekend with some of my mates. Can you do us a jug of beer?'

'Course I can, my love. Having a party?' She began pulling pints into a large jug.

'Wake, more like. This guy's getting married.' Andy jerked a thumb at his sheepish-looking friend.

'Should be you, by rights. Your mum and dad were saying you needed to find a nice girl and get settled.'

'Plenty time for that. I'm still young . . .'

Georgia wiped off the jug and set it down. 'Getting older all the time, petal. Still, make the most of it.'

'Trust me.' Andy winked, then noticed Christie was standing patiently beside the bar. 'Oops, I'm sorry,' he said. 'This young lady was ahead of us, Georgia.'

'Sorry, dear,' Georgia echoed. 'What's it to be?'

Christie saw 'Andy' was looking at her properly for the first time. 'Put it on my slate, Georgia,' he said. 'An apology for queue-jumping.'

He had a great smile. Christie smiled too. 'No need. But . . . oh, just a Becks, thanks.'

'Cheers!' he said, pouring out beer for himself and passing the jug to one of his friends, but he didn't rejoin the group. They introduced themselves: he was Andy Macdonald, from Kirkluce, and his mates, after sidelong looks and some pointed remarks, settled at the end of the bar, with a bit of good-natured jostling.

Then the bomb went off. Christie screamed, a piercing, full-blooded scream, looked wildly about her, then dived under the nearest table with her hands round her head. An absolute silence fell.

Then Andy's arms were round her. 'It's all right, Christie, it's all right. One of these idiots just burst Dave's balloon, that's all.'

Half dazed, she sat up, then felt a hot tide of embarrassment flood right through her, turning her face puce. 'Sorry,' she mumbled. 'Oh God! How humiliating.'

Conversations began again, with sympathetic murmurs and glances. Some people had obviously seen the TV programme, though Andy clearly hadn't. As he helped her up, her face still aflame, one of his friends who looked almost as uncomfortable as Christie felt came to apologise for bursting the balloon.

'Sorry' seemed to be the key word tonight. He said it several times, she said it several times, each politely laid claim to total stupidity, then he went back to the group with obvious relief.

Christie's heart was still pounding and her legs were shaky. She needed to sit down before she fell down and made a fool of herself all over again. She headed for a window seat.

'I'm fine now, thanks,' she said to Andy, who was still holding her arm. 'You go back to your mates.'

'I'd rather talk to you.'

They squeezed on to the narrow seat and he said, 'Right. Tell me what all that was about.'

When Matt Lovatt, his dog loping alongside, appeared on his way to the boat half an hour later, Lissa was still sitting there. He waved, not slowing down, but she scrambled to her feet.

'Are you going to the island? I'll come.'

He groaned inwardly. He loved being alone on his island on a soft night, when colour had gone from the sky and it became a place of shadows and ambiguity, when his pretty dappled deer could slip into the trees and mysteriously vanish, when the offshore breeze died and everything went still.

He knew, too, why Lissa wanted to go – she only ever had one reason, which always broke her apart all over again. Anyway, Matt would have liked to check before she did – he'd found a nasty little message sprayed on the headstone recently.

'Won't you be cold like that, Lissa? And it's getting dark. I'm just dumping concentrate for the deer and coming straight back.'

She shook her head. 'No. I want to take him these. He'd like them.' She bent to pick some harebells, making a dainty posy.

'Fine,' Matt said. She followed him to the jetty, walking on the grass verge in bare feet. At a gesture, the dog jumped into the motor boat, sitting like a figurehead in the prow. Matt helped Lissa aboard and started the engine.

Her eyes were fixed on the island – wide, hungry eyes. Matt glanced at her, then glanced away. With hindsight, he'd been crazy: he could easily have said a burial on the island wouldn't be allowed. It was unfortunate he'd remembered the consecrated ground around the tiny ruined chapel, with a couple of old headstones weathered to anonymity, and exploited that to get permission. Close by was the burial cairn and the Norse graves; Matt had liked to think of the child, who had never lived and now was little more than a scar on his mind, in the company of the old warriors.

If he was honest, it had been a bid for permanence. For the first time in his life he had felt rooted; the island was his place. Lissa would never want to leave if the grave was there. It hadn't occurred to him that his salvation might be his wife's destruction.

He swept round to bring the boat in, jumped ashore to tie up and held out his hand to help Lissa ashore. In her other hand the fragile flowers were losing colour, wilting already, dying in front of his eyes. The symbolism was deeply uncomfortable.

Matt clicked his fingers and the dog came to heel. 'I'll go to the bothy then come back here. Don't hurry – I'll wait for you.'

'Aren't you coming?'

In the deepening dusk he couldn't see her face, but he knew the look – the one he had seen so often, asking for something he couldn't give and filling him with guilt at his failure. If there was graffiti on the headstone, it was too late to do anything about it now.

'No,' he said gruffly.

Lissa paused briefly then set off on the grass in her bare feet, ignoring the track which curved round the hill then ran from one end of the island to the other.

Matt watched her go before he followed the track to the

bothy. Sheltered by the trees at the seaward end of the island, it had housed a shepherd in his grandfather's day. Matt had made it weatherproof with a storage area below and basic accommodation above where you could doss down if you had a sick animal or an orphan fawn.

There were a couple of does moving about, browsing and nibbling at low scrub. Dawn and dusk were their times; they were happier in half-light, like all prey animals. One raised her head as he passed, pricking the ears that looked far too large for the neat head, her tongue going out to moisten the shiny, plastic-looking nose. Then she went back to her bushes. They were used to him, and even to the dog at his heels, though sometimes it sniffed the air as if some atavistic memory stirred.

Matt did his errand, then returned to the boat. He had no idea how long Lissa might be and with the dog again in the prow, he settled down to wait.

From across the water he heard a brief, strange, coughing roar, and his head came up, listening. It wasn't repeated, but Matt smiled. They'd have to bring in the stags tomorrow and isolate them; the rut was beginning. It wouldn't be long before the buck on the island was barking his intentions too.

It was only minutes later he saw Lissa coming back down the hill, pale dress glimmering like a ghost in the gathering darkness. He bent to start the engine. It meant he didn't have to see the tears he knew would be trickling down her face.

From the wooden chalet above Fleet Bay, Derek Sorley trained binoculars on the island – the island he now refused to call Lovatt. He had only recently learnt the old name – Tascadan. It was Gordon Lovatt, Matt's great-grandfather, who'd changed it in 1883, and the locals still hadn't forgiven him for his arrogance.

The sound of the motor boat had brought Sorley to the picture window which was about the only good thing about this shabby, gimcrack place, with doors that had warped and gaps round the ill-fitting windows that the draughts whistled through and sometimes even the rain, with the wind in the wrong direction. And there was the dirt-cheap rent too, admittedly – modern holidaymakers demanded standards his landlord was too mean to provide.

Sorley would have preferred to live in Kirkcudbright where he had a job at the moment driving a van for a stationery company, but with a piddling wage, docked anyway by the Child Support Agency for that vampire bitch, his ex-wife, all he could afford was a room in someone else's house and having got rid of one nagging woman he'd no wish to acquire another. At least here he'd the place to himself.

Seething with loathing, he watched the Lovatts and the devil dog heading for the island. It was the dog had sniffed him out that day, all but given him a heart attack, staring at him as if sizing him up for attack – shouldn't be allowed, having an animal like that. Then Lovatt had come to see where his precious dog was and lost it completely, yelling at him, making accusations, ordering him off his land. With the dog growling, Sorley wasn't going to stay to argue.

He'd been so careful, too. He'd checked that Sunday: he'd seen Lovatt make a visit and return before he tackled the causeway of rocks and shingle which made the island accessible at low tide. There was no reason Lovatt should have come back unless he'd been tipped off – and strangely enough, Cal Findlay's boat had been in the bay earlier.

What made Sorley sick was he'd just had a reaction from his second-hand metal detector, there by the burial cairn. Gold, it had signalled – gold! His heart had flipped, then turned a couple of somersaults. Things like that didn't happen to him – but maybe his luck had turned. Norse gold was big, big money.

Lovatt had no right to ban him. Scottish Right to Roam legislation should mean no private property any more beyond your garden, but when he'd taken it up with his local councillors – without mentioning the metal detector – they weren't interested.

If only he'd got there before Ma Lovatt popped her clogs. No one ever went near the island then. She'd a tenant farmer, Hugh Donaldson, whose croft adjoined Lovatt land; he'd retired just before Ma Lovatt died, and his son Steve had thrown up his job in Paisley to come home and take over. Then Matt Lovatt arrived and wouldn't grant a new tenancy, leaving Steve with no job and a scruffy croft that didn't offer a decent living. There was only one man hated Matt Lovatt more than Derek did and that was Steve.

Sorley's fingers were drumming on the window sill. He wasn't going to accept this. He could see it so clearly – armlets, twisted brooches, dirty after years buried, but rubbed with his thumb revealing the dull tint of old gold.

He'd offered at the time to split proceeds but Lovatt hadn't listened, red in the face with rage, apart from the scar that stayed deathly pale. That, as well as the devil dog, had spooked Sorley.

Steve's croft had some burial sites as well – barren sites, unfortunately, when Sorley had checked. But if he could get at the stuff on the island – if he took it across to Steve's place . . . The sort of money you'd be talking, he wouldn't grudge splitting it two ways for provenance. An amateur trying for a no-questions-asked sale could be stitched up, cheated on the price, definitely – maybe shopped to the police too. Legal and above board was safer, and more profitable as well.

But how could he dig there? He could slip across – as indeed he had, to leave his poisonous message in revenge – but disturbance round the graves would soon be spotted.

As the drumming of his fingers became a thumping with his fists, an idea came to him. The island must be abandoned again and there was only one way: drive the bastards out.

His brow furrowed in thought, he took out his mobile and tapped in Steve's number, but frustratingly there was no answer.

Sorley went back to his binoculars. The woman was climbing the hill, heading for the grave, no doubt. His mouth flickered in an unpleasant smile. She'd be running back down soon, sobbing. '*We must leave this awful place!*' he imagined her saying. But there she was, sitting down instead.

His smile faded. Someone must have cleaned it off. Disappointed, he turned away and his eye lit on *Gaelic for Beginners* lying on the rickety coffee table. He might as well put in a bit of time on that. There certainly wasn't anything better to do.

He'd started learning Gaelic because the Scottish Nationalist government was shovelling money in that direction and, if he got fluent, there were cushy jobs for the asking. But who'd have thought his studying would have such an early benefit? It was how he'd discovered the meaning of the island's name, Tascadan: it came from *taisgaedan*, the Gaelic for treasure.

Kerr Brodie had unlocked the gun cupboard, tipping some bullets into his hand from a box of ammunition then dropping them into a capacious pocket of the shooter's waistcoat on a peg alongside. He took a .243 rifle from the rack to check it over; he was fanatical about preparing his equipment and he was irritated when the phone rang. He propped up the gun and reached the kitchen extension just in time to stop the answer service cutting in.

Brodie glanced at the number that came up – not one he knew, but the Glasgow code. 'Yes?' he said.

The voice was husky, tentative. 'Sarge?'

Brodie frowned. 'Who is this?'

'Crawford. Fergie Crawford.'

The frown deepened. 'Crawford? What are you wanting?'

He didn't sound encouraging, but a frantic outpouring came from the other end. He listened with increasing concern.

'No, no, don't do that. Give me a moment.' Kerr was scowling now. Then he said, 'OK – I'll tell you what to do.'

He gave instructions, then rang off and swore violently. This he didn't need. He walked back to the gun cupboard in an evil mood.

It was half past eleven when Marjory Fleming drove up to Mains of Craigie. The outside lights were on, but the rest of the house was in darkness, apart from the middle window above the front door where a light was still burning. Cat's bedroom.

Her heart lifted just slightly. At least she could go and apologise, maybe even have the chat she'd missed at supper. She hurried in, dumping her shoes in the sink in the mud room. She'd felt sickened on the way home by the lingering smell.

Marjory ran upstairs and tapped on Cat's door. 'Hi, darling. Back at last! Sorry about that.'

There was no response. When she opened the door, the room was in darkness and her daughter was only a hump under the bedclothes, her back to the door.

She hesitated. She could say, 'Cat, I know you're awake,' and insist they talked. But Cat wasn't a child any more; she was a young woman about to begin her own life and if this was her decision it ought to be respected. Anyway, Marjory couldn't think it was likely to prove a constructive conversation.

She closed the door again. She could understand Cat's resentment, of course, but if she'd put a family supper ahead of a case that might prove to be murder, her bosses would seriously question her priorities. A woman's place is in the wrong, Marjory reflected bitterly, as she went to have a long, scented bath to get the stench of the day out of her nostrils.

It was one o'clock in the morning when Jamie started screaming.

I didn't   scream

CHAPTER THREE

'What on earth is the matter, Jamie?' Tony Drummond, startled out of deep sleep, was more annoyed than sympathetic.

His wife Rosie pushed him aside, giving him a death stare as she hurried to her son. 'Darling! What's wrong?'

Jamie was bolt upright in bed, hair tousled and damp with sweat, mouth square as he uttered scream after scream, his eyes wide and staring. As his father snapped on the light he put up his hand to shield them.

Rosie, alarmed herself, sat down and took him in her arms, rocking him like a baby. 'Sssh, sssh! It's all right, sweetheart, just a bad dream, that's all.'

The screaming stopped, but he began to cry shuddering wails.

'He's getting hysterical,' Tony said. 'Jamie! You've had a nightmare, you're awake now. Nothing's wrong.'

Rosie looked reproachful at the sharp tone, but the boy's sobbing died down a little. 'Tell you what,' she said soothingly. 'We'll go downstairs and I'll make you hot chocolate, with lots of marshmallows. Would that be nice? Come on, then.'

Jamie, shaking violently, allowed himself to be led towards the stairs, still crying. His father followed them out of the bedroom, then hesitated.

'Er . . . not much point in us both losing sleep. If you've got it covered . . .'

'Oh – *men*!' Rosie gave him a withering look, but she didn't insist.

Five minutes later Tony was sound asleep. When she woke him again, he was confused. 'Did the alarm not go?'

'Don't be silly. It's half past one. Jamie's still freaking out, but he won't tell me why. I need you.'

At the kitchen table, Jamie had stopped crying but was still shaking uncontrollably. At the sight of his father he bit his lip.

What was that about? Frowning, Tony drew up a chair beside his son, who wouldn't meet his eyes.

'OK, Jamie, let's sort this out. You'd a bad dream, right?'

The boy nodded.

'Dreams aren't real, you know that.'

Another nod.

'Do you want to tell us what it was about?'

He shook his head violently. Rosie said, 'I've tried. He won't.'

'Hmm. So there's something else, is there? What is it?'

Jamie's eyes flicked to his father's face, then away again.

'Something you don't want to tell us.' Tony thought for a moment. 'Is it something you've done that you shouldn't have?'

The child's head sank down. His parents looked at each other.

'We promise we won't be angry, darling,' Rosie said reassuringly.

Tony's reaction was less comforting. 'Better tell us before we find out. What were you and Craig up to this afternoon?'

'F-fishing,' Jamie faltered. He began crying again, and then it all spilt out.

Which was why Tony Drummond was in his boat at first

46

light, heading for the cave on Lovatt Island, eyes gritty from lack of sleep. He wasn't upset, though. From the sound of it he was on to a good story.

Smugglers, ancient skeletons, adventurous kids, nightmares – it had all the ingredients, a gift to a journalist. Good visuals as well – this could be one for BBC Scotland, even national, maybe, a soft tail-ender for *News at Six*. In a spirit of keen anticipation Tony steered the boat through the mouth of the cave.

He'd glanced inside once, years ago, but seen nothing to tempt him further. Now he couldn't see anything either and for a moment wondered if he was chasing a figment of a child's vivid imagination. It was still fairly dark, though, and like Craig he got the torch out of the locker and shone it round – nothing. Then Tony shone it above his head.

And there it was. The rock shelf it was lying on was man-made, definitely – wide and deep, with a couple of empty shelves above it. The skull was close to the edge, and when he stood up in the boat he could see the ribcage, too, and leg bones. And horribly, a lower arm bone and a lower leg bone hanging, clamped to the wall by iron staples.

He had time to think, 'Poor bastard!' and wondered what ancient crime had merited such a hideous punishment. Then he noticed what was still round the arm, resting on the staple.

Marjory Fleming put the bacon in the pan on the Aga, then fetched eggs from the larder. There were mushrooms to chop too, and she'd better not forget baked beans. It was the full works today, with Cat going off.

She'd shed some quiet tears feeding the hens this morning. Tomorrow night there'd be three in her family, not four. Cat's visits would be frequent, no doubt, but just that – visits. Catriona Fleming doesn't live here any more. Her precious daughter was going out into the world alone – willingly, eagerly, without a backward glance over her shoulder. Just as she should.

The thing was, Marjory thought mutinously as she put plates to warm beside the sausages in the oven, no one ever explained as they put the tiny, utterly dependent creature into your arms – *your* baby, flesh of your flesh – that you were at the start of a relentless process of giving her up, to nursery, to school, to friends. Imperceptibly, a whole new life developed, where you had no part any more. Of course, she'd never been *yours* at all – it had just felt like that during the long years when you had her on loan. Having to face the reality felt almost like bereavement.

Marjory was swallowing hard when Bill came in.

'Ah! Best smell in the world, that!' He was looking unnaturally tidy in a tweed jacket with a checked shirt and even a tie.

'Mmm.' His wife prodded the sizzling bacon with a fork. 'Any signs of movement upstairs? I don't want to fry the mushrooms too soon, but you could open the beans and dump them in a pan.'

She hadn't turned to look at him. Instead of obeying instructions, he came and put his arm round her shoulders.

'Finding it tough? So am I,' he said. 'My wee girl – do you remember when she couldn't say "mushrooms" and—'

'Bill, stop it!' Marjory said sharply. 'Go and be sentimental somewhere else. If you want Cat to find us snivelling over the sausages, I don't.' She paused. 'How was she – last night?'

Bill grimaced. 'Subdued. She'd set her heart on the last family meal—'

'And I let her down again. I know, I know,' Marjory said unhappily. 'All for a domestic, and the woman's recovering. Still, we can have a nice leisurely lunch in Glasgow today before we get her settled in at the residence.

'Can you check Cammie's getting up? I woke him, but he always goes back to sleep.'

Bill went to shout up the stairs as Marjory started putting bacon on to a plate in the oven. When her mobile rang, she froze. Had the wretched woman died after all?

She fetched it from her bag and listened. 'How extraordinary!' she said at last. 'I'm off-duty today – get DS MacNee down there to check it out, and report to me. I'm going to Glasgow but I should be back late afternoon and I'll call in then. Doesn't sound as if there's much urgency about this one.'

Eddie Tindall was always at his desk by seven-thirty in the office which was the hub of his extensive motor trade business, with branches right across the Midlands. Saturday was always a busy day, and his PA came in at nine.

Marianne Price had been with him twenty years, a small, tough Scouser with a bright-red frizz of hair and a penchant for tight skirts and stilettos. She was competent, discreet and utterly loyal, though she'd made it plain her loyalty was sorely tried in relation to his second wife. Discouraged perhaps by chilly courtesy, Elena almost never came to the office and he was surprised now when Marianne announced she was there.

'I'll show her in, shall I?' she said.

Eddie jumped to his feet. 'I'll come. Didn't know she knew nine o'clock even existed.'

He laughed, and Marianne gave a thin smile as he hurried past her. He felt, as he always did, a little thrill of pleasure when his wife appeared unexpectedly, but anything unusual was enough to make him worry too.

Elena was standing in reception beside the red plastic bench seating and the coffee table covered with brochures and slightly dog-eared motor magazines, tall and elegant in a navy linen shift dress with a jade cashmere cardigan draped over her shoulders and lots of chunky gold costume jewellery. She looked exotic and seriously out of place.

Eddie came over to kiss her. 'Nice surprise. Got a busy day, doll?'

She smiled at him. 'Just a plan. Thought I'd take off for a bit of me-time, if that's all right.'

'Of course,' he said instantly. 'Need any money?'

Elena shook her head. 'I'm fine. You really are a sweetie, Eddie. I'll be in touch.'

'You do that, my love. Have a good time. Take care.' He took her in his arms and she allowed herself to be kissed.

As she left and Eddie headed back to his office, Marianne's mouth twisted into a cat's bum of disapproval. She hated seeing him jerked around by that little slut.

Eddie didn't settle straight back to work. He hadn't asked where Elena was going – he never did. Not after that first time, when she had burst out that if their relationship was to continue, sometimes she just needed space, without accounting for herself to anyone. At first he'd wondered about a lover; if that was her price he'd put up with it, as long as she came back afterwards.

But if he didn't ask, he always knew. She probably hadn't thought of it, bless her, but paying her credit card bill told him what she'd done – a stay at a spa hotel, a few days in London perhaps. The other expenses would be shopping or theatre or meals for one person. He'd relaxed long ago. If she needed to feel a free spirit, fine – just as long as he knew exactly where she was and what she was doing.

But Eddie still craved reassurance. Now, he phoned to ask for the statement, but this time there was no reservation deposit. She didn't usually go on spec. Frowning, he called up their joint bank account, but Elena only ever used it for ATM withdrawals – two hundred pounds every few days, the last two days ago. He clicked it off, disappointed. He'd just have to wait to follow her trail, then – it wouldn't be long.

But there was that niggle at the back of his mind: the way she had looked last night. He could always tell when she was stressing, even when he'd no idea why, and where Elena was concerned anything out of the ordinary set his nerves on edge.

'Where?' DS MacNee said. 'Never heard of it.'

He jotted down location and details from the officer in Kirkcudbright, put down the phone with a groan then checked on the huge Ordnance Survey map on one wall.

He was alone in the CID room. He'd managed to farm out interviews arising from last night's fracas and after an extended shift yesterday felt smugly entitled to a quiet morning with a wee bit of gentle catching-up and maybe a chat to Sergeant Jock Naismith, always abreast of the station gossip. Now with Andy Macdonald off on leave and Ewan Campbell out doing interviews, he'd have to take this one himself – at least an hour's journey with a boat trip at the end. MacNee could feel sick going 'doon the watter' on a Clyde ferry, and that was before they left the pier. He set off thinking bitterly of Campbell, out on what now looked like a real doss, just standing listening to folk for a while before he came back for his pie and beans.

The sunshine and the scenery didn't cheer him. MacNee had a townie's distaste for anything involving fresh air and mud, and the tractor drawing a horsebox which kept his speed to nineteen miles an hour on a narrow road bounded by stone walls for a quarter of an hour didn't improve his temper.

The local constable was obviously getting his knickers in a right twist. A couple of messages had come through from HQ asking for an ETA, and MacNee's responses had got sharper and sharper. With the time the victim had waited already, another half-hour wasn't going to make a whole lot of difference. Anyway, a historian was likely to be more interested than the police.

But here at last was the small village he was looking for – just a wee street of houses straggling along the edge of the bay. Bonny enough, MacNee admitted grudgingly, with the islands out there and the sun shining.

The Smugglers Inn was halfway down the street. There was a badged car in its small car park with a young constable beside it, looking spare. As MacNee drove in, he turned, a hopeful expression on his round pink face.

It wasn't easy to get space to park, with three other cars and too many people around, and MacNee noted darkly that one had a professional-looking camera. He slotted the car in beside a shrub with small pink flowers, swarming with wasps. He batted at them irritably as he got out.

The constable hurried across. 'DS MacNee? PC Hendry, sir. Glad to see you. It's been a wee thing tricky—'

He was immediately joined by the man with the camera, holding up a card. 'Tony Drummond. Press. You took your time!'

MacNee assessed him sourly: mid-forties, balding a bit, paunch, but with sharp brown eyes. Not with a national; he recognised the name from his byline in the local paper and he probably acted for a news agency too. That explained Hendry's anxiety – he'd be pressured by the man trying to protect his scoop.

'Well, Mr Drummond,' he drawled, 'I can't tell you anything till I've had a word with the officer here. So perhaps you'd let me do that, while you wait, say – over there?' He gestured towards the wasp-infested bush. Seemed appropriate.

Drummond laughed. 'Ah, Sergeant, that's where you're wrong. I'm the one you want to talk to, not Doug here.'

The look MacNee gave Hendry at this evidence of fraternising with the enemy reduced him to stammering. 'Mr Drummond – it was him found the body – well, the bones.'

'I see,' MacNee said stiffly. 'Better give me the facts, then, sir. Constable, have you arranged a boat?'

'No need,' Drummond said promptly. 'I'll take you out myself.'

'Good of you,' MacNee said, with an ill grace. It was entirely unsatisfactory, but what else could he do? And those others – interested locals, no doubt, half a dozen men and one woman with blonded hair who was giving him a friendly smile.

MacNee didn't return it. He went to speak to them. 'Right, lady and gents. Any useful information, speak to PC Hendry here. Otherwise, you may as well go home. There'll be nothing happening for a good wee while.'

There was some disgruntled muttering, mainly from a big man wearing farmer's dungarees and a surly expression, but they moved off to stand in a huddle at the other end. The woman hesitated.

'I'm Georgia Stanley, the licensee. I'll be opening at twelve. If you want a cuppa before then, just come round the other side and knock on the door.'

MacNee produced a grin. 'Thanks. I might take you up on that.'

Georgia looked a little doubtful but MacNee was used by now to that reaction to his gap-toothed smile. He turned to Drummond.

'Right. Let's get on with it. Not far, is it?'

Elena Tindall left without acknowledging her husband's secretary. She never did, if she could help it – impertinent old bag! She'd hinted

53

to Eddie about getting rid of her but for once he'd been adamant: business was business and Marianne was the best you could get. Elena had backed off. She didn't care that much, anyway.

Outside, she hailed a taxi. 'Primark,' she said.

The driver looked at her with some surprise. She looked more the Selfridges type, but he reckoned keeping his mouth shut was the way to a decent tip. The iceberg type seldom appreciated a bit of banter.

It paid off: she tipped him a fiver. He watched as she disappeared inside, shrugged, then drove on.

Half an hour later Elena came out carrying several large bags, hailed another cab and gave her home address.

When she got out of the lift into the elegant lobby on the penthouse level, she held her breath as she opened the front door. If Lola was polishing the hall floor . . .

She wasn't. The parquet was gleaming, the huge, shaggy, white chrysanthemums in the Chinese vases were fresh that morning, the mirrored console table sparkled, but there was no sign of her housekeeper. She wasn't in the master bedroom either, and Elena could get the bags through to her walk-in closet unnoticed. She touched a wardrobe door; it swung open and she tucked them out of sight.

It wasn't that Lola spied on her, or anything. Lola was just very chatty and when Eddie came home he'd pump her for every detail of Elena's departure. Oh, Elena knew he kept tabs on her, but it didn't bother her. She didn't have a lover; she'd had more than enough of men. She just needed breaks when Eddie's obsessional devotion began to stifle her, and with nothing to hide she'd made it easy for him to check. Not this time.

'Morning, Lola,' she said, walking into the Philippe Starck kitchen where Lola was wiping the polished marble worktop. 'Could I ask you to do something for me just now?'

Lola, a bright-faced Spanish woman in a neat pink overall with a navy butcher's apron on top, turned immediately. 'Yes, of course, Mrs Tindall.'

Elena found Lola very restful. She was suitably aware of having a good job and a generous employer, and she did what she was asked without discussion or fuss.

'Could you please run round with this to the cleaners?' Elena was holding one of Eddie's suits. 'I think he might want it tomorrow, so if you could get them to do the express service then pop it back in his closet . . .'

Lola agreed with alacrity, removing her apron and taking the suit from her employer. As she went, Elena called after her, 'Oh, by the way, I'm going to be away for a little while. Look after Eddie for me, won't you?'

'Sure, madame! I get something good for his dinner tonight – you know how not happy he is when you go away.'

She smiled. 'Thanks, Lola.' A moment later she heard the front door shut and smiled again. Lola wouldn't hurry back: a friend of hers had a coffee shop nearby, and Lola always enjoyed an excuse.

Elena returned to her bedroom. She glanced at the huge bed, with its Egyptian cotton sheets and soft down pillows, with a wry twist of her mouth. It wouldn't be like that tonight. *What care I for a goose-feather bed . . .*

She did care a bit, actually. She gave a little shiver.

As she took the bags out of her closet and pulled out her purchases, she glanced at her watch; the agency would be open now.

She had no difficulty booking a chalet, and she could pay in cash when she reached Kirkcudbright. She'd reserved a hire car, using the credit card Eddie didn't know she had and a pay-as-you-go phone. She'd a secret bank account too; it wasn't difficult to build it up when you regularly withdrew money but paid for everything on a credit card, and she'd a useful arrangement with a dress agency for her last season's clothes. Eddie was never interested in what she spent. He was buying her presence, and he was a generous man.

Elena had no idea how long she would be away this time. He'd be terrified she'd left him and keeping him happy would be hard work. She'd have to be meticulous about keeping in touch or he'd start calling in private dicks, the police – the army, if he could swing it.

Unclasping the costume jewellery, Elena put it in a velvet-lined drawer in her dressing table. She folded the cashmere sweater and laid it on a shelf with others in a dozen colours and styles. The linen dress went into the laundry basket, but she didn't take off the Elle Macpherson underwear. There were limits.

Cheap jeans – she'd forgotten how uncomfortable they were. And the T-shirt wasn't sewn quite square – dreadful fabric, too. She hesitated; surely one T-shirt was much like another except to the person wearing it and she had a drawerful – but no. She must play the part to the point where she wasn't playing a part any more, where she *was* the girl she'd been before Elena was born, when new clothes of any sort had been a treat.

She stuffed the rest of her purchases into a holdall and gathered up the bags they'd come in. There were bins in the garage basement and if she took the lift down there the concierge wouldn't see her leaving and wonder. Eddie would talk to him as well.

At the door, she hesitated. She was afraid, for all sorts of reasons. Even now, she could cancel, head for a spa hotel instead . . . Luxury had always been her drug of choice.

Like any other addiction, it solved nothing. The gnawing

inside was only briefly assuaged and its destructive effect was increasing. Elena was struggling, and here at last was her chance of closure. Just a chance – but nothing else seemed to give her peace of mind. Peace of mind – how beautiful that sounded! All she needed was courage, and a bit of luck. Perhaps she'd just had the luck and she'd proved long ago she had courage.

Yet still she hesitated. Then, very slowly, as if it were almost against her will, Elena went back to the velvet-lined drawer. Right at the back there was a dainty Victorian penknife, silver and mother-of-pearl; she looked at it for a moment before picking it up. She opened it, checked the razor edge of the slim, shiny steel blade and clicking it shut again put it in a pocket of her jeans. As an afterthought, she picked up two wide cuff bangles of engraved silver, tucked them into the holdall and left.

There was no one in the lift, or in the basement garage. With the bags safely disposed of, she loaded her luggage into her silver Mercedes coupé, then drove up the ramp and out of the building.

MacNee noticed with relief that the island indicated, Lovatt, was only a few hundred yards offshore – only to have his hopes dashed as Drummond headed the boat towards the farther end.

'The cave's round the other side. There's a ridge of rocks between the island and the shore at this end, a sort of causeway – you can walk across it at low tide.'

MacNee nodded. Speaking didn't appeal at the moment. The sea, which had looked billiard-table flat from the shore, seemed to have nasty little bumpy bits when you were speeding across it.

Drummond was clueing him in and it helped if MacNee concentrated on that. It was a straightforward enough story; nasty shock for the poor kids, though. He was even preening himself on getting his sea legs when Drummond said, 'There it is,' and headed for a hollow in the cliffs. Surely in there, sheltered from the waves, it would be better too.

It wasn't, of course. In the confined space the waves bounced off the walls, swirled and jostled, slapping playfully at the sides of the boat. MacNee turned green just as Drummond said, 'There's one little detail I didn't mention to the constable.' He picked up the torch and shone it up.

The skull grinned down. Drummond moved the beam to the wall behind, focusing it on a limb pinned to the wall, caught by the iron staple. The hand bones had fallen and only an arm bone was left, and round it, also resting on the metal, was an unmistakably modern man's wristwatch.

At which point MacNee, to his utter humiliation, vomited.

'Cat, if you're taking anything more, it won't fit into the car,' Bill said. 'You'll be home again in a week or two. You're not needing everything you're going to want for the next five years.'

'I'm not!' Cat said defensively. 'I just don't know exactly what I'll want yet and if it's too much I can always bring it home again. Anyway, this is the last.'

She held out a cardboard box. Bill looked doubtfully at it, then at the boot.

'It'll have to go inside between the two of you.' Cat, shrugging, put it into the car where Cammie was already sitting waiting.

'Go up and take another look round, why don't you?' he suggested. 'I bet there's like another trunk or two of clothes you really really need. And of course this is a mega-cool way of spending a morning – sitting in the car.'

Cat pulled a face at him. 'I'm ready now, anyway. Where's Mum?'

'Give her a shout,' Bill said.

Cat disappeared back into the house. 'Mum! We're ready!' she shouted.

Marjory called back, 'I'm right there.' Pressing the button to start the dishwasher, she headed out of the kitchen.

Then the phone went.

MacNee watched as Drummond, smirking, swung the boat round and headed back. He was standing on a ledge just to the side of the cave; above him a steep slope of rocks and rough grass, below him the sea.

Drummond had been reluctant to leave him there, but anything was better than sailing right round the island again, no doubt giving Drummond even more humorous copy for his rag – though at least he'd directed the man to lose his camera before they'd set out. From the other side of the island, it really would only be five minutes back to Innellan, and he'd have time to recover while he waited for Fleming to be brought out and shown the site.

He glanced up again. There were plenty of footholds, but they weren't necessarily stable and he was no mountaineer. And the further he climbed, the greater the drop below.

But it was dry land. MacNee comforted himself with that. He'd made his decision: Drummond mustn't come back to find him still there, being feeble about climbing as well as sailing. *Welcome what thou can'st not shun*, he reminded himself, having his usual recourse to Scotland's Bard. Reaching above his head, he tested a handhold and began the climb.

The worst thing was the nausea and dizziness. It hadn't stopped when the boat did, and soon he was having to cower into the slope, taking deep breaths before attempting the next step. It made MacNee careless; he put his foot on a tuft of grass which had grown on a loose stone. With a cry and another lurch of his suffering stomach he felt it give beneath his weight and bounce down, down into the waves below.

His desperate grip on a more stable rock above saved him. He thought he might be sick again from sheer terror, but with an act of willpower controlled it and after a moment or two found a safer foothold. Doggedly, he began the climb once more. There wasn't much else he could do.

Don't look down. Test. Don't startle when you test and it breaks off. Don't pass out. Look up. The top's nearer now, nearer . . . With one last, frantic effort he heaved himself up on to the level ground beyond, digging his nails into the friendly turf as if to clamp himself on.

At last MacNee sat up, feeling a bit better – experiencing a certain pride, even. It prompted him to crawl across to look back over the edge, then he regretted it. Even from a safe position, the drop was stomach-churning.

Enough! He'd a job to do. MacNee got to his feet and found his phone. He hated to do this to the boss; he knew what was at stake for her with Cat, who'd always been demanding. But with Drummond going to file his story anytime now, he could hardly tell him the Senior Investigating Officer would be along when she got back from taking her daughter to the uni.

Fleming's voice went absolutely flat as she agreed that yes, she would have to come. MacNee had just put his phone back in his pocket when he heard the shot.

He took off, sprinting towards the sound, sending a couple of deer leaping away in fright. He reached the top of the hill and paused, breathing hard.

Near the trees, a man with a rifle was standing over a fallen deer. Close by, two others were browsing in the undergrowth, apparently unmoved, until MacNee's headlong arrival sent them, too, starting away.

'What the hell do you think you're doing?' he shouted.

The man turned, lowering the rifle. 'I could say the same to you, Jimmy. This is private property.'

It was a familiar accent. And now MacNee looked, he recognised the man too. And he'd have been glad never to see him again.

'Well now, Brodie,' he drawled with evident distaste, 'this is an unexpected pleasure. Poaching now, is it?'

Brodie looked more closely. 'Oh God, MacNee! What did I do to deserve this?'

– I did not scream. Today my hand's painful, yes, but already it feels freer since I wrote the words – I did not scream. I've never been able to tell anyone that I could have screamed.

When he left, I was shaking in terror. He had gone – I could call out now . . . But I was too afraid. My twin needed my help, but all I did was cry, burrowing my face in the pillow to stifle the dangerous sound.

Then I don't remember anything, until I woke next morning, thinking it was a dream. Even now, I wonder if my memory is totally clear – but what I do know is that when I sat up in our bedroom, with the pink gingham curtains blowing in the breeze from the sea outside, my sister's toy elephant, Nellie, loved into formlessness, was lying on the floor by her bed. But she wasn't there.

Even then I didn't scream.

CHAPTER FOUR

Andy Macdonald heard the shot too as he walked along the shore on the mainland opposite Lovatt Island, ostensibly having an aimless stroll. He glanced about but wasn't sure of the direction. The sound wasn't unusual around here anyway – someone out potting rabbits, probably.

It was years since he'd come down to Innellan, but here he was walking in the footsteps of his childhood self. Every picture told a story: the little cove where they'd managed to swamp the boat; the rock he'd jumped off for a dare and broken his arm; the beach where his ten-year-old self had made a first incompetent attempt at kissing a girl, and got roundly slapped . . . He smiled as the memories flooded back of those holidays in the family caravan with the gang of other kids who were all but feral by the time the summer was over.

The other guys were still asleep. There'd be sore heads later when they surfaced, but Andy's head was clear enough. He'd spent the evening talking to Christie while they got on with the solid boozing; he'd had to take relentless ribbing afterwards but he didn't care.

She intrigued him. His own job as a police officer had its dangers – last year's tragedy had been a stark reminder of that –

but hers, living with the immediate certainty that people were trying to kill you, demanded a whole different order of courage. And the working conditions: forty degrees heat, no proper accommodation and no proper showers – *no showers!* – for days on end. In a way that seemed almost worse. You'd develop techniques for blanking out danger, but keeping up morale while being sticky and stinking was something else.

Christie had talked compulsively about her army experience, but an innocent question about her background had been stonewalled. 'I don't want to talk about it. It wasn't great' was all she said and Andy had changed the subject immediately.

She'd said something earlier, though, about the army having 'saved' her, a phrase which in his experience often indicated a brush with the law. So when she asked what he did, he said he worked in public service. It was an evasion he sometimes used – not exactly untrue and sounding so boring that follow-up questions were rare. There'd be time enough to confess if the relationship developed. He was hoping it would.

The only thing was, she'd been evasive herself about meeting again. Christie would be working, and when he suggested dropping by the farmhouse she'd recoiled. It wasn't her house, she was just a guest, she didn't know when it would be suitable – excuses, excuses. She might perhaps be in the pub at night, if Matt didn't need her.

There was something about the way she said 'Matt' . . . Andy knew little about the man, except that he'd inherited from his grandmother. And that he was married.

He'd had a starring role in Christie's conversation – generous, sensitive, courageous. One of the youngest ever majors in the British Army. It was hero worship, certainly, but her disparaging tone when she mentioned Lovatt's wife made Andy wonder if there was more to it than that.

He wasn't about to back off, though. Dogged by nature, he was dogged by training now too and he was scanning the sloping fields above the shore as he walked in the hope of seeing her. It seemed strange to see deer browsing where there had always been cattle – the little black-and-white-belted Galloways, alarmingly fierce with kids who took liberties when there were calves around.

And there was Christie now, coming down one of the higher fields towards a gate. She was holding a basket of potatoes, shaking it temptingly, while behind her, and towering over her, stalked a huge stag, his head crowned with majestic antlers. There was terrifying power in that massive frame.

Andy caught his breath. Neither Christie nor the animal had seen him, and he was afraid to move. Even if it seemed to have little interest in anything apart from the potatoes, there was no saying how it would react to the arrival of a stranger. From a distance he admired the magnificent beast: the summer coat glinting red in the sunlight, the creamy underbelly and scut, the bristle of mane down the back of that powerful neck.

They were nearer the farmhouse now and Christie was leading the stag into one of three paddocks enclosed by planking, laying a trail of potatoes and watching patiently as his greed betrayed him, until she could slip through the high gate and secure it. Andy saw the stag look up and then as if in defiance give a rasping roar.

He hailed Christie just as she turned and saw him. 'Well done! That looked a bit scary.'

She waited for him to reach her. 'Only looked,' she said. 'Rudolf's a pussycat really. Hand-reared, and he'd sell his soul for a potato. But the rut's starting and then the stags get seriously unpredictable. I wouldn't be doing this once he gets wound up by being beside his rivals.'

Andy was interested. 'I've heard that roaring a few times since we came down yesterday.'

'They'll be doing that night and day soon, challenging each other and announcing to the hinds that they're ready to mate. We've three stags. They've to be separated or they'll fight. There's a fallow buck on the island too, but he hasn't any rivals so we can just leave him to it.'

Deer husbandry had its limits as a topic of conversation. 'What about you today?' Andy asked. 'Any chance of meeting me at the pub at lunchtime?'

Again Christie seemed hesitant. 'Kerr's going off to Kirkcudbright later. I'm not sure – Matt's bringing in the other two stags that aren't so tame. I should probably hang around—'

'Just a drink? Half an hour?' Andy persisted.

'Well, I could ask, I suppose. I wouldn't like to stand you up, but if I'm needed . . .' She shrugged.

'OK. I'll hope for the best.'

She headed towards the farmhouse. Andy walked slowly back to the caravan site.

Why hadn't he just told her not to bother? There were plenty of eager girls around; he'd never wasted time on reluctant ones. Until now.

'What's all this about, anyway?' DS MacNee looked at the dead doe, neatly shot in the head, its eyes glazing over. 'Have you a licence for that thing?' He pointed to the rifle.

Kerr Brodie looked at him coldly. 'Of course. This is part of my job – slaughtering deer.'

MacNee eyed him in genuine horror. 'By *shooting* them?'

'It's the kindest way. This one never knew what hit it, and the others paid no attention. You coming blundering up scared them a lot more. Try loading them in a van, taking them to the abattoir – they're terrified.

'So like I said, what are you doing here, MacNee?' He was bristling like a dog ready to defend its territory.

'Crime scene,' MacNee said laconically, and watched with interest the other man's sudden stillness.

'Crime scene? What're you talking about?'

'Body in the cave down there.' He jerked his thumb over his shoulder. 'Know anything about it?'

'No, of course not. Whose body?'

'Ah well, that's just a wee bit hard to say. It's got no clothes on.'

'A naked body?'

'Not exactly.' MacNee was playing with him. 'It's not got any flesh on either. Just bones.'

Brodie gave him a look of disgust. 'You've not improved, MacNee. But then I never thought you would.'

'Our ways parted a long time ago. You picked yours, I picked mine. And it's my job now to ask you some questions. How long have you lived here?'

'Two and a half, nearly three years.'

'Visited, before that?'

'Never even been to the area till Major Matt set up the deer farm. Knew me from the army, offered me a job when he heard about this. Bosnia – landmine.' He pulled up the leg of his trousers to give MacNee a view of his artificial leg.

He made no attempt at conventional sympathy. 'Lucky to get a job, then.'

'Aye.'

'Your gun skills coming in useful too.'

Brodie's eyes hardened. 'I don't know what you mean, MacNee.'

'Aye, do you!' There was real bitterness there.

'It's a long time since Glasgow. And it was your word against mine.'

'Mine was the truth, Brodie.'

The man gave a snort of impatience. 'If there's nothing else you want to ask in your official capacity, I've work to do even if you don't.'

There was a small tractor with a forklift, MacNee now noticed, parked nearby. As Brodie broke his gun and limped towards it, he called over his shoulder, 'See much of your da these days, MacNee?'

MacNee's hands balled into fists at his side. It was an effort to turn away, but if he didn't, Brodie would succeed again in what he'd been trying to do since they were scruffy kids living on the same stair of a Glasgow tenement – provoke MacNee into doing something he'd later regret.

He turned his back and went to sit on a rocky outcrop looking over towards Innellan, brooding.

Marjory Fleming was in an embittered mood too as she drove down the single-track road which led only to Innellan and the sea. Cat wouldn't even kiss her goodbye and the worst thing was that Fleming knew there was no real operational need for her to be here – just a cosmetic job, because of the reports that would appear in the media if she didn't, with a journalist there on the spot. She'd suffered at the hands of the press before and she was conceiving a violent dislike already for this particular representative of the breed.

She'd arranged for the pathologist, photographer and scene of crime officers to be summoned – though how, precisely, you were to secure a crime scene and carry out an effective investigation in a sea cave, and what you could hope to learn from it after so much time had clearly passed, was a whole other question. But at least that was their job, not hers.

Maybe this was a local missing person and it would all be

straightforward. She certainly hoped so, since otherwise you were talking DNA analysis and dental records and forensic anthropology, and with no immediate urgency this would go right down to the bottom of the list. It could take weeks to have any hope of ID, and of course, estimates of time of death would be in years, not hours. They wouldn't get that information quickly either.

The only upside was that the press was always impatient. If there was nothing immediately, the story would go cold. Fleming's main task today would be to quash expectation.

When she reached the Smugglers Inn she was surprised not to find MacNee there to greet her, only an embarrassed-looking young constable and the journalist who took pleasure in describing her colleague's problems.

Eying the distance between island and shore, Fleming felt the irritation of the good sailor who sees *mal de mer* as something of an affectation. Presumably MacNee hadn't done it deliberately, but really! The press was ready enough to mock the police, without making them a present of choice material.

There was no alternative to accepting Drummond's offer to take her across to see for herself, then bring back MacNee. PC Hendry was dripping around like a wet sheet, the concept of initiative being clearly foreign to him. Muttering under her breath, Fleming sent him to investigate boat hire. A fushionless gomeril, as her mother would say.

Still, at least on the trip out she could fill in on background. She didn't know this area, and since Drummond lived here, he should be a good source. Journalists always knew the dirt and he might be persuaded to dish it.

It was, at least, a glorious day, with the sea deep blue and sun sparkles on the waves. As they headed out into the bay, a flight of Manx shearwaters came past, skimming the surface on stiff wings and Fleming had to stifle a cry of delight. This wasn't a trip round the bay on the *Nancy Belle*.

'Is Lovatt one of the National Trust islands?' she asked.

According to Drummond, it wasn't. The Matt Lovatt who owned it was a relatively recent arrival, from England somewhere. Fleming's knowledge of decomposition was sketchy, but she would hazard a guess that if he'd only appeared three years ago he could have nothing to do with the case, though she'd have to interview him as owner of the property.

Drummond was more than ready to outline Innellan society. 'There are two families of incomers living here year round – we're one of them,' he said, pointing out a newish house on rising ground above the village. 'It was dirt cheap, fantastic views, great place for a kid to grow up and as long as you don't expect any contact with the locals beyond good morning if they're in a particularly loquacious mood, that's fine. Suits us – my wife and I both work, the kid's at school all day.

'What can I say about the natives?' He shrugged. 'Scrambled ashore when the Ark grounded, I reckon. Intermarried, naturally – you never say anything about anyone because they're all cousins. And if you're going to be wanting information from them, I can only say good luck. If they think – rightly or wrongly – that one of their own might be involved, you'd get more out of a chat with the deceased.

'And you'd have to think it would be a local crime, wouldn't you?' he asked innocently.

Fleming gave a non-committal smile. 'No comment,' she said.

'Just thought it was worth a try.' He made a rueful face.

Rather against her will she found herself warming to him. 'How's your son? Must have been an unpleasant experience for him.'

'Better in the daylight. What it'll be like tonight, goodness knows. He'd got hold of ghost stories from somewhere which has made it all worse.

'It is a bit macabre, mind you. See for yourself.'

They were round the seaward side of the island now and he throttled back the engine as he steered the boat into the mouth of the cave.

It was dim inside even on this bright day and their eyes took a moment to adjust. The tide was higher now and the ledge was just above their heads. As Drummond swung the torch around Fleming felt a twinge of sympathy with Tam as her own stomach turned. Not at the clean bones, no, but at the hideous reality of the torment those clamps represented. How long had it taken him to die – days, a week, straining, lacerating himself, screaming unheard, with the heavy watch on that painfully suspended wrist marking the slow excruciating hours? If the place was haunted by a restless ghost it would hardly be surprising. What sort of monster could inflict this sort of torture?

There was no evidence of clothes. The man had been stripped naked and left to die of exposure or starvation. She cleared her throat. 'The shelves.' It was a safer subject. 'Man-made, obviously. Know anything about it?'

'Not specifically. Oh, there's stories about smugglers running cargoes in from the Isle of Man – maybe this was somewhere to leave barrels for later collection. Maybe they're just stories. But it doesn't look recent, does it?'

'Hard to say, in these conditions.' Fleming looked around and spotted a ring driven into a rock nearby. Her usual caution about the press made her pause before drawing his attention to it, but he had been more than helpful and deserved a reward.

'Someone's tied up a boat here, look. Rusted iron – new or old? Corroded, certainly.'

Drummond shone the torch directly on to it. 'Looks as if

there's been some sort of older fixing here, then a new ring added later on.'

'You're in the wrong job,' Fleming said, smiling at him. 'We have guys who'll be able to date it. And the watch, of course.'

Again, he obligingly directed the torch on to it and they both studied it. Apart from being a relatively modern man's wristwatch with a date display they couldn't make out, it told them little.

'Thanks,' Fleming said. 'That's all I need to see.'

Drummond turned the boat cautiously, then opened up the throttle and they headed back round the island.

'Look, Inspector,' he said, 'I've done you a favour on this. When you get reports, will you keep me in the loop ahead of the others once they catch up with the story?'

'I'll see you get a favour in return. On one condition. That you leave out the funny section on my seasick sergeant.'

'It was going to be good,' Drummond said wistfully. 'But OK, it's a deal. I can understand you want to spare him public humiliation.'

'Partly,' Fleming said. 'And even more than that, I'm a bit short just now of something that gives me a hold over him and this is perfect.'

MacNee sat gloomily on his rocky perch. It was going to be a long time to wait, outside here with nothing to do except appreciate the beauties of nature and the sea air. His lungs weren't really adapted to that kind of strong stuff.

Not long after his exchange with Brodie, he saw a man come over from a jetty across the bay in a flat-bottomed boat; the slaughtered deer was loaded into it and ferried back to the mainland. Brodie drove the forklift back to a sort of bothy, left it there, then went back down and took off himself in a smaller motor boat. He didn't offer to take MacNee back. MacNee wouldn't have accepted if he had.

A little later there was another shot, from a field across the water, and later still a tractor and trailer came along the rough track by the shore. MacNee wasn't close enough to see, but that presumably was another deer despatched. He'd seen for himself that they hadn't time to suffer, but even so it looked kind of a brutal business. The one shot here was a pretty beast, kind of like Bambi's mother with its spotted coat and big soft brown eyes. He liked his meat unrecognisable, in wee polystyrene trays with cling film over the top.

At last he saw Drummond's boat, with Fleming on board, come out from the little pier at Innellan and head off in a curve around the island. Big Marge hadn't been exactly cheerful last night; she'd be worse today.

It could be half an hour before they fetched him and MacNee didn't fancy just sitting here contemplating her reaction to Drummond's no doubt gleeful account of his disgrace. He might go and check out the bothy, if only to have something he could tell the boss he'd done.

As he neared the cottage, a browsing doe looked up, but didn't startle away. He'd never been this close to a fallow deer before, though he'd seen one or two red ones killed by cars – and a dead man, too, after a sudden encounter with one of them on a country road. They could do more damage than you might think.

The bothy was built of rough stone, with a corrugated-iron roof which extended over a lean-to for the miniature tractor. The window glass had long gone and been replaced by slats roughly nailed in place. The front door, its wood scoured to bare timber by the elements and rotted along the bottom, stood open on a barn-like room, and when MacNee stuck his head inside, the musty smell of animal feed greeted him. There was none of the usual farm disorder, though; in the dim light he could see sacks arranged with military precision and racks and cupboards for tools.

From the middle of the room rose a rough staircase with a solid modern door at the top. It had a lock, but when MacNee turned the handle it opened and he stepped into a loft running the full length of the building, with a small window at each end; these too had been boarded up. One of the slats had slipped and a ray of sunshine played on the dust motes stirred up by his entrance.

The roof beams came low down and only a strip in the centre gave reasonable headroom, but at one end a thick mattress with a sleeping bag and blankets was tucked under the eaves, with a camping Gaz lamp beside it. There was a very basic lavatory and basin behind a partition and at the other end a table with a camping stove on it as well as a couple of plates, a mug, a frying pan, kettle and a few utensils. There was a shelf with tins too, MacNee noticed. Beans with pork sausages, ham, corned beef; a comfortable enough set-up, if you'd to be here overnight for some reason – sick animal, or something, MacNee supposed vaguely.

And eggs. And butter. And a loaf of bread. MacNee frowned. You didn't leave stuff like that for an emergency. Someone must be staying here.

He didn't know enough about deer to know if they needed babysitting. Or maybe one was ill now. He shrugged and went back downstairs.

But as he did, it came to him that he wouldn't really like to spend much time here. There was something uncomfortable about the atmosphere. Or maybe it was just the dim light and the draught of air coming through the window that was making him feel chilly.

* * *

Steve Donaldson, lounging against a car in the Smugglers Inn car park, threw away his cigarette and straightened up, looking at his watch and scowling.

'For God's sake, that's after five to twelve! When's the silly cow going to open up?'

He was a big, powerful man gone soft, with dark hair badly in need of trimming and a roll of fat round his thick neck. His fleshy mouth was permanently set in discontented lines and there were the marks of temper between his brows.

Derek Sorley, a puny figure beside him, said, 'Scared of the polis. She's only got a licence from twelve. Anyway, what do you think about what I said?'

Donaldson grunted. 'Oh, I'll go with anything that gets that bugger off the land I should be farming, by rights.'

It wasn't what the lawyers had said – the lease agreement had lapsed, and Donaldson hadn't been working the farm with his father – but Sorley knew better than to remind him.

'If the plan works, I'm sure he'd be glad for you to take a lease afterwards.'

That only seemed to provoke further rancour. 'Aye, and I'd be expected to be grateful to him. "Yes, sir, thank you sir!"' He put on an affected voice, then added savagely, 'And get back where you came from, you Sassenach bastard!'

Sorley, who now considered himself an authority on Celtic culture, interrupted him. 'Ah now, that's not quite right. The Gaelic *sasunnach* doesn't mean English, it means lowlander, non-Gaelic speaker. To a highlander, you'd be one.'

The dangerous look on his companion's face brought him up short. 'Ah, well.' He saw with some relief the pub door opening. 'Look – there she is now. The other thing – I'll come round this afternoon and we'll talk about it.'

Donaldson grunted and moved on ahead. To his further

annoyance he found he wasn't first to the bar; the sergeant, MacNee, was sitting on a stool there already with a woman beside him.

'That's nice,' he sneered. 'One law for the polis and another for the rest of us, eh?'

MacNee held up his china mug in a mock salute. 'Not really, pal. Just a wee fly cuppa.'

Georgia Stanley bristled. 'I don't serve alcohol to anyone before twelve o'clock. Since it's that now, I'm ready to take your order. The usual?'

She pulled pints for the two men. Once they had carried them to a corner table she returned to the other end of the bar, pulling a face.

'Sorry about that. Not two of my favourite people,' she confessed, then as the door opened again and an elderly man appeared, groaned quietly. 'And there's another – Steve's father. I always make sure I've got the counter between me and him.'

MacNee and Fleming turned to look. Donaldson senior looked to be in his seventies, shorter than his son but not unlike him in appearance. His sagging jowls had tufts of an old man's weak, greying stubble after a careless shave and the leer he gave her from his watery eyes explained Georgia's reaction.

'Pint. Bring it over to me, pet, will you?' he said with a smile revealing broken and discoloured teeth.

A little knot of people coming in gave her the excuse to say, 'Hang on, Hugh. You'll have to take it yourself – I'm going to be serving.'

There was a lot of interest in Innellan's most sensational event since a summer visitor trying to launch his boat had beached his new Jaguar below the high tide mark two years ago, and the buzz of talk rose.

Fleming heard a woman say, 'Well, it's just a skeleton, isn't it?

76

Not like a *body*, or anything.' Her friends laughed comfortably.

She was wrong. It was exactly the same as a body – a body whose identity had been ruthlessly stripped away, right down to the very flesh on its bones.

'That's it,' Matt Lovatt said, closing the gate on the last of the stags. 'Nothing more to do, except leave them to get worked up for the next couple of weeks. I can smell them already.'

And Christie could too, now she thought about it. There was a taint on the air, rank and pungent.

'Smells a bit like goats,' she said.

'A bit – stick around! They really start to stink. Gets the hinds excited – sort of like guys putting on aftershave when they're going out on the pull.'

'Takes more than that to do it for me,' Christie said saucily, which made Matt laugh as they headed towards the farmhouse. She loved making him laugh – he didn't laugh often enough.

'What else is there today?' she asked. 'Kerr's gone into Kirkcudbright.'

'I know. But there's not much – concentrate to take out later and there's some fencing needing attention. But take some time off – I don't want to be a slave-driver.'

He gave her his lopsided smile – lopsided, because one side of his face didn't work very well any more – which always went to her heart.

'You're not!' she protested. 'Are you going in to lunch now?'

The arrangement was there were packets of instant soup in the cupboard, cheese and ham in the fridge, and you took your own when it suited you, eating with whoever was there or taking it to your room, if you liked.

Christie cherished days when she and Matt coincided at the kitchen table alone. She still knew little about him as a person;

77

he was very reserved, but gradually she was piecing together the tiny scraps of information he let fall. They couldn't discuss the art films he liked and she'd never seen, or her favourite pop videos, but they could agree they could barely even look at a poster for a war movie.

Matt glanced at his watch. 'I'll probably take a break around twelve-thirty. I was up early today.'

Christie nodded, then said casually, 'Did Lissa go with Kerr?'

'No. She's found some crab apples – says she's going to make jelly, but I wouldn't depend on it for your "piece" at teatime.'

She'd be in the kitchen, then. Christie smiled. 'That's very brave. If you don't need me I might pop round the pub for half an hour.'

'Fine, fine. See you later,' Matt said absently, and went on towards the house. In the pen in the yard, his dog was waiting, padding from foot to foot and swinging its tail. He let it out and it pranced round him as he went inside.

Feeling somehow deflated, Christie watched him go then walked down the farm road leading to Innellan.

It was quarter past twelve when Andy Macdonald reached the pub. He was alone; the other guys were still doggedly eating the fry-up they hoped would make them ready for the next beer.

He registered the surprising number of cars in the Smugglers' car park without looking at them closely, but the police car drew his attention. When was the last time he'd seen one here? Probably when he and his delinquent mates had taken the underwear off Mrs Chalmers's washing line and draped her impressively large knickers and bras over the gravestones round the old church. In keen anticipation of another local drama, Andy went in and headed for the bar.

'What's going on, then, Georgia? Anyone exciting under arrest?'

'Andy Macdonald! What are you doing here?'

The sudden materialisation of Big Marge at his elbow threw him completely. 'Er . . . boss! What . . . oh, I'm . . . I'm in a caravan with some mates, along there.' He jerked his head, then noticed MacNee. 'Hello, Tam. Well, er . . . this is a bit of a surprise.'

He was babbling. Georgia, whose sympathetic expression suggested that given a chance she'd have warned him, put a pint in his hand. He took a steadying sip, then said, 'A stag weekend, that's all. What's happening?'

'Bones,' MacNee said in suitably sepulchral tones. 'Old bones. And watch what you say – we've the press breathing down our necks.' He raised his tea mug in an ironic salute to Tony Drummond, who had edged closer.

Fleming drew Macdonald into a corner and was briefing him in a low voice when Christie Jack came in. She looked round, and Macdonald said awkwardly, 'Sorry, boss – someone looking for me.'

He went over. 'Good to see you – I wasn't sure you'd make it. A Beck's?'

'Thanks.' She was looking puzzled. 'What on earth's going on today, with all the police and stuff?'

Macdonald was saying uncomfortably, 'Well—' just as MacNee hailed him.

'Come on, Andy, introduce us to your friend.'

Macdonald turned with obvious reluctance. 'Christie Jack. This is DS Tam MacNee and DI Fleming.'

Christie's eyes flickered over their faces, then went to his. 'How . . . how do you know them?'

Macdonald winced. 'I'm in the force.'

'Detective Sergeant,' MacNee put in helpfully.

'Oh,' Christie said flatly.

Macdonald's face fell. 'Let's go and sit down,' he suggested. 'There's a table over by the window.'

As they moved away, Fleming said coldly, 'You really are a sod, Tam. That wasn't kind.'

MacNee conceded that. 'No, but it was kinna fun. Should have told her at the start, shouldn't he?' He went on sententiously, '*The honest heart that's free frae a' / Intended fraud or guile, / However Fortune kick the ba' / Has ay some cause to smile.*' He did just that, favouring Fleming with a choice specimen.

'A man who threw up on a journalist isn't in a strong position to sneer at others,' Fleming pointed out and saw with satisfaction the smug grin disappear.

Kerr Brodie drove into the car park near Kirkcudbright harbour, looked round, and swore. His instructions had been clear enough. Where the hell was the man?

It wasn't a good day. As if things weren't problematic enough already, this was seriously threatening to his plans. It was tempting to drive away and leave the stupid bugger to his fate – but a loose cannon careering round the deck could sink the ship.

Ill-temperedly he parked, got out and went into a bar with a window he could watch from, but he'd finished his sandwich and almost finished his pint when a lorry drew up and a painfully skinny young man climbed down from the cab with a bulging carrier bag in his hand, waving a thank you to the driver. As the lorry drove off, he looked round him with a sort of helpless misery.

Brodie drained his glass and hurried out. 'What kept you?' he snarled. 'Get in the car. Over there.'

The youth's face cleared. 'Thanks, Sarge. I didn't know what to do—'

'Spare me.' Brodie slammed the car door and took off almost

before his passenger was inside. 'Shut up, and take on board what I'm telling you, Crawford. It's important. Get it wrong and you're done.'

Crawford's pinched face registered alarm as he listened to Brodie, but he didn't speak until Brodie finished. Then he only said, 'Right, Sarge.'

They drove on in silence. At last Crawford ventured, 'Don't suppose you've got a smoke, Sarge?'

Brodie gave him an exasperated look, then jerked his head towards the glovebox. 'Tin in there.'

The young man rolled a joint with shaking hands, took a long draw and sat back, his hunched shoulders relaxing as the tension drained from his slight frame.

I have to go on. Now I've started, I mustn't stop. Or all the pain, all this dreadful remembering – pointless.

There in the bedroom that was too quiet, I heard the morning sounds of movement. My mother's voice, shrill, angry with my father. A familiar sound. Her footsteps, brisk, annoyed, clipping along the wooden floor of the landing. I hid under my covers, rigid with fear.

The door opened. 'Come on, you two – time to get up.' The voice, as always, with that slight hint of barely controlled irritation.

I sat up, rubbing my eyes as if I had been asleep.

'Where's your sister?' she said. 'Did she get up early?'

I remember I said, 'I was asleep.' I remember I got dressed as usual but remember, too, shivering as if I was cold though it was a sunny morning.

After that, things are blurred. I don't know how long it was before the house was full of strangers and the questions started. I answered them all with tears and shakes of my head. After that I kept to my room, I think, but I can't be sure of much in the hazy unreality of the days that followed.

It's like a series of snapshots: lying in bed, in that same room, unable to sleep for terror, unable to tell anyone why; hearing my mother screaming at my father, screaming and screaming – but that was nothing new; a kitten, I think – did someone bring a kitten to cheer me up, or is that just a dream that came from an unfulfilled longing?

Then there came a night – I don't know how much later. I had been asleep, I think, and I got up and went out of my room. The house was silent and –   too difficult I can't

CHAPTER FIVE

Georgia Stanley glanced out as a large van drew up in the street outside the Smugglers Inn.

'That's the telly again,' she said. 'They'll be thinking they live here.'

'Right. Tam, let's move.' DI Fleming put down her mug. 'I want to see this Major Lovatt anyway and clear our lines before anyone else arrives on his property. Thanks, Georgia.'

MacNee followed her out of the back door, with a glance back at Macdonald and the girl, who seemed to be having a rather stilted conversation. Outside, PC Hendry was keen to assure the boss that boats were coming from Kirkcudbright and would stand by until required. The pathologist was expected in around half an hour.

'That's more like it, Constable,' Fleming said. The lad looked relieved as she turned and headed towards the house Georgia had pointed out.

It was a brisk five-minute walk away, standing on a rise above the rough farm road which skirted the shore: a substantial, white-harled farmhouse in its own garden, a little apart from farm buildings and enclosures and with a small wood of mature broadleaves round about it. The original, more modest house had been extended with a wing at the back and spoke, if not of wealth, then certainly of solid prosperity. It was well maintained and the garden was laid out to grass and paving, to an effect undeniably more military than artistic. Near the house there was a spacious dog-run and kennel, surrounded by chain-link fencing and empty at the moment.

Matt Lovatt answered the door himself. Georgia had prepared them for his disfigurement, but even so the taut, shiny skin under his right eye distorting his cheek was shocking, perhaps partly because he would otherwise have been a good-looking man: tall, dark curling hair with a hint of a widow's peak, very dark grey-blue eyes. Fleming found it hard to assess his age; he probably looked older than he was. He seemed surprised by their warrant cards, but waved them in without question.

The square hall was panelled in varnished pine and dark after the sunshine outside. Fleming, glancing round, encountered a pair of pale amber eyes, glowing in the light from the open door, and recoiled.

There in the shadows of the staircase was – surely not a wolf? But those eyes, slightly slanted, the ruff of silver-fawn fur, the huge feet . . .

'My God!' MacNee spoke first. 'What the hell is that?'

Fleming sensed Lovatt stiffen and saw the creature's ears prick. 'My dog,' he said flatly.

'It's not a dog, it's a frigging wolf!' MacNee exclaimed.

'I don't know what his father was. His mother was a German Shepherd of sorts.'

The Wild Animals Act, 1976 – the words hovered in the air. Fleming said, 'A hybrid? Do you have a licence, sir?'

'I have no reason to suppose the father was a wolf.' Lovatt

was defensive. 'Look, Inspector, I was in Bosnia with the army. This stray came into the camp and produced pups, two of them, and she died along with the other one. I raised this fella myself.'

The dog, sensing it was being talked about, moved to stand beside its master and Lovatt fondled its head.

'There are plenty of dogs like this around the Bosnian villages. OK, he could be second-, third-generation wolf – how would I know? Maybe more. The point is, he's domesticated, he's intelligent, he's extremely well trained.' At a hand gesture, the animal sat.

Lovatt was clearly familiar with the legislation. First-generation wolf, licence needed. Second generation, fine.

'How did you get it into the country?' Fleming asked, and saw his face take on a wary look.

'I spent a bit of time in France, and he came over on a pet passport.'

'Vouched for by an army vet, do I take it, sir?' Fleming's tone was dry.

'As it happens, yes.' Lovatt met her eyes squarely.

'I see. Well, Major Lovatt—'

He interrupted her. 'I don't use the rank. I prefer Mr or Matt – that's fine.'

'Mr Lovatt, then. I've seen the provision for the dog as we came in and I believe it would comply with the regulations anyway. I take it there have been no complaints?'

'No,' he said firmly.

'Then I think we can leave it at that.'

Fleming noticed the dog's pricked ears relax even before the man nodded and said, 'So what can I do for you, Inspector?'

The door was standing open on a room looking out over the bay, and she could see chairs and sofas. 'May we . . . ?'

As she spoke, a door at the back of the hall opened and a woman appeared. She was slightly built, with long dark hair, pale-blue eyes and an air of helplessness.

'Matt, I need you,' she said.

Lovatt turned with evident irritation. 'What's the matter, Lissa? I've got people here—'

'It's the jelly.' Her eyes filled with tears. 'It's not gelling – it's all runny. I need you to come and see . . .'

'I can't come just at the moment,' he said with elaborate patience. 'I'll come when I've finished here – all right?'

She gave him a tragic look. 'Oh, I know. It's not important, is it? Fine.' She drifted back through the door under the stairs.

Fleming blinked. Wow! Straight off the 'passive aggressive' page in the psychology textbook. Still, not her problem. She followed Lovatt into the sitting room.

It was a big, square, very traditional room – fireplace in the middle of the wall opposite the door, double sash windows across the front of the house – and very traditionally furnished and decorated too. The deep sofa had chintz covers in a Jacobean print and there were armchairs and occasional tables which were definitely antique. The Regency-striped wallpaper, celadon green and gold, was faded and rubbed in places, with darker patches where pictures had once hung. It was a functional, indeed comfortable room, but clearly one which had not benefited from recent attention.

On the to-do list, perhaps, Fleming reflected. Setting up a deer farm couldn't be cheap and there would be other priorities. Running it as a sort of unofficial charity, as Georgia had told them he was, wouldn't help cash flow either.

MacNee was asking him about the island, and Lovatt looked puzzled.

'Yes, I'm over there most days – if not me, then Kerr Brodie who is . . . well, my foreman, I suppose you could call him. We've fallow deer over there.'

'Ever been in the cave round the back of the island?'

Fleming eyed Lovatt narrowly. The rigidity of the damaged side of his face made for a certain lack of expression, so it was hard to be sure, but she couldn't see any sign of sensitivity to the question.

'The little cave? I took a boat in once, shortly after we got here, but it's not much of a cave really, just a hollow in the rock face.'

'Didn't notice anything?'

Fleming stepped in as Lovatt shook his head blankly.

'Mr Lovatt, I understand you inherited from your grandmother. Did you visit regularly?'

'Well, no. My parents divorced when I was young and my mother never got on with her. I don't think there were even childhood visits, unless I was too young to remember.'

'So the first time was after she died?'

'Yes. The will, frankly, was a shock. I knew my father came from Scotland and nothing else. But I was just coming to the end of my commission and I'd always wanted to farm – perhaps it's in the genes.'

'And your father – would he have expected the farm to come to him?'

'I don't know. Perhaps, but we're not in touch – I lived with my mother and they were estranged. But can I ask what all this is about?'

Fleming gave him the bald facts, and he looked amazed.

'And it's been there for years? It was there when I went into the cave?'

'We're not in a position to say just yet. But depending on the tide it was above eye level, so it certainly could have been. You have no idea who might have had access in past years?'

She wasn't hopeful of an enlightening answer and she didn't get one. 'Anyone with a boat,' he said, and she knew that already.

'Tell me about Brodie,' MacNee said suddenly. 'How did you come to employ him?'

'Kerr? He was in the regiment. NCO, short-service commission. Stood on a landmine a month before he was due to leave. Unbelievable bad luck. Then when I was setting up here I talked to a vet who pioneered deer farming in Scotland, and when he told me about the research showing that shooting the animals on site was more humane than sending them off for slaughter, I thought of Kerr Brodie immediately. Handy man with a gun, Kerr.'

'I can imagine,' MacNee said dryly and Fleming looked at him sharply. There was something about the way he said that . . .

'He was at a pretty low ebb,' Lovatt went on. 'But this place helped him, like it helped me. And he helped us – Lissa and I both have had . . .' he hesitated, 'Well, problems of one sort and another. Kerr's been very helpful in the past.'

In the past? Fleming noted the curious phrase, but said only, 'And you're giving a chance to other soldiers, I hear.'

He looked awkward. 'Oh, well – we can manage one, or perhaps two – and of course they help round the farm. I just hope the TV interview won't raise expectations we can't fulfil.'

'The television people are back today again, which may be even less welcome.' Fleming got to her feet. 'Thank you, Mr Lovatt. There will be officers dealing with the situation on the island, but they shouldn't have to trouble you here.'

As they walked back towards the inn, Fleming said, 'What did you make of him? Seemed straightforward enough.'

MacNee was more cynical. 'Oh, an officer and a gent, no doubt. They're always so good at the surface stuff you never get to see what's underneath. And if he's a pal of Kerr Brodie's,' he almost spat the name, 'you'd better count your fingers after shaking hands.'

So she'd been right: there was some sort of history with this man. But with TV cameras and some obvious reporters waiting around the inn, it wasn't exactly the moment. Fleming groaned.

'The vultures are gathering. Take a deep breath, Tam, and count to ten before you open your mouth.'

He muttered something about whisky and facing the devil – Burns, presumably, but she didn't stop to listen.

There was something mesmeric about driving at speed up the sweeping northern motorway, the traffic thinning as she crossed into Scotland and on through the brooding moorlands of the Borders. Elena Tindall had the car radio on but lost in her own thoughts she was hardly aware of it.

Until the news bulletin. She gasped. It couldn't be! Not now! The car behind her blared its horn as she suddenly slowed down. Shaking, she got out of its way and it flashed past her with another angry blast.

She drove on in the inside lane until she reached a lay-by, then pulled in thankfully. She collapsed over the steering wheel, dizzy with the thoughts whirling in her head.

It was so cruel, when she had at last a chance of healing the wounds that had tormented her for so long, when she had everything in place and her way clear. To abandon it now . . .

But why? The question came from somewhere in that steely core that had saved Elena from going under long ago. It needn't matter; viewed from another angle it could even be an advantage.

She still felt shaky, but she sat up and started the car again. All she needed to do was stay calm and confident.

* * *

Christie Jack walked back from the pub in a thoroughly bad mood. Andy Macdonald had apologised for his deception several times while she assured him it didn't matter – which wasn't true – until at last she snapped, 'Look, let's talk about something else, OK? Why are your pals here anyway?'

Once he'd told her about the skeleton on her lovely island, which she'd have preferred not to know, the conversation stalled. It got stickier and stickier until at last she'd finished her drink and could leave.

Oh, it wasn't that she'd any particular problem with the police. Some of her own early experiences had been, well, unfortunate – Andy must somehow have picked up on that – but she'd been in the army since and her attitude to authority had changed. His job was like any other – you got good cops and bad cops. There'd been some right psychopathic bastards in the army.

Christie just couldn't take being conned. He'd sized her up and decided to deceive her. Maybe he'd reckoned once she got to know him she'd be too charmed to walk away, or maybe he wasn't planning to be around long enough for it to matter. Either way, it wasn't a good start. In any case, right now she wasn't looking for involvement with anyone. Anyone else.

Not that Christie was what you could call 'involved' with Matt Lovatt. He treated her like just another army comrade, and sometimes she wondered if he even noticed she was female. A couple of times, though, they'd really connected and he'd laughed like she'd never heard him laugh before.

It had been just hero worship, a teenage-type crush on this really great guy. Even though he and Lissa slept in separate bedrooms – separate wings, in fact – how their marriage worked was none of her business. Maybe he snored. Or she did.

But then, last night . . .

Last night, Christie had come home late from the pub. She'd enjoyed talking to Andy; she hadn't talked and talked that way since she left the army and she was high on the unaccustomed pleasure. Her head was buzzing and there was no way she could sleep until she'd come down.

She went to sit at her bedroom window, as she often did, looking out over the bay towards the islands. The moon had gone down and as the Innellan street lights went out the night sky suddenly become a pitch-black background to a million million stars. Yet even with that deep peace, broken only by an occasional startling bellow from a stag, Christie's mind was still sparking and fizzing.

Tea – that was the answer. She'd make a cuppa – and grab a biscuit or two as well. It was a long time since supper. She opened her door, then heard another door being quietly opened. She drew back, closing hers over, and swore silently.

That would be Lissa. She and Christie had the only two bedrooms to the front of the house; Matt's was in the wing towards the back, up some stairs which came off the landing on the main flight, and Kerr had a bedsitter and bathroom on the ground floor, near the kitchen.

For a moment Christie paused. She'd rather stay awake all night than sit with Lissa at the kitchen table – but maybe she was going to the sitting room or something, and Christie could sneak past unseen. She was getting fixated on the idea of tea now, and the Hobnobs were calling her.

She opened the door again and tiptoed across the landing to look over the banisters. She could hear the wheezy ticking of the grandfather clock in the hall below, and also stealthy footsteps padding down the stairs.

But it wasn't Lissa. It was Kerr Brodie in his dressing gown, and he'd come from Lissa's room.

Stifling a gasp of shock, Christie shrank back hastily in case he should feel her eyes upon him. She was a little afraid of him already and he'd take it badly. She retreated, waiting until she could be sure he was out of earshot before she risked closing her door.

What the hell was going on? Did Matt know about this? And if he did, did he care?

She went back to her seat, oblivious to the stars and the night sounds, struggling with this unwelcome knowledge. She felt protective anger thinking of Matt being hurt, Matt who was the soul of honour and decency in her eyes. Lissa was his wife, after all; sure, their relationship was rocky, but that didn't give Kerr the right to take advantage. What a bastard! Matt had given him a job, a life, even, and this was his repayment. She'd always been wary of Kerr – not wrong there!

But maybe Matt knew. She'd heard of open marriages, of course, though she always wondered how you dealt with possessiveness and jealousy. She was damn sure she couldn't do it.

Either way, it changed things. If Matt accepted it, he was free to enjoy sauce for the gander. And if he didn't, he'd suffer less if there was someone to hold his hand when he found out. Her, for example.

She thought about it as she walked back after her awkward meeting with Andy. Actually, she'd been thinking about it all day. She'd rather not have known, and facing Kerr over breakfast hadn't been easy, especially when Lissa came in.

'Sleep well?' he'd asked her.

'Very well, by my standards,' Lissa had said, giving him that faint, weary smile that always made Christie want to slap her.

So Christie had no scruples. She'd worked out her strategy; now she only needed campaign tactics that wouldn't utterly humiliate her if Matt wasn't interested.

Take it gently, she decided. First objective – get him along to the pub, where they could get to know each other better over a beer or two. Lissa wouldn't come and if Kerr came he'd get talking to the locals as he always did.

Yes, that was it – a series of small strategic objectives. Not tonight – Andy would still be around tonight, and that could scupper her plans. Tomorrow night, then. Her stomach gave a little nervous jump at the thought.

Catriona Fleming looked round the bleak double room. The furniture – two beds, two wardrobes, two desks, two chests of drawers, two chairs with sagging webbing and wooden arms – was way past its best and the walls, an indeterminate shade of grey, were daubed with abandoned Blu-tack, the surface lifted in places by illicit Sellotape. Her room-mate hadn't arrived yet – just as well, since all the floor space was taken up by Cat's belongings, dumped by her father and brother before they left.

She'd a hollow feeling inside, thinking of her comfortable room at home, of her family, irritating but always there when she needed them – but she mustn't start feeling homesick already! She'd been counting the days to the start of Life with a capital *L*. She was nervous about the room-mate, but then Cat got along with most people OK.

She was disappointed Will wasn't here to meet her. She'd texted him, but his hours at the hospital were so irregular, he could be sleeping. His phone had been off the last couple of days.

Without much hope Cat phoned him and her spirits soared when his voice, not his voicemail, answered.

'Will!' she exclaimed. 'I'm here, at the residence. Where are you? Can you come round?'

'Hi, Cat,' he said. 'Right, right. Er . . . tell you what, I'll be there in twenty minutes. OK?'

'Brilliant. See you.'

With renewed vigour, Cat set about unpacking, shoving everything into the wardrobe to be sorted out later. The older residence was a lot cheaper than the newer, smarter ones, and once she'd a few posters up and her own things round her, the room would be fine. It just needed TLC, and indeed was looking better already with the floor cleared and the bed made up.

She was spreading a brightly coloured rug over it when Will's knock came at the door. She flung it open.

'Ta-ra! Get me – Catriona Fleming, real, genuine student! At last!' She flung herself into his arms, holding up her face to be kissed.

Will fielded her awkwardly, planting a kiss somewhere near her mouth, then moved her aside to survey the room.

'God! A bit dismal, isn't it?'

Feeling deflated, Cat shut the door. 'It'll be fine once I'm settled in.' She linked her arm through his. 'Now, Will Irvine, there's work to be done. That case has to go on top of the wardrobe—'

'Cat, we need to talk,' he said, and something in his look and voice turned her heart to stone.

She sat down on the bed abruptly, and listened while he told her about the other medical student who had been working at the hospital with him. She listened in silence, afraid that if she opened her mouth she might start screaming, or be sick, or something equally humiliating.

Will, her lovely Will, was saying, 'We've always been straight with each other and I knew you'd prefer not to get stuff like, you know, "I think we need a bit of space." Then you'd hear about Elaine and it would be worse that I hadn't told you face-to-face . . .'

He seemed to be patting himself on the back for heroism.

'Oh, you think?' Cat muttered. Her throat felt so tight she could hardly get the words out and her lips were oddly numb.

Will looked sheepish. 'Well, it was just a boy-girl thing, Cat. You can't have expected it to last.'

A boy-girl thing? This from Will, the love of her life, who had always talked about 'for ever'? She found her voice.

'Get out! Get out right now. I never want to see you or speak to you again.' She jumped up and seized her mobile from the desk with trembling hands. 'See? There's your number – I've deleted it. If you phone me, I won't answer. I'm deleting you from my life as well.' She flung the phone down on the bed.

It was a good line. She was rather proud of it, as Will, murmuring some crap about having hoped they could be friends, departed.

'Good riddance!' she shouted down the corridor after him, and slammed the door. But then the tears came.

Ten minutes later, Cat was still crying. Her nose was blocked, her eyes were swollen and her chest was aching as if her heart, indeed, had broken. And there was no one to go to for comfort. Will had been her only friend in Glasgow, and now she had no one at all. She had never felt so lonely, so utterly wretched. She wanted her mother.

Mum had always been great when bad things happened – when Jenny had said she didn't want to be best friends any more, when the boy she really, really fancied in Year Ten told her he didn't fancy her because she had spots. Mum could make you see it wasn't the end of the world, and then she'd say something acidly funny about them that made you laugh. She badly needed a laugh at the moment. Cat reached for her mobile again.

But what was the point? Mum was in the middle of a murder inquiry and that took precedence over everything – like Cammie almost crippling himself that time or her daughter feeling suicidal now.

She didn't, quite, of course. Cat wasn't about to give Will Irvine the satisfaction of knowing how he'd hurt her. And it did hurt – how it hurt! She flung herself down on the bed and buried her face in the pillow.

When the door opened, Cat sat up, blinking and sniffing. The girl in the doorway was very skinny, all in black with her face so pale that her eyes, dramatic with jet-black eyeliner and mascara and iridescent eyeshadow, looked like dark holes above her purple mouth. There was a stud in her nose and half a dozen metal rings down one ear, and another through her brow. She was trailing a huge black canvas bag on wheels, which she parked beside the other bed, and looked in some surprise at her room-mate.

'Got a problem?'

Licking her dry lips, Cat said, 'I've just been dumped.' Forming the words for the first time made her feel worse and the tears started again.

'Bummer,' her Goth companion said, not unkindly. 'Boy next door?'

'Sort of.'

'Better without him.' She was looking round the room. 'Jeez, what a hellhole. Still, don't plan on hanging out here much.'

There was something bracing about such breezy indifference. Cat found a tissue and blew her nose hard. 'I'm Catriona Fleming – Cat,' she said.

'Lily.' She sketched a salute with one finger. She kicked at her bag. 'This can wait. Fancy checking out the scene?'

Cat put a hand to her blubbered face. 'Not sure I'm up to it.'

Lily gave her a long look then went to the wash-hand basin in one corner of the room and ran it full of cold water. 'Stick your head in that. And then I've got something that'll make you feel better.'

Cat did as she was told, but said hesitantly, 'I-I don't do drugs.' Will had been really against them, and as for Mum . . . !

'This isn't "drugs".' Lily sketched quotation marks. 'Strictly legal. Bubbles, it's called. Or miaow-miaow. Give you a bit of a lift.'

Cat, lifting a dripping face and groping in a drawer for a towel, was under no illusions. But what did she care now what Will thought? Or Mum, for that matter. Doing something Mum would disapprove of was a sort of revenge.

Cat drew a deep breath. 'OK, Lily, I'm cool with that.'

It was six o'clock by the time DI Fleming had detailed uniforms to start on house-to-house enquiries and liaised with teams arriving. The pathologist, muttering about work conditions, had performed the official bit and the photographer, also muttering, had done what he could from a bobbing boat. The scene-of-crime officers were out there now doing what was possible at the cave before it got dark, trying to get the remains removed by tonight if the tide allowed. She could only hope they'd better sea legs than Tam.

She'd given a statement to the media, warning them that little would emerge over the next few days, but she knew they'd be hopefully trailing her officers round the houses – if they could tear themselves away from the Smugglers Inn, now doing a roaring trade.

There wasn't anything else for Fleming to do here, but there would be plenty back at the headquarters in Kirkluce, and the sooner she got there the sooner it would be done. She headed back to the car.

She'd thought about Cat on and off all day, and before

Fleming drove off she took out her mobile to give her a call – luckily there was a signal here. There was no answer so she left an affectionate message on voicemail. Out on the town, doubtless. She smiled as she thought, with just a touch of envy, of Cat and Will, celebrating the first night of Cat's student career.

If she'd been more sensible herself when she was young, she'd have gone to university too, and it was a permanent regret that she hadn't. Lucky, lucky Cat!

She hadn't realised how tough it would be, how difficult even on a physical level. In her hired Peugeot, on the roughly gravelled parking area outside the hired chalet, Elena Tindall sat wondering if her body would obey her when she tried to get out of the car. She was taking shallow breaths, her chest hurt and her legs felt weak and useless.

She didn't have to do this. There was nothing to stop her turning the car and heading off to a decent hotel, then going back to an ecstatic welcome from Eddie tomorrow. She must be mad, not just to accept his generous love and the life he offered her and be grateful.

But Elena was going mad anyway, silently but steadily, more and more trapped in the prison of her past, spiralling slowly down until one day she would take the little silver penknife and slit her wrists in earnest. So what was a risk fraught with danger – more, even, than she had thought there would be – when set against a certainty?

She was panicking, hyperventilating. Elena put her face in her cupped hands, breathing steadily until her heartbeat slowed. When she opened the car door the air was unexpectedly still and warm, almost oppressive; it felt somehow unhealthy, like a lusciously ripe fruit on the point of rotting. She told herself not to be fanciful as she steadied herself against the car until she was sure her legs wouldn't buckle.

The chalet was one of perhaps twenty or thirty, set in the hillside up behind Innellan and straggling along the curve of the bay. Wooden structures weathered to silver-grey, they had picture windows looking out over Fleet Bay and the islands, and on this golden evening, as light slowly drained from the sky, the view was incomparable. Elena did not turn to admire it.

She brought in her bags from the car and looked disparagingly around her. This was IKEA-chic, she supposed – family-friendly accommodation, clean and well maintained, but hardly what she was used to. But then, once upon a time having a place like this all to herself would have seemed like paradise.

She had driven from Salford without a meal stop and she was hungry and tired and grubby. What she needed first was a hot shower, letting the force of the water wash away the stresses of the day. Without unpacking, she went through to the spartan bathroom.

The shower was hot, admittedly, but a feeble apology compared with the power showers she took for granted now, and the towels provided had synthetics in with the cotton which made them slippery and too soft instead of absorbent.

How quickly luxury became essential! Damp and irritable, Elena dressed again and went through to the kitchen.

It was fairly basic, but she wasn't planning on cooking much; for tonight at least she had food she'd bought in Waitrose before she left. It was soothing to have prosciutto crudo, manzanilla olives and good bread with Normandy butter to set on the clumsy white plates.

She'd brought a case of wine too, and the Barolo tasted good even from a thick cheap glass. Elena drank the first one fast, the second a little slower. It was a long time since she had done more than sip a little well-chilled white wine and already she could feel the first effects: a loosening of tension, the faintest lift of light-headedness. She must phone Eddie before she got drunk, as she fully intended to.

There were three messages on her mobile when she switched it on. No need to check to see who they were from: he answered before the end of the first ring.

'I've been waiting to hear from you, doll. You all right? Your phone was off.'

'Eddie, I'm fine. Just starting to chill out. I've been feeling very stressed lately and this is the perfect place, a sort of retreat. I can feel it doing me good already.'

'You'll be patient, won't you, darling? Don't know how long it will take, but I'll come back so relaxed you won't know me.' That wasn't exactly a lie; she hoped it would be true.

'Of course, of course.' He sounded deflated, and she could sense his struggle not to break the rules and quiz her. 'If it's what you need, it's all that's important to me. You know that.'

'You are a love,' Elena said, and this time she meant it.

'Oh . . .' Eddie gave a little, awkward laugh. 'Just so you come back to me at the end of it. Promise? And keep in touch.'

'Of course I will.' But when he said, 'Love you, angel,' she said only, 'Night, darling. Sleep well.'

After the third glass of Barolo, Elena got up and went at last to the window. She closed her eyes, drew a deep breath and then opened them. Her grip on the glass unconsciously tightened.

The light had all but gone now and a huge harvest moon was rising, a curious deep red-orange in colour. The lights of Innellan shone below, as well as the lights from a house further out along the shore – and there were the islands, dark shadows on a pewter sea.

Suddenly, the silence was shattered by a sound which made

the hairs stand up on the back of her neck – a long, spine-chilling howl. A dog, Elena told herself, just a dog, baying at the blood-red moon.

But when at last, a little unsteadily, Elena went to bed, she dreamt of wolves she could not see apart from the eyes that glowed in the darkness of the forest where she was being hunted, and she woke with a dry mouth and a thumping head just as a grey shape leapt from the shadows towards her throat.

I've taken Valium. I think it's the only way. I need to finish this now.

That night, I woke up suddenly. I don't know what broke my sleep, because the house was quiet as it hadn't been since it all happened. There was no noise of people moving about downstairs having those frightening, hushed conversations, no sound of my mother sobbing or screaming at my father. Perhaps it was the unnatural silence that woke me.

I got up and walked out of the room. The house seemed to be holding its breath as I went downstairs, noiseless on my bare feet. I crossed the hall and went into the dining room – somehow I knew that was where I had to go. The door seemed heavy as I opened it.

On the big table where we ate Sunday lunch there was an open coffin, white shiny wood, catching flickering reflections from the thick candles burning in white candlesticks at head and foot.

And there she was: her face expressionless like wax, but her eyes were wide open – eyes so exactly like my own. Her hair was spread out on a sort of pillow – dark, wavy hair, just like mine. Her hands, with the same long fingers as I had, were crossed on her chest and I saw the thumbnail she had bruised when we were moving stones to build a dam in the stream in our garden that ran down to the sea.

My sister, my twin, my other self. The popular one, the clever one, the one who lived in the sunshine – not the quieter, stupider, awkward one, her shadow. It should have been me.

I remember the flood of sick horror that came over me. I don't remember going back to my room. Did I sleep? Did I lie all night, grinding the scene into my consciousness so that now it plays like a film when the 'recall' button is pressed?

I remember, sometime later, my mother echoing my own

thought, my mother who had become a dishevelled, swollen-faced, hysterical stranger as she screamed at me, 'It should have been you!'

After that, I think I was sent away to stay with an aunt, but that time is a blur. And afterwards – that's not part of the story. This is just my confession, my attempt to make peace with her troubled spirit and my own.

I have read it through – 'my confession'. I reached the end, and I burst out laughing.

Oh, I could see how much it had cost me, the pain I had felt, the agonised attempts at truth. But in my state of chemical calm I could also see what wasn't there.

Because there is still a lie, a lie by omission. I couldn't make myself write the last, most terrible secret. I must still be able to tell myself I made it up, or dreamt it, and committing it to paper would give it some sort of objective reality.

So perhaps this has all been pointless pain. It hasn't brought dramatic relief – how could I believe it would? All I can do now is pay back what I can, by way of restitution. But how can you hope for absolution from a ghost?

CHAPTER SIX

The concrete floor was stained with dark oil patches. Fergie Crawford could smell it as he lay, his head pillowed on the plastic bag which now held only a spare pair of trainers. He was wearing every other stitch of clothing, but still he was shivering as dawn light seeped under the swing door.

At least it was light enough to see his surroundings. Since nightfall, he'd been in pitch darkness with no idea of the passage of time. He hadn't slept much, constantly jerking awake with the pain of stiffness and cold, usually in rising panic until he figured out where he was.

That had been the pattern since he started sleeping rough. He'd slept on hard ground often enough in the army too, but then he'd been well fed and physically exhausted enough to crash out and he'd always had a warm softie jacket and a roll mat. The thin rug the sarge had chucked at him hadn't looked at the problem.

While he could still see to do it, Fergie had arranged the unmarked cardboard boxes stored in the lock-up garage to form a shelter against the draught that whistled under the door, but that hadn't helped much. He got up slowly, rubbing at his arms and stamping to get feeling back into his numbed feet. His cramped muscles screamed as he stretched.

He perched himself on a pile of the boxes, keeping his feet up out of the draught and draping the rug round him. There was nothing to say what was inside them, but he'd a pretty good idea that if he broke into one and helped himself he wouldn't even notice his miseries any more.

He didn't, of course. OK, he might not be the sharpest knife in the drawer, but he wasn't mental. When Brodie had told him he'd better shut his eyes so he couldn't tell anyone where the lock-up was, he not only shut them but covered them tight with his hands, so there was no mistake.

Knowing stuff was dangerous. Taking cash for flogging what Brodie and his pals gave him was fine, but after Brodie took a hit and got his discharge, the trouble started. The boss who took over got greedy and clumsy and the redcap monkeys who lifted him were looking for Fergie now too.

He'd gone on the run in a panic, never thinking where he could go. He'd never had a father – he doubted if even his mother knew who it was. She was an alkie and her current boyfriend was too – violent with it. He'd nowhere to call home, so seeing Brodie on the telly had been like a miracle, when he'd been sleeping rough and begging in the street, all but starving.

He felt like he was starving now. Brodie had left him some scoff but he'd eaten it last night in one go – not that it had been that much anyway, for someone who hadn't had a square meal in three weeks.

What time was it now? It seemed to have been daylight for hours, but he couldn't remember when it got light at this time of year. Brodie'd said he'd be back sometime in the morning, when he could get away.

Fergie bent his knees and hunched himself over them, draping the rug round and tucking his hands into his armpits to warm them up. It wasn't quite so cold now the sun was up; maybe he could doze off again, to help the time to pass . . .

When he woke up, the light was stronger. He'd no idea how long he'd slept. What time was it now? When would Brodie come?

And what if he didn't come at all? He'd spelt it out that Fergie was a problem and Brodie wasn't the sort to put himself out for you. He could just have gone off, leaving him here till Fergie got tired of waiting and left of his own accord.

Feeling panic rise again, he fought it down. Course Brodie wouldn't do that. Fergie just had to trust him – what else could he do? On the other side of that door, in the scary outside world, there was the same old stuff: nowhere to sleep, no food, always being terrified the monkeys would find him.

He could give himself up. But then they'd ask all the questions he knew it was dangerous to answer, and somehow they'd make him answer them anyway and then . . .

Brodie had said he'd a plan to sort it out. Fergie had to hold on to that. It was just the waiting that was getting to him.

If he maybe took a peek outside, he'd get some idea what time it was from the sun. True enough, it was safer if he'd nothing he could tell, but if he just opened the door for a minute it wouldn't tell him much. Before he was told to shut his eyes, he'd glimpsed the row of lock-ups in a back lane where weeds were growing up round most of the other garages.

Just a quick look, that was all. He'd feel better once he'd been out in the sunlight instead of this greyish half-light – warmer, too.

Fergie went to the door. It was hard to see against the light coming in round the edges and he felt down for the handle – in the middle, he seemed to remember, having seen Brodie close it as he left.

It wasn't in the middle. He must have been wrong. He patted along the back, along left, along right, up, down, top to bottom.

There was no handle. Why would there be? He was trapped inside.

And the question he had asked returned with devastating force – *what if Brodie didn't come back at all?*

Fleming glanced round the officers assembled for the morning briefing. It was Sunday and the room wasn't crowded – she hadn't put out an expensive overtime call to off-duty officers, as would normally be the case in a murder inquiry. Superintendent Bailey, pursing his fleshy lips, had been very definite about that.

'They're just old bones, Marjory. You know how tight the budget is this year, and we can take our time over this one.'

She hadn't argued. Door-to-doors in such a small place wasn't labour-intensive; there would be a lot of fiddly stuff for the civilian staff, following up records of owners and visitors to the caravans and chalets, but that could wait until they knew the timescale. The pathologist had confirmed the skeleton was adult and male but refused to speculate further in conditions like these, so they hadn't much to go on as yet.

The photographer had done his stuff, though, and on the huge whiteboard on the back wall his blown-up shots of the pathetic skeleton in its shackles, with the watch, that final refinement of torture, hanging from the arm bone, had produced shudders of distaste as the officers gathered.

'I've glanced at reports from the door-to-doors so far,' Fleming told them. 'It's a close-knit community and it'll need low-key, persuasive interviews. And a couple of names suggest a follow-up and I'll be getting on to them today.

'Apart from that, I can't see much more to be done until we start getting forensic stuff. Any questions?'

A female DC put her hand up. Hepburn: fairly new; young, sharp-eyed with olive skin and very dark curly hair that looked as if she'd been pulled through a bush backwards.

'Is there any particular angle you'd like us to concentrate on?'

Genuine enquiry, Fleming wondered, or the sort of 'sucking up' question to get attention that every teacher is familiar with? Giving her the benefit of the doubt, Fleming said, 'Just use your initiative. Anything else? No? Then the other areas I want covered today . . .' Fleming went on briskly to detail them, then finished the meeting.

At the end she called over Andy Macdonald who, to her surprise, she had seen sitting with Tam MacNee and Ewan Campbell.

'Thought you were on leave,' she said. 'I wasn't expecting to see you today, Andy.'

'Reckoned I might as well come in, boss. Didn't fancy getting the third degree every time I went round the pub, and stag weekends tend to run out of steam anyway.'

Fleming couldn't resist asking, 'And what about your lady friend?' Andy had a bit of a reputation for putting them through his hands.

Macdonald pulled a face. 'Don't think she ever was, and she certainly isn't at the moment. But . . .' He paused, as if afraid of saying too much.

'But?' Fleming prompted, intrigued. 'Don't worry, I won't tell Tam.'

'I'll see him later. Anyway – well, I'm not giving up. She's quite a girl.'

Smitten, was he? She didn't let her amusement show. 'Good for you! But listen, Andy. You obviously spent time in the place. Any useful contacts?'

Macdonald shook his head. 'Hardly even met the locals,

except the man who used to run a Johnnie-a'-things. He'd a range of the most lurid sweeties you've ever seen – we were probably high on E-numbers all summer. But it closed long ago and I don't think he lived there anyway. The kids I knew all came from the caravans and chalets.'

'Too much to hope for. No point in you coming down to Innellan, then – there's just two or three people I want to see at the moment and Tam and I can cover that. Make the most of your day off. Away you go and have Sunday lunch at your mum's.'

'Oh, help me! Help me! Don't go!' Aileen Findlay sobbed. 'Don't leave me! Stop him, stop him!'

She was propped up in bed, grossly overweight with straggly grey hair and demented eyes. The carer, a scone-faced girl in a pink overall, looked helpless, her jaws rotating as she chewed gum.

Her son didn't conceal his exasperation. Cal Findlay's swarthy complexion and dark eyes made him look dour at the best of times and now there was a line of temper between his brows.

'I've got to go. Just carry on with the routine.'

Doubtfully, the girl approached the bed, but Aileen slapped at her with a hand like a wet fish. She stepped back, out of reach.

'Don't think she wants me. Maybe if you—'

'She doesn't "want" me either,' Findlay snapped. 'She hasn't a clue who I am. She's just unsettled this morning. She'll be fine once I've gone.'

He left, shutting the door on the carer's protests, and drove to Kirkcudbright harbour in a black mood. At least today he could nurse it on his own in the small boat, checking lobster pots – he'd a strict quota for the prawn fishing.

Yes, his mother was unsettled. She'd seen the police from the chair by the window where she spent her days and had started rambling, blurting out the random thoughts, disconnected and dangerous, which were all she had nowadays.

She'd been like that for ten years – years of pure purgatory for her son, which wasn't to say that theirs had been a good relationship before that. They were bound together in a devil's embrace of need and past events.

Findlay parked then walked to the pier, giving unsmiling nods in response to greetings from acquaintances. He knew they thought he was a moody sod. He didn't care. He had a lot to be moody about.

He'd come back from working on trawlers on the Cumbrian coast to live at home, buy his own boat and be his own boss; if the fishing hadn't been kneecapped by the EU, he'd have had his own place too. But here he was, heading for fifty, still at home with his mother, barely able to service the loan on his prawn boat and pay a deckhand, inheriting the house when Aileen died his only hope for the future.

She'd still been in her fifties when dementia struck. Sometimes Findlay wondered if it was a punishment for her actions – or perhaps, more realistically, a result of them. He knew his mother had suffered from guilt, and so she should.

She'd have been in a home long ago, if he hadn't known she'd be made to sell up to pay for it. So she had to be there in the house, her presence seeming to suck light and even air out of the place, however determinedly he ignored her – sitting in another room, sleeping in the most distant bedroom with earplugs in. Oh, he'd thought of the pillow over the face, but he wasn't a fool. It would be a sure way of letting her ruin his life from beyond the grave.

Yes, she was his mother. But yes, he had reason to hate her. She had used him when he was too young to understand, had condemned him to the sort of half-life he was leading now. Once he'd had a young man's dreams; now all he wanted was peace and security – and a mind free from the fear that had stalked him all these years. Once he had thought of it as a figure on the distant horizon, easy enough to ignore; now it was a presence at his shoulder, dogging his steps.

The police wouldn't have got much out of yesterday's questioning. Innellan was a place of closed doors and closed mouths when it came to outsiders. But if you put a stick into a muddy pond and stirred the water, there was no telling what would come bubbling up.

Findlay cast off, started the motor and headed out into the Solway Firth. He wouldn't be going towards the islands today.

'Thick as thieves,' Georgia Stanley had said when Fleming and MacNee consulted her, having failed to find Sorley at the run-down chalet. 'They'll be together.'

And that, indeed, was where Sorley was: at Steve Donaldson's house. It had clearly been a labourer's cottage, a meanly proportioned box built of concrete slabs. There was a traditional croft house nearby, presumably still occupied by Donaldson Senior.

An unsavoury-looking crew, Fleming thought, as she and MacNee joined Sorley and the Donaldsons, father and son, at the kitchen table where they were drinking coffee. The table looked as if it had come down in the world, too large and expensive-looking for this narrow, basic room.

At Sorley's suggestion Steve's wife Josie, a wispy woman with an embittered expression, left after setting mugs of instant before the officers with a bad grace. It had been made with cooling water and little undissolved grains floated on top; Fleming pushed hers away, though MacNee didn't seem to have noticed and was drinking his with no evidence of distaste.

They had received a cautious welcome and preliminary questions were answered readily enough: they knew nothing of the cave, they had no suggestions about identity. But Sorley, with an eager expression on his weaselly face, was keen to enlarge on his theories.

'Like I told the officer yesterday, it all fits now. I could tell there was something, the way he wanted to keep folks off the island, when it's our right by law to go where we like in our own country. Anyone could go anywhere in your day, eh, Hugh?'

Sucking his remaining teeth, Hugh Donaldson agreed. 'Funny thing, that, right enough. What's he got to hide? And he's been like that, right from the start. This deer farming nonsense – he'll never make it pay, and I made plenty for the old woman, I can tell you that. So what call did he have to refuse my boy the lease? Something funny there, you'd have to say.'

'Funny's not what I'd call it.' His boy, sitting slumped over his paunch, suddenly flared up. 'The bastard screwed me. I'm not used to living like this, you know.' He made an angry gesture round the cramped room. 'I'd a job and a good house and a future. Gave up the lot to come here and farm, going to build a new house and all.'

Fleming, having heard the story from the invaluable Georgia, cut his lamentations short. 'Why do you think he was trying to keep you off his property?'

'You'll have to tell us that, Inspector,' Sorley said. 'But in the light of what's happened, maybe there was someone he wanted rid of, and knew the right place to put him.'

'Who?' MacNee said. He made no attempt to disguise his scepticism, and Sorley bridled.

'You lean on him and maybe you'll find out. But what I can tell you is what happened to me. I went over, just walked across at low tide. Next thing I know, there he's threatening me with that wolf. And that's another thing you want to look at.' Sorley was warming to his task, his scrubby ponytail bouncing up and down to emphasise his points. 'Keeping a wild animal – shouldn't be allowed.'

'We have that in hand,' Fleming said.

'Do you think maybe it was the vandalism made him a wee bit unfriendly?' MacNee drawled. 'What do you know about that?'

The blank looks on their faces might have been more convincing if Sorley hadn't changed colour and Steve Donaldson's hand hadn't gone up as if to loosen the already open collar of his checked shirt.

'You see,' MacNee went on, 'I'd be downright antisocial myself, if there were folk around putting graffiti on my wee baby's headstone.'

Hugh Donaldson's watery eyes met MacNee's unflinchingly. 'Who told you that? Never heard anything about that. It's likely a story Lovatt put around to cover himself.'

Admittedly, Georgia had got the story from Kerr Brodie, but to Fleming it had the ring of truth, especially after meeting the pond life. Having established the accusations against Lovatt were prompted by spite not evidence, it was tempting to leave and find a hot, cleansing bath. Still, they were in a position to give her information Georgia didn't have.

'Mrs Lovatt Senior,' she said. 'What was she like?'

'Toffee-nosed old bitch,' Steve Donaldson said.

His father's eyes were cold as a snake's. 'She was a mean, grasping, greedy old besom. Bled me dry with rent over the years, then cut out her own son when it came to her will.'

'You know him?' Fleming asked with interest.

'He's a good lad – grew up here, but I haven't seen him for years. They never got on – she threw him out, told him he was never to come back. I thought maybe when she died Steve would get a better deal on a new lease from him, with us being pals. But oh no! The old bitch saw to it she'd carry on buggering up our lives, even once she'd gone.'

It was an interesting example of the sort of feud Georgia had said Innellan specialised in. This one looked set to run for a generation or two. At the very least.

With a glance towards MacNee, Fleming got up. 'Thank you for your cooperation,' she said formally. 'That will be all for the moment, though of course there may be more questions later.'

As they walked back down to Innellan, MacNee said, 'Nice guys, eh? See what's wrong with the law in this country? We can't lock them up and throw away the key just because we'd all be better off without them.'

'If you ruled the world, Tam, there'd only be about three people left at liberty and I'm probably flattering myself that I'd be one of them. And your friend Brodie – he certainly wouldn't be, would he? I've been meaning to ask you, what was that about? Has he previous?'

MacNee grunted. 'Not that I know of.'

His manner was discouraging, but Fleming persisted. 'You obviously know something about him, though.'

'Aye. All of it bad.'

'Tam, if I enjoyed pulling teeth I'd have gone in for dentistry. What sort of bad?'

With a sigh, MacNee said, 'You know how, if you buy a stick of rock in Rothesay, it has "Greetings from Rothesay" all the way through? That kind of bad.'

She wasn't going to be brushed aside. 'How do you know?'

'He lived in the same tenement as me. He was in with some bad stuff.'

Remembering MacNee's earlier reaction, Fleming said, 'Guns?'

'They never pinned anything on him. But guns, aye, and the other stuff that goes with them. That's all. OK?'

Fleming was sure that wasn't all, but from the shut look on MacNee's face, she was also sure it was all she was going to be told. She changed the subject.

'Where, I wonder, is Tony Drummond?'

'Drummond? You want him?'

'No, I specifically don't want him. I want to go to his house when he's not there, officially to hear directly from his son what happened. In reality, I can't think there's anything useful either he or the other boy, Craig someone, could tell us.'

'So? Why do you want to see him, then?'

'I want to find out more about this story of the island being haunted – who told him, where the rumour started. And I don't want a headline "DI seeks occult explanation for mysterious death".'

'Right,' MacNee said slowly. 'Think someone's used scare tactics, then?'

'Frankly, we're clutching at straws here. Sorley's was the only interview yesterday that offered anything to follow up.'

'See them?' MacNee jerked his head towards the village they were approaching. 'If you dangled a treacle scone in front of their noses, they'd be afraid to take a bite at it in case a word slipped out.'

Fleming laughed. 'So what is it they're afraid might slip out?'

'Maybe they don't know themselves. Maybe it's nothing. Maybe someone brought the man from somewhere else completely and dumped him here to die,' MacNee said gloomily.

'I know why I bring you along. It's to keep me cheerful and motivated. That's the Drummonds' house there, and there's no car in the drive. Any chance he's away and the family aren't?'

* * *

Elena Tindall shivered as she came out of the chalet. Last night's honeyed warmth had disappeared, and though the sun was still shining there was a sharp breeze and her cheap jacket was too thin to give protection. It looked as if a change in the weather was on the way; there were small waves ruffling the surface of the sea and away on the horizon a line of clouds was massing.

She had a lingering headache and after all she had drunk last night it wasn't surprising she'd slept only fitfully, and the rags of the dream about wolves at her throat hung about her still. Everything seemed fractionally out of focus this morning, as if a sheet of glass had come down, separating her from reality. She could be grateful for that, she thought, as she walked down the rudimentary gated road that led from the chalets and caravan site down to Innellan.

The village was very quiet. Elena saw a tall woman and a much shorter man coming out of the house tacked on to the Smugglers Inn, but there was no one else around when she took the track that ran round the shoreline, past Lovatt's Farm.

She became aware of a strange, echoing sound, intermittent but persistent, and broken by barks and grunts. The deer, of course; she knew stags bellowed sometimes, and there were enclosures up towards the house. They seemed to be challenging each other, roaring and replying.

As she looked in that direction, a woman appeared in the yard at the other side, a thin woman with wavy long brown hair. She was carrying a bag of rubbish which she put into a bin before going back inside. It wasn't the woman she'd seen on TV.

Elena stood very still, watching her for a moment unseen. As she walked on a man appeared, coming down over the rough grass towards the track she was on, a tall, dark-haired man. He wasn't the man she'd seen then either.

Matt Lovatt?

He was playing with a dog, a huge, handsome, wolf-like creature, tussling and pushing it. It was joining in the fun with, Elena thought, a certain measure of respect, and the man was laughing; the bond between master and dog was evident. As the game came to an end the man gave an order and the dog immediately lay down. He rolled it on to its back, holding it there with his hand across its throat for a long moment, before allowing it back on its feet.

Catching sight of Elena he stood up, looking faintly embarrassed, and she saw with a severe sense of shock that his face was badly disfigured by what looked like burn tissue.

'Sorry about the display of dominance,' he said as she reached them. 'He's a big fella – has to know who's boss.'

The dog was standing beside him, ears alert, extraordinary slanted eyes fixed on Elena. The man ruffled his head with obvious affection and pride.

'He's beautiful. Would he let me pat him?'

'Of course. Mika, stay.'

The dog did not turn its head as she went over and stroked the thick, soft ruff of fur round its neck. It showed no interest, no sign it had even noticed her touch.

'A nice enough morning,' its master said pleasantly. 'But I've a feeling the weather may be on the change.'

She replied in the same vein. 'Not too soon, I hope. I'm staying in one of the chalets.'

'Wonderful view from up there. Hope you enjoy your holiday.'

He nodded and moved off, the dog at heel, heading back to the farmhouse. Elena continued her walk, with that light-headed feeling of unreality even stronger than before.

There was a rough path leading off to her left and she followed it through the whin bushes towards the shore until it came out in a small, pretty, sandy bay, unexpected on this rocky shore. The tide was going out and on the coarse sand a trail of little shells showed the high-water mark.

Elena bent to pick one up. The twin shells were still joined butterfly-style, pink and perfect with a pearly sheen, and she studied them as if some extraordinary secret they held would yield to her scrutiny. A fit of shuddering took her. It was close to decision time.

She took a long, deep breath. Then slowly, deliberately, she crushed the pretty shells to fragments between her fingers and dropped them on the sand. She didn't notice a sharp shard piercing her finger until she saw a smear of blood on her hands.

She walked briskly back up the hill to the chalet and got into the car without going inside. She needed petrol and a warmer jacket and she wanted, anyway, to see what Kirkcudbright had to offer.

The hunger was a gnawing pain in Fergus's belly now, and knowing the time had become an obsession. He tried to tell himself it wasn't very late, it was just that with nothing to do time passed slowly.

Anyway, what could he do if Brodie meant to leave him here to die? He could batter the door and scream, but it could be weeks before any of the owners of the lock-ups came here again. He'd come under fire in Iraq but he'd never been as scared as he was now.

A sort of fatalism possessed him. From the start he'd never had any luck in his life, until he joined the army where everything was arranged for him and he'd a bit of money to spend. He'd blown that now.

So what was the point of all the pain and the misery if this was where it finished? *What was the point?* That was all he wanted to know, before the end came.

CHAPTER SEVEN

Rosie Drummond was looking harassed when she opened the door to DI Fleming and DS MacNee, her plump face creased with anxious lines and her fair curly hair wild, as if either she hadn't had time to brush it or had run her hands through it since. There were shadows under her brown eyes. There was no sign of her husband.

'Oh dear,' she said, in tones of helplessness. 'More questions? Jamie's been up half the night and I've just settled him on the sofa with a DVD in the hope he'll drop off.'

'You look as if you could use some sleep yourself,' Fleming said sympathetically. 'Look, I don't want to upset the poor kid again. The officers yesterday took his statement, so perhaps we could just have a chat with you meantime?'

Rosie's face cleared. 'Oh, thank you. Yes of course. Come through to the kitchen. Coffee?'

The house had obviously started out as a traditional two down, three or four up, but the ground floor was now open-plan, in an L-shape. Everywhere there was the comfortable clutter of a family too busy getting on with life to be obsessive about tidiness, and Rosie made disjointed apologies as she took them through to the kitchen area, lifting a basket of washing off the island unit as she waved them to stools by the breakfast bar.

The sound of shrieks and canned laughter came from the sitting area round the corner and Rosie went to peer anxiously round.

'It's all right,' she reported. 'He's gone to sleep. Now, coffee . . .'

Fleming noted the smart coffee-maker with relief, and MacNee's face brightened too as Rosie set a packet of chocolate digestive biscuits down in front of them, asking what they needed to know.

'I just wanted to get events clearer in my own mind,' Fleming said untruthfully and allowed Rosie to give a dramatically enhanced version of the official report. Once they reached the account of Jamie's nightmares, Fleming felt she could broach the subject that interested her.

'By the way, there was something in Jamie's statement which rather intrigued me – something about the island being haunted? Is this a local legend someone's told him?'

Rosie looked embarrassed. 'I'm afraid it was me. Oh, I'm kicking myself now, I can tell you.'

'Really?' This was an unexpected bonus. 'Where did you get it from? Is it a good story?'

'Not . . . not really. It's just – well, wailing and stuff.'

'Sounds interesting,' Fleming said lightly. 'What sort of wailing?'

MacNee very quietly got out a notebook as Rosie said, 'I know it sounds silly, but I first heard it years and years ago. My family had a house here that we came to for weekends from Glasgow. I was probably – oh, twelve, thirteen maybe.'

What age was she now? Early forties, probably, but Fleming didn't want to interrupt the story to ask.

'It was my sister and me. We were out along the shore,

mucking around when it was getting dark one night. It wasn't late – must have been March, April maybe, because I remember going back for tea afterwards.

'It was quite a still night, no one about, and then we heard the wailing. It was just . . . sort of crying, on and on, not like anyone calling for help or anything, coming from the island. But no one lived there, and it was really creepy. We just ran away home and didn't tell anyone.' Rosie shivered in recollected terror.

'We used to make up stories about it to scare ourselves but we weren't brave enough to go there again before we went back home. We never heard it after that and I sort of forgot about it. And of course, I don't believe in ghosts – not really.'

The disclaimer lacked conviction. She went on, 'But years later, I'd a nephew staying who wanted to go out fishing one evening, and Tony had stuff to do so he babysat while I took Johnny out in the boat. We were round the other side of the island and we heard it again – sort of groaning this time. There was no one to be seen, and it totally spooked me. I didn't want to scare Johnny – he was only seven or eight, I think, so I just said it was the sort of noise the wind made sometimes. Maybe it was, even, but it didn't sound like that.'

MacNee's pen had frozen on the page and he looked up. Fleming felt a chill run down her spine, and it took quite an effort to sound casual. 'It sounds very alarming! Was Johnny convinced?'

'I don't know. I never asked him. Well, he's probably forgotten anyway – it's a long time ago. Goodness, he's . . . what, nineteen now, I suppose. I can't believe he's that age! More coffee?'

Fleming passed across her mug, trying to work out how to phrase her next question so that it wasn't an accusation. 'But . . . Jamie heard the story somehow?'

Again, Rosie looked embarrassed. 'I just didn't think. He came in a few weeks ago – he'd gone out after supper, and it was getting dark, and he said he'd heard someone crying and wailing on the island. And of course, they'd been talking about the poor Lovatt baby being buried there – you know what ghouls kids are – and he was all set to tell his pals it was the baby's ghost.

'I'd have hated that to get back to them – they've been finding things difficult enough here, without that sort of stupid gossip. So I told him about the other times. God, I wish I hadn't now! I can't think how we're going to get it out of his head.'

There was a lot of material there, opening up several promising lines of enquiry. But Fleming wasn't ready to do the sort of probing about times and dates that Rosie would tell her husband about, and have him asking questions long before she was ready to answer them.

'It's easy with hindsight, isn't it?' she said with a smile. 'I hope your husband's sympathetic – I'm not sure mine would be!'

'Sympathetic? Tony? I haven't told him where Jamie got the story – he'd go crazy!' She looked alarmed. 'You won't – you won't tell him, will you?'

Fleming looked at MacNee, now on his fourth chocolate digestive. 'I don't know what you've found to write in your notebook, Sergeant, but if Mr Drummond comes in suddenly, you may have to tear out the pages and swallow them.'

With Rosie laughing, and Jamie still asleep, they got up to leave.

The question was, when did you decide to start yelling? If Brodie had only been delayed – or worse, if he came back while you were beating on the door with your bare fists – you'd look a right eejit. Or worse, he'd go radge and then anything could happen.

Fergie bit at his last remaining nail. He couldn't quite believe this was really happening – that he'd been shut up in this place to die. It wouldn't happen quickly, either. Death from starvation could take days, especially if you'd access to water. He didn't, though. There wasn't a tap.

He knew all about dehydration, after Afghanistan. You could die of dehydration in – like, about ten minutes there. He'd never heard of anyone dying of dehydration in Scotland, but if there wasn't any water, you could. How soon would it start? Suddenly he felt a raging thirst.

What time was it? If he ever got out of here, he'd buy a watch. He'd never needed one before. Either he was in a situation where time didn't have much meaning, or else the place was full of people who'd order you to move when you had to move.

He didn't know what to do. He'd never been good at decisions. The ones he'd made himself were mostly bad, and now there was no one to make this one for him. He began to cry, in a dismal, hopeless sort of way.

Fergie was still crying when the garage door was flung open and he sat blinking in the sudden flood of light.

Brodie stood in the aperture, eying him in disgust. 'What the hell's the matter with you, Crawford?'

'I-I thought you weren't coming back,' he snivelled.

'Wasn't coming back? For God's sake, man, I told you I'd be here in the morning, and it's twelve o'clock!'

'Twelve o'clock?' Fergie knuckled his eyes. 'I thought – I didn't know what time it was.'

'Get yourself a bloody watch! And get in the car.'

Fergie stumbled out after him. So life didn't end here, in this brick-walled prison. He just didn't know what would come next.

'We certainly got more than we bargained for there,' Fleming said to MacNee as they drove away from Innellan.

'*Embarras de richesses*,' MacNee said with a smug expression and an execrable French accent.

'*What* did you say?' Fleming stared at him, dangerously taking her eyes off the narrow road just as she rounded a corner.

'*Embarras de richesses*. It means so much good stuff you don't know where to start.'

'I know what it means, thank you very much. I was actually quite a star when it came to Higher French, and if I can ever persuade Bill to take a holiday for long enough to let us get across the Channel, I intend to prove it.' Then she paused. 'If I can remember any of it, that is.'

'You could brush it up. Have a chat with Louise.'

'Louise?' Fleming again risked their lives on a tight corner. 'Who's *Louise*? Does Bunty know?' It was said jokingly, but there had been problems last year when MacNee's adored wife Bunty had suffered badly from depression, though according to Tam she had made a good recovery.

'Don't be daft,' MacNee said scornfully. 'Hepburn – just started in CID, you know? She's all right.'

High praise indeed, from MacNee. 'Of course I know Hepburn. Didn't realise that was her first name.'

'Her mum's French. When I dumped a pile of reports on her desk, that's what she said – "*embarras de richesses*".'

'If she's managed to start teaching a chauvinistic Scot at least some elements of a foreign language, I'll make a point of getting to know her.'

'Ah well, that's *French*,' MacNee said. 'The Auld Alliance – the happy days when the Scots and the French fought the English.' As a clincher, he added, 'I read in a book about Rabbie Burns that he spoke French. He told someone his wife thought he was "*le plus bel esprit et le plus honnête homme du monde*".' The accent was even worse this time.

'Did they add what his wife actually said about him – "Our Robbie should have had twa wives"?' Fleming asked dryly.

'Anyway, why are we talking about Burns, for goodness' sake? This stuff – I'm a bit dazed. Spectral cries and groans coming from the island – what did you make of that?'

'Hardly know where to start. By Rosie's account, there's been someone in distress there maybe twenty-five, thirty years ago, depending what age she is, then around twelve years ago and again just recently. Is this maybe some sort of thing the teuchters do? Like kind of ritual sacrifice?'

'I resent that. Despite being denied the glories of culture as practised in the backstreets of Glasgow, I think even us hayseeds would have noticed if people were disappearing regularly,' she said acidly. 'But Tam, seriously, are we to assume there were three separate episodes, years apart, that there was an ongoing cause for cries that were occasionally heard, or that Rosie and her son just have vivid imaginations? Do you suppose other people have heard it too?'

'Two wee girls, scaring themselves on a dark night, and a laddie who knows a baby's buried on the island – if the wind was blowing through a crack or something, you could easy convince yourself it was someone crying. But I tell you what's getting to me—'

'You don't need to,' Fleming said heavily. '"Round the back of the island" – it was chilling when she said that. The shape of the cave would amplify the sound, of course. It could have been that poor tortured guy dying, too weak to scream for help. If she'd just gone to see, if she hadn't that silly idea about ghosts in her head, she might have investigated and saved his life.'

'If you gave Rosie a penny for her thoughts, you'd be wanting change,' MacNee agreed. 'Nice lady, though.'

'Give you a chocolate digestive and you're anyone's,' Fleming said absently, then went on, 'We'll get some sort of confirmation about date of death, of course, but the timing sounds plausible to me. Once we get it, we can start questioning to see if anyone else heard strange sounds around that time.

'I'd like to investigate the most recent one too. Oh, I know Jamie may have imagined it, but it's worth asking. And if Lovatt's keeping everyone else off the island, we should check out his household to see if anyone there has a rational explanation.'

'No time like the present,' MacNee suggested, but Fleming shook her head.

'I've got a meeting this afternoon. I'll get Andy and Ewan to come down tomorrow. It's not what you'd call a matter of urgency – nothing's going to happen if we don't make use of the "golden hour" on this one.'

MacNee gave her a pitying look. 'Will you never learn?' he said.

Elena Tindall swung across the heavy metal cattle gate and bolted it. It was a laborious operation: getting out of the car, opening the gate, driving the car through, getting out to go back and shut it before driving on to repeat the process a few yards on. There were two of these gates enclosing a field, each having to be latched to stop cattle from straying. She was nervous about the cows too, though the great black beasts grazing nearby didn't even lift their heads to look at her.

Still, it had been a satisfactory expedition to Kirkcudbright. She'd got what she needed, found a reasonable deli and a newsagent which had *Vogue, Marie Claire* and *Vanity Fair* as well – a pleasant surprise. And it had occupied part of what could be a long, empty day too.

She stowed away her purchases, then fetched another bottle of Barolo from the case and took it, along with a glass and her copy of *Vogue*, to the chair by the picture window overlooking the bay.

As Elena set down bottle and glass on the window ledge, she

noticed binoculars, half-concealed by the curtains – a thoughtful provision for visitors, presumably. She put them to her eyes and adjusted the focus.

They were high-magnification lenses and the road below, running through Innellan, became suddenly close and so clear that she could have counted the pansies in the Smugglers Inn window box. She could see round the bay, along past the Lovatts' farmhouse. And she could see the island.

With uncanny clarity she saw a deer lifting a back leg to scratch its ear, like a dog. She watched it for a moment, then swung the binoculars along.

There was the stand of trees at the far end and close by, the cottage. It looked deserted, the door standing open and the windows boarded up. She had only just focused on it when a motor boat starting up made her turn towards the sound.

The man steering was definitely the man she'd seen on television – grey hair, stocky. In the boat was something covered by a tarpaulin, but she couldn't make out what it was.

He guided the boat in neatly to the jetty then walked with a lurching gait uphill towards the cottage. There was a small tractor with a trailer parked beside it which he hitched to the back, then drove it down on to the jetty.

It blocked Elena's view of the boat, but when he heaved the tarpaulin package on to the trailer she saw it was long, narrow and clearly heavy – heavy and oddly flexible. Almost . . . almost like . . . a body?

Now she really was losing touch with reality. It was this terrible place. She shouldn't have come – she shouldn't have come.

But she had to. She'd decided.

The man was driving it back up the hill now, the trailer bumping behind. He swung it along the front of the cottage, then with impressive skill reversed the trailer through the doorway, with only inches of clearance on either side.

Elena put down the binoculars and picked up her wine glass, but she didn't open a magazine. She was still watching ten minutes later when he drove out again, parked the tractor, then got into the boat. It sped back to the jetty below Lovatt's Farm, where a car was parked. He drove it up to the farmhouse.

What had she just seen? She didn't know. Perhaps it was nothing to do with her. But for her own safety, it would be wise to know everything she possibly could about what was going on here.

Christie Jack tipped the sachet of instant French Onion soup into a mug and topped it up from the kettle. She'd made her sandwich – cheese and chutney – already, but she was dragging her feet, being in no hurry to join Matt and Melissa Lovatt at the table. They weren't talking, but the atmosphere between them seemed to get unhealthier by the day, until you felt crushed by it just from sitting beside them.

Lissa was toying with cottage cheese, lettuce and tomato as if it was almost too much effort to eat. Matt was making munching a ham sandwich look like duty not pleasure.

Christie put the soup packet back in the old-fashioned press. Like the rest of the house, the kitchen hadn't been done for years. There was an old coal-fired Aga and the Belfast sink wasn't the new smart kind you saw in design magazines; it had the chips and scars of use and the old brass taps were green round the base with verdigris. Above the scrubbed wood table hung a pulley, draped with drying clothes. Useful, of course, but oppressive when you were underneath it.

Lissa often complained about the kitchen – not forcibly, but in that sighing, helpless way that set Christie's teeth on edge. No wonder Matt had learnt to ignore it. Knowing what Christie knew now, she wondered if he'd developed the skill by ignoring other, more important things. It could hardly make him happy, though – which showed in the lines of strain on his face. She felt a flame of anger on his behalf as she went to join them.

She had just sat down when Kerr Brodie arrived. Lissa suddenly sat up straighter, and watching Matt under her brows Christie saw him glance towards Kerr, then without speaking go back to his sandwich.

'Everyone's very quiet today,' Kerr said jovially. 'What's happened – somebody died?'

Matt looked up. 'You could say,' he said stiffly. 'The police were here earlier, asking about the bones found in the cave.'

Kerr put two slices of bread in the toaster. 'Och aye. Nothing to do with us, though. They've finished over at the island, right?'

'As far as I know. Were you ever in that cave, Kerr?'

Kerr was slicing cheese. 'Now, what would I be in there for?'

'I didn't even know there was a cave until today,' Christie chipped in. 'Round the other side, I suppose.'

'I went in once, when we came here first,' Matt said. 'Nothing to see, I thought – just a hollow in the rock.'

'I was with you,' Lissa said suddenly. 'I remember. Such a beautiful day and I wanted to go out and see the seals basking on the rocks out in the bay.' Her blue eyes were dreamy. 'I used to love doing that – before . . .' She bit her lip.

Matt got up, pushing his chair back abruptly. 'Yes,' he said flatly and went to the door, then turned to Kerr and Christie. 'Couple of things we need to discuss before the afternoon rounds. The office in quarter of an hour – OK?'

Kerr gave an affirmatory grunt as he grilled the cheese on his toast. Christie said, 'I've finished. I can come now, if you like.'

She was rewarded with one of Matt's rare smiles. 'Doesn't do to be too keen, you know,' he said teasingly. 'You always get the worst jobs.'

'Oh, I don't mind,' Christie said blithely. She didn't see Kerr's sardonic look as she followed Matt out.

The meeting had dragged on, as meetings do, and it was almost five o'clock when MacNee, hovering near the door of the CID room, intercepted Fleming as she returned from it. He was holding a piece of paper.

'Interesting development, boss.'

'I like that word, "interesting". It would make a change from the last two hours, when I thought the clock had stopped. Is that a printout?'

She took it from him and they walked up together to her fourth-floor office; Fleming liked it, with its outlook over the plane trees lining the main street in Kirkluce.

She sat down and started reading, while MacNee explained. 'It came in around two, and I phoned to have a word. One of the guys in the lab has a sideline speciality in watches and couldn't resist prioritising. You'll see there – date on the stopped watch, 12th October, 1999. Silver oxide battery – a life of two to three years, apparently.'

'So – a possible date of death anything up to three years before. But we don't know how long it had been in the watch already – six months, a year . . .'

'1997?' MacNee said. 'The nephew Rosie talked about was seven then and he's nineteen now. Twelve years ago.'

'Mmm.' Fleming tapped her front teeth with a fingernail, a habit she had when thinking. At last she said, 'They're very rough figures, of course. We'll have to get more detail from Rosie – talk to the nephew too, if he remembers anything. Time of year, for a start, though if they were fishing after supper you'd assume summertime.

'Andy and Ewan can pursue that as well tomorrow. And I tell you something, Tam. We're going to nail the sadistic bastard who did this, step by step.'

The rain came on in late afternoon – sharp, stinging rain with a cold breeze. The clouds were low and heavy and at half past six Elena Tindall peered out into the gathering gloom without enthusiasm.

She had just made her nightly phone call to Eddie and had spun it out longer than usual, letting him ramble on about the business. His familiar, loving voice, his anxiety for her happiness, had left her shaken in her resolve. It would be so easy to slip back into that cosseted life . . .

Half-life, which she spent rigidly exercising the control that Eddie mistook for tranquillity. And quietly going mad until the day when she couldn't take it any more. It would be different afterwards; Elena was pinning everything on that. Afterwards – she hardly dared think the word.

She must take the next step, now. Before she could weaken and sit down with a glass of wine at the TV, she grabbed her new waterproof jacket, pulled the hood up and walked out into the chill of the autumn evening.

Georgia Stanley pulled a pint and set it in front of Cal Findlay.

'Not a night to be out, is it?' she said pleasantly. 'We'll likely be quiet anyway after all the excitement, and most of the weekenders will be heading home. At least they got the weather when it mattered.'

Findlay agreed but made no contribution to the conversation. With professional tact, Georgia moved to the other end of the bar where three more of the locals were sitting chatting. Last night the talk had all been about the bones in the cave, but that was yesterday's news now. With only low-key police activity there wasn't much more to say and the multiple iniquities of the local council were a more interesting topic.

Georgia was polishing glasses when the door to the main street swung open, admitting a gust of wet, cold air. A woman she had never seen before came in, closing the door behind her quickly. Her jacket had great dark wet patches on it and when she pushed back her hood she had to wipe her face with her hands.

'Hang that up by the fire, love,' Georgia called to her. 'It'll dry quicker.'

'Thanks.'

As the men at the bar watched her with casual interest, she draped the jacket over a chair then stood with slim hands held out to the blaze, rubbing them to warm them. Then she came over to take a bar stool just one away from Findlay.

'Red wine,' she said, in answer to Georgia's query. 'Whatever you have.'

'Just the house red – Chilean merlot?'

'Fine. Large glass.'

A lively interest in people, Georgia often thought, was all that made this job bearable. Pouring out the wine, she took stock of her newest patron.

Very good-looking, undoubtedly, in a glacial way – dark-blue eyes, chiselled nose, blonde hair scraped back into a ponytail held by an elastic band – the sort of natural-looking sun-streaked honey-blonde you only got in expensive hair salons. And those perfect, perfectly white teeth – she hadn't got those on the NHS.

What was intriguing, though, was the cheap clothes, markedly out of place with the glossy, high-maintenance appearance. She wasn't wearing a wedding ring, though as she paid for her drink Georgia noticed the slight narrowing of the fourth finger which long-term wearing of a ring produces. Divorced by some wealthy bastard who'd stopped paying?

Feeling stirrings of sympathy, Georgia said, 'On holiday, are you? Shame the weather's changed.'

'Yes, it's a pity. It's so lovely around here. I'm staying in one of the chalets up above here – Spindrift, it's called. Very comfortable.'

'Been here before?' Georgia asked.

'Oh, long ago. A couple of times. Just brief visits.'

Her sideways glance included Findlay. He hadn't been in a mood to talk earlier, but he'd changed his mind now. Like most men, he responded to a good-looking girl – though looking more closely Georgia reckoned she was quite a bit older than at the first glance.

The bar started to fill up a little; clearly some visitors hadn't gone, including the rest of Andy Macdonald's stag party. Georgia was kept busy dealing with them, and when she turned back to glance at Findlay and the woman, they were still in conversation.

But what on earth had she just said to him? He was staring at her with what almost looked like horror.

Elena was on her third glass of wine when the back door of the Smugglers Inn opened and three people came in. One was the limping man she'd watched on the island. The girl ex-soldier she'd seen on TV was there too, and the man she'd met earlier that day. He gave her a half-smile of recognition, then sat down with the girl at a table near the fire while the other man came to give the order.

He nodded to Elena. 'Terrible night,' he said. 'Georgia, pints for me and Matt, bottle of Beck's for Christie.'

As he waited he turned to look at Elena and she saw his eyes kindle in that way men's eyes always did.

'Visitor?' he said. 'I'm local – along the road. Kerr Brodie.'

Feeling the familiar bone-sapping weariness at having to respond, she smiled, but didn't encourage him by offering her own name in exchange. 'Yes, just visiting.'

Georgia came back with the drinks. Brodie moved off with a wink to Elena and, 'Catch you later, eh?'

Findlay had left and Elena was on her own at that end of the bar. She couldn't face the weather and the walk home just yet. Another drink after this one, and she should be reaching the stage where she could go back to the chalet and crash out. She drained her glass and held it up, catching Georgia's eye and saw her give a doubtful glance. She served her anyway, with a chatty remark, but didn't try to pursue a conversation.

A few minutes later the door to the main street opened again and another group came in: a big slob of a man, a short, balding man with a straggling ponytail and an elderly man, fat as a toad, with hooded, rheumy eyes. They were in high good humour, laughing as they came up to the bar.

The old man's eyes lit on Elena, then lingered with an expression she recognised, producing in her a wave of revulsion and horror so physical that she thought she might be sick. She got to her feet, pushed back the stool clumsily and abandoning her drink went over to grab her coat, in her haste stumbling over an umbrella. She heard a guffaw as she hurried out.

The rain was still relentless and the street lights were shrouded in halos of mist. The shock of cold air made Elena gasp as she huddled into her jacket; the icy freshness made her head swim even more. It seemed a long way back to shelter and solitude and a door she could lock behind her. And pills that would let her sleep.

Her head down, Elena trudged up the track to the chalets. It was unlit, uneven, but she just had to take one step after another, trying not to think, trying not to feel.

It was as she was reaching the first gate that she heard the footsteps behind her – strange footsteps, light and quick and clacking. She glanced fearfully over her shoulder but the ground behind declined sharply and she could see nothing.

She quickened her pace. She was probably being neurotic, but . . .

Her hands were cold and wet and clumsy and the heavy bolt resisted her attempt to shift it. And whoever was behind was gaining on her now.

At last the gate yielded and swung back. She didn't pause to close it; she was running now, though with the steep ground and the mud underfoot it felt like running in a dream where no matter what effort you make, you get nowhere.

Then a smell reached her on the air – a rank, feral stench, and suddenly the sound of a coughing roar.

Elena turned. Panic, in the oldest sense of the word, seized her as she saw it breasting the slope below – a massive stag. It stopped when it saw her ahead, as if startled, then its mouth opened wide as it roared and roared again. It began tossing its great head, lowering the crown of rapier-tipped antlers in a threatening, sweeping movement.

The second gate was just ahead, blocking her path as she struggled frantically with the bolt. It wouldn't shift – and with a sudden trotting charge the beast was on her.

All she could do was to scream and scream and scream.

CHAPTER EIGHT

Christie's plan was working out just as she had hoped. Kerr had turned to talk to the people on the next table and she and Matt were left together.

He was so controlled it was hard to get near him. He managed to conceal the suffering his disfigurement must still be causing him and she longed to know his secret, which might help her to master her own mental turmoil. Meditation, perhaps? Or medication, even?

She tried to draw him out about himself – most men's favourite subject – but he shied away from personal questions. Christie could understand that: she didn't allow rooting around in her past either. It had been bad enough at the time, and until recently confining her memories to an iron-bound chest with several padlocks in a dusty corner of her mind had worked well enough.

Matt clearly had his own iron-bound chest, and his marriage was off-limits too. There was plenty of common ground, though: the army, the farm, the animals with their individual personalities.

Rudolf was Christie's particular favourite, and Matt was telling her about his moment of glory as star of a TV whisky commercial when his mobile rang. He took it out of his pocket, glanced at the number, then with an irritated apology, answered it.

'Lissa? Is there a problem?'

The problem, Christie thought sourly, is that he's having a nice time for once and she wants to spoil it. But as she watched, Matt's face changed.

'*What!*' he said, sounding horrified. 'Oh, for God's sake! Which one? Go and see.' He was on his feet, shrugging on his jacket, jerking his head to Kerr and Christie. 'Yes, I know it's raining. I noticed. Find a jacket or something, go and look and call me back.'

Kerr and Christie, eying him in alarm, put on their own jackets.

'One of the stags is loose,' Matt said, tight-lipped. 'And apparently some woman's got between him and where he wanted to go. Lissa's finding out which one it is. Kerr, get the dart gun and you'd better bring the rifle as well, though I don't want to shoot him unless there's no alternative.'

Kerr nodded and went out of the back door. Christie lingered, her heart in her mouth. She'd been in charge of Rudolf; had she failed to secure the gate, somehow?

Matt had gone up to the bar and was banging a beer mug on the counter to get silence.

'Sorry to interrupt your evening, but one of my stags has somehow got loose. We're going now to get him rounded up, but please don't leave until we've found him. They're a bit edgy at this time of year.'

There was a mutter of talk, and Christie could see unfriendly looks being directed at Matt. He wasn't popular and the idea of dangerous animals at large in Innellan wasn't going to help his reputation. However, when he said, 'The drinks are on me,' there were some muted cheers, particularly from Andy Macdonald's friends.

Christie followed Matt out into the darkness. He was walking fast, splashing through puddles, and with her shorter legs she broke into a trot to keep up.

'Keep your eyes peeled,' he said tersely. 'He could be anywhere, and if he's upset and confused he could think you were a rival.'

His phone rang again. 'Yes?' He listened, then said heavily, 'Rudolf. Right,' and Christie bit her lip. 'We're on our way. Kerr's ahead of us.'

They were running now and Matt was faster than she was. She knew what he must be thinking – stupid, careless woman! But now she thought about it, she was sure she'd bolted the paddock gate properly after putting in his feed – quite sure, because she'd been edgy – Rudolph had been pawing the ground a bit and he was really stinking already. She was hardly going to leave the gate on the latch and have him come after her.

As he could be doing, even now; she could hear bellowing. That was probably just the other two stags, but even so Christie couldn't help a nervous glance round the edge of her parka hood as she ran up the drive to the farmhouse, shadowed by trees. Matt was well ahead of her, and she remembered the sage advice, 'You don't need to run faster than the bear chasing you, just faster than your companion.'

It was quite a relief to reach the lighted garden area round the house. In its pen nearby the dog, alerted by the bustle, was at the chain-link fence watching her with amber eyes.

Matt was already talking to someone on the phone when she came in. 'Up on the track to the chalets? Right. We'll be there.'

Lissa was standing beside him. She was soaked through, cotton dress clinging to her and hair plastered to her head – a mute reproach to show how unreasonable Matt was, asking her to go outside on a night like this?

If that was her motive, it didn't work. Absorbed in his phone call, he wasn't even aware of her. He was listening to what seemed to be a tirade. 'Yes, of course. Yes, I do appreciate that. I'm very sorry. We'll be there in five minutes. Just don't try to go near him . . . No, I suppose you wouldn't. But if you've shut the gates he'll be highly unlikely to jump them.' Then, at something else that was said, Matt's voice became bleaker. 'Oh, have you? I see. Yes, of course. Naturally. Anyway, I can only apologise. We're on our way.'

Kerr came in, carrying his .243 and another elderly-looking rifle. 'What's the situation?'

'He's in the field area between the two gates on the track to the chalets at the moment. He's attacked a woman – don't know how seriously, the woman on the phone was a bit hysterical. They've sent for an ambulance. And the police.'

'Oh,' Kerr said. 'Hoped we might have dealt with it ourselves.'

'We've probably got twenty minutes before they arrive and say we have to shoot him. Knocking him out before then is our only chance.'

Matt went to the key board beside the back door, detached one, then chucked it to Christie. 'Medicine cupboard. Pack of Immobilon. There's Revivon with it, and we need something called Narcan as well. Packet of rubber gloves, veterinary darts, metal storage box. OK? Fetch them. I'm going to get the trailer on to the forklift and then I'll come back and explain what we do next.

'Kerr, take the car and get up there. Try and keep them happy if you can.'

Her heart pounding, Christie hurried through to Matt's office. She had to steady her hands to unlock the medicine cupboard. She took the pack marked Immobilon down from the shelf – etorphine hydrochloride, it said below the name – and there was an alarming warning emblazoned on it. She shuddered, assembled the rest of what Matt had asked for and went back to the kitchen. Matt came in just as she set them down.

Unlike her own, Matt's hands were rock-steady. He donned the thin gloves, took out the darts – for all the world like some strange form of shuttlecock – and the glass ampoules, one holding the immobiliser and another the drug to revive the animal afterwards, scribbling a note on a label to identify them. He explained the steps to her as he prepared the darts, spelling out the dangers. Even a drop on the skin could be immediately fatal for a human and Narcan, the antidote, also had to be ready.

He put the darts in a metal box, collected up the empty ampoules, wrapped them in kitchen roll and put them in a plastic bag with his discarded gloves. 'Dangerous waste,' he said to Christie and she nodded, hurrying through with it to the enclosed bin, marked with skull and crossbones, at the back of his office. When she returned, he was ready, holding the box and the Narcan.

When they left, Lissa was still standing there, her mouth downturned and with a little rivulet of rainwater trickling from her hair down the side of her face.

Supper was over, but Marjory and Bill Fleming were lingering at the kitchen table over coffee. They were alone; Cammie had been coy about his plans for the evening, but Marjory suspected there was a girl involved.

'To be honest,' Bill said, 'I'm just putting off going to do the evening rounds. It's such a filthy night.'

'I suppose we can't complain – it's nearly October, after all. But we got spoilt with those weeks of lovely autumn weather.' Marjory glanced towards the collie asleep in her usual position, as close as she could get to the elderly Aga. 'I doubt if Meg wants to go either.'

At the sound of her name, the dog lifted her head lazily, glanced at her owners, then with a sigh put it back down again. They both laughed.

'I'll take that as a no, shall I?' Bill said. 'Mind you, she'll be up and dancing around whenever I make a move. What are you doing this evening?'

Marjory leant back in her chair, stretching luxuriously. 'I'm happy to say, not a lot, for once. Karolina and Mum between them have everything running like clockwork, and we're not under the cosh with the new investigation, the way we usually are. I've just got a few reports I want to read through again. And I thought I'd phone Cat. I've tried a couple of times but it's always on the answerphone.'

'Too busy enjoying herself. She sounded quite excited when I spoke to her last night.'

'I hope she realises how hard she'll have to work. Vet's a tough course and there's not much scope for mucking about.'

Bill smiled. 'Killjoy!' he said, getting to his feet. 'We were young once too, remember?'

'I remember all too vividly,' Marjory said tartly. 'And I don't want Cat going down that road.'

'Speak for yourself. Come on, Meg – sooner we go, the sooner we'll be back.'

He went out. Marjory fetched her phone and called Cat's number, then listened to it ringing out yet again. She didn't leave a message; she'd done that twice today.

She sat back, frowning. Was it paranoid to think Cat was punishing her? Yes, probably. It wasn't much more than twenty-four hours since she'd seen her daughter, and Cat was probably, as Bill had said, high on the excitement of independence.

And anyway, if Cat was annoyed, it was hardly unnatural. Marjory had never managed to fall out with her peaceable, gentle mother, but she'd certainly had plenty of spats with her father. Given time, Cat would forget about it, since Marjory didn't plan to foster hostility, as her father had done.

Consoling herself with that thought, Marjory stacked the dishwasher and picked up her reports. She went through to the sitting room, lit the fire and settled to read.

The new case was slow-paced but intriguing: as the pieces of evidence started coming in, it would be a matter of fitting them together like a jigsaw puzzle – and it looked as if Rosie Drummond's ghost story and the information about the watch were forming at least a small corner of the picture.

Clinging to the side of the trailer as it bounced up the track behind the big forklift truck, Christie could see the lights of torches ahead and as she got nearer, hear agitated voices. There were three chalets fairly close together beyond the second gate, one still dark but the others with lights blazing and front doors standing open.

Kerr's car was parked by the first gate with its headlights illuminating the scene. Matt stopped the truck and jumped out carrying his equipment and Christie climbed down from the back with a tin bowl full of potatoes – her own idea.

There was no sign of the stag. She could see Kerr standing on the farther side of the second gate with a little knot of people and they went through to join him.

With an expression of rigidly controlled irritation, Kerr was listening to a small woman with a frizz of permed hair, flanked by a tall silent man and a youth, presumably their son.

'You have to shoot it, now!' she was saying in hysterical tones. 'It's a monster – it could have killed her!'

'Yes, pet,' Kerr said. 'But if you could just tell me where he is, I could maybe do something.'

'Up that way.' The youth stepped forward, pointing up the steep ground of the field. He certainly seemed calm enough. 'It kind of snorted a bit and then trotted off, that was all. My mum's just mental.'

'Yes, but he could come back,' his mother insisted. 'He could leap the gate and—'

Matt stepped forward. 'I'm Matt Lovatt, the farmer – we spoke on the phone. I promise we'll deal with this safely. But I'm very concerned about the injured lady. What happened?'

'Well!' The woman began her recital with relish. 'We were in our sitting room there when we heard screaming – terrible, terrible screams. Made my blood run cold, didn't it, Martin?'

The silent man nodded and she went on, 'And when we came out, the lady from Spindrift was on the ground with that evil creature pawing at her, ready to run her through and through with its horns. I just screamed and yelled, and it looked up – I thought it would come right at me, over the fence – and she somehow managed to wriggle under the gate and escape.

'Then it attacked the gate and I thought it would break it down and we'd all be murdered, but then it sort of gave up and went away. But you'll have to kill it, now it's got the taste for humans—'

Her son burst out laughing. 'Oh, yeah, like it's a man-eating lion? Hello? And it so didn't attack the gate, just, like, butted it a couple of times like it was confused, that's all. Anyway, the woman wasn't that much hurt.'

She turned on him. 'How do you know, Barrie? With internal injuries you can say you're all right, then ten minutes later, bang! You drop down dead. Isn't that right, Martin?'

Martin nodded, though with a little less conviction this time.

Lovatt said tautly, 'Where is she? Perhaps I could speak to her.'

'I wanted her to come in with us, but she wouldn't.' The

woman was clearly disappointed. 'She went back to Spindrift, said she was fine, she didn't want a fuss—'

'So you go, "Right, right," then call 999,' Barrie jeered. 'Cool idea! Just want your name in the papers, you do.'

His mother bristled. 'I don't want her on my conscience if something goes wrong, that's all,' she said shrilly. 'I know what's right.'

Still, Christie felt a little more cheerful. It sounded as if the woman's injuries were minor, and as if she wasn't hell-bent on revenge either. Maybe Matt could sweet-talk her with an offer of compensation.

He was having a low-voiced conversation with Brodie. Lovatt was holding the dart rifle and as he put on the gloves again and loaded it, she heard him say, 'So don't kill him unless you have to,' as he handed it to Brodie before heading off towards Spindrift.

Brodie nodded, but even so started to load the .243. The woman exchanged a triumphant glance with her son, but Christie felt sick – Rudolf, normally so sweet-natured, who had been an abandoned calf, hand-reared by Matt himself! As Brodie opened the upper gate, she went through behind him. 'Matt said only to shoot if absolutely necessary,' she reminded him. 'I heard him.'

He turned on her. 'For God's sake, woman, get out the way! Last thing I need is you in the way when I'm lining up a shot.' He glanced at the bowl of potatoes. 'And he's not a dear little Santa Claus Rudolf right now. He's a raging sex maniac and I'm not planning to risk my life for a few tons of venison on the hoof.'

Brodie limped off with the two guns. He was afraid – Christie knew the scent of fear and she could smell it on him now. And of course he was right – the calves that Rudolf might sire weren't going to live a long and happy life as pets, so why should he be different?

Even so . . . Christie waited until he had stumped out of the pool of light from the headlights and been swallowed up in rain and darkness, then looped round the opposite side of the field, peering ahead from under the shelter of her parka hood. She could see the black bulk of the cows, whose field it was, lying down, close enough for her to smell their warm grassy breath, and she stood in something that squelched unpleasantly, but there was no sign of the stag's familiar outline.

Rudolf could be anywhere – concealed by that great bank of gorse, say, crazed by his hormones and confused by the night's events. Days ago he had nuzzled her for potatoes; once the rut was over, he'd do it again – if he was still alive. And Matt must feel even worse about this than she did.

Christie was afraid too, but fear was no stranger to her. She'd experienced it many times in action, and she had trained responses. She was in action now and she could handle it.

'Rudolf!' she called, rattling the potatoes in the tin bowl. 'Rudolf!'

The door to Spindrift was standing open. Matt Lovatt tapped on it, called a greeting and came in.

He recognised the woman in the chair by the window as the holidaymaker he'd met on the shore earlier today. Her face was ashen and smeared with mud; she was shaking, and her thick weatherproof jacket was torn. A long rip in her jeans showed a bruised and bloody gash on her leg.

The look she gave him was cold. 'I'll be all right. I don't need anyone.'

He looked at the injury with dismay. 'You need that seen to, just for a start. Did he gore you?'

'No. Not for want of trying. I managed to roll under the gate so he couldn't reach me. This was from a hoof.'

'I'm so sorry. I'm Matt Lovatt – the animal's mine. And I know – apologies aren't nearly enough,' he said helplessly.

'No.'

He was floundering now. 'I will, of course, pay compensation—'

The woman actually laughed. 'And you think that would make it all right? *You would!*'

'No, of course not.' Lovatt found himself becoming unreasonably irritated. If anyone had a right to be difficult, it was this woman. She was clearly in pain and in a state of shock, but that was a personal attack. 'Do you want us to kill him?' he asked stiffly.

Suddenly, she seemed very tired. 'Do what you like. Just get out of here and leave me alone.'

'Of course. I'll get in touch tomorrow when you're feeling better. The ambulance and the police will be here shortly, I'm sure.'

She sat up, galvanised. '*What!* What did you say? Oh no, that *fool* of a woman!'

There was an empty wine glass on the window ledge beside her. In a sudden spurt of energy she jumped to her feet, picked it up and dashed it to the ground.

As the shards flew, she shouted, '*Now* will you go?'

Without a word, Lovatt left.

Elena walked through to the bathroom. She didn't know whether she was still shaking from shock or from purest rage. She had been controlling herself so rigidly for so long that she wasn't sure she could recognise rage any more.

That moronic bitch! She'd expressly said that she didn't want a fuss, and the resultant publicity. Stag attacks woman – it was the sort of story the press might pick up, and if Eddie caught a whiff of it he'd arrive in a protective frenzy before she could say 'I'm perfectly fine'.

Wincing, she washed the gash on her thigh with soapy water. Mercifully, it had been a glancing blow; a sharp hoof that fully connected would have meant stitches at the very least. She always carried first aid and she smeared on antiseptic, then wound round a lint bandage. She was used to dealing with minor wounds.

The jeans were past repair. She binned them, pulling on another pair. She'd come with a good stock, planning anyway to throw them out once they were dirty and it was much more irritating having ripped her jacket – that would have to be replaced.

There were the sirens now! Elena swore. She so didn't need this; she just wanted to lock the door she had foolishly left open when she staggered through it, take two pills and go to bed.

But if she did, then by morning the story would have grown. If she went out now, said it was a fuss about nothing, it would kill it.

They'd ask her name and address for a statement, though. But then she knew – who better? – that a name was only what you called yourself, and an address could be anything you liked. They wouldn't be demanding ID, after all.

In his loft in the bothy, Fergie Crawford too heard the sound of sirens and whimpered in fright. They were coming for him! Somehow they had tracked him down – How? Brodie?

He still didn't trust the man who'd given him a roof over his head and food to eat, which at one point had been his only concerns. But Brodie always had some scam going – jake, if you fitted in with it. If you didn't, you were dead meat.

Fergie was huddled into his sleeping bag, happed up with blankets. He'd been lying there since it got dark, banned from lighting the lamp in case someone saw a flicker of light where no light should be. Brodie had said he'd have to live like that until the next shipment from the Isle of Man was due; he'd take him out then to meet the fishing boat and they'd put him ashore in Ireland where there were folk he could work for. He was still uneasy, though.

Yes, he'd done a good job for Brodie and his pals, reliably keeping his mouth shut, not trying to make a bit extra on the side like some other runners did. So he could be useful – though in the creepy darkness he sometimes thought he might be more useful dead.

But dead was one thing, shopping him was another. Surely Brodie wouldn't – Fergie knew too much.

The sirens had stopped. They'd be finding a boat to bring them across to the island, and locked up here he couldn't even hide – 'Can't have you going stir-crazy and deciding to take a wee walk,' Brodie had said with a mirthless smile.

It was a very sturdy door with a solid lock. Fergie went and shook it, but not hopefully, then knelt by the window looking towards the mainland. There were gaps between the slats, and he squinted through.

The flashing blue lights were not, as he had feared, by the jetty. They were on the hill behind the village where there were buildings and a lot of lights.

A great sigh of relief escaped him. His legs went weak as the fight-or-flight adrenaline surge subsided and he turned to go back to bed. But it had made him hungry too; he peered in the darkness at the stacked tins. He felt for one with an inset opener – spaghetti hoops – and groped for a spoon, then went back to his sleeping bag to eat them.

At least his belly was full when he lay down again. And soon he'd go to sleep, and not have to lie there staring at the shifting shadows, which made him feel as if there was another presence moving just outside his line of sight.

* * *

'Rudolf!' Christie called again. 'Rudolf!'

From behind her, she heard Matt's shout. 'Christie! For God's sake, come back here,' and she ignored it.

'Rudolf!'

Then, from the darkness at the end of the field, she heard a bellow and moved towards it. 'Potatoes, Rudolf!' she cried idiotically, shaking them in the tin to make the sound he would recognise.

The bellow came again, definitely closer. It was scary, but she held her ground. If she could keep ahead of him, keep him moving until he was in the lit area near the gates, Kerr could get him darted.

Christie could see something moving now, still at a distance. She peered into the darkness, and against the skyline could see antlers.

Then a shot rang out.

CHAPTER NINE

Christie's shoulders slumped in dismay. She'd been sure Kerr would ignore Matt's instructions; no doubt he'd claim Rudolf had made to attack him. As perhaps he had – how did she know?

She became aware of police sirens away in the distance, but she could also hear Brodie's furious swearing and then saw him stomping back towards the gate. In the darkness, and possibly even feeling nervous about how immediately his damaged body could respond in an emergency, he had missed.

Now Christie could see the stag clearly, his bulk looming against the paler night sky. He'd been unsettled; he was snorting and skittering, then began coming towards her at a fast, purposeful trot that swiftly ate up the distance between them.

She rattled the potatoes in the bowl, still calling, 'Rudolf!' but gave a quick glance over her shoulder towards the circle of light from the headlamps, calculating the distance. Lovatt was standing there.

'He's coming!' she shouted. 'I'll try to bring him to where Kerr can dart him.'

'Get back here!' Lovatt yelled, fury in his voice. 'Run!'

The stag was twenty yards away now, lowering his head. He didn't look as if he was interested in potatoes.

Christie ran. It wasn't far to the gate, but he was effortlessly gaining on her. She heard the shrill, panicky screams of a woman behind the gate and knew she couldn't reach it in time. Automatically she threw herself to the ground, offering less of a target, protecting her head. She could feel the ground shaking, like muffled drumbeats under her ear.

Then there was another, quieter shot. As she lay there, she felt the shock go through her as the stag's body slumped to the ground a few feet away.

'Quiet evening?' Bill Fleming said as he and Meg came into the sitting room after their evening round, and Meg made a beeline for the rug in front of the fire. 'You look very comfortable, anyway.'

Marjory smiled at him, curled up in one of the shabby chairs they were always vowing to replace and somehow never did. 'Very quiet, for once. I've had a chance to go through my reports, and even watched an old *Taggart*. Do you think we could get them to come along and give us a few tips on wrapping up a crime in under an hour?'

Bill sat down. 'Good idea. Did you speak to Cat?'

'No,' Marjory said slowly. 'She's ignoring my messages. Am I being punished, Bill?'

It had been on her mind all evening. She wanted him to mock her, tell her she was imagining it.

He pulled a face. 'It's possible,' he said. 'She was seriously pissed off yesterday.'

Sometimes a husband who was straight as a die, open and incapable of telling an untruth – admirable as this might be – wasn't actually what you wanted. Marjory was just about to point out the virtues of the tactful lie when they heard footsteps in the hall.

'There's Cammie,' she said. 'Wonder how his date went?'

'Date?' Bill said.

'Yes, date. Mark my words.'

Cammie opened the door. Marjory still found it hard to believe that over what seemed about ten minutes, he'd started towering over her. Girls were bound to feature in his life soon.

'Hi,' she said. 'Good evening?'

'Yeah,' Cammie said.

'Were you out with David?' Marjory asked, naming his best mate with apparent innocence.

He was still standing in the doorway, moving from foot to foot. 'Er . . . no.'

Bill, notoriously less sensitive, at least where his son was concerned, demanded, 'Are you just going to stand in the doorway, letting in the draught?'

'Er . . .'

Marjory smiled at him. 'What were you going to ask, darling?'

Cammie looked at her gratefully. 'Er – could I bring someone for supper? I'd like you to meet them.'

'"Them?"' Bill raised his eyebrows sardonically. 'When you say "them"—' then subsided at a glance from his wife that suggested completing the sentence would be a mistake.

'Of course you could!' Marjory said warmly. 'When would you like to bring her?'

'Tomorrow, maybe? Some time when you're going to be around,' Cammie said. 'I know it's not always easy to say, but—'

'That's fine,' Marjory said quickly. 'As far as I know, it's not a problem, and if it is I'm sure we can rearrange it.'

'Yeah. Thanks, Mum.' He turned to go, then turned back. 'There's just one thing . . .'

He was looking quite pink and embarrassed. It was very sweet; how young he still was!

'Whatever it is, it's fine, I promise,' Marjory said, and saw his face clear.

'Oh good! She's a vegetarian.'

It was very hot in the nightclub. Very hot, and the smell of sweat was pretty gross. There was kind of a creepy guy checking her out and Cat moved away to break eye contact. Where was Lily?

She'd felt OK at first tonight, kind of crazy and free, and there were all these great people who were crazy and free as well, but she was beginning to feel tired and a bit sort of sick of it all – maybe she should go home . . .

But it wasn't home. It was back to a bare room where she'd be alone with the thought that her life had just been, like, totally wrecked. Where *was* Lily? Maybe if she was going back too, they could talk a bit before they went to bed.

But Lily didn't look like she was planning to do that any time soon. When Cat found her, she said, 'You're coming down. I can fix that.' And before Cat knew where she was, she was having, like, a really fab time all over again. Simples!

For a moment Christie wasn't sure she could move. She was sending messages to her legs but they didn't seem to be receiving them. Realising that her face was resting in a cowpat, though, provided the necessary impetus. She sat up hastily, groping for a tissue to wipe it.

Matt came hurrying through the gate towards her, his face grey in the artificial light. He grabbed her arm, ungently pulling her to her feet. 'I can't believe how bloody stupid that was. Are you all right?'

'Yes, yes, of course.'

'No "of course" about it,' he snarled. 'If Kerr hadn't got into position—'

Christie turned her head. Brodie, his face black with rage, was stumping over. With his back to the interested audience, he swore at her in a vicious undertone.

Lovatt was turning away. 'I'll bring the tractor in. I've got the Revivon. Sooner we get him back and bring him round again the better.'

'Sorry, Kerr,' Christie said as humbly as she could. 'And thanks. You maybe saved my life there.'

'Not sure why I bothered,' he said ungraciously. 'Without you interfering we wouldn't be having to start on antidotes and monitoring him half the night afterwards to make sure he's all right.'

'Sorry,' Christie said again, but she wasn't. If she hadn't brought him into Matt's line of sight, Kerr would have killed Rudolf by now.

Lovatt was bringing up the forklift attachment ready to move the inert animal on to the trailer. The police sirens weren't far away now.

'Here.' Brodie thrust the dart rifle into her hands. 'Take care of that.'

Christie took it and headed back to the gate where the family from the chalet above were still watching the free show, though looking damp and cold in the continuing rain.

Barrie came across as she opened it. 'Hey! That was seriously cool, the way the big guy just came crashing down.'

'Mmm.' Christie wasn't feeling inclined to be chatty. She set down the rifle, ejected the dart then turned to fetch the rubber gloves she needed to handle it. She caught movement out of the corner of her eye, spun round and saw Barrie bending to pick up the dart.

'Don't touch it!' she screamed in a panic. 'Get back!'

The youth jumped, then drew back, putting his hands up. 'OK, OK!'

She turned on him, shouting, 'What the hell do you think you're doing? Get a spot of this on your hand and you could be dead in five minutes.'

'All right, all right.' He was looking a bit shaken himself, and his mother stepped forward belligerently.

'Shouldn't have stuff like that, lying around for people to touch. It's just all of a piece, the carelessness, letting wild animals roam around the place. This whole thing's an outrage.' Getting into her stride, she raised her voice. 'That's what it is – an outrage! That creature should have been shot – look what it did to that poor lady—'

A cool voice came from behind her. 'I'm fine, actually. Just a graze, that's all. I can't imagine why there's all this fuss.'

Christie turned and saw a woman approaching from the other chalet, a slim woman walking a little stiffly and wearing a torn jacket with a hood pulled up, not quite covering her blonde hair. The victim, obviously, but she certainly didn't look like an ambulance case.

As Barrie's mother bridled and bleated that you couldn't be too careful, Christie went on clearing up, stowing the dart safely in the metal box, along with the surgical gloves. The police arrived as she picked up the Narcan, mercifully unneeded.

Lovatt jumped down from the forklift and went to meet the two uniformed officers. Christie heard him say, 'So you see, it's important to revive the animal as soon as possible.'

They seemed to accept that, taking his name and address, then came up towards the group at the gate.

'Where's the injured lady?' one called.

The blonde woman came forward, putting her hand up to

shield her eyes from the headlamp beam. 'That's me. But there's absolutely no need for all this fuss. It was just a minor accident.'

'No need for an ambulance, then?' The policeman's tone was dry, and Christie saw the woman colour in annoyance.

'I didn't send for it – or for you!' she said fiercely, casting a look of contempt at Barrie's mother. 'I suppose it was this woman here. I told her I was fine.'

'How was I to know? Could have been worse than she seemed, isn't that right, Martin?' The older woman was sharply defensive.

'Cancel the ambulance, Constable,' one of the officers said, then as his partner nodded and went back to the patrol car, added, 'I'll need statements. Is there anyone else likely to have been a witness to how the animal got out?'

Christie cleared her throat. 'Er . . . there were people in the pub at the time. They might have seen something.'

'Right. We'll get down there after we've finished here.'

'We can go down to the pub too, out of the rain. You could talk to us there.' The silent Martin spoke with sudden animation, startling everyone. 'Need a drink after the shock.'

His wife looked at him askance. 'Anything for a drink with you, isn't it?' Then, as a thought occurred to her, 'I suppose we could. People'll want to know what's happened, won't they?'

'And you want to tell them,' Barrie jeered. 'Tragic, you are.'

The blonde woman cut in on the domestic discussion. 'I'd be grateful if you could take my statement first, officer. I'm still slightly shaken and I'd like to get to bed.'

'Of course, ma'am.' He turned to Christie. 'What about you?'

'I live at the farm. I've got hazardous waste here, and I need to get back to dispose of it safely.' She held up the metal box.

He nodded. 'On you go,' and Christie hurried off down the path.

At least it sounded as if it wouldn't be a major problem. But now she began turning her mind to what had happened in the first place. She knew, absolutely knew, she hadn't left the gate unlatched. So who had opened it? Who was bent on causing trouble for Matt?

He wasn't popular in the village; she knew that, though she wasn't clear why. But what she'd seen for herself was the growing hostility between Matt and Kerr, presumably because of Lissa – was it possible Kerr had done this, just to cause trouble? He'd been keen to shoot Rudolf, when in fact a killing shot to the head or neck was much more difficult in these conditions than a dart that would be effective wherever it hit. Rudolf was a great favourite with Matt . . .

Perhaps Christie was over-refining. Perhaps, as Kerr said, it was just that he didn't want all the bother. And perhaps she should leave it to the police to find out what had happened and get on with the job in hand.

Cal Findlay's sitting room was on the side of the house, looking inland across the roofs of Innellan. Originally a bedroom, it was dark and poky and only merited its present designation by virtue of an armchair, television and computer. Its one advantage was that Cal didn't have to share it with his mother.

He had been sitting in darkness watching a sci-fi movie, though, if challenged, he could not have recalled a single detail of what passed for a plot. The sound of police sirens brought him instantly to his feet and he went to the window, his nerves jangling.

The flashing blue light was moving up the hill on the far side of the hamlet where the chalets were, and now he saw that there were other lights there too, the headlamps of stationary vehicles. What was going on?

Probably, Findlay told himself, it was just one of the minor disturbances that happened from time to time and the police were bigging it up as an excuse for blasting along on sirens. It could be kids mucking about – or, now he thought about it, a stag party getting out of hand. He'd seen a group of young men in the pub.

Even so, an emergency . . . And his nerves were in tatters already. He had to find out what was happening.

They'd know down at the Smugglers. Without even switching off the TV he left the room and grabbed a jacket from a peg in the hall. As he opened the front door, his mother's voice moaned, 'Help me, oh help me!'

Her usual cry. He hardly heard it now.

Georgia Stanley had never seen the pub so full of locals and everyone was in a rollicking mood. Word of free drinks had obviously got around, since many of the people had arrived later and she'd seen the Donaldsons on their mobile phones. Tony Drummond was coming in now too, journalistic antennae bristling.

Cal Findlay had just arrived as well. It was most unusual for him to make a repeat visit late in the evening, but he didn't join anyone, just going to edge himself into his usual place at the far end of the bar. Maybe he'd heard the police sirens and come to see what the fuss was about.

Like a good landlady, Georgia told him and served him his free drink, to his obvious surprise. She was beginning to worry about the bill that would be waiting for Matt Lovatt and had started restricting the supply for people trying to stack them up – like the Donaldsons, naturally, who were getting more obnoxious by the minute. She took an anxious glance at the clock; it was a while yet till closing time and at this rate the poor guy would need a second mortgage to pay his bar bill.

The arrival of Martin and his family caused an immediate stir. As his wife came in, clutching at her heart dramatically, she proclaimed in carrying tones, 'You'd better get me a brandy, Martin. I was never so terrified in my life!' Within minutes a fascinated group had gathered, with the Donaldsons, Sorley and Tony Drummond well to the fore. There was a reverent hush as Barrie took over to describe in minute detail his near-death encounter with the poison darts.

He had just reached the point where the girl had said, 'I shall have to dispose of this hazardous waste,' when the back door of the pub opened and Matt Lovatt came in, gaunt with tiredness and strain.

He seemed surprised at the silence, but it allowed him to say, 'Thanks for being so patient, everyone. The stag's safely back in his pen.'

'So I'm afraid you'll have to pay for this yourself,' Georgia said with considerable satisfaction as she set down a pint in front of a scowling Steve Donaldson. He fumbled for the money with a dirty look at her and at Lovatt.

The buzz of talk started up again as Lovatt said, 'All right, Georgia, what's the damage?'

'I hate to tell you, Matt. But look, I'll split the difference on the wholesale price. It's been great business for me this evening.'

He looked taken aback, she thought, as if kindness was beyond his expectation. His 'That's very generous of you. Are you sure?' sounded stiff, though she had no doubt that his gratitude was genuine.

'Least I could do,' she said. 'I think word got round.'

He looked round the bar ruefully. 'Yes, I can see that.' Then he lowered his voice. 'Could I just ask you – did you hear anyone say anything about how the stag got out? Christie swears the gate was latched and I'm inclined to believe her.'

With some regret, Georgia said that she hadn't. 'But I can tell you, there was a lot of joking and sniggering from the Donaldsons and Derek Sorley just after you went out to deal with it.'

Lovatt sighed. 'Doesn't prove anything, of course. But . . .'

'Exactly,' Georgia agreed. She hesitated for a moment, then said, 'Maybe I shouldn't say this, but you should be warned. That lot really hate you, you know. They'll do anything they can to harm you.'

'I know that,' he said wearily. 'I've lived with it since I came here. Now, what do I owe you?'

She worked it out and he paid with a credit card, then thanked her again. As he walked out, there was a gale of unpleasant laughter from the Donaldsons' table.

Georgia bit her lip. She'd said all she could say to Lovatt, but he hadn't picked up on her feeling that the resentment which had simmered for three years was for some reason coming to the boil.

Christie came back from the farm office to the kitchen and went to the sink to scrub her hands, feeling that you couldn't be too careful.

'I'm glad to have got rid of that scary stuff,' she said to Lissa, who was sitting at the table with a cup of herbal tea, looking damp and reproachful. 'Are the men still busy with Rudolf?'

'Kerr is. Matt's gone back to the pub to pay a huge bill we really can't afford. And all for such a simple thing as a gate not being shut properly . . .' She gave a little sigh, her limpid gaze an oblique accusation.

Christie was too exhausted and upset to be anything but blunt. 'Are you accusing me? Because it's not true. I know I shut it.'

'Did you?' Lissa said vaguely. 'Oh, well . . .'

With a tightened jaw, Christie said, 'I'll just go and see how

Rudolf is.' She headed to the door; she always came off worst in these encounters with Lissa.

'Kerr's cross with you,' Lissa volunteered. 'Poor man – he's going to have to spend half the night looking after it.'

Again, there was that sly hint of blame, impossible to refute. 'I'm quite happy to take his place,' Christie said crisply. 'Matt can tell me what to look out for.'

'He'll probably stay himself anyway. That would suit you, wouldn't it?'

It was too pointed to ignore; it had to be challenged. 'What do you mean by that?' Christie said, hoping that a blush wouldn't betray her.

'Oh – nothing, really.' Lissa gave a small, tight smile.

If they were going to play games, it wasn't going to be under Lissa's rules. Her voice flat, Christie said, 'There's nothing between me and Matt, if that's what you're implying. More's the pity – he deserves someone whose first thought isn't always "poor me!"'

Lissa's pale face flushed, and for a moment she showed temper. 'How dare you!' Then she smiled. 'Oh, dear, how sad! You see Matt as a romantic figure, I suppose, because of his face. He's not, you know. He's a very difficult, moody person. You've no idea how cold and cruel he can be. I've had a lot to put up with.'

'Poor you,' Christie said sarcastically, and saw that little spurt of temper again as Lissa said with uncharacteristic sharpness, 'No, poor you, really. Don't you think if you just decided to leave, it might be easier?'

'Easier for you and Kerr, you mean?' Christie had a temper too.

Lissa went very still. 'I don't know what you're talking about.'

Perhaps Christie shouldn't have said it, but it was too late to

161

take back the words. 'I know about your affair. And from the way Matt's been this last bit, I reckon he's guessed too. So maybe it will be you and Kerr that are leaving.'

Lissa's face showed real alarm. 'Oh, but I couldn't leave! Not ever – there's the baby, you see.'

She'd done it again – left Christie feeling insensitive, brutal, even. 'Oh, well . . .' she said awkwardly.

But Lissa was saying, almost to herself, 'If he asks me, I'll tell him – he'll understand. He knows what I've been through, how hard I find it to cope. If this brings me comfort, he won't push me into despair – he knows what that's like. I'd kill myself, rather than leave. I know he won't make me.'

She got up and with a smile she left the room.

Christie stared after her. She couldn't interpret that smile. Was it mocking? Triumphant? Or was Lissa just satisfied that she'd found the solution to an awkward problem? As an excuse for a *ménage à trois* it was cheek of a breathtaking order.

Would Matt really go along with that? She didn't know him well enough to say. And perhaps he was moody and difficult; she knew what the after-effects of trauma had done to her, and she wasn't reminded of what had happened every time she looked in a mirror. He certainly wouldn't have had much support from a wife who'd established a monopoly on suffering. Christie's feelings for Lissa had been a mixture of irritation and, yes, contempt. Now they crystallised into a clearer emotion: purest hatred.

It was still raining steadily. She pulled her hood over her head and hurried across the yard. She could see a light in one of the sheds; they'd have put Rudolf in an inside pen. Tired though she was, she'd be happy to sit up with him. Anyway, if she tried to sleep in her present disturbed state she knew how she would be punished.

* * *

162

Elena took her sleeping pills along with a glass of wine which she took to the chair by the window. Her usual seat – though of course she had only come yesterday. How odd it was, that habit kicked in so quickly. The territorial instinct, perhaps. My chair. Mine. I can do what I like with what's mine . . .

She caught herself up. She was so tired, she was rambling. And shocked. And drunk, a bit.

She'd dealt all right with the police, though. They had seemed indifferent, almost bored, and all those years of strict control had paid off. It had just been what she'd heard described as 'a little local difficulty'. She liked the phrase, but she couldn't recall who said it. A politician, probably, caught up in one of the usual scandals . . .

God, she was rambling again. She had to rehearse what she'd told the police, just in case. Natalie Thomson – it had come easily to her lips.

Of course it had. Natalie Thomson had come to grief long ago on the streets, a terrible warning – but Elena had believed she'd blotted out that time. She didn't care for the thought that somewhere it was lodged in her consciousness. It was, though, along with everything else. She'd given them an address, too – 14 Church Street, Solihull: an address which didn't exist – or at least she hoped it didn't. She'd never been to Solihull. She wasn't actually entirely sure where it was.

So even if something did appear in the press there would be nothing to attract Eddie's attention. He was getting restive and inquisitive, making his frequent phone calls more difficult to handle, as he constantly pressed her to say when she would return. Elena knew why: she'd covered her tracks this time so he couldn't trace her through her plastic. He thought she didn't know he did that, so he couldn't admit it and it was probably driving him mad. She'd told him this was a retreat and she'd be switching off her phone for long periods. If necessary she could even say she was going into a few days of silent meditation to get Eddie off her back.

Silent meditation. Peace. How good that sounded! A mind scoured of memory, aware only of this moment . . . and this . . . and this . . . She found she was drifting, her eyes starting to close as the pills began to take effect. She shook her head to clear it, and got to her feet.

Peace! Elena's mouth twisted in a cynical smile. The only peace she could know came from chemical oblivion and—

She didn't want to take the other route. Yet when she reached her bedroom, her eyes went to the chest of drawers. She couldn't look away; as if drawn by a string she crossed the room and opened one of the small top drawers. There it was, the pretty shiny thing that gave her so much power, over herself if nothing else. For a moment she resisted, then she picked it up and snapped it open. She drew the little wicked blade across her arm, felt the sting of pain and saw the thin line of blood rise with a sigh of exquisite relief.

CHAPTER TEN

Eddie Tindall was, as usual, at his desk by seven-thirty. It had been a struggle today – after a restless night, he'd fallen into a deep sleep shortly before the alarm went.

This was the happiest part of his day, normally. He could shift twice as much with phone and email switched off, and today, too, he was engaged in a favourite occupation: assessing a report on a business he might add to his ever-growing empire.

He wasn't concentrating, though. Eventually he stopped trying and logged on to the bank account he'd checked last night. He wasn't really expecting it to be different this morning; it was just a neurotic twitch.

There had been no activity in their joint account since Elena withdrew a couple of hundred pounds in the middle of last week – a standard amount for taxis and tips, stuff you didn't use a card for. He logged off again.

He'd phoned to check her credit card account last night, and she hadn't used that either, not even for petrol. He'd got a printout detailing her recent mobile phone calls: most were to his own number and the ones he didn't recognise proved to be a hairdresser's, a couple of restaurants and several surprised women friends whom he had to fob off with a story about Elena wanting them told she'd be away for a few days.

Elena's rules had always been clear: she would come back, but he mustn't ask where she went, and she wouldn't tell him if he did. Until now that had been fine – he'd always traced her anyway. Knowing where she was gave him a reassuring sense of possession and now his failure was sending him crazy. *He needed to know!*

Could she be deliberately covering her tracks? He shied away from the question, too afraid of the answer staring him in the face even to consider it, putting up a barrier with every possible counter-argument. A retreat, she'd said; that suggested something religious, so maybe there was no charge – a donation at the end, perhaps. She could have seen it in a magazine and booked by post. And if it wasn't very far away, she wouldn't have needed much petrol. How many times had Eddie gone through that reasoning? A hundred – more? It was running like a loop in his head, faster and faster because if it stopped, unwelcome thoughts would intrude.

He could break her rule and ask her straight out, but when he'd hinted a question on the phone, her voice had gone cool and distant. If he pushed her too far, she could just stop taking his calls; he suspected she'd blocked some already.

So he'd just have to be patient until she came back, Eddie told himself firmly, but another voice whispered, '*And what if she doesn't?*' What if he could never again come home to that still pool of serenity she created, could never again make love to her and then lie and watch her sleep, in awed disbelief at his good fortune? How could he bear it? He groaned.

This was no good. He picked up the report again, forcing himself to consider the questions it raised. Yet even so, the loop was still playing in the background.

* * *

Marianne Price was wearing red today: red polka-dot blouse, red pencil skirt, red stilettos. She always chose red when she'd a busy day ahead. It got her going, she said, and she swept into Eddie's office in a whirlwind of activity.

'You've that Jakie Butler coming at ten,' she told him, 'and there's these forms – lawyer wants them this morning. Told him he'd be lucky, but—' Then she stopped. He was frowning over the papers he was reading and he'd only grunted instead of giving his usual greeting. There were bags under his eyes – well, Eddie always had bags under his eyes, but you could pack these for a weekend in Torremolinos.

'Not get much kip last night?' she asked.

Eddie looked up, rubbing his hand down his face. 'Does it show?'

'Does to me. She still away, then, is she?' Marianne seldom referred to her boss's wife, and never by name. 'That Woman' served if she was talking about her to someone else.

'Yes, she's just having a bit of a break. At a retreat.'

'Retreat? What's she needing to retreat from, then?'

'Feeling a bit stressed lately.' Marianne's silence was eloquent and he hurried on, 'Do her good to get away from her old man.'

'Where is she, then?' Eddie had confided his checking-up habit to her long ago. 'Just to make sure she's all right,' he'd said, defensively, then made her promise not to tell Elena – not difficult, since Marianne confined conversations with That Woman to monosyllables as far as possible.

'*I don't know!*' The words burst out as if Eddie couldn't help himself. 'It's just I never ask her straight out – you know. And this time she's not booked anywhere, or withdrawn any cash, or used her credit card. Oh, it's maybe that she's not needed to – if it's a religious place maybe they don't charge, and . . .' He went on to recite the arguments, gone over so often they seemed threadbare even to himself, then saw her sceptical face. 'You don't believe that, do you? You think she's gone off with someone.' He sounded utterly dispirited.

Though tempted to punch the air and shout, 'Result!' Marianne restricted herself to a non-committal, 'Couldn't say, really. Been in touch, have you?'

'Oh yes!' he said eagerly. 'Just says she's tired, needs a bit of peace and quiet, but she'll be back for sure once she feels rested.'

That would figure, she thought grimly. Poor Eddie! Dead decent fella, but soft in the head when it came to That Woman. She'd have her fling, then come back to her meal ticket, no doubt. Marianne hadn't the heart to tell him, though, so she played for time. 'If that's what she says, why shouldn't it be right?'

'Because if you're on your own, you can't do anything without money. So someone else is paying.' Then another thought occurred to him. 'Unless she's got another source I don't know about. Do you think she's found out I check up on her?'

'Not from me,' Marianne said, feeling a twinge of sympathy for the woman. If she did know about Eddie's activities, it might feel uncomfortably like being stalked by your own husband. She hesitated. 'Say there was someone, would you have her back afterwards?'

'If she'd come,' he said simply. 'I don't care. What I can't bear is not knowing where she is, feeling she might just disappear and I wouldn't be able to find her – it's doing my head in.' He rubbed his forehead, as if to ease some physical pain.

Maybe the woman was entitled to a bit of privacy. On the other hand, Marianne had no doubt where her loyalties lay, and if her advice wrecked the marriage, she wouldn't be weeping into her champagne.

'Why don't you give Clive a call?' she said.

Eddie looked shocked. 'Clive? I couldn't . . .' he said, then slowly, 'But he's always very discreet, isn't he?'

'Very,' Marianne confirmed. As she left the office, she saw him lifting the phone.

Nothing new had come in this morning. DI Fleming hadn't expected anything; labs wouldn't be working over the weekend and useful information from other sources was unlikely. She laid out the notes she'd made at home, ready to task Macdonald and Campbell before they went to Innellan this morning, then started preparing for the morning briefing. There would have to be an extensive follow-up to Friday's domestic and there had been an off-licence break-in that would mean leaning on the usual suspects.

Her phone buzzed. 'There's a Tony Drummond asking to speak to you, ma'am. He says you know him,' the Force Civilian Assistant said.

'In a manner of speaking. He's a journalist. Put him through anyway.'

Fleming didn't blame him for trying to safeguard his investment, but it wasn't going to do him any good. She wasn't ready yet to talk about what the watch battery suggested about timing and she wasn't going to drop poor Rosie in it either, so she'd nothing fresh for him.

'I haven't forgotten we owe you,' she said in greeting, 'but you'll have to be patient. I'm not expecting reports before the middle of the week at the earliest.'

'Fair enough,' Tony conceded. 'But I really wanted your comment on the incident last night.'

'Incident?' Fleming said sharply. 'What incident?'

'You mean the local police haven't reported to you? I should have thought anything happening at a murder scene would have relevance.'

'It depends.' She was wary now. 'Details?'

'One of Matt Lovatt's stags got loose and attacked a holidaymaker.'

'Badly hurt?' Fleming was startled.

'No, apparently not. Though of course she could have been.' There was a distinct note of regret in Drummond's voice.

She laughed, relieved. 'Mercifully the police aren't expected to deal with could-have-beens. I'm sure the Kirkcudbright officers can deal with negligent accidents.'

'Yes, but was it an accident? That's the question.'

'What does that mean?'

'Georgia Stanley said last night that the girl looking after the stag was adamant that the gate was properly closed. And she says there are elements in the village who really have it in for Matt Lovatt.'

'And you have some idea this links up with the murder?' Fleming did not try to hide her scepticism.

'You don't think it does?'

She grinned. 'Nice try – "DI dismisses incident as irrelevant"? Sorry, no comment.'

'You're not a lot of fun, you know that?' Drummond complained. 'Come on, give me a quote I can use.'

'I'll give you an exclusive. "Detectives are being sent to pursue enquiries." And the reason it's an exclusive is that no one else will bother to ask me.'

Fleming was smiling as she put the phone down. You had to hand it to Tony – he tried hard, and she quite liked the man. She scribbled, 'Stag attack', as a reminder on the notes for Macdonald and Campbell, then went back to her preparation.

Tony Drummond pulled a face. Fleming was nobody's fool; he hadn't actually thought she'd play along with the idea that last night's fuss was linked with what he was trying to promote as the 'Cave Man Mystery', but he needed something to keep the story alive. He'd done well with the stuff over the weekend – the sadism of the watch had gone down particularly well with the tabloids – but if it just went quiet as Fleming had suggested it would, generating interest again wouldn't happen unless the findings were sensational.

He glanced at his watch. Half past nine: time he headed into the *Galloway Globe* to do what he could with his limited copy. Last night he'd only gone to the pub when he heard police sirens, by which time the action was over. The family who'd witnessed it had overwhelmed him with details, and then some, but when he'd phoned Lovatt this morning for an interview and photo of the stag, he'd got a very brusque refusal – rude bugger!

There was the injured woman, of course – Natalie Thomson. The police had given him her name last night, but said she'd taken a sleeping pill. He'd have to go up there and interview her before going in to work.

When Drummond reached Spindrift, there was no sign of life. Glancing in at the picture window across the front, he could see the sitting room was empty. Still sleeping off the pills, probably. He hesitated, then glanced at his watch again. He didn't want to antagonise her, but he wasn't driving all the way back later, when she might well have gone out. He rapped on the door. There was no response, and after a minute he banged on it harder, shouting, 'Hello? Natalie, are you there?'

From the curtained room next to the front door he heard the sounds of someone wakening from deep sleep: a couple of groans, and then muttered swearing. Drummond grinned to himself and waited expectantly.

The woman who opened the door looked groggy, her hair a bird's nest and her half-shut eyes smudged with last night's mascara. She was huddled in a black towelling robe with the Dior logo and she was eying him with naked hostility.

'What the hell do you want?'

He switched on the charm. 'Oh God, I'm sorry, I'm sorry! Were you asleep? And I guess you must have been pretty shaken too.' He held up his press pass. 'Tony Drummond. It'll only take a moment of your time—'

'Press?' she said thickly. 'Piss off.'

The door was slammed so hard it almost got his nose. Aggrieved, Drummond retreated. OK, she'd been asleep, but there was no call for aggression. Her and Lovatt must both have taken their nasty pills this morning, unless it came naturally.

He'd just have to pad the article with suggestions of foul play – and he could make something of the phrase, 'Detectives are being sent to pursue enquiries', especially if he linked it to Innellan's other news story.

Elena Tindall leant against the door she had just slammed. She felt like death. Her stomach was heaving and the gash on her thigh was throbbing in time to the pounding of her head. She struggled to the sofa at the back of the sitting room and sank on to it, glancing anxiously towards the window in case the scum was poking a camera at it, but a moment later she heard a car drive away.

Water. She needed water. Her lips were parched and her tongue was sticking to the roof of her mouth. With infinite caution she raised her head, waited for the room to stabilise, then staggered through to the kitchen.

The water was good, very good: icy cold, fresh and without the stale chemical taint city water always had. Elena drank greedily then filled a jug, found some paracetamol and went back to the sitting room. Her legs were shaky, but her discomforts gave her an excuse not even to try to process the various shocks which had hit her. She had drunk too much, of course, but she was punch-drunk too.

It had all seemed so clear and simple when Elena made her plans. She only had to be invisible; the name she had given to the letting agency as she paid in cash was not her own, and once she had left there would be no trace.

It had taken steely resolve not to turn back on her journey north, but now that was faltering. There was just too much. *She could leave, now*, tempting whispers were saying. *Drive home to Eddie, back to the comfort of his adoration.* Eddie – perhaps that comfort was the closest thing to love she would ever know. But at what price? The maelstrom of emotions behind the calm and smiling front she always presented to him was destroying her and to return with the issues unresolved would, she surely knew, kill her, in one way or another.

So she'd nothing to lose. Nothing to lose – and to gain? Debts repaid? A slate wiped clean? Unfinished business completed? Her tortured mind, at last, at rest? Elena had to believe it.

If she was going on with this, she had to stay calm, clear-headed. No more storms of rage, like last night. No more drinking. Ignoring her still-aching head, she got up, found the remaining bottles of wine and poured the contents down the kitchen sink. She put the kettle on for coffee and went to run a shower.

When her mobile rang she didn't answer it, assuming it was Eddie. Her voice was probably still rough and he'd fuss about her health. She had her shower, swallowed some coffee, then picked it up. He'd only go on phoning until she spoke to him.

Then she realised that it hadn't been this phone ringing, but the other one, the pay as you go Eddie didn't know about and couldn't monitor, the one whose number she had given Cal last night. She listened to the message, chewing her lip. He was right: they had to meet, and the sooner the better. 'This afternoon,' she said when she rang back. She couldn't afford to go out now and be breathalysed.

No going back now. Elena stood for a moment staring out at the island, and the tiny flame of anger that always burned in her soul flared up into vigorous life.

'What did he do?' DC Ewan Campbell said.

Fleming and Macdonald looked at him. She had just detailed the interviews she wanted done and outlined the tentative theory that Rosie Drummond might well have heard the man's dying groans.

'You mean his job?' Macdonald asked, puzzled.

'No, you don't, do you, Ewan?' Fleming said slowly. 'You mean, what did the man do to merit such an unspeakable punishment?'

Macdonald was inclined to be dismissive. 'Psychopaths get their kicks out of inflicting torture. You can't deduce something from the method and start blaming the victim.'

'But it's a new line of thought,' Fleming argued. 'I hadn't looked at it from that angle. Don't psychopaths also get their kicks from watching their victims suffer? Whoever did this left him there.'

'Could be he didn't want to watch,' Campbell said. 'In case.'

'In case of *what*?' Macdonald said in some irritation. 'It's all very well being the quiet type, Campbell, but you're starting to sound like Mystic Meg.'

This time Fleming made no attempt to interpret, and let the silence lengthen. At last Campbell said, 'Well, in case he relented.'

Matt Lovatt was doing accounts, sorting bills into one pile, invoices into another. Money in, money out, never quite seemed to match up, and he winced as he thought of the bill for last night's largesse. Lissa had been complaining already that they couldn't afford what she called 'army waifs and strays', but he was adamant. It was a debt of honour and Christie, and her successors, were repayments to the account.

Kerr had gone into Kirkcudbright to buy stout padlocks for the gates of the stags' pens. That way, if it happened again it would plainly be criminal damage, not negligence as the police obviously believed.

But if it wasn't that, it would be something else. The scheme to drive the Lovatts out had started whenever they arrived as 'white settlers' and continued sporadically over the years – tacks tipped on to the drive, a load of manure ordered in his name, insults scrawled on walls. Just petty vandalism – he'd no doubt the Donaldsons were behind it but he'd never bothered to report it, reckoning it would probably make matters worse and they'd give up when they saw it wasn't working.

This was different. He could pinpoint when the atmosphere had changed: after he'd turned Sorley off the island with his cheap metal detector and his pathetic, avaricious delusions. The local reference section in Kirkcudbright library held a report from an archaeological dig in the seventies, and if there was a hoard of Viking gold they'd managed to keep it remarkably quiet.

The venomous graffiti on his son's grave and the dangerous freeing of the stag had Sorley's fingerprints all over. The Donaldsons weren't very bright; Sorley was much sharper. So what would he come up with next? Surveying his vulnerabilities, Lovatt's eye fell on Mika, lying in his basket. The dog opened its eyes as his master turned his head, then half-closed them again.

Lovatt had been careful not to look into the parentage of the pup he had reared. Its mother had clearly been living rough, probably another pathetic victim of the Bosnian conflict, and given the area – and the appearance of the pups – a wolf father was possible. Importing a hybrid was complicated, though, and if the animal had to be quarantined for months he'd almost certainly have lost any hope of domesticating it.

He had no illusions about what he'd taken on: a half-wild creature who must never discover that a challenge would succeed. But out of the daily dominance rituals – a vital tool of management – had grown an emotional bond, the most satisfying Lovatt had in what had become a bleak existence. He shied away from describing it as love – love was a concept entirely foreign to the dog, who understood only loyalty to the alpha male. But Mika certainly meant more to him than any human being, and there was a danger that, picking up subliminal clues, the dog might decide to try to assert his favoured status in his human pack, so Lovatt invariably kept him either at his side or securely in his pen – and now he thought of it, he must call Kerr and get him to buy an extra padlock for that. 'Wolf on the loose' would make another good story for bloody Drummond.

Oh yes, it was all starting to get very nasty indeed. Maybe he should just give up, pack it all in, let the bullies have their way. He was tired, tired, tired, and starting again to have the nightmares that left him afraid to take the sleep he needed.

He'd never get Lissa to leave her son's grave, though. Lissa . . . He sat back and ran his hand through his hair. What, in God's name, was he going to do about her and Kerr?

She'd had a breakdown before they were married. She'd always been vague about the causes but he didn't talk about his problems either; it was their mental struggle that was their common ground.

'You *understand*!' she'd said on their first date, her blue eyes shining. 'I've never met a man who understood.'

He'd convinced himself no woman would take on a man with

a face like his, least of all one as delicately pretty as Lissa, and a month after their first meeting they were engaged. Had he ever loved her, or was it just that her responsiveness was balm to his wounded spirit?

At that time it had felt as if they were perched on a cliff edge, clinging together so that neither should fall. Building each other's confidence, supporting the lapses into despair, had been a shared purpose in those early days, something he realised later had disguised their total incompatibility. Lovatt had hoped a child would provide another focus, but after the tragedy there was no hope. He had seen Lissa coming closer and closer to that edge; he'd feared she might even try to kill herself, yet struggling with his own stability he couldn't help her. It was Kerr's arrival that had brought her back to ground that was at least relatively safe.

Lovatt had no idea how long the affair had been going on. Perhaps if he'd still been emotionally involved with his wife he might have been more observant, but what he felt for Lissa now was mainly exasperation. He had only realised what was going on the other day, when he'd seen them kissing in the garden in clear view of the farm office. He'd drawn back so they wouldn't see him, but he'd felt betrayed – by Kerr, though, rather than by her. Of course they were out of the army now but there was a code among comrades-in-arms which he had, in some unformulated way, thought would still apply.

Had their kiss been a careless action, with a subconscious wish to be discovered, perhaps? Or was it more deliberate, representing – a dark thought, this – a sort of challenge from Kerr, as if, like Mika sensing a weakness in his authority, he had taken him on? With everything else just now, Lovatt had no stomach for confrontation. It would have to wait till he felt stronger. He tried not to think what the result would be with Mika if he did that.

What had he done to deserve all this? *No*, a quiet voice in his head murmured, *don't go there*.

With a half-groan, he turned to what he must deal with today. That woman, for a start. Would he have to go up and see her again?

She'd been on his mind in his wakeful hours through the night. Smashing that glass – such rage, such a strange and violent act! With so much direct and somehow personal hostility, Lovatt had felt that grinding it into his face wouldn't have been beyond her. '*You would!*' she had said, as if she knew him, her dark-blue eyes blazing, yet their brief meeting the previous morning had seemed a pleasant, casual encounter.

There was something about her that affected him at a level he couldn't quite explain. Had they met somewhere before? Not that he could remember, certainly, and he couldn't afford to let it bother him. She'd been in shock, after all, and perhaps was a bit unstable anyway.

That settled it. He'd order flowers to be sent to her with another apology, and let her take it from there.

You could go pure mental, shut up in this place on your own. A military prison where you'd other guys to talk to would be better than this.

Fergie was pacing up and down the loft. He'd worked out an exercise programme of marching to and fro, push-ups, sit-ups and squat thrusts, to do four times a day. He hadn't worked out like this since he was a recruit with a sadistic bastard as RSM, and he wouldn't call it enjoyable, but it was better than staring at the wall. Brodie had brought him some paperbacks, but reading wasn't Fergie's thing. It was kinna hard to get the story when you needed your finger to follow the lines. He'd begged to have the door unlocked but Brodie wouldn't hear of it.

'You'd get yourself caught,' he'd said, 'and I'm not having you dropping me in it.'

Fergie completed his marching. Now, push-ups. He lay down. One, two, three . . . He was panting hard by the time he'd reached a hundred.

Suddenly he heard movement from below. Poised at the top of a push-up with his arms straight, Fergie froze, then lowered himself noiselessly. In his exertions, he hadn't heard a boat coming. He could only hope it was Brodie, though he'd get grief for not keeping a lookout and making a noise.

The visitor was walking across the room. Still flat on the floor, Fergie turned his head to follow the movement. He heard a door open, then shut – a cupboard, maybe? – and then footsteps coming back.

And now, they were on the stairs. The ninth step creaked – he had counted as Brodie came up with supplies. There, that was the creak now. Fergie held his breath. Could the pounding of his heart be heard on the other side of the door? There was no sound of a key in the lock – not Brodie, then – but the handle turned and the door was rattled.

After a gruelling minute, the footsteps retreated, and he sagged with relief. If the door had been unlocked, he'd have been caught like a rat in a trap. He could hear more movement downstairs, then it sounded as if someone was walking away. With infinite caution, Fergie crept to the window with the broken slat and peered out.

A man he didn't know was walking up the hill, carrying a bucket – feed for the deer, likely. There was a huge, scary dog, German shepherd or something, loping alongside. Fergie sat down on his bed, feeling shaky.

What would happen now? Would the man come back, with another key? He felt sick with nerves, just sick.

* * *

Matt Lovatt put the dog into a sit-stay, then went up the hill to shake feed pellets into a wooden trough. He could hear the buck barking in the wood somewhere, but a couple of does came trotting up. He watched them for a moment, then called the dog and headed back to the boat.

He'd need to speak to Kerr. There must be rats in the cottage again; he'd heard scuffling movement that had stopped as he walked in, but when he fetched the poison from the cupboard to put down upstairs, the door was locked and the key wasn't in its usual place – in one of Kerr's pockets, no doubt. If they didn't get bait put down immediately, half the feed would disappear.

CHAPTER ELEVEN

The woman who opened the door to DS MacNee, a hard-faced blonde in her forties, gave him a less than enthusiastic greeting. In fact, it was a long time since MacNee had heard such a varied selection of swearie-words. Respect!

He grinned. 'Nice to see you too, Shirlee. Where is he?'

Shirlee produced another colourful selection to attach to Bar-L as well. Billy, it appeared, was in Barlinnie on remand until his trial for a robbery in Paisley.

'Och well, hen,' MacNee said cheerfully, 'there's a silver lining to every cloud. I was here to have a word about an off-licence break-in and if he'd not been banged up, no doubt he'd have had another offence to be taken into consideration.'

Shirlee didn't seem to appreciate this comforting reflection. With a cheery wave at the slammed door, MacNee went back to his car.

That suited him just fine. He'd a wee bit of business to deal with on his own account, and no one would be expecting him back at the station for a while. He'd driven to Newton Stewart already to find Billy; now he drove on down the road towards Borgue.

Kerr Brodie. MacNee had never been in the top rank of good haters. Folk did bad things, time passed, you shrugged your shoulders and let it go.

In general, that was his rule. For Brodie, he made an exception. For Brodie, a visceral loathing festered. Brodie had wrecked Tam's father's life and that he hadn't wrecked Tam's as well seemed even now a sort of miracle.

Unbidden, the image rose of the Glasgow tenement: the Brodies on the ground floor with two bedrooms and their own toilet, the MacNees on the top floor in a wee poky room-and-kitchen, with a shared cludgie on the stair. He thrust it away; he never thought about those days if he could help it, and he blamed Brodie that he was being made to think of them now.

He'd run an illicit check on the man on the quiet, but he didn't have previous, something of an achievement given what MacNee knew of his early associates and activities. Maybe Brodie had been clean since then – and maybe pigs would grow wings and hold a fly-past in his honour.

No, Kerr Brodie, damn his black soul, could no more decide to go straight than a corkscrew could decide on a new career as a skewer for shish kebab. So he wasn't just cannon fodder – and he probably had friends in the right places too, MacNee reflected grimly. They didn't pay coppers so well that they'd turn down a few quid in used notes for just not noticing.

So what was Brodie in on, down here? Drugs? It usually was. Scotland was bidding fair to be drug abuse capital of Europe, and if you did it in a quiet way and didn't go flashing the cash, you'd be on to a very nice little earner. There'd been smugglers of one kind or another on the Solway coast since Rabbie Burns was an exciseman – and before. Easy access to the Isle of Man and Ireland, a straggling coastline, wee isolated places accessed by a dead-end road so you knew who was arriving and had a view of the sea in case they came that way – ideal.

Places like Innellan. And an island – an island, if Sorley was to be believed, whose owner didn't like trespassers. Brodie and Lovatt, with the deer farm as a handy, money-laundering enterprise?

The stuff could come straight in and go straight out again, but in MacNee's experience there was usually leakage in the local area. Cutting out the middleman on at least a proportion of the supply was almost irresistible.

Brodie had arrived less than three years ago, so it should show up around here. And MacNee knew the man who could tell him: PC Danny Tait, a handy man with the arrows, like MacNee himself, who'd be happy enough to have an unofficial chat with a pal.

The police office at Borgue, just along the road from Innellan, was scheduled for closure next year – one of the tiny local stations run, basically, by a man and a boy. Tait was an idle beggar, putting in time till retirement, working office hours and no weekends, and there were plenty who envied him his quiet life. MacNee, though, looked with a curled lip at the pretty church and the pleasant cottages with their neat gardens. He'd likely have to put a doily under his coffee mug.

Tait was, indeed, happy to be interrupted and produced coffee, though with no genteel extras. 'So what are you after, Tam?' he asked, the pleasantries over. 'Not trouble on my patch, I hope?' He was looking alarmed at the thought.

'No, no, Danny,' MacNee reassured him. 'Just a general query, that's all. Have you had more drugs problems around here over the last two or three years, say?'

The man looked blank. 'Not more than usual, as far as I know. It's pretty quiet – and that's the way I like it.'

'Deals done in country pubs, maybe? And you've a lot of caravan sites. Anything with the holiday visitors in places like Innellan, say?'

Tait seemed keener to hear about the dramatic events there than to address himself to the question, but MacNee brushed that aside. 'Any figures on drug use in the area?'

With some reluctance, Tait heaved his corpulent body out of his chair. 'I don't, offhand, but I know a man who does.' He went over to open a door and stuck his head round it. 'Pete – a word, if you don't mind.'

He came back and sat down again with a grunt. 'FCA Pete Ogilvie – great guy. Does all the work around here, don't you, Pete?'

Ogilvie was a tall, thin young man with a shock of black hair and sharp, watchful eyes. 'Certainly do.'

That was probably right, MacNee thought, and from the way Ogilvie spoke he didn't think it was as much of a joke as Tait did.

Tait introduced him. 'DS Tam MacNee. Looking for the stats about drug offences – got them at your fingertips, have you?'

'Anything special you're looking for?' Ogilvie asked.

'We're interested to know if you've seen more drug-related offending in the last couple of years or so.'

Ogilvie pulled a face, shaking his head. 'Nothing out of the ordinary. That answer your question?'

The tone was dismissive, which made MacNee stubborn. 'Have you the figures? I'd be interested to see how they compare with the general pattern. And have you had any luck recently?'

'Arrests, you mean?' Ogilvie glanced at Tait, who shrugged.

'You'll remember better than I will, Pete.'

'Two, maybe three,' Ogilvie said. 'The odd small pusher but no big guys in the area. Coming in from Glasgow as usual.'

Was he stonewalling? He hadn't answered MacNee's question

about the statistics. Tait had noticed the omission and was about to say something, but MacNee said smoothly, 'Aye, right enough. Not a lot we can do about that unless we searched every car coming down the A77 and I can't see the budget stretching. Anyway, appreciate your help, Pete.'

'My pleasure.' He disappeared back into his office.

MacNee got up to leave. 'Thanks for the coffee, Danny.'

Escorting him to the door, Tait said wistfully, 'Don't suppose you're going to give me the low-down on the Cave Man Mystery, are you?'

'*Cave Man Mystery?*' MacNee was revolted. 'Where did that come from?'

'Our local reporter, Tony Drummond. *The Sun*'s taken it up.'

'Typical!' MacNee's view of Drummond was inevitably jaundiced. 'Well, forensics won't be in a hurry and it'll go pretty quiet till then.'

He went back to his car very thoughtful. He was opening the door as a white van pulled up and a weaselly-looking man with a straggly ponytail got out. MacNee changed his mind, and shut it again. 'Good morning, Mr Sorley. Got a problem?'

Sorley gave him a tight smile. 'Just making a complaint.'

'Anything I can help you with?'

'No,' he said flatly. 'I want this logged officially. Lovatt's negligence over dangerous animals is endangering our community.'

'Dangerous animals? His dog?'

'His wolf, you mean. Oh, that too. But after the stag attack last night it's time the authorities took action.'

It was the first MacNee had heard of it, but he wasn't going to admit that. 'Right, right. I won't detain you, then.'

He drove off, frowning. Had Drummond found a story to keep the pot boiling? He was tempted to drive on to Innellan and find out, but Macdonald and Campbell would be there already and more police would generate more interest. In any case, MacNee was uncharacteristically keen to get back to his desk. The stats that Ogilvie was reluctant to disclose should be on record at HQ and it would be easy to compare the Borgue drugs statistics with what they had been four years ago, before Kerr arrived in the district. He was ready to bet something would show up.

Kerr Brodie's mobile rang as he was paying for the four padlocks in the ironmonger's in Kirkcudbright. 'Brodie. Yes?' he said, then listened to the brief message. 'Half an hour, by the harbour. Right.'

He took the receipt from the assistant and went out with an uneasy feeling in the pit of his stomach. He didn't like the sound of that; didn't like it at all.

Pete Ogilvie went through to the main office where PC Tait was working on the computer – at least he was doing something, though his guilty movement suggested it was more likely solitaire than an official document.

'OK if I take an hour out, Danny? I've had toothache and the dentist's got a cancellation.'

'Sure, sure,' Tait said. 'No need to hurry back – you'll be feeling a bit groggy. See you in the afternoon.'

Whenever he left, Tait switched off the computer, switched on the answerphone and locked up. He'd logged Sorley's complaint, but it wasn't exactly urgent. If anyone wanted him they could push the bell, which rang in his house. There was golf on the telly and a beer in the fridge.

'I think we'd better head for Lovatt's Farm first,' Macdonald said.

Campbell was driving; Macdonald had the report on the stag

incident as well as Fleming's notes and had been filling him in on it as they drove to Innellan.

'Four people there,' he went on. 'Matt and Melissa Lovatt, Kerr Brodie, Christie Jack. I'd like to talk to her as soon as possible.'

'Aye, MacNee told me.' Campbell was apparently concentrating on the narrow road.

Macdonald flushed. 'Don't know what he told you but it's a load of bollocks anyway,' he said stiffly. 'We need to establish she wasn't responsible before we interview anyone else, and then we can ask about noises from the island. Right?' He directed a challenging look at Campbell but got no response.

'The other interviews – straightforward enough,' he went on. 'The Donaldsons, Sorley – though presumably he works? May be hard to get hold of.'

They were reaching Innellan now. 'Turning on the right, just beyond the pub,' Macdonald directed. 'We'd better drop in to the Smugglers to see my friend Georgia afterwards. She'll tell us who to interview to see if there's a tradition about ghosts on the island.'

'Does she do pies?' Campbell's face brightened.

Macdonald shook his head. 'Crisps, sandwich, maybe, if we can sweet-talk her.'

'Is there another pub?'

'What's wrong with a sandwich? How come you're so obsessed with junk food?'

'Wife's into healthy eating. Up here?' Campbell gestured towards the short drive up to the farmhouse.

'Mmm. Try driving on a bit. If we want to see Christie first, she's likely out around the farm.'

They bumped along the badly made road round the bay. The tide was almost at the full, the sea a sullen grey and the sun a silver ball hazed over with cloud, struggling to break through but without success.

'There she is!' Macdonald said, pointing to a field beyond a bank of whin and bracken.

Christie Jack was standing beside a drystone dyke with a fallen section, turning a large stone in her hands and frowning, like someone with a jigsaw piece that doesn't seem to fit anywhere. She turned her head at the sound of the car, and when it stopped by the gate into the field, put down the stone and came slowly towards them.

Macdonald reached her first. Their greeting was constrained, and when Campbell arrived Christie eyed him unsmilingly. She was heavy-eyed and pale; as she waited for their questions she squared her shoulders and tilted her chin, an attempt at confidence that somehow only made her look more forlorn. Macdonald fought down a surge of protective tenderness; there was a job to do.

'Can we have a few minutes of your time? Just one or two questions.' He smiled.

She didn't. 'I don't have an alternative, do I? What do you want to know?'

'I don't need to go over the information you've given already,' Macdonald said. 'But last night—'

She interrupted him. 'You're going to say, am I sure I shut the gate properly. Yes, I am. I'm really, really sure. I know I did. Someone else let the stag out deliberately.'

'Who?' Campbell, as usual, was brief and to the point.

'*I* don't know. That's your job, isn't it?' Her tone was hostile.

'Of course,' Macdonald said soothingly. 'The local police will be dealing with that.'

'Will they? Haven't seen them checking for footprints, and it rained during the night so there's probably no point now. But if they're going to check fingerprints I'm happy to have mine taken for elimination.'

The chances that further action would be taken, when the only injury had been to a woman who said it was trivial and she didn't want matters taken further, were zero. Macdonald said awkwardly, 'I'm sure they have it in hand,' earning himself a look of contempt. He went on hastily, 'I gather you had no direct knowledge of what happened?'

'No.'

'Any ideas?'

'Not much point in playing guessing games, is there?'

He struggled on. 'Do you know Hugh and Steve Donaldson? Or Derek Sorley?'

'I know who they are.'

'Did you know there was bad feeling between them and the Lovatts?'

'Yes, I heard that. Kerr Brodie told me there'd been nasty stuff went on.'

At last she had volunteered something to follow up. 'So do you think they were behind this?'

Christie shrugged. 'Guessing games, like I said. I told the police they'd come into the pub laughing not long before we heard the stag was out.'

Campbell said, 'But you're still guessing? Someone else in the frame too?'

'Not necessarily. Don't see the point, that's all.' But she clearly had another idea, something she didn't want to say.

Recognising her discomfort, Macdonald couldn't bring himself to make it worse. What was she doing to him? 'Fine, fine,' he said, and saw his colleague giving him a sharp look. So? If Campbell was wanting probing done, he could try doing it himself for a change.

Macdonald went on, 'There's something else – a rather odd question. Have you ever heard strange noises coming from the island – screams, wailing, that sort of thing?'

Christie stared at him. 'Screams and wailing? What on earth's that about?'

'I know, I know. Sounds crazy.' He smiled at her again, hoping she might smile back, but she still resisted. 'The thing is, we have a report that a month or two ago someone heard noises like that coming from the island.'

Her scepticism was obvious. 'I certainly haven't. I—' Then she stopped. Her hand went to her mouth and her face turned red.

Macdonald and Campbell exchanged glances.

'Changed your mind?' Campbell said.

'Not . . . not exactly. But – well, if it was a couple of months ago it could have been me.'

'*You?*' Macdonald was startled.

'It was just after I came here. I was . . . I was just a total mess. If it hadn't been for Matt Lovatt I don't know where I'd be now.'

Macdonald noticed jealously that her mouth softened as she said his name.

'He told Kerr to give me the key for the bothy on the island with the instruction to stay till I was ready to come back. I . . . I sort of went mad. I threw rocks in the sea and yes, I suppose I cried and yelled. It was beautiful weather and on a still night sound does carry across water.' She looked from one to the other defiantly. 'OK, so it sounds crazy, but it worked. The island's a healing place.'

Macdonald smiled. 'I'm glad it worked for you. Perhaps you need a rest cure there again, after all this.'

He got the briefest flicker of a smile, before her face darkened again. 'If stuff like last night's going to happen, I'm not leaving Matt to face it alone.'

190

With a heavy heart, Macdonald thanked her. Christie turned to go, then paused. 'You . . . you won't have to tell everyone, will you? I'd feel a right plonker.'

Macdonald reassured her. She nodded, then headed back to her challenging task. As they went back to the car, Macdonald said defensively, 'I know you thought I should have pushed her more. But Big Marge said it was just a matter of ticking the boxes for the local press.'

Campbell ignored that. Instead, he said, 'Alone, eh? And where does that leave Mrs Matt?'

Catriona Fleming stirred in her sleep, groaned, and flung an arm across her eyes against the bright light. God, she felt terrible!

Without lifting her head from her pillow, she half-opened her eyes. The bed opposite was empty; Lily must have got up early and gone out. Or not come back at all – that was more likely.

Cat couldn't remember much about last night. Sunday had passed in a sort of blur, hanging out with Lily's chums, and she vaguely remembered coming back with some guy from the residence, giggling and talking, and someone yelling at them to shut up, making them laugh even more. It had been very late, and now she looked she hadn't even undressed, just collapsed on to her bed.

Not good. Naughty. Must do better. What on earth time was it? She'd better get a move on – she'd registration at ten, a meeting with her tutor at eleven and the introductory lecture at twelve.

Cat sat up and blinked at the clock on her bedside table. It was saying half past twelve – it must have stopped. But it hadn't stopped; the second hand was sweeping jerkily round the face. It must have gone haywire! The alarm was set for eight-thirty. She grabbed it up.

It wasn't set. She'd been so wasted last night that she hadn't started it, and now it was half past twelve and she'd missed everything, all the official stuff. What would happen? They wouldn't throw her out, right away, would they? She'd have to ask Will—

She'd forgotten. Her misery overcame her like a great wave and she fell back on her bed again, sobbing. What was the point? He'd been key to her dream and now he'd gone it was turning into a nightmare.

She should go to see her tutor now and apologise. But that would be a great big black mark before she even started, and she'd probably be yelled at. Cat couldn't face that, not the way she was feeling at the moment. Her clothes smelt disgusting and there were mascara smears on her clean sheets. She ought to strip them off, take them down to be washed – but later. She couldn't face the hassle right now.

Once she'd showered and changed, she'd go back to the pub where Lily and her friends hung out. Someone there would know what she should do.

There was, Macdonald thought, something surreal about this whole set-up: the thin little woman with her great tragic eyes who might once have been chocolate-box pretty, the man who would be handsome apart from his ravaged face, the animal that should have been lurking in the shadows of some Russian forest, assembled in this old-fashioned sitting room with faded wallpaper and worn loose covers on the chairs. Oh, and with two police officers asking them about ghost stories.

They'd taken that question first this time. Matt Lovatt had looked blank; Melissa Lovatt had said the island was always haunted for her by her dead child.

'And certainly I cry there,' she said, her soft mouth trembling. 'I cry a lot, but quietly, naturally. No one could possibly hear me.

192

And of course my husband never does. He hardly goes up to the grave at all, do you, Matt?' There was an interesting hardening of the voice as she said that.

Lovatt didn't respond, only saying, 'There are old Norse graves there so there could be a local tradition – I wouldn't know. I never came here before my grandmother died and we don't mix much with the locals.'

Macdonald nodded. 'I see. That brings me to the incident last night. We've spoken to Miss Jack, and she says she shut the gate properly. What's your opinion of her?' The proper, professional question would concern her reliability, but he couldn't resist phrasing it in a way that might reveal whether Lovatt's feelings reflected Christie's.

'If we were in action in a tight spot, I'd trust her with my life, without hesitation. The stress disorder was a tragedy for her. She's the best sort of soldier – courageous, loyal, honest, a good comrade. If she says she shut the gate, she did.'

Macdonald felt as if a load had been lifted. Lovatt's assessment was anything but lover-like – yet Lissa gave a little sigh and raised her eyes to the ceiling.

'You don't agree, Mrs Lovatt?'

She fluttered. 'Oh . . . oh yes, of course, of course. Lovely girl. But it's not easy – things you do automatically, so hard to be definite. And of course she's had all these . . . problems. But if she says she did, well, I'm sure . . .' Her voice trailed off suggestively, and her husband gave her a look of irritation.

'Christie's both competent and collected. I don't believe she would forget to shut the gate.'

'So,' Macdonald said, 'someone with a grudge?'

Lovatt looked rueful. 'You could say. I wanted to farm the land myself, you see. The tenant's lease had elapsed and I refused to agree a new one with his son.'

'The Donaldsons?'

'I'm afraid so. There have been niggles over the years but recently I fell out with Derek Sorley, who was up by the graves with a metal detector. I was afraid the next thing would be digging them up, so I banned him from the island. He didn't take it well.'

'We'll have a word with them. Anyone else?'

Again, like Christie, Lovatt seemed to hesitate, before he said quickly, 'No, not specifically, though they're not very fond of us generally in the village.'

Lissa sighed. 'But Matt was determined we would come to live here, Sergeant.'

Stung by the implied criticism, Lovatt retorted, 'You wanted it too, Lissa, don't forget.'

She fluttered again. 'Oh, of course, I didn't mean . . .'

Lovatt didn't look at her. Macdonald suspected he was afraid his eyes would betray his anger; the air felt thick with it.

As they left, Campbell said, with surprising venom, 'Poisonous woman!'

'Poisonous? I'll give you manipulative, but a bit pathetic, I thought.'

'That's the worst kind. Meet my mother-in-law.'

'Mmm,' Macdonald said. Perhaps he was biased, but he thought there could be stuff going on under the surface with Lovatt that wouldn't be very pretty in the light of day. His wife could have reasons for being the way she was.

At the Smugglers Inn, Georgia Stanley was, as always, welcoming. The bar was quiet, with only one or two tables occupied. She had, she said, some leftover cooked sausages and Campbell beamed at the promise of a sausage butty with ketchup.

The sandwiches, though, were all she had to offer them. She'd never heard stories about the island being haunted, and she had never heard anything herself. Georgia was eager, though, to put the knife into the Donaldsons and their crony, and had no doubt that they'd released the stag.

'And I'm warning you, it's not going to stop there.' She was very serious. 'There'll be more trouble, and last night it was only luck that the woman wasn't worse hurt. Or killed, even.'

Macdonald grimaced. 'We can hardly set up a protection unit, but I hear what you say. We'll duff them up a bit when we talk to them. But about the ghost stories – who could we talk to that might know?'

Georgia looked surprised that they were persisting, but gave it some thought. 'Best just knock on doors, quite honestly. There's some holiday cottages and two or three houses with newish people like the Drummonds, but the rest have been here for ever.'

Macdonald groaned. 'That takes care of our afternoon. Hurry up and finish that, Ewan.'

Reluctantly, Campbell obeyed, saying thickly, 'Great sandwich,' as he followed his sergeant out.

'We'll start at the far end,' Macdonald instructed. 'There's a house up there, look, on the hill round the bay. There's the track, off to the left.'

From its isolated position, above a steep drop to the shore, it looked as if it had been a traditional croft house: grey stone, sturdily built but with small, deeply recessed windows and an upper floor with dormers. There was no sign of any farming activity now, and when Macdonald knocked the door was opened by a grey-haired woman in a pink overall.

He showed his warrant card. 'Are you the householder?'

'Och no,' she said. 'I'm just one of the carers. It's Mrs Findlay owns it, her and her son.'

'Either of them in?'

'Just her. And she's not exactly – well, you ken what it's like.'

'Would she be able to talk to us?' Macdonald asked.

'Oh, she'll *talk* to you, right enough. It's just it'll not maybe make much sense.'

Campbell said, with unbecoming eagerness, 'Oh well, then—'

But she cut him short. 'Och, she'd like fine to see visitors for a wee change, I'm sure. Gets awfy dull for her, never seeing anyone but us and her son.' She gave a disapproving sniff. 'And not much of him either. Come away ben.'

Macdonald, feeling not a lot more enthusiastic than his constable, followed her into the front room to the left. As he entered, he had to control his recoil from the frowsty atmosphere, compounded of overheated air, stale human sweat and a faint tang of urine – the smell of old age. He heard Campbell cough behind him and guessed that he, too, was trying not to gag.

There was a neatly made bed in one corner. By the window, a woman was sitting in a lug chair on a rubber sheet; there was a framed photograph of a man on the small chest of drawers beside her. She was grossly fat, with an unhealthy purple tinge to her complexion and though she looked at them, her eyes were vague.

'Help me, oh help me!' she moaned, sending a chill down Macdonald's spine.

'She does that even on, but it doesn't mean anything,' the carer said reassuringly. 'We're all here to help you, dearie!' She raised her voice and patted Aileen Findlay's hand. The woman pulled it away petulantly.

Macdonald cleared his throat. 'We're from the police, Mrs Findlay. Just wanting a little chat.'

She became visibly agitated. 'Police!' she cried. 'Oh God, no! He didn't. It was wickedness. Evil. Evil. Pretty, too. Cruel, cruel. Wrong! And he was a liar!' Her voice rose. 'A liar, I tell you! I couldn't – but I should. Wrong, wrong! Evil! Wickedness!' She was screaming now, at the top of her voice.

The carer, alarmed, said, 'You'd better go. You're upsetting her – I maybe shouldn't have let you in. But—'

'That's all right,' Macdonald said hastily. 'We're on our way. Hope you manage to get her settled down again.'

Campbell was out in the hall already. As they left, the wild shouting died and again they heard the wail, 'Help me, oh help me!'

Macdonald said, 'Well, what do you make of that? What's been going on there?'

Campbell was shuddering as he started the car. In an unusual burst of loquacity, he said, 'Don't even want to guess. Let's do these calls quickly. I don't want still to be in this place once it gets dark.'

As they drove on through the village Macdonald said in rallying tones, 'Come on, Ewan, don't come over all fey on me. She's just a daft old woman and you're letting the ghost stories and the Hammer House of Horrors setting get to you.' He gestured as they passed the abandoned church with its tumble of gravestones.

'It's not the dead folk bother me,' Campbell said. 'It's the living ones.'

CHAPTER TWELVE

All the computer terminals in the CID room were in use. With a practised glance around, DS MacNee homed in on one of the younger DCs and tapped him on the shoulder.

He looked up, dismayed. 'Aw, Sarge! Ten minutes, OK? I have to get this—'

MacNee shook his head. 'Hop it, sonny boy,' and the detective logged out and got up, muttering under his breath about abuse of power.

Grinning, MacNee said, 'Kind of the point of being a sergeant, ken? That and the money.'

'It's us should get paid more for getting kicked around by you lot,' his victim grumbled.

'You could be right there, laddie. I'd pay for the privilege, myself,' MacNee said genially, sitting down in the vacated seat. He called up the figures for drug offences broken down by district, and looked at Borgue's first.

Contrary to his expectation, it seemed there had been fewer arrests, not more. OK, the numbers were small, but the past two years showed a marked drop. Frowning, he scrolled down to the returns from the comparable small police office in the

Machars, on the other side of the Galloway area. Here, with minor fluctuations, there was a slow increase, pretty much in line with general trends.

Maybe, after all, this was more about himself than about Brodie. Perhaps the man was clean – but MacNee's gut was telling him different. He sat back in his chair, thinking. The dispossessed DC looked up hopefully, but seeing the sergeant's expression thought the better of any attempt at reclamation.

MacNee brooded. There were other criminal activities Brodie could be engaged in – other kinds of smuggling, even. There was a thriving black market in cigarettes, for instance . . . Yet with what he knew of Brodie's background—

A thought struck him and he went back to the screen. Brodie would be savvy enough to keep his doorstep clean – indeed, he might easily have swept out the dealers operating there before, which would explain the figures. Kirkcudbright was next door; their stats might be more revealing. Eagerly, he accessed them, along with the earlier returns, and made the comparison.

These, too, told a remarkable story. Up to three years ago, offences had shown the same depressing rise that marked the war against drugs being slowly but surely lost across the country; after that arrests had suddenly fallen, and the improvement had been maintained.

Good policing? The lads out there, nipping it in the bud, keeping the dealers off their well-patrolled patch? Maybe. But they'd all tried that, and no one else had succeeded. And as MacNee scowled at the screen, a face came to mind – a narrow face, with sharp, watchful eyes. Ogilvie.

Sleekit, had been MacNee's immediate verdict on the man: sly, not to be trusted. The FCA was pretty much running the Borgue office, with PC Tait's complacent approval. Certainly, he'd been interestingly reluctant to discuss the drugs scene, and he'd be party to information about ops being mounted in the area; a few phone calls would be all it would take to make sure no one had unexpected visitors.

But MacNee had nothing to go on, and the Kirkcudbright lads might take it unkindly if he challenged the sort of figures that would have the chief constable beaming and directing them to share best practice. Still, what else could he do? MacNee yielded the computer to the hovering DC and found a phone in a quiet corner.

He had been tactful – in as far as he ever was – and was unprepared for a blast of rage from the normally equable Inspector Michie.

'Drugs figures! Don't talk to me about drugs figures!'

'Sorry!' MacNee was startled. 'I suppose everyone's asking how you do it.'

'How we do it?' Michie gave a bitter laugh. 'Tam, we've had an explosion in drugs use this last bit. We've had more petty offenders slapped on the wrist with an unrecorded fiscal fine than ever before. It's becoming a hotbed, but we make fools of ourselves every time we launch an operation. They always know we're coming, and I can't find out who's tipping them off.'

MacNee could feel the warm, satisfying glow which usually came from a good malt spreading right through him. 'Well now, Graham,' he said cordially, 'I think I can maybe help you there. Try again, but this time, just make sure that none of the information gets through to Borgue.'

'Borgue? PC Tait?' Michie was frankly sceptical.

'Not Tait. An FCA called Ogilvie, who's being allowed to run the shop. And what's more, I could maybe give you a wee steer about where to look for the big man.'

It was raining now, slanting silver spears making tiny pockmarks on the surface of the rock pool at Cal Findlay's feet. Sitting on the promontory below his house and staring out across the bay, he barely noticed he was getting wet.

The tide was going out. Below, a chain of rocks was becoming exposed, dark and jagged, draped with seaweed; in an hour or so they would form a rough causeway out to the island. Over there the trees were on the turn, green giving way to pale yellow and brown, waiting for the first frost to turn the leaves blazing scarlet and gold. It was autumn, just as it had been summer and would be winter: the unalterable pattern of the seasons, the eternal landscape, the inescapable routine of daily life – you came to feel nothing could ever change.

It could, though. A cliff could fall, a hurricane could tear in and level every one of those trees. Cal felt as if he was in the teeth of one now, with the wind rising to a shriek that almost deafened him.

He had come here looking for peace and silence to clear his head, but even now, with the only sound the quiet hiss of rain and the rattle of stones being drawn back by the retreating waves, he couldn't think straight. He too was being sucked back into the past, a past never forgotten, but suppressed with a sort of dogged desperation, like someone with an ugly symptom hoping if not believing that it can be safely ignored. He couldn't ignore it now. Now, it was unimaginably worse than his worst imaginings.

The rain was getting heavier, soaking him through. He shivered, only partly with cold, and stood up feeling bleakness seeping into him like the grey veil that was obscuring the landscape in front of him. There was no point in trying to think of a way out, because there was none. It was too late. Ten years too late. Or longer than that – yes, much longer.

With leaden steps he climbed back up to the house and the daily horror of living with his mother. His mouth twisted in an ironic smile at the thought that going on in the same soul-sapping way was the best he could hope for now.

To his surprise the carer's car was still there. He'd seen it when he'd parked his own, before walking down to the shore. Usually once whoever was on duty had given his mother her tea, she would leave, only returning when it was time to put her to bed. But today she was looking out for him, opening the front door before he could.

'Oh, there you are! Oh, Cal, I've had just an awful job with your mum this afternoon!' Then she broke off. 'Dearie me, what's happened to you? You're drookit!'

'Went out for a walk and got caught in it,' he said tersely, stepping past her into the hall. He could hear the moaning from the front room. 'Sounds much the same as usual. What's the problem?'

The woman was still distracted. 'Are you wanting a towel, or something?'

'No, I'm fine.' Controlling his irritation with difficulty, he said again, 'What's the matter with her?'

'Well, I maybe did the wrong thing,' she admitted. 'Thought it'd cheer her up a wee bit to see some different faces, ken? So when the polis came chapping on the door—'

'The *polis*?' He thought his heart would stop, but somehow he managed to say, rather than scream, 'What were they after?'

The woman frowned. 'Oh, I never thought to speir what they wanted. Just said could they talk to Aileen.'

'And you *let them in*?' This time he did raise his voice.

She became defensive. 'How was I to know she'd go daft? You never said no one was to be let in to see her.'

Tight-lipped, he asked, 'What did she say?'

'Och, just a whole load of blethers about evil and wickedness – rubbish like that. You know Aileen gets kind of thon way sometimes. They were only a few minutes before they realised, but I thought I'd better stay on and warn you – she'll quieten down for a while and then she's off again.'

'Right. Thanks.'

Thanks for nothing, his tone said, and the carer became huffy. 'No need to take that tone with me, Cal. It was maybe a mistake, but we all make them, don't we?'

He didn't reply, and she flounced off to fetch her coat. He opened the door of Aileen's room, then stopped dead. Without turning, he said, 'Where the hell did that photograph come from?'

She peered past him. 'Oh, that? It was there when I came in today. She must have had it in a drawer. I've never seen it before.'

'OK.' Cal stood rigid in the doorway, not moving until he heard her car drive away.

His mother turned her head. 'Help me, help me!' she cried. 'The wickedness! Cruel, cruel!'

He was at her side in two strides, snatching up the photograph on the chest of drawers.

'You evil, dangerous old bitch!' he screamed at her. His hand, almost of its own accord, swung back to hit her, but he stopped himself. Bruising that would be reported by whichever carer came to settle her down tonight would hardly improve the situation.

Cal stormed out of the room, out of the house. The rain had stopped; there was a brisk wind now, whipping the clouds across the sky. He threw the photo to the ground, smashing the glass, then stamping the frame to fragments.

The man's face looked back at him, distorted by the angles of the shards, muddied with footmarks, yet still that same face with its dark, flashy good looks and the slick, arrogant smile.

Risking his fingers on the broken glass, Cal picked the photograph out then shredded it into strips, lengthwise, then across, into tinier and tinier scraps that fluttered to the ground. He bent to gather them up then walked to the retaining wall above the cliff at the edge of the garden. He tossed them into the air and watched the wind take them, fluttering down towards the rocks below.

You couldn't describe the evening as a success. It was unfortunate; Cammie's Zoë was a delightful girl, bright and thoughtful and very, very pretty with a creamy complexion and huge brown eyes. And sensitive, too. That was the problem.

When Marjory Fleming went to welcome her, the brown eyes were brimming with tears, which Zoë was doing her best to blink away.

'Oh dear! Are you all right?' Marjory asked, concerned.

'Sorry – yes, yes of course, Mrs Fleming.' Zoë bit her lip.

Cammie, whose face showed agonised embarrassment, said gruffly, 'It's just the stirks. She asked if they were going to be milking cows and I had to tell her.'

'I thought there were just sheep,' Zoë said, a little defensively. Clearly stirks being blatantly fattened for market had come as a shock.

Bill, who had fetched them after school activities, obviously felt he had been cast in the role of First Murderer and had lost his usual ease of manner. Cammie, spellbound, spent most of his time just looking at her and though Zoë responded readily to Marjory's efforts to keep the conversation going, it was definitely sticky, with the spectre of the abattoir an extra presence at the table.

The food didn't help, either. As part of her housekeeping duties Karolina kept the freezer well stocked, but there was no demand for vegetarian meals from the Fleming household and Janet had failed her daughter this time, having a few days away in Pitlochry with friends.

Marjory was on her own, and even she couldn't claim her veggie lasagne was a success. Some vegetables were hard, some mushy, and bits of the pasta had come out of the sauce and were crunchy.

Bill, who had lapsed almost into silence, said, 'Er . . . what is it?' He was pushing his food round his plate.

'Hard to say,' quipped Cammie, cracking a burnt edge. 'Hard – get it?'

Zoë looked appalled. 'That's so mean, Cammie! It's very . . . very nice, Mrs Fleming,' she said, truth yielding to good manners.

'You're extremely polite, Zoë,' Marjory said, 'but I'm afraid my cooking is a family joke. I can fry a good rare steak, but that's about it.' As the words left her lips, a little silence fell as each person round the table had a vision of the steak oozing blood, though with presumably different feelings. Bill's and Cammie's, Marjory was fairly sure, were simple hunger.

No, the evening had not gone well, and when he and Bill got back from running Zoë home, Cammie went straight up to his room.

'I've got a meeting in Kirkluce the night Zoë's coming to supper again,' Bill said.

Marjory looked surprised. 'Is she? When?'

'I didn't say she was coming to supper. I said I would have a meeting that night, whenever it was.'

'Bill, that's not fair,' Marjory protested. 'She's a lovely girl! When you think what some of them are like, you should be grateful. And being veggie's actually a more moral stance in lots of ways than eating meat, you know.'

Bill sat down at the table. 'Yeah, fine. But it's hard to enjoy your food when there's someone opposite who sees blood dripping from your hands. Actually, it's hard to enjoy a vegetarian meal cooked by you anyway.'

'You say that whatever I cook.'

'Not about bacon and eggs,' he shot back. 'Any chance?'

'I took a lot of trouble with that, you know,' Marjory said. 'But – well, I have to admit I didn't eat much of it either.'

As she put in the bacon in the frying pan, she said, 'Have you spoken to Cat today, Bill? I've left messages and she still hasn't phoned back, so I'm not going to pester her if she's sulking. I'd like to know how she's getting on, though.'

'Yes, she phoned home around lunchtime. Sounds fine.'

Really, men! Marjory looked at him with some exasperation. She didn't want to have to spell out how much she was missing her daughter, with an almost visceral sense of loss. 'Details?'

'That was about it, really. She's OK, the residence is fine – didn't say a lot else.'

'Did she say if she was coming home at the weekend?'

'Oh, that's right. She said she wouldn't be home. There's a party or something.'

'Right,' Marjory said slowly, prodding the bacon. 'I was wondering about her, because it was a bit odd. I was shopping at lunchtime and saw Mary Irvine. I haven't seen her for ages, and I wondered if she'd heard from Will. She barely stopped – said she was dashing to a hair appointment, but it wasn't like her. Usually I can't get away from her, once she starts. You – you don't think there's anything wrong there, do you?'

Bill looked alarmed. 'I'd hate to think so. He's almost one of the family now.'

'I know. And it would be awful for Cat, starting out somewhere new, if . . . Do you think we should pop up to Glasgow to see how she is?' She made the suggestion hopefully, trying not to show that she was grasping at any excuse just to see Cat, to have her physical nearness – always supposing Cat would allow a hug, in her present frame of mind.

'No, I don't,' said Bill firmly. 'You've got to accept that she's left home. And if you're uptight because Mary didn't stop to talk, it's daft. Maybe she did have an appointment.'

'I know, but I've got a feeling—' Marjory was saying, when the kitchen door opened and Cammie appeared.

'Is that bacon I smell? Oh, great!'

His father grinned. 'Better than rabbit food, eh? Pity it didn't work out. She's a nice enough lassie.'

'Mmm,' Cammie said, but looking at him with a mother's eye Marjory wasn't as sure as Bill was that the spell cast by those big brown eyes had been broken.

Eddie Tindall let himself into the darkened flat with a heavy heart. In the lounge, where in his mind's eye his wife was always sitting smiling up at him, her gold hair gleaming in the pool of light from the lamp on the table behind the sofa, there were only great luminous patches of pale orange on the polished floor from the street outside in the oppressive, artificial silence the double glazing created. He pressed the switch to turn on the lamps and reflexively clicked the TV remote, though he went back out again immediately.

Clive hadn't called him, and Marianne had kept Eddie too busy to have much time to think about Elena. He was thinking about her now, though; he'd been late back, so perhaps Clive had left a message here. But through in his study there was no red light blinking on the phone.

Without expectation, Eddie checked the bank account, but there were no new transactions. He could phone and check the credit card again, but it was a lot of effort to make, knowing it would be pointless. He was feeling very tired tonight, tired and old.

He wandered through to their bedroom, then into Elena's

walk-in closet. Perhaps there might be a clue in what she had packed. But as door after door swung open to his touch, he looked helplessly at racks of skirts, dresses, trousers, piles of shelved sweaters. For all he could tell, she might have taken half her clothes with her, or nothing at all.

Jewellery – he was more familiar with that, having bought most of it himself. The good pieces were kept in the built-in safe in his study, but when he opened it nothing was missing. A guarantee of her return? He tried to console himself with the thought, but though Elena enjoyed luxury, she had never been acquisitive.

He could phone her. Hearing her voice would be the highlight of his evening, but he was becoming afraid to try her number. What if she didn't answer? What if she never answered again? What if she did, and told him it was all over? 'Eddie, I'm sorry, but . . .' He buried his face in his hands.

She'd barely been away two days. She'd often gone for three or four in the past, and she'd warned him she planned a longer break. So why did it seem like a crisis? He was being a fool. A stiff drink, that was what he needed. A drink, and a good talking-to.

Back in the lounge, he poured himself a Scotch. On the big plasma screen, some birdbrained woman was simpering and giggling at an equally birdbrained man. Irritably, he killed the sound, though the flickering images were company, in a strange way.

Sitting there with his whisky soothed him, same as always. OK, Elena wasn't there and without her the flat was bleak and empty, but in another week or so she'd be back. He'd be able to laugh at his fears, unless he blew it now by overreacting. The problem was with his own idiotic imaginings. As if someone else had spoken the words, Eddie nodded affirmatively.

But it didn't convince him. The bank account and credit card were evidence that this time was different; he just didn't know why, or what it meant for his marriage, and it was getting to him. He downed the Scotch in one and went for a refill.

The phone ringing startled him so that he almost dropped the glass. Clive, was his first thought, but no – it was Elena. She usually only phoned when he'd been trying to reach her.

He tried to sound casual, unsurprised. 'Hi, doll! I was just going to call you. How are you doing?'

She was fine, it seemed, thoroughly enjoying the peace and quiet, having long walks. She wanted to know how he was, what kind of day he'd had, what Lola had left him for supper, and when he said he hadn't eaten yet, warned him not to get stuck into the Scotch when she wasn't there to keep an eye on him. At the end of the conversation, when he said, 'Love you, sweetheart,' she said, after a tiny pause, 'I miss you, Eddie.'

He switched off the phone and sat down again. On the screen, a woman was yelling at a girl with a trout pout and a Croydon facelift.

He should be feeling reassured. Elena had said she was missing him. She'd been concerned, affectionate, forthcoming if not explicit about where she was and what she was doing there.

His Elena was cool, reserved, detached, almost. This was totally unnatural. What could it mean? His hand was shaking as he brought the glass to his lips. What was he to do? He had to do *something*. Maybe Clive had found some clue, some promising line of enquiry. He could phone Clive – he had his mobile number.

Clive, though, was not helpful. Eddie was a good client, but even so his irritation at being disturbed in the middle of his supper came through. Yes, he had feelers out and was hopeful. No, it was too early to expect results and he'd certainly contact Eddie immediately he'd anything to report.

So there was nothing Eddie could do but sit there, amid the trappings of his wealth and success, meaningless now that they could no longer buy him his heart's desire.

Elena switched off the phone and grimaced, feeling drained and faintly nauseated. She just hoped this wifey-wifey performance would keep Eddie happy, stop him getting twitchy for a bit, at least. She didn't need worry about him on top of everything else.

She felt as if her nerves were being stretched taut, and then stretched some more, until they might snap at any moment. She was becoming irrational. Any sudden sound outside sent her heart racing; this evening she had drawn the curtains before it was even dark, and checked twice that the door was locked when she knew it was. But if she was locking some of her fears outside, she was locking herself in with the rest.

Cal had seemed badly stressed. She'd been relying on Cal, Cal who before had seemed solid, imperturbable. Today he'd gone on a lot about his mother; she'd been driving him to the edge for years, and Elena was afraid that might actually tip him over – really afraid.

Calm. She had to be calm. She had plenty of practice in that too, even when she was having to drown out the screaming inside her head.

Yoga. That helped; sometimes she even felt her sanity depended on it. She sat down on the floor, took a deep breath, and tried to relax.

The only problem was that as she lowered her head gracefully she found herself looking at the broad cuff bracelets on her wrists, which reminded her that in the drawer in her bedroom there was a pretty little knife which held the promise of even greater relief.

* * *

Brodie was late tonight bringing fresh scoff, much later than usual. Fergie had meant to pluck up courage and ask for a radio, just for company – he'd keep it low, of course, and watch for any boat coming across.

After one look at Brodie when he eventually arrived, Fergie thought the better of it. The man's face was black with temper and he dumped down the carrier bag as if he had some personal grievance against it.

'Thanks, Sarge,' Fergie said, but very quietly, and he wrapped his arms across his thin body as if to make himself smaller and less visible. Invisible, preferably. Brodie looked ready to lash out, and famously wasn't particular about his targets.

He was eying even this diminished Fergie with distaste. 'We've got a problem,' he said with venom. 'You.'

Fergie shrank back, which seemed to rile Brodie even more. 'God, how did I get myself into this? Sooner or later, you pay for every good deed – that's the truth. There's people sniffing around, and we can't bring in a boat till we've neutralised them. You'll have to stay here for as long as it takes.'

Dismay made Fergie incautious. 'Can you not just get me out of this place? Sometimes I feel like I can't breathe. Being alone all the time's messing with my brain.'

It gave Brodie the excuse he needed for venting his fury. 'Your brain? Your *brain*? Don't make me laugh!'

Fergie quailed under the tirade of obscenity that followed, putting his arm up to cover his head as if he were being physically attacked. 'Sorry, Sarge,' he whimpered when his assailant paused for breath.

Brodie looked at him with contempt. 'You really are a snivelling little sod. Just get this into your tiny head – I won't turn you in because you'd come apart. And I won't knock you on the head and push you off the cliff because you'd come ashore on the current and they'd come around here asking questions. You've got food and shelter – think yourself lucky. Do as you're told and it'll all come right in the end.

'These are your orders. Keep a strict watch. I'm giving you a key so you can lose yourself in the wood if someone's coming that might search the building. And I don't want it looking lived-in. Nothing left visible. Clear?'

Fergie could feel Brodie's eyes boring into him. 'Right, Sarge,' he said.

Brodie maintained his laser gaze for a long moment. 'And don't go wandering about for the fun of it,' he warned as he left. 'Anyone sees you, we're buggered, both of us, and don't think you won't pay.'

As the door shut, Fergie's knees gave way and he collapsed on to the mattress on the floor. He'd always been wary of Brodie, and Brodie when things were going wrong was seriously scary.

He'd counted on the boat coming any day now. The way Brodie talked, it could be weeks – weeks of solitary in this creepy place. He felt a tightness in his chest and started taking gasping, shallow breaths as if there wasn't enough oxygen in the air.

It was getting properly dark now. The moon was casting beams of pale light on the splintery floor through the gaps between the slats. Under the eaves the restless shadows shivered. Fergie got up and went to look out.

In bright moonlight the familiar landscape seemed strange, bleached of colour, with black spectral trees and dark mysterious hollows in the grass, but the air coming in was fresh on his face, damp and cool. His breathing quietened.

For the first time, Fergie could go out and walk around. He'd heard the boat take Brodie back. He'd be disobeying orders, but who would know? Just a little walk. Freedom to take more than ten paces backwards and forwards. Freedom to look at something more than four wooden walls.

He opened the door as quietly as he could, winced at the squeaking step, though there was no one to hear. Downstairs, the storeroom was musty with the smell of the feed for the deer, but once outside in the clear air he snuffed it like an animal. Trained not to offer a target, he kept close to the house and only moved towards the wood when he had the building between him and the mainland.

From inside it had looked inviting, but under the sheltering branches it was deeply dark. The undergrowth was dense, and he tripped on an unseen tree root and almost fell. As he saved himself, a bramble raked the back of his hand and he licked at the ragged scratch, wondering how he'd explain if Brodie noticed it. Maybe this hadn't been such a great idea after all.

The noises unsettled him too, stealthy noises from movement he couldn't see. The deer, of course, it was just the deer, he told himself, but he didn't know much about them anyway. Could they attack, if they took against you?

Perhaps it would be better just to go back. He'd had his breath of air, and when he got that suffocating feeling he was free to come out. He turned, retraced his steps.

As the trees thinned out, the moonlight caught eyes, glowing from a bush nearby. He jumped, stepped on a stick which cracked like a pistol shot. He heard a bark, like an angry dog, and giving a shout of fright himself, stumbled back to the bothy without a thought for any watcher on the mainland. His heart was pounding as he stumbled up the stairs, flung himself into the room and shut the door, like a captive animal rejecting freedom for the security of its cage.

CHAPTER THIRTEEN

It was mid afternoon on Thursday before the DNA analysis of the bones in the cave landed on DI Fleming's desk and she seized on it eagerly. She'd been trying to temper expectation; while you could learn a lot from DNA, it didn't come with name and address attached.

Usually. But this one did – a name, at least. Delighted at this stroke of luck, Fleming read on.

They had scored a hit with one on the police database in Manchester. There was no further information, no indication of a date or of any offence he had been charged with.

Perhaps there wasn't one. In Scotland, unless there was a conviction samples were destroyed after three years, but in England they were kept indefinitely, even if no charge followed the arrest. So that was another stroke of luck; innocent or guilty, they had his name, Andrew Smith.

Andrew Smith. She said the name under her breath. It held the ghost of a man, where before there had been only dry, anonymous bones. If he had a record, she could flesh them out from interviews, details of associates, addresses – a treasure trove for investigation.

If not . . . In that case, the missing person's register would be almost their only hope, since trawling through phone books and voters' rolls for one particular 'Andrew Smith' wasn't likely to prove rewarding.

She mustn't be pessimistic, though. At least they had a starting point: a request for information from Manchester. But official channels were hardly noted for their speedy response, and it wouldn't be easy here to argue for top priority. They'd have to be patient, and Fleming had never been good at that. She sat tapping her finger on her front teeth, thinking.

She had a contact in Manchester, DCI Chris Carter, who had worked with her on an earlier case. They'd hit it off a little too well, and she'd discouraged his attempts to keep in touch, but that was years ago. He was probably married by now with a couple of kids, and she was pretty sure he'd do her a favour. She still had the number of the North Manchester Divisional HQ somewhere. She tracked it down, then keyed it in before she could change her mind.

She crossed her fingers as she asked to speak to DCI Carter. Given Sod's Law, he would probably be off duty, or even not there any longer . . .

But that was his voice saying, 'Marjory Fleming? Well, well! That's a name from the past. How are you?'

'Fine, thanks. How's the scene in Manchester?'

'Oh, same old, same old. Kids have gangs now instead of families – doesn't make for an easy life.' He sounded weary.

'Sorry to add to the workload, but I'm looking for a favour. We've an interesting one at the moment,' Fleming said. 'Skeleton in a cave.'

'I read about it,' he said. 'Made the nationals with the creepy little detail about the watch.'

'Yes. Pretty sick, that. But it turns out from the DNA report that he's one of yours – one Andrew Smith.'

Fleming could almost hear his shrug. 'Doesn't immediately ring a bell. Common enough name, of course.'

'That's the problem. We're reckoning he's been dead twelve years, give or take, but they've given me a reference for the sample. Any chance you could run a check for me? It'll take weeks if I make it official.'

'Sure. I'll get someone on to it . . .'

Fleming crossed her fingers again. 'Any chance you could just press a few buttons right now? You're obviously at your desk . . .'

Carter groaned. 'If you could see my desk, you wouldn't ask.'

'Yes, I would. I'm gallus.'

'Gallus?'

'Shameless, with an added dash of chutzpah.'

'You're certainly pushing your luck. Well, I suppose, just for you, Marjory. Give me the number. I'll call you back.'

'You're a star,' she said gratefully, and switched off the phone. This was definitely her lucky day; she ought to stop and buy a lottery ticket on the way home. She had glanced at her watch impatiently several times, though, before Carter called back.

'I hope you realise crime in Manchester has been going unsolved while three overstretched DCs work for the Galloway constabulary,' he said. 'Half an hour, that took. I should bill you for their time.'

'Tam MacNee's all yours, any time you ask. But go on,' Fleming prompted.

'It's certainly an interesting one. Goes back to 1998 – quite an early sample.'

'What did he do?' Fleming asked, suddenly hopeful.

Her luck wasn't that good. 'Nothing, officially. Seemed to have been in the wrong place at the wrong time in the wrong company, and got swept up.'

Her spirits sank again. 'So – no record?'

'Sorry, no. But I can tell you he had some very nasty little chums – about as nasty as it gets. They were into all the vice stuff in the city – gambling, drugs, prostitution – you name it.'

'But he wasn't charged?'

'No evidence. There was a big clampdown and he was arrested after a raid on a bar, drinking with a couple of them, but there wasn't anything to say he was involved. Like I said, found in bad company.'

'Right,' Fleming said slowly. 'Thanks, Chris, I owe you one.'

'I'll get them to send you on the reports, and do a bit of a sniff-around as well.'

'Brilliant. I'll keep you posted.' She paused, then added lightly, 'So, how's life down there?'

Carter's voice warmed. 'Good, thanks – very good, in fact. I'm engaged now – great girl. You'd like her, Marjory.'

Fleming smiled. 'Glad to hear it! Come up to Scotland for your honeymoon and visit us.'

'Might do just that. Good hunting!'

She was still smiling as she rang off. Chris deserved a great girl and he'd sounded truly happy. Her mind, though, was already racing ahead.

Lack of evidence wasn't proof of innocence. Maybe Andrew Smith had just been careful – or lucky. The sadistic manner of his death had made Campbell ask, 'What did he do?' Carter had just suggested what it might be.

There would be victims of the vice trade, and their relatives, who might well feel no suffering was too great. But there would also be men, dangerous and utterly ruthless, who might feel that Smith escaping justice was unfair—

Or even, she thought suddenly, suspicious. He's in the bar along with these guys. Suddenly it's raided, he's taken in along with them and then released. Could he have been grassing?

Fleming seized a pad and began scribbling. There'd be no records kept at that time, of course; a snout would just talk directly to an officer he knew, be rewarded with some greasy notes, or a promise to overlook a crime, say . . . And to safeguard him, they'd arrest him and then let him go. She felt a surge of excitement; she could really be on to something there. But what was the connection with this remote, all but unknown Scottish island?

Brodie? MacNee had talked of some bad stuff there. She could get him to dig about a bit. If Manchester came up with names of associates, someone would have to head down there, but right now they could find out if any Innellan residents knew Andrew Smith.

Or at least, they could ask. Finding out might be something else.

Kerr Brodie was simmering with barely suppressed fury as he left the Kirkcudbright police station, which he had attended 'by invitation'.

That always sounded polite, but it was no tea party. He had been grilled for an hour about his past activities and his present activities and had left with the warning ringing in his ears that his future activities had better be confined to knitting and the perusal of the less inflammatory sections of the Bible, if he didn't want to find himself with the sort of problems that would make the trials of Job look like a walk in the park.

Brodie was fairly sure the local busies were all piss and wind. They'd got nothing on him – his record was clean and better men had tried and failed to rattle him. It was his guess that now they'd put the frighteners on him they'd relax.

But even if Ogilvie hadn't tipped him off, he'd have guessed who was behind it. MacNee would do anything in his power to destroy him, and he certainly wouldn't give up. While MacNee had him in his sights, there'd be no chance of bringing anything in – or getting anyone out. He couldn't keep the wretched Fergie in the bothy indefinitely.

So MacNee had to be neutralised – at least for as long as it took to call in the boat without finding a customs cutter waiting. And suddenly, as Brodie was driving back, the idea came to him. He was fishing for his mobile when it rang.

He glanced at the number. 'Lissa,' he said, without enthusiasm. 'What do you want?'

There was a sort of twitter from the other end. He gritted his teeth. 'I asked what you wanted, Lissa? Right, if it's nothing, I'll ring off. I've stuff to do.'

She had started to cry before he switched off the phone, and he grimaced. He'd begun to realise recently that he'd dropped himself right in it, there. She wanted to make it some great love affair, when it was just a sort of sly marking of his territory as alpha male. She now seemed hell-bent on creating some witless drama, without understanding that it would probably lead to them both – or him, at least – being kicked out, which would be a disaster. Lissa's hysteria could bring everything crashing down about him. She had to be stopped.

But there were more immediate problems to deal with. He scrolled through his phone book.

'Sammie? I've a job for you. Go down round the usual places and see if you can find old Davie. I've a wee job for him.'

Christie Jack was passing through the hall on her way to the kitchen for her tea break as the doorbell rang. When she saw two uniformed officers on the doorstep, a sergeant and a woman constable, she was pleased at first. Admittedly, she almost said, 'Better late than never,' but she was inviting them in politely as Matt came through from the office, Mika as usual at his side.

The officers looked askance at the dog as Lovatt stepped forward, but it sat on command and neither said anything, though Christie noticed the constable keeping a wary eye on it.

They had come, she then realised, not to investigate the gate which had been deliberately opened, but 'acting on a complaint from a member of the public' about negligence in keeping dangerous animals. No, it was not policy to disclose the name.

No prizes for guessing who, though. Looking up at Matt, Christie saw his jaw tense and his face go red, apart from the burn area, starkly white in contrast. For a moment she thought he would lose it completely – she would have – but with a restraint that made her admire him even more, he said calmly, 'Let me take you out and you can see for yourself what precautions we take. We've just improved the security.'

He led the way down the short drive and along the rough road by the shore, Christie beside him and Mika at his heels. The officers followed, the constable making sure she was as far away from the dog as possible.

In the field nearest the farm buildings, the red deer hinds were restless, roaming to and fro and sniffing the air, ready for mating. The barking roar of the penned stags as evening came on was so familiar to Christie now that she barely registered it, but she could never get used to the musky, acrid stench and she heard the sergeant gagging. Served him right!

Still, the separate enclosures were gravely inspected. The stags became unsettled, more aggressive – and indeed they were an alarming sight, dripping saliva as they bellowed a challenge. Matt pointed to the heavy padlocks on the gates, and they were solemnly rattled in turn.

'That seems quite satisfactory,' the sergeant said. 'Thank you, sir. We won't take up any more of your time.'

Christie could sense Matt's frustration, but he said, mildly enough, 'What progress have you made about finding who turned the stag loose on Sunday?'

From the blank look on the young woman's face, Christie guessed that she knew nothing about it; the sergeant said, indifferently, 'I understand the injured lady doesn't want to make a complaint, so there won't be any follow-up. Maybe you should have installed the padlocks sooner, but—'

That was when Christie lost it. '*She* doesn't want to make a complaint? Well, *I* do. I was in charge of that animal,' she pointed towards Rudolf with a shaking finger, 'and someone deliberately opened the gate I had shut. I had to put myself in danger to stop him having to be shot. Someone is victimising Major Lovatt. What more has to happen before you take all this seriously? Someone getting killed? And you could try looking at who's behind it—'

'Christie!' Matt's voice, the voice of military authority, cracked across her like a whiplash, stopping her in mid breath. 'That's enough.'

Blinded by tears, she turned away and half-ran back to the house, stumbling up the stairs to throw herself on her bed. What a fool she was, what an idiot, losing her temper when Matt was trying to keep the police onside! It made her sound hysterical and unbalanced.

And perhaps she was. Christie had been badly shaken and she was having problems again, not sleeping because she was afraid to dream.

The atmosphere in the house, too, was growing more toxic day by day. Lissa was blatantly flirting with Kerr, sometimes with a sidelong look at Matt as if she were taunting him. She kept making sly little gibes at Christie too, the sort you couldn't reply to without sounding oversensitive, but they were demoralising.

Christie hadn't had a full-blown flashback for weeks now, but though she did her best to avoid the thoughts that might prompt it, she could sense them hovering in the dark recesses of her mind, along with the other things she had resolved not to think about, waiting, waiting for the barriers she had tried to put up to crumble.

'Good news tonight,' Fleming said as she started the evening briefing. 'First, break-in at the off-licence. Our two prime suspects' alibi was that they were drinking all evening at the Brig Inn in Newton Stewart along with a third, who confirmed it – except he said they were at the Masonic Arms.'

Amid laughter, she went on, 'And curiously enough none of the bar staff in either pub remembers seeing them, so with any luck they'll cop a plea. We're not exactly talking master criminals here, but it all improves the clean-up rate. Well done that team.'

There was a ripple of ironic applause and one of the younger detectives went pink with gratification.

'More importantly,' Fleming said, 'we now have a name for our victim in the cave – Andrew Smith, from Manchester. No criminal record . . .' She explained the background, then added, 'There'll be a press statement tomorrow, but I'd rather it wasn't local gossip until then. I'll be giving out detailed tasks in the morning and when we get lists of his associates from Manchester we'll have a power of work to do there.

'Right. Next thing, I want a follow-up on that domestic last week. Wife's just out of hospital so there's a chance she might be sober enough to give a statement – if she wasn't so drunk then that she can't remember.'

She tied up a few more loose ends, and finished the meeting. Macdonald and Campbell followed her out.

Campbell was, as usual, looking impassive but Macdonald said eagerly, 'Would you like us to make a start on Innellan tonight, boss? I've no commitments and Campbell's dead keen to get out the house – his mother-in-law's cooking, and she's into boiled fish.'

Fleming smiled, wondering if Macdonald's enthusiasm had anything to do with a certain young lady, but she wasn't going to tease him. 'Well, I'm sympathetic, naturally, Ewan. It doesn't justify overtime, though – nothing's going to happen before tomorrow. Then you can try to establish some sort of connection. It's reaching a bit to imagine Manchester villains found Lovatt Island with a pin. OK?'

As she left them, Macdonald turned to Campbell. 'I did my best for you. Bad luck.'

'Bummer,' Campbell agreed. Then he said, 'They don't know that, mind.'

'A couple of pints and a game of pool? You're on.'

'And a pie,' Campbell said firmly, and went to make his phone call.

The black Granada was driving very slowly around the warren of streets behind Glasgow Central station.

'There he is!' the passenger cried. 'Stop!'

'About bloody time, Sammie,' the driver grumbled. 'I've more to do than chase sodding alkie deadbeats all over Glasgow.'

'Favour to a friend. The kind of friend you don't say no to.' Sammie got out and approached a man sitting on some old bits of cardboard, propped against the wall in a dark, urine-smelling close.

There was a chill wind whipping down the alley and his mittened fingers were blue with cold, but they were clutching a not quite empty half-bottle of cheap whisky and he looked as if he was feeling no pain. His stubbled cheeks were brick red, roughened by exposure, blotched and mottled, with a bluish tinge around his thin lips. His grey hair was long and wild, caught in a rubber band at the back, and he was wearing a filthy ancient overcoat, held round him by a piece of string.

223

As Sammie approached, he narrowed bloodshot, rheumy eyes at him suspiciously.

'Wha' are you after?' he slurred. 'Lea' me alone.'

Sammie wrinkled his nose at the smell as he bent over him. 'I've a job for you, Davie. Come on, upsy-daisy.'

With some reluctance, he grasped his arm and tried to urge him to his feet.

'I'm no' – I'm no' wantin' a job. Lea' me alone.'

Ungently, Sammie levered him up. He was no more than skin and bone, a small man, light as a bird. He clutched wildly at the cardboard he had been sitting on. 'I'm needin' that. And ma bags . . .'

Sammie glanced at the three plastic bags that had been stacked beside him, full of dirty rags. They stank too.

'We'll get you some gear. You're not needing them.'

'I am so! I am so!' The old man, weaving on his feet, was shouting now, starting to attract attention from a couple of passers-by.

Grim-faced, Sammie grabbed the bags and bundled Davie, still clutching his bottle and his cardboard, across the pavement to the car.

Davie stopped in alarm. 'Here – wha' the hell's this? Where're you takin' me?'

'To get a drink.' Sammie used the magic word.

Davie's face cleared. 'I wouldna say no, if you're offerin'.'

'Here!' the driver protested as Sammie opened the back door to chuck in the bags, and Davie, preceded by his unique aroma, climbed in. 'You never said I'd to have him in the car. Take me weeks to get rid of the smell.'

'All right for you,' Sammie said bitterly. 'I've to take him back to my flat and drive him down to Brodie tomorrow.'

* * *

224

DI Fleming was getting up from her desk when she paused with a sudden thought. Tony Drummond.

He'd been on her mind; she'd been annoyed that he'd tried to spice up a fading story with her remark about detectives being sent to pursue enquiries about the stag attack, but she still owed him a favour. She had some sympathy with him, too, having his big local scoop annexed by the big guys. The rest of the press would get the DNA story tomorrow, and if he got it tonight, it would be her quid pro quo to keep him happy.

'The polis with the wrong end of the stick, as usual!' Kerr Brodie gave a hearty laugh. 'It'd be Sorley, no doubt. Have to hand it to him – getting the police to check out us instead of them has a bit of style. I think it's quite funny.'

'Do you? I don't.' Matt Lovatt clamped his mouth shut, as if afraid of what he might say next.

'Oh, goodness, Matt,' Lissa tittered. 'You have to keep a sense of humour! Come on, Kerr, we won't let him get us all depressed with his moods.'

The look Kerr gave her was profoundly discouraging. Lissa's eyes grew big with hurt and she withdrew into pained silence. Matt's face was expressionless.

Christie was working at the stove as the others sat at the kitchen table. She had the sort of headache you get on oppressive days that need a storm to clear the atmosphere, and she was afraid one would break any minute now. She'd have given supper a miss if it hadn't been her turn to cook.

She brought the plates over, then sat down herself. The sausages and mash hadn't really worked: the mash was lumpy and there was too much Bisto in the gravy. The men ate stolidly, but Lissa, tasting it with a fastidious grimace, pushed the plate away with a little martyred sigh. Christie wouldn't have minded a 'God, this is disgusting!' – would have agreed, readily enough – but at this typically Lissa reaction she felt a flood of loathing for the woman.

It was Kerr who broke the silence with a conciliatory remark about the progress of the rut, as if he was afraid of going too far. Matt's reply, though, was brief and cold, and when they disagreed on precisely when the stags should be put to the hinds, the argument developed an edge and bitterness that was out of all proportion.

With a sick, cold feeling, Christie realised this wasn't what they were really arguing about. They were squaring up over Lissa, like a couple of stags, neither quite ready to make a challenge. She had believed Matt cared little for his wife – could she, hideously, be wrong?

She felt she was struggling to breathe. The moment the men had finished she got up, put out yoghurts and biscuits and cheese, then cleared the plates, scraping the uneaten food off her own and Lissa's and stacking the dishwasher before she said, as lightly as she could, 'I'm just going out for some fresh air. I've a bit of a headache.'

It was almost dark outside. The nights were drawing in fast now and over in Innellan the lighted windows and the street lamps made a bright chain round the edge of the bay, but it was too early for stars. There was a chill wind blowing and Christie shivered even as the fresh night air cooled her cheeks. Her nerve endings still felt charged with tension, as if her fingers might crackle if she touched metal. So many emotions, swirling around – some of them her own.

Perhaps it was her anger that was making her head ache: anger at Lissa, anger at Kerr, anger at herself most of all. Anger, and humiliation.

She'd seen all the signs of a broken marriage: separate

226

bedrooms, Lissa's relationship with Kerr, Matt's indifference to his wife, almost bordering on dislike. Had Christie read it wrong? Was this just a kind of marriage she didn't understand? Most dreadfully of all, had Lissa been right in accusing her of being a dumb romantic, cherishing a teenage-style crush? Had Lissa and Matt talked about how to handle it – had a laugh about it, even?

She clenched her hands so that the nails bit into her palms. She'd always had problems with rejection. Maybe she should leave now, before Matt told her, oh so sympathetically, that she must leave.

Like hell she would! Christie was a soldier and she'd been in plenty of fights with steeper odds than this one. She wouldn't give in until there was nothing more she could do.

She mustn't let it get to her. She'd been in a very bad place before and if she wasn't careful she'd be back there. Very deliberately, she unclenched her fists, spread out her cramped fingers and shook the tension out of her hands.

Perhaps she needed the island cure again. She could ask for the keys to the bothy and just retreat. But working out her emotions like she had last time had attracted an audience – she couldn't do that again.

The island was no more than a dark outline tonight and the stretch of water between was inky black under the lightless sky. It looked menacing, not like her beloved refuge at all, and Christie gave a little shudder, with the odd feeling she had heard described as a goose walking over your grave.

There was a smirr of rain on the wind now, and there were clouds gathering too, grey purple in the night sky. She considered going to the pub, but she didn't fancy a wet walk back. The company in the house wasn't appealing either, but she could slip upstairs to her room unseen.

As she walked back, she saw that though the light in the kitchen was still on there was no one there. There was a light behind the drawn curtains of one of the rooms in Kerr's little flat between the kitchen and the sitting room, and she wondered if he and Lissa were together. Matt had probably withdrawn to his office and she thought of going there to speak to him. But no, everything at the moment was just too complicated, too murky. She went in through the kitchen then headed upstairs.

There was a light under Lissa's bedroom door, next to her own. Christie paused, wondering whether, perhaps, Kerr was beginning to back off. And if he did, would Matt and Lissa make an effort to save the marriage?

Matt Lovatt was sleeping soundly when the rain came sweeping in a little after midnight. He didn't hear it – or the tinkle of glass breaking at the back of the house in his office, or the muffled *crump!* as the petrol caught fire.

And nor did anyone else.

CHAPTER FOURTEEN

Georgia Stanley was sleeping only fitfully. She'd wrenched her shoulder manhandling a keg too enthusiastically, and as she turned over a stab of pain shot through her, waking her completely. She groaned, failed to find a comfortable position and decided painkillers were the answer. Still half asleep, she plodded through to the bathroom, found the Neurofen and ran the tap for a glass of water. It was only as she stood at the basin that she looked out of the window above it.

It took a moment for her to register what she was seeing. There was a light in a downstairs window at the end of the back wing of the Lovatts' house, a strange, flickering yellow light. Flames! The room was on fire, and all the other windows were still in darkness. With a cry of dismay she dropped the glass, not even noticing as it shattered in the basin, and ran back to her bedroom, stumbling in her haste, and dialled 999.

The flames had found the pitch-pine panelling in Matt Lovatt's study and attacked it greedily, licking at the heavily varnished surface, speeding along, up, behind, as the resiny wood caught.

The room became an inferno; a window broke and with a roar that sounded like a cry of triumph the flames billowed out and up.

Inside, too, it was making its way behind the plaster of the walls, devouring the flimsy laths and reaching up into the gap between the floors. As the old, dry beams began to smoulder, the lethal black smoke crept and swirled. A joist collapsed, breaking down the ceiling below. The rest of the windows had broken now too; the office desk, reduced to a skeleton outline, crumpled to the floor.

In his room off the corridor above, Matt Lovatt was heavily asleep, deep in a disturbing dream where he couldn't move or cry out, where he was sinking deeper, deeper—

Someone was shaking him, moving those helpless limbs, shouting, shouting. He was too tired to be bothered, too tired. He sank back again, but the shaking and the shouting went on. He was being pulled upright, and at last he struggled to the surface. It was Christie, yelling, swearing, trying to haul him out of bed. His head was swimming, he felt sick . . .

Christie was wrapping a wet towel around his face, then around her own. She was choking as well – on the smoke, the smoke that was making him cough too now. Fire! That was what she was telling him – and the adrenaline of fear gave him the strength to stand, to stagger across the room. The floor under his bare feet was hot and Christie was urging him on, the fear in her own voice showing, but his lungs were labouring, his limbs didn't want to obey him and moving was hard, so hard and so slow.

The light in the upper hall was on, and there was more air here; the smoke was wispy rather than dense. His eyes were streaming and smarting, but at least he could breathe and his head became a little clearer as Christie supported him down the stairs. The fire was below in the wing behind him, where he could hear the cracking of timbers and a crash as something down there fell; it would soon spread across the stairwell to the rooms at the front.

'Lissa?' he croaked.

'It's all right. I told her before I came for you. Come on, come on, we're nearly there.'

He supported himself against a wall as Christie fumbled with the bolts on the front door and at last flung it wide. Air, pure fresh air, damp with the teeming rain outside, poured through the opening and he tore off the towel and gulped it as if it was water and he was dying of thirst. Christie shoved him out, then followed and collapsed on to the grass, burying her face in it, groaning and clenching her fists.

Matt barely noticed. He felt as if his head might split; the nausea was making him dizzy and his sight was blurred. He sat down on the wet grass, barely noticing the rain that was soaking him through.

But a thought forced its way into his clouded brain. The bolts! Christie had unbolted the door – but Lissa would have done that, surely, on her way out? Where was his wife? Had she gone through to the back to warn Kerr? In the flat by the kitchen he should have been far enough from the site of the blaze to be safe, and they could have left the house that way. Matt screwed up his sore eyes to focus better in the lurid, demonic light.

He could see Kerr now, coming out of the kitchen door on crutches; apparently he hadn't taken time to put on his artificial leg. But he seemed to be alone.

'Lissa?' Matt yelled, and Kerr shook his head, made a shrugging gesture.

Oh God! He looked back at the house. Thin threads of smoke were coming out of the front door now. He could hear shouts as people came hurrying from the village, but this couldn't wait and Kerr, in his present state, couldn't help. Matt grabbed up the towel, wound it round his face again and went back into the building he had just escaped.

The lights gave a flicker, and then went out. In the thick darkness, the only illumination came through the staircase window, from the wing which was well ablaze. The noise was terrifying, like an express train; the smoke on the landing now was no better than the corridor had been.

He took the stairs two at a time and burst into Lissa's bedroom, shouting her name. Incredibly, she was asleep – or had the toxic fumes got to her already?

She was still breathing, but impossible to rouse. Matt began to gag and the carbon monoxide headache was almost blinding now. If he lost consciousness, they'd both die.

Lissa was, at least, small and slight. He grabbed her in a fireman's lift and struggled out on to the landing. Her flimsy nightdress caught on the finial at the top of the staircase, jerking him to a standstill. Confused, he struggled, then almost lost his balance as the cloth suddenly ripped. His head was swimming, every breath a struggle in the thickening air, and he could feel his legs buckling. With the flames outside casting a flickering, red, angry light, the dark pit of the stairwell below looked like a vision of hell.

Smoke rises. Crawl, he told himself – he wasn't sure his legs could hold him up much longer anyway. He put Lissa down, then collapsed beside her, and began to inch like a caterpillar backwards down the stairs, dragging Lissa with him. Her head bumped on each step, but there was nothing else he could do. The wet towel had fallen off at some point and his lungs hurt as he sucked in the sooty air, desperately seeking oxygen. Willpower alone was keeping him going; one more pull, one more, just another one . . .

He was nearing the bottom now and the air from the open door began to reach him at last. Kerr, impotent on his crutches, was standing in the hall, shouting.

'Keep going, keep going, you're nearly there! Can you make it?'

'Have to,' Matt groaned. He reached the threshold and with a mighty effort stood up, pulled Lissa out of the house then reeled over to fall on the wet grass. He was retching and coughing but not caring about the rain, not caring about his smarting eyes, his painful throat, his shattering headache, his churning stomach, just being thankful to breathe. And miraculously, that was the sound of sirens now as fire engines went screaming through Innellan and hurtled up the drive, men leaping from them and running out the hoses.

A fireman sprinted over and lifted Lissa from where she lay inert on the gravel, picking her up as if she weighed nothing at all and carrying her to where another was spreading a tarpaulin out on the grass in the beam of the lights they were setting up. They had an oxygen mask on her face in seconds – big, gentle, efficient men.

They started playing fountains of water on the flames, the fire hissing and spitting defiance as clouds of smoke changed to steam. Hoses were being trained on the main part of the building as well, soaking the roof and the walls. The wing was all but gone already; they were working to save the rest of the house.

Matt's pyjamas were sodden, his hair was plastered to his face and he was chilled through, but he still felt too shaky to get up off the wet grass. Christie, similarly groggy, was sitting up now too, looking ghastly.

He managed a smile. 'Well done, soldier,' he rasped, patting her hand. 'We'd have died in there, if it hadn't been for you.'

She bit her lip. 'You nearly did die. I-I didn't realise Lissa was still inside. I banged on the door and yelled at her, so I just thought . . .'

'Of course,' Matt said soothingly. 'You mustn't blame yourself for that.' But there was just a trace of hesitation in his voice as he said it.

Innellan, wakened by the sirens of fire engines, three police cars and an ambulance, turned out in force to observe this latest sensation. Fire, raging uncontrollably, has a compelling attraction and people, huddled under umbrellas, stood mesmerised in little groups, talking in suitably hushed voices. Some had come down from the chalets as well, Derek Sorley among them and Elena Tindall too, with the hood of her new parka pulled up against the rain. On the further side of the crowd Cal Findlay stood silent, a little detached from the others. There was no sign of the Donaldsons, father or son.

They watched as Melissa Lovatt was taken away in an ambulance, and paramedics escorted her husband, Kerr Brodie and Christie Jack, blackened with smoke, soaked to the skin and wrapped in survival blankets, over to the Smugglers Inn where Georgia Stanley had hot soup and brandy waiting for them.

But when, a little later, Derek Sorley came up to join a group, saying jokily, 'Well, it's good entertainment, you have to say,' he was met with stony silence.

Then one man said, 'You've gone too far this time, you and Steve. Folks like you aren't wanted here.'

'What do you mean?' Sorley was instantly defensive. 'You watch your mouth! This is nothing to do with Steve or me. Say that again and I'll take out a writ. I've witnesses.'

'None that would testify,' said another voice, and faced with a row of turned backs, Sorley retreated.

* * *

Elena Tindall walked back up to Spindrift along with the woman who had called the police on Sunday night, her husband and son silently bringing up the rear. It was very late; Elena was tired and cold, and disinclined to make polite conversation.

However, it was not required of her. The woman kept up a shrill rant about the defects of Innellan and her determination to get a refund with compensation on top until they reached her chalet, and Elena, with a weak smile, could walk on.

She let herself in, but didn't put on the light. The room was still lit by the livid glow of flames and the flashing orange lights of the fire engines. In any case, she didn't like the idea of standing illuminated in the picture window, like a figure on a stage.

She heard the noise of loud voices and laughter before she saw them appearing up the track: the weasel-faced man, along with his companions in the pub on Sunday night. The two younger men had their arms round each other's shoulders; the older man was walking alongside, but they were clearly all in high good humour.

Elena shrank back into the shadows. *Something wicked this way comes . . .*

'What the hell is going on at Innellan?' DI Fleming asked DS MacNee next morning. It was a repetition of the question she'd been asked earlier by a distinctly tetchy Superintendent Bailey, but he hadn't got a satisfactory answer and she didn't either.

'God knows,' MacNee said, and they both bleakly contemplated the day ahead when everyone, from the victims to the already-encamped media, would be asking the same.

'The first thing they're going to ask is whether it's connected with Smith's murder, or just coincidence.'

'And what'll you tell them?' MacNee asked with some interest.

She groaned. 'How would I know? On the face of it, why should it be? That was a coldly sadistic crime, committed maybe ten years ago. Hard to see any connection with what looks like a long-standing campaign of minor harassment that got a bit reckless last week, and now looks to have progressed to fire-raising on a grand scale.'

'The Donaldsons and Sorley starting to get desperate when Lovatt still hasn't got the message?'

'Desperate indeed,' Fleming said grimly. 'It's pure chance that the lot of them weren't killed. The fire chief's at the scene this morning so we'll need to get down there. He'll be able to pinpoint how and where it was started – and you never know, it could just turn out to be an electrical fault.'

'Aye, that'll be right! You don't believe it any more than I do.'

She sighed. 'No, I don't. But fire-raising's tough to pin on anyone. An inferno like that – what have you got left for forensics? Then you've had every fireman in the county tramping about the scene, inside and out, so it's hopelessly contaminated. It's a smart choice of crime.'

'Sorley's not daft, and he's gallus with it – complaining about dangerous animals, when it's a pound to a bawbee it was him and his pals let the stag out.'

'Chief suspects, certainly. We'll get them in today and lean on them.'

'Steve Donaldson first,' MacNee suggested. 'He's the weakest link.'

'Right. Then maybe someone noticed something last night, or the fire chief might give us a lead. But think about it, Tam – they'd have to be crazy to pull a stunt like that so soon afterwards.'

MacNee was stubborn. 'That'll be what they'll want us to think. Gallus, like I said.'

'Fair enough. But look at it the other way – we find Smith's body, and suddenly all hell breaks loose. Neither Sorley nor Steve Donaldson was around ten years ago, and Hugh was, as far as we know, contentedly farming as tenant to old Mrs Lovatt. This could have a Manchester dimension. Say Smith grassed on his nasty chums, and—'

'Hmph.'

She gave him a sharp look. 'No?'

'Let's just say, it's kinna elaborate. Knife in the back, body left in a gutter in a backstreet – I'll buy that. Bullet in the head, even, and a trip to a nearby quarry – OK. Carrying a prisoner all this way to meet a lingering death on a remote Scottish island that no one south of the border's ever heard of . . .' He gave a dismissive shrug.

Fleming resented his rubbishing of her precious new theory. She resented it even more as she thought about it herself and it crumbled.

'Put that way,' she said stiffly. MacNee grinned, but wisely said nothing.

'Since you're so smart, what's the connection between Smith and Lovatt's house being set on fire?'

'There isn't one. Sorley's got off with everything he's done so far. He's the wee boy! That's how he sees it. And here – maybe he really thinks there's gold in them there graves and he's going radge because he can't get at it. Burn the house to the ground, Lovatt has to leave, temporarily at least, and he has time to do his searching undisturbed.'

'That's plausible,' Fleming conceded. 'Anyway, at least the news about Melissa Lovatt's good this morning. They were lucky, though. If the girl hadn't raised the alarm she and Lovatt would both have wakened up dead.'

'Oh, Andy can pick 'em,' MacNee said, grinning. 'Is he away down to see her now?'

'Yes, he and Ewan were scheduled to do interviews there anyway. In fact, they wanted to make a start last night, but I didn't feel it merited overtime. I actually said nothing would happen if they waited till the morning. I'm feeling guilty about that – maybe if I'd let them go it wouldn't have happened.'

'Or maybe it would,' MacNee said firmly. 'Don't beat yourself up. When do we go?'

Fleming glanced at her watch. 'Half an hour? I've a couple of things to do first—'

She broke off as her phone rang. It wasn't a long call; MacNee raised his eyebrows as she said, '*What!*' but she didn't meet his eyes. Her face was sombre as she put the phone down.

She said awkwardly, 'Tam, you're needed downstairs. I'll come with you.'

MacNee said sharply, 'What's happened?'

But she only said, 'I'll explain on the way down,' and preceded him out of the room.

The ashes were cooling but still not cold when DS Macdonald and DC Campbell arrived at Lovatt's Farm. One fire engine was still standing by, ready to extinguish any flare-up, but the weather at least was favourable: dry, with a touch of autumn sunshine, and so far at least, with no sign of wind to breathe a smouldering beam into sudden life.

The back wing of the farmhouse was a hollow shell, with empty windows like dead eyes and a roof reduced to spindly blackened struts and sagging slates at the end nearest the main building. The rest of the house was, remarkably, intact, though there were smoke streaks in the stonework and every door and window was open to try to clear the air. Smoke damage would be extensive, and water damage, too; the ground area round about was a boggy mess. The leaves on the trees, great broadleaves in a sheltering half-circle a few yards from the house, were shrivelled from the heat, though the heavy rain had saved them from greater harm.

Firemen with thick boots and rakes were working in what had been the office, clearing debris and carrying out a few metal items which, though buckled and blackened, had survived more or less intact. A twisted filing cabinet was lying on the ground where it had been dumped, papers spilling out of the drawers.

The fire chief, Angus Williamson, was a burly, grey-haired man also in heavy boots and wearing a helmet which he took off as the detectives joined him.

'Wicked business, this,' he said heavily. 'Pure chance that it's not a murder inquiry.'

'Deliberate, then?' Macdonald asked.

'No question. I've been in there this morning – unmistakable.'

'How was it done?'

'An accelerant of some sort. Petrol, almost certainly – yellow flames and oily black smoke observed in this area last night. And then with all the wood, it'd go up like a Christmas tree.'

'Someone chuck a Molotov cocktail?' Campbell suggested, but Williamson shook his head.

'There were multiple points where it was splashed around – the fluid dynamics of the blaze are quite clear. Someone broke in first – there, we think.'

He led them across to what remained of the glass-panelled back door of the office. It had fallen outwards as the fire destroyed its fixings and though damaged was still relatively intact. He pointed to the square immediately above the door handle.

'Here, you see? There was glass among the ashes right on the threshold. 'All the rest of the glass was blown out, but this fell inwards. There's still the jagged edges from where it was smashed, look. I've warned the lads not to touch it.'

There was a key still in the keyhole, too. 'Not much thought about security, anyway,' Macdonald said. 'Simple enough to break in.'

'Casual about smoke alarms too. Don't know what they had in this wing, but the ones in the main house have dead batteries.'

'Never think it could happen to you, do you?' Macdonald said uncomfortably, making a mental note to buy batteries on his way home. 'Thanks, anyway.'

He was turning away when Campbell spoke. 'Why spread the petrol around? Chuck something in a window, let it blaze – easier.'

Williamson looked at him. 'Certainly. Not as quick, though. This would spread in seconds.'

Macdonald, his mind on Christie Jack, felt sick. 'Right,' he said hollowly. 'Thanks, Chief. We'd better get on. We've a lot of people to see.'

'Good luck,' Williamson said. 'You want this one behind bars as soon as possible.'

Matt Lovatt, his dog at heel, walked along the foreshore. He was avoiding the path; too many of the neighbours were out gaping, some blatantly, some making the excuse of 'just being out for a stroll' when they saw him. He tended to prefer the blatant ones.

He still couldn't get the taste of smoke out of his mouth, and he had slept little in one of Georgia Stanley's spare rooms. He must be looking as bad as he felt; Brodie, who had got a bed from a friend in the village, had taken one look at him and said he'd take charge.

'You and Christie take the day off – I'll easy manage. I've an errand to do first, but there's nothing special needs doing today.'

Lovatt didn't feel strong enough to argue. The dog, unsettled last night by the smoke and noise and strangers, needed a proper run, and then he'd go to Dumfries to see Lissa. She was on the road to recovery, but they planned to keep her for another day. It was frightening to think how close she had come to death.

He would have died too, but for Christie, but Lissa had come closer. Christie had tried to wake her, of course she had. She'd said that. But Lissa had spelt out to him before, in malevolent terms, that Christie had what she termed a 'crush' on him. Was it possible . . . ?

No, of course it wasn't. But how come he, half-suffocated by smoke, had realised the bolts hadn't been drawn back and she, who had half-dragged him out and down the stairs, hadn't noticed?

She'd done the best she could in the circumstances, he told himself. Perhaps Lissa had taken sleeping pills – she sometimes did. That would be it, of course. Comforted, he walked on. He'd check when he went in to see her later.

Matt had outdistanced the gawpers now. With a gesture, he set the dog free to roam and clambered over one of the groynes of rock going down to the sea. This was one of his favourite places; a neat little bay beside a curving promontory which, like a protective arm, sheltered it from storms sweeping in up the Solway. It had a special tranquillity, on a morning like this—

He was sharing it with someone else. And to his dismay, it was the strange woman who had been attacked by his stag and now was being approached by his dog, which could cause alarm even when right beside him. If she complained . . .

'Mika, here!' he called, his anxiety putting an edge on his voice, and the dog immediately obeyed. 'I'm sorry,' he said to her stiffly. 'He won't hurt you.'

She seemed faintly amused. 'I met him before, and I'm not scared of dogs,' she said. 'I won't make a fuss.'

Embarrassed to have betrayed that his concern was for the dog rather than for her, Lovatt said hastily, 'Of course not. It's just he looks ferocious, though he isn't.' He ruffled the animal's fur affectionately, then said, 'Er – I hope you've recovered from your ordeal?'

'I could say the same to you,' she said. 'I gather no one was hurt?'

At least she was being civil this morning. 'No, thankfully. My wife's all right, but they're keeping her under observation for the moment.'

'That's good.' The woman nodded, then turned away.

'Hope all this isn't ruining your holiday,' Lovatt called after her, then turned back himself. He wasn't going to get the peace he so desperately craved so he might as well go home.

Or he could go to the island. He headed back to the jetty, untied one of the boats and snapped his fingers to Mika, who jumped into position at the prow.

Lovatt needed the quiet to think. Guilt, guilt, guilt – that familiar refrain. His wife had almost been killed and a damaged girl been drawn into deeper danger, under his roof, because of him. It felt like a punishment – but how could he complain he didn't deserve it? The charge sheet against him wouldn't be hard to write.

From the shore, Elena Tindall watched the boat speed over to the island. It wasn't cold this morning, but she was having to brace herself to stop shivering. She was half-slept, of course, and her head still seemed to be ringing with the noise of the sirens.

She left the beach and walked back along the path past the farmhouse. The smell of smoke was heavy on the air here and she felt colder than ever, looking at the destruction – cold with fear.

Her car was outside the chalet door. She could be in Salford tonight, loved and safe, not lonely and utterly, utterly vulnerable.

But that was false security; the enemy within was the greatest threat, and she had sensed it becoming more powerful by the day. She could have no refuge until it was vanquished.

There was a wall of pigeonholes on one side of the entrance to the university hall of residence. It looked innocuous enough, but Catriona Fleming approached it as if confronting a savage beast. Yes, there was something in hers. Taking a deep, shaky breath, she took it out and opened it.

It was from her tutor, just as yesterday's had been. This one was angrier, and mentioned a time which – Cat glanced at her watch – had passed already. She didn't know what to do – well, she did, really, but it would mean going to see an angry woman who, the note said, had twice come to the residence looking for her.

She couldn't face it. She could walk out now, give it all up. She could be back home in two, three hours, back to Dad who would make it all right. Mum would be angry, but Cat was still Dad's little girl.

But he couldn't make it all right, could he? She wasn't a little girl any more, and she'd screwed up her whole career. He was so proud of her; how could she tell him she'd let him down? Her phone rang.

She took it out and looked at it suspiciously. If it was Mum again – but it wasn't; it was Lily, and suddenly everything seemed better.

'Sure,' Cat said. 'See you in half an hour.'

Fleming held open the door for Tam MacNee as, looking shocked, he went into the reception area. There was a man sitting there, an old man with a drink-ravaged complexion, unkempt and smelling.

It was far from unusual. Galloway had its share of down and outs. But what was different was that this one had a journalist with him: Tony Drummond, his eyes bright with anticipation. A photographer stood, camera at the ready, behind him.

'DS MacNee, this man says he's your father. Can you explain how he comes to be destitute on the streets of Glasgow, without any help from you – or even contact? He tells me you washed your hands of him twenty years ago.'

CHAPTER FIFTEEN

'Thanks for letting us in,' DS Macdonald said with real gratitude as Georgia Stanley opened the door of the Smugglers Inn just wide enough to admit them, then shut it again hastily. 'Thought they were going to eat us alive.'

'I checked out of the window first. They've been driving me demented, ringing the bell and banging on the windows. What on earth is it about? A fire, even arson, no one really hurt – you'd expect a report in the *Herald*, a photo, maybe – but this?'

'They're linking it to the bones in the cave,' Macdonald said. 'Some of them followed up on the stag story and now this'll mean headlines like "Village of Horror".'

'Not wrong there,' Campbell said with feeling.

Georgia gave a little shudder. 'It's all right for you. You'll be going home at night, but I live here. What's going to happen next? Honest, my loves, it's really scary. The atmosphere—' She broke off. 'But you haven't come to listen to me rabbiting on. You'll be wanting a statement, I expect. Not that there's much to say – woke up, saw flames from the bathroom window, dialled 999. Anyway, come through to the house. It's a bit quieter at the back.'

She led them beyond the bar and into the little kitchen adjacent to it, then stopped, lowering her voice.

'Christie's through there having her breakfast, looking like a ghost, poor kid. I've just made her toast and coffee. I offered her bacon, eggs, anything, but . . .' Georgia shrugged.

Seeing a gleam in Campbell's eye, Macdonald shot him a look which dared him to speak, and he subsided.

In the cosy sitting room at the back, a log fire was burning and Georgia had drawn up a table beside it where Christie was sitting, clasping a mug. The toast was untouched.

Macdonald's heart went out to her. She looked so pitiful, drawn and white, her blue eyes bloodshot and her lips dry and cracked. She was trembling so that when she set down her mug it clattered against the plate. He went over and before he could stop himself took her poor, shaking hands in his.

'You're in a bad way,' he said gruffly. 'Have you seen a doctor?'

Taken by surprise, perhaps, she didn't resist. 'Not a lot of point. It's just reaction. I'll get over it.'

'What happened?'

He was still holding her hands. She seemed only now to notice and pulled them away, looking from one officer to the other.

'Is that an official question?'

As Macdonald coloured, Campbell said firmly, 'Yes.' He pulled over a chair and took out a notebook; as Georgia discreetly withdrew, Macdonald sat down too, trying to switch into professional mode. He led her through the sequence of events – straightforward enough, up to the point where she had led Matt Lovatt out of the burning building. Then she stopped.

'And . . . ?' he prompted.

'I-I don't know.' Christie was looking flustered.

Campbell glanced up sharply. 'You don't know?'

'I . . . well, I had a flashback,' she said reluctantly. 'It . . . it just hit me. Probably the heat set it off, like I was back in Afghanistan.'

'Right,' Campbell said. 'I'll write that down.'

Sensing scepticism, Macdonald said sharply, 'A horrible experience, I can imagine. So what happened afterwards?'

Christie nibbled at a piece of dry skin on her lip; she pulled it away, then licked at the raw patch. 'When I . . . when I came round, sort of, Matt had gone back to rescue Lissa.'

Macdonald was startled. 'But . . . you said you had roused her first?'

'I . . . I banged on the door, opened it and shouted. The fire was on the other side of the landing, where Matt's bedroom was. He was the one in danger.'

'Waken her, did you?' Campbell said.

'Apparently not.' Christie was on the defensive now. 'She must have taken pills or something. I didn't go and shake her, if that's what you mean. She wasn't at risk then, and Matt was. I hadn't time to go fussing after her.'

'Don't like her much, do you?' That was Campbell.

She didn't answer. She tore another piece of skin from her lip.

'So,' Macdonald said, 'you had every reason to suppose she had left the building while you were rescuing Matt, and then once you had got out you were hit by the flashback?' He could feel Campbell's eyes on him, but he didn't look up.

'Yes,' Christie said gratefully.

'Then Matt realised she wasn't there, and went back in for her?'

She nodded, but didn't say anything.

Macdonald looked at her uncomfortably. There was something there, something she wasn't telling them. He should probe . . .

'What are you not telling us?' Campbell said.

Tears came to Christie's eyes, but she said fiercely, 'You'll find out anyway. I should have noticed – when I went down with Matt the door was still bolted. I was in a state – it was terrifying. I'd probably have realised she was still in there once we were outside, like he did. But—'

'Oh yes, the flashback.' Campbell nodded, and Macdonald was seized with a sudden desire to hit him.

There wasn't much more she could tell them. As they left Macdonald said, remembering his instructions, 'Just one last question: does the name Andrew Smith mean anything to you?'

Christie looked at him blankly. 'No. Should it?'

'Just routine. Thanks, that's all.'

The interview with Georgia didn't produce any surprises and the detectives left to run the media gauntlet again. When at last they outdistanced them, on their way to conduct the interviews at the farther end of the village, Campbell said bluntly, 'You'll need to keep out of this. At least where she's concerned.'

There was an eloquent silence. Then Macdonald said, 'I know it looks bad. But I don't believe for a moment she left the woman in there to burn. It's not in her nature.'

Campbell's silence was even more eloquent than his own had been.

MacNee's face looked, Fleming thought, as if it had been carved in stone. 'No comment,' he snapped.

The old man blinked blearily up at him. 'Tam? Is that you? Here, son – you wouldn't have a drink for your old man, would you?'

Tony Drummond said, 'He was found in a backstreet in Glasgow, in the state you see him in now. Look at him – does it not make you feel ashamed?'

Involuntarily Fleming's eyes went to the tattered clothes, filthy with stains she didn't want to think about, the cracked hands with their broken nails, ingrained with dirt, the pathetic face with its drinker's complexion and a ragged growth of old man's stubble. One of his eyes, watery with age, spilt moisture like a tear and Fleming heard the camera click.

MacNee's hands were clenched at his side and the muscles in his jaw tightened visibly as he forced out, 'No comment.'

Drummond was visibly enjoying himself. 'No comment – that's the best you can say to the father you haven't seen for twenty years?'

MacNee took a half-step forward, his clenched fist coming up. Fleming stepped in front, blocking him.

'DS MacNee has said he has no comment,' she said icily. 'There will be a statement put out by the press officer later – to *all* the press. In plenty of time for them to catch their evening editions.'

Drummond's face, as he saw his exclusive disappear, was comically crestfallen.

Fleming smiled, walking over to the outside door and holding it open. 'Bad move, Tony. I don't know who arranged this pantomime, but you've just killed the goose who might have been prepared to lay an egg or two for you in the future.'

Sullenly, the journalist and his sidekick left, the FCAs at the reception desk watching in frozen silence. In ten minutes' time this would be all round the station.

'Right,' Fleming said briskly. 'Interview room.' She took the old man's arm, trying not to wince at the smell. 'This way, Mr MacNee.'

He peered up at her suspiciously. 'Here! Where're you taking me? I'm no' a vagrant – I've money, look!' He pulled a five-pound note out of his pocket. 'I'm just needing to buy a wee drink.' From the fumes on his breath, it wouldn't be the first that day.

'It's all right, we'll see about that later,' she said, propelling him, still protesting, out of the reception area.

MacNee followed them, a stricken look on his face. His father turned to say over his shoulder, 'You'll look after old Davie, won't you, son? I dinna like this place. We'll away and have a wee bevvy, just the two of us, eh?'

It was with some relief that Fleming deposited him on a seat in the interview room and said, 'You stay here, Mr MacNee. I'll get you a cup of coffee.'

'Coffee?' He gave a snort of disgust. 'I'm no' needin' *coffee*.'

Ignoring a pleading look from MacNee, Fleming headed back to reception to order it. After all, there must be things father and son had to say that didn't need an audience. Surely?

There was a buzz of talk at reception that died as she approached. She thought of saying something, then decided there was no point. This would be all over the tabloids tomorrow.

Returning to the interview room she paused at the door, listening. The last thing she wanted to do was intrude – and if she was honest, the second last thing she wanted to do was open it. But there was no sound of conversation inside and with a sigh she went in.

Davie had fallen asleep in his chair. His son was sitting on the other side of the room, still with that stricken expression. He didn't turn his head until Fleming said gently, 'Tam?'

'I know what you're thinking,' he burst out. 'What kind of a son is he, to leave his father drunk in a gutter? That's what everyone will be thinking.'

'I'm not. I know you wouldn't.'

'I wouldn't, no. But it's come to the same thing, hasn't it?'

'Why don't you tell me about it?'

He hesitated. Fleming leant forward, her voice coaxing. 'You'll have to have a statement for the press officer. Tell me, and we'll work on it together.'

MacNee buried his head in his hands. 'Give me a wee moment,' he said.

She sat in silence. Davie gave a snore and half-woke, then subsided back.

At last MacNee sat up, squaring his shoulders. 'The thing is, it was him cut *me* off. Wouldn't have anything to do with me after I joined the polis. He was doing fine at that time, if you didn't ask where the money came from, but I was asking. I won't say what he told me I could do to myself, but you can maybe guess.

'I've wondered where he was, what he was doing – of course I have. I've still got pals in the Glasgow force I can ask to check the records for me and there's been nothing for years now. I just thought maybe he'd decided to go straight – or got better at not being caught. But, of course, if folks end up on the streets, minding their own business, they drop off the radar – a caution, even a fiscal fine, maybe, but no criminal record.'

'Can't have been easy for you, deciding to join the force with influences like that as you grew up.'

MacNee gave a cheerless laugh. 'That's the joke. He wasn't the bad influence – I was. He used to rant on at me about the company I was keeping. Guys like . . .' he drew in his breath '. . . Kerr Brodie.'

'Ah,' Fleming said. 'I wanted to know about Brodie.'

'We lived in the same tenement. They'd the swanky flat on the ground floor. His old man did favours for folks. You didn't ask.

'Mine worked in the shipyards – unskilled, so he didn't bring home a big wage. But he was straight, so we'd just the wee room and kitchen flat at the top of the stairs. After my mam died it was just him and me. He told me to keep clear of the Brodies, but Kerr was . . .' MacNee paused, then said slowly, 'Kerr knew all the big names. He'd always money, he – put things my way too.'

He didn't elaborate, but Fleming saw his face darken – with shame, perhaps? But he went on, 'Glasgow was in a bad place at that time – the ice cream wars, T.C. Campbell, the Doyles. There was a big stushie about a shooting, but I didn't think anything about it when Kerr showed up at the door one afternoon. Said he'd a message for me, and he wanted to come in. My dad had been on an early shift so he was around and I mind it was awkward – he wasn't best pleased, but Kerr could be good company when he wanted so he sat down and we'd a bit of a crack. Can't remember what the message was – nothing much.

'They came that night with a warrant, and of course they found the gun they were looking for in the chair where Kerr had been sitting. I told them, but they wouldn't believe me. They took him away in handcuffs.'

Davie stirred in his sleep and started to snore. MacNee turned his head to look at him, and Fleming saw his face soften, as if he were seeing for a moment the man his father had once been in the sad ruin before him. His voice was harsh as he went on.

'He'd been stitched up, good and proper. The gun was hot, of course, but he'd a lucky alibi so he went down for possession – seven years, and that was when you served the full term. By the time he came out, Bunty and I were married and I'd joined the force. I wanted revenge on the folk like Brodie, and Bunty wouldn't let me do it any other way.

'When he came out he was – destroyed. He'd been paid sweeties all his working life, but he'd been an honest man. "*The noblest work of God*", as Rabbie says.' MacNee's voice faltered. 'And his reward was to be screwed – by the establishment, as he saw it, and there were the Brodies standing by to offer him a kindly helping hand. I tried to make him see that for what it was, told him it wasn't an apology, just a plan to use him in the future like they had last time.

'But . . .' MacNee shrugged. 'He never wanted to see me again. I tried, a couple of times, when I heard he'd gone down, and got a good swearing. Nothing I could do.

'And Brodie's behind this now. I knew he'd joined the army after it all happened – probably had some nice little scam going there. He knows I'm out to get him and he wants me off his back.'

It wasn't the moment for a lecture on police ethics. Fleming said gently, 'What are you going to do now?'

'Take him home to Bunty.'

Of course. Bunty, who had never been known to turn away a homeless cat or an abused dog, would see her father-in-law as just another project. 'She'll get him sorted out,' Fleming said, smiling. 'I'll get the press officer to draft a statement. But Tam, however she words it, there's flak coming your way.'

MacNee compressed his lips, as if he didn't trust himself to speak. Then he turned to the old man and put a hand on his sleeve. 'Come on, Dad,' he said. 'Wake up. You're going home.'

Davie sat up, blinking. 'Home? Where's that?'

'You've made an appointment for that moron Jenkins. I didn't want to see him till I'd all the details to hand.'

Marianne Price gave her boss an appraising look. Eddie Tindall had been in a cantankerous mood when she arrived this morning and since there wasn't a cat for him to kick he was taking it out on her. That Woman's fault, no doubt.

'You always say if an employee wants to speak to you, the door's open.'

Eddie grunted. 'Not this employee. Not at the moment.'

'I'll just tell him that, shall I?' Marianne made as if to leave.

'Oh, I suppose . . . Since it's in the book . . .'

Stifling a smile, she said, 'Fine. Do you want me to get his line manager on the phone, then?'

'Right.' Tindall picked up a report from his desk and began to read it without enthusiasm.

Marianne went to the door, then turned with artistic casualness. 'Heard anything from Clive, then?'

She really shouldn't tease him, poor old bloke. She knew perfectly well he hadn't, or it would have been the first thing he'd have told her when she came in. She'd steered clear of mentioning his missing wife for the last couple of days – she'd had enough of his agonising over That Woman – but now, given the chance, it all poured out.

'I'd like to know what I'm paying the man for! Not a word, and when I phone him all he can say is "making progress". Progress! Not that I can see.'

And there was more. Elena, he disclosed, had been very chatty on the phone recently, wanting to know what he was doing, how he was getting on. She'd even asked once what Lola had left him for supper!

'That's nice, isn't it?' Marianne said, uncertainly.

It wasn't, apparently. As he explained his concern, she got a new insight into that strange marriage. What a cow! It could only be the sex, she concluded. Sex addled the heads of even sensible, decent guys like Eddie. Till he got her back – *if* he got her back – Marianne would suffer. Maybe she should get an office cat – but Eddie would just go soppy over it, and she'd still be in the firing line, having to take out litter trays as well.

When the call came from Clive, she put him through with some relief. Maybe if he'd solved the mystery, Eddie would go back to thinking of something else – like his business, for instance.

Five minutes later, Eddie's office door opened. He was frowning.

'Don't know what to make of this, Marianne. Clive's persuaded someone to track Elena's mobile. She's up in Scotland. What does she want to go to Scotland for?'

'A holiday?'

'Some place called . . .' He glanced at the sheet of paper in his hand '. . . Kirk-cud-bright.'

'Kirk-coo-bray,' Marianne corrected him. 'I've a friend had a holiday there. Nice place, she said.'

Eddie pounced on that. 'So you think she maybe just went there for a holiday?'

She was fond of Eddie. She'd been with him a long time. He was a good boss, and he paid her well, but sometimes she thought she earned every penny, and there were limits. 'That's what I said, isn't it?'

'You see, I was just thinking I might go up and take a look myself. But Clive could only tell me the general area, and it's big. What do you think?'

What Marianne thought was that the divvy sponging on poor Eddie should come back and earn her keep, and let everyone else get on with life. With exemplary tact, she suggested it might not be a good idea.

'If you don't know where she is, there's not a lot of point, is there? And supposing you found her, how'd you explain how you knew she was there?'

Eddie was struck with this. 'That's right,' he said. 'Could be awkward, couldn't it?'

'Certainly could,' Marianne said heartily. 'She's probably just looking for a bit of peace and quiet.'

And she could fancy a slice of that herself, to deal with the work that was piling up on her desk while she played agony aunt to her boss. And maybe the most useful thing she could do would be to find the Blu-tack, make a model, and stick drawing pins in the vital organs.

Kerr Brodie switched off his mobile, scowling. Lissa Lovatt was rapidly becoming a major problem. She'd called him from the hospital phone trolley before she'd even phoned her husband, expecting him to rush instantly to her side to check for himself that he hadn't lost her. Lost her! Chance would be a fine thing.

He'd better things to do today – these, at least, seemed to be going according to plan – and he'd tried to choke her off, but he could hear her voice rising, and she could go all dramatic on him any minute. God, he hated hysterical women!

He'd have to deal with her sooner or later, but for the moment all he came up with was laying it on thick about Matt's devotion and romantic heroism in saving her life, when Christie had left her inside the house to burn. Lissa had seized on that. It might give him a breathing space if she turned her attentions back to Matt.

The success of his other venture was more important, though. This was his chance, with the local police running round like chickens with their heads cut off and MacNee otherwise occupied. He gave a small, self-satisfied smirk.

The lads in the Isle of Man could do a quick run, removing the wretched Fergie, and once all the fuss died down, it would be back to business as usual – if Lissa wasn't planning to cause trouble. If she was . . . His scowl returned.

MacNee kept the car windows open as he drove across town. At his side, Davie kept up a constant stream of complaint and he was feeling chilly himself, but even with the flow of fresh air it was hard not to choke.

The physical cold wasn't as bad, though, as the cold misery inside. He felt guilty and ashamed, even as he told himself angrily there was nothing he could have done. Davie had deliberately disappeared from his life, but he knew how to find Tam, knew too, surely, that his son would always see to it he had a roof over his head. Still, to see his dad like this . . .

It was the drink, of course. The younger druggies wouldn't make old bones, but with this generation their addiction didn't kill them outright, just sucked the life out of them till all that was left was a pathetic husk, to be finished off by a cold night on the streets. It was amazing he'd survived this long.

You couldn't change the past. You just had to take it from here, work out what to do next. Davie needed rehab, but Tam wasn't taking him to a clinic until he could go there with dignity: cleaned up, well clad, and properly fed. He'd have to take him back to Bunty, and he had deep misgivings about that.

Not that he doubted her good heart – never that. But he'd been terrified a year ago when Bunty had a breakdown, and though she was fine now, even seemed quite like her old self, it all depended on her medication. Tam had an almost superstitious reverence for the magic pill, but he wondered now if its effects were powerful enough to counteract the stress of an alcoholic, down-and-out father-in-law. If she got that way again . . . Tam winced at the thought.

But there was no alternative. If he didn't take him straight home, Bunty would get stressed over what the neighbours would think of headlines suggesting Tam wouldn't even let his poor old father over the doorstep. No, he'd just have to do his best to cushion her from the worst effects, and keep Davie discreetly topped up for the moment. The last thing they needed was him with the screaming abdabs.

Brodie was behind it, of course. MacNee knew that, as well as if he'd heard him making the phone calls that had brought Davie to the police station. He could guess, too, what it was about: Brodie must have stuff waiting to be brought in. If MacNee was taken out, the surveillance he was prompting would slip, especially with all that was going on just now. He could read Brodie like a book.

But Brodie could read him, too. Their shared culture went bone-deep and they both knew that this duel at a distance would be fought with no holds barred – every kid on a Glasgow street knew that, in the catchphrase, there are no rules in a knife fight.

But Brodie wasn't going to win this one. This told MacNee he'd touched on a nerve, and he'd been right all along: Brodie was running drugs, and to nail him, he just had to outsmart him. If the motivation had been strong before, now it was all-consuming.

They had reached the road end. As he turned in, Tam said, with forced heartiness, 'Here we are, Dad. Bunty'll give you a hot drink to warm you up.'

'Hot drink? Och, I'll not trouble her. Just a wee tot – that'll warm me up fine.'

With a sinking heart, he drove up to the house.

Melissa Lovatt was asleep when her husband knocked tentatively on the door of the side ward. Her dark hair was loose on the pillow, and when she opened her bloodshot eyes, they looked too big for her pinched face. Seeing him she smiled tremulously.

'Lissa, I'm sorry about all this. How are you?' He took the chair by the side of the bed. An oxygen cylinder with a breathing mask stood on the other side, and she looked very fragile as she struggled up against her pillows, eyes filled with tears.

She seized his hand, and kissed it. 'You saved me!' she cried, her voice roughened and husky. 'That woman left me to burn to death, and you risked everything to save my life. Kerr told me.'

They had been in touch already, then. Lovatt said as lightly as he could, 'Oh, he was exaggerating—'

But she went on. 'Oh Matt, we've drifted, I know. But that showed me how much you really, really care – enough to die for my sake! It's not too late, is it?'

'Of course not.' What else could he say? The hollow feeling spreading through him was – inappropriate, and he fought it down. Reconciliation might – or might not – lie in the future, but for the moment, there was something that must be cleared up.

'Christie didn't leave you to burn, Lissa. She thought she had wakened you, and at that time the fire was only in the wing.'

Lissa withdrew her hand, giving him a contemptuous look. 'Matt, you know what I'm like. You know we have separate rooms because every time you turned over it woke me and I couldn't get back to sleep.'

Lovatt's impression had been that they had stopped sleeping together when the contrast between the remoteness of their daily dealings and the intimacy of the marital bed became too stark to be tolerable for either of them, but he didn't argue. Instead, he said, 'I just assumed you'd taken sleeping pills, and there was no reason for Christie to know that and try harder to wake you.'

There was a tiny pause, and then Lissa smiled. 'Oh, is that what she told you? Darling, I've said this before – she's got a massive crush on you, poor thing.' She gave a little cough, turned to pick up the glass of water at her bedside and took a sip. 'Sorry, my throat. Oh, maybe she didn't start the fire just so she could get rid of me and rescue you, but it must have seemed the ideal opportunity.'

Lovatt stared at her. 'You don't think that, do you? You often take pills—'

She cut across him. 'Well, I didn't last night. I'd had a stressful day, I was tired, so I didn't need them. I'm sorry if I'm shattering illusions about your little soldier, but I almost died, you know.'

Her voice had taken on that whingeing tone of self-pity that set his teeth on edge, but she coughed again, reminding him of what she had been through. He said lamely, 'Of course I know. And I can only be thankful you didn't.'

It was a relief when a nurse came in with a chart and some medication, giving him an excuse to leave. Lissa was likely to be released next day, apparently, and she would phone him when she knew the time.

Lovatt felt more depressed than ever as he drove back to Innellan. Surely what Lissa had said couldn't be true? There had been an unpleasant, spiteful tone to her voice and certainly he'd dismissed previous comments about Christie out of hand. He wasn't a vain man; he'd seen nothing more in their relationship than friendship between comrades.

But now he began to remember small things: her lingering over her lunch if they were in the kitchen alone; her going on the rounds with him if she'd nothing else to do, but never going with Kerr; her pressing him to come to the pub the other night when it was obvious Lissa wouldn't go . . .

He'd had a lot of experience in assessing young people, and he'd been good at it. You had to be, in his job, otherwise your men ended up dead. Christie had always impressed him as a great kid, straight as a die, the best sort of soldier: cheerful, competent and certainly brave – she'd risked her life to stop Rudolf being shot.

Yes, she had. But that wasn't exactly rational, was it? And there was plenty of evidence that the ideal qualities for a soldier weren't always ideal when it came to civilian life, especially after the sort of experiences combat put them through. Achieving your objective was drilled into you from day one, and if you weren't seeing things quite straight . . .

He couldn't afford to think like that. He put it firmly out of his mind; he'd plenty of other things to worry about. Georgia had offered them her spare rooms for as long as they needed them, but they couldn't impose on her indefinitely. Then there would be insurance claims, too, and the work of the farm still had to go on.

The gawpers, at least, had lost interest by the time he got back to Innellan. A policeman was still on duty by the blue-and-white tape, but the site was quiet. A couple of firemen were checking on loose masonry, under the supervision of Williamson, the fire chief, but all the engines had gone.

The smell of smoke, and the stark skeleton of the wing, in its sea of mud, brought back the horror. Lovatt's stomach churned, and when Williamson came over to him, it took a mighty effort to make the appropriately grateful noises.

The fire chief was almost offensively cheerful. 'Yes, they did a great job, the lads. Of course, the wing's a hazard – have to be demolished as a priority – but we've saved the main house for you. Get the joiners to block it off, and it's a cleaning job after that, once the worst of the smoke has cleared.'

'Something to be grateful for, certainly,' Lovatt said. It sounded as if he, at least, would be able to camp there before long. He walked round to the back where once his office had been, while Williamson explained exactly what had happened.

It was more than he could bear to hear just at the moment. He made an excuse as soon as he decently could, and was turning to go when his eye was caught by a sturdy metal cabinet standing with the rest of the rubble, still intact though warped and twisted by the heat.

He pointed to it. 'There's some dangerous stuff in there,' he said. 'Veterinary medicines – it'll need proper disposal. And there would be a metal bin as well, with hazardous waste – skull and crossbones on the top.'

'Thanks, sir. I'll see to that.' Williamson walked over to give the instructions as Lovatt plodded off towards the Smugglers Inn.

'No sign of any bin, Chief,' one of the firemen called. 'I've raked through the ashes, but it's not there.'

'Not a lot we can do, then,' Williamson said. 'They carted away a lot of stuff already. That's fine, lads. Finish up, and I'll get you back for your dinner.'

CHAPTER SIXTEEN

The press conference went badly. DI Fleming had appeared, along with the press officer, to explain that DS MacNee would have been there himself but had taken his father home to be cared for, though the press officer had warned that this wouldn't go down well. The press liked their prey served up fresh and preferably bleeding, she said, but conceded that MacNee in his present state of mind was unlikely to do himself any favours.

Fleming's explanation provoked a ripple of scornful laughter. 'Bit late for the caring son bit now, isn't it?' one hack sneered, and it was clear that as a plea in mitigation, the carefully worded statement had failed to temper the sentences they would write.

At least press conferences didn't last for ever. Fleming was figuratively mopping her brow as she escaped, but frying pans and fire were in her mind as she headed towards the super's office for the second time that morning.

The first time hadn't been much fun either. Donald Bailey, who tended to take professional problems as a personal insult, was tetchy about events at Innellan. He had been particularly irritated that the recent incidents, unconnected to the murder, that had caught the media's attention were regularly giving them material to run the story for yet another day.

'What I want to know, Marjory, is what's *behind* it all,' he had said, sitting back in his chair and steepling his fingers across his well-rounded stomach. 'And it's not enough for you to say you don't know. It's your job to know.' His plump cheeks were pouched by a moue of disapproval.

Fleming looked at his corrugated brow, which seemed to have an ambition to reach the back of his head, and found herself eying the heavy paperweight, topped with crossed golf clubs and an artistically placed ball, which lay on his desk with a certain longing.

But she said, in placatory tones, 'We're doing our level best to find that out, Donald,' and proceeded to give an extensive, detailed and boring report on deployment, until he showed signs of restiveness and interrupted, 'Yes, yes, I'll leave that to you. Let me know immediately of any developments. The chief constable is anxious about it, you know.'

Fleming had left, congratulating herself on having sustained only surface wounds. She hadn't, however, reckoned on returning so soon with more bad news. Bailey's fear of hostile headlines was all but pathological, and this sort of tabloid scandal would leave him irascible and unreasonable for days.

'Gardening leave,' was his immediate reaction. 'I can't imagine how the man could let this happen to his own father—'

'I did explain—' Fleming put in, but he cut across her.

'I'm not interested in the sordid details. Just see he's off the premises for the next bit. Put out a statement that he's been granted compassionate leave – that should put us in the clear.'

She was dismayed. 'Donald, we're under strength already. We've three fewer detectives than we had this time last year—'

'In a time of economic stringency,' he said portentously, 'we all have to exert ourselves to work that bit harder. The job has to be done, Marjory, and it's your responsibility to see that it is. But I don't want to see MacNee again till this blows over. And that's final.'

Trying vainly to think of an instance of Bailey exerting himself – or even missing a single golf game – Fleming left muttering resentfully. MacNee was her most effective officer and she needed all the manpower she could muster at the moment.

There were half a dozen messages waiting when she got back, but she didn't sit down at her desk. She went to the window and looked out at the plane trees, the leaves turning golden now, and down on to the busy high street, without really seeing the townsfolk of Kirkluce going about their daily business. Unconsciously, she was tapping her finger on her front teeth.

She was getting a very, very bad feeling about Innellan. The island, with its strange voices and its nasty secret. A dangerous animal set loose. A house burning down.

It was easy enough to find a rationale for the latter two, especially in the light of a campaign of persecution. Macdonald and Campbell were, she hoped, even now giving the Donaldsons and Sorley a hard time. But perhaps that was too easy?

Andrew Smith. The Manchester force had done an official check now, but it turned up no more than Carter had told her informally: there was no Andrew Smith on the Missing Persons Register and media publicity hadn't produced anyone claiming to know an Andrew Smith whose body this might have been, apart from a few of the usual nutters who could be discounted. If he'd had a more distinctive name it would have helped, but even now they weren't in a position to flesh out the bones which had been stripped of everything.

Was there a pattern to the events, a pattern she just wasn't seeing? If there was, she reflected grimly, the next figure in the tapestry was unpredictable – unpredictable, and almost certainly ugly.

Hatred. The word suddenly came into Fleming's head. Hatred had left Andrew Smith to die a hideous death. Fire-raising as an expression of hatred and anger was a psychological cliché. The stag incident had risked innocent lives to strike at Matt Lovatt.

She needed to talk to him again. She knew what he would say – that it was the result of the Donaldsons' grudge against him. Certainly, there was precedent: over on the west coast a house belonging to an impresario had been burnt to the ground a while ago, and that was almost certainly local resentment. They'd never managed to find enough evidence among the ashes for a prosecution, though, which wasn't an encouraging thought.

Despite that, something was telling her she needed to dig deeper with Lovatt. He was a strange man, with what popular psychology liked to term 'issues', and certainly MacNee had thought there was something going on beneath that polite and pleasant exterior.

MacNee. She was going to have to phone and tell him of Bailey's ukase. Could she see him meekly accepting it? Could she hell! So she'd then have to spend time and energy making sure neither the superintendent nor the press found out that he hadn't.

'Just routine questions, miss, if you don't mind.' Macdonald and Campbell introduced themselves, and Elena Tindall waved them inside.

'I don't think I can tell you much, but you'd better come in.'

A good-looking woman, Macdonald thought, as they went into the sitting room with its huge window on to the bay: slim, blonde, elegant even in casual jeans and long-sleeved white T-shirt. Good-looking, yes, but remote, forbidding – no, that wasn't the word. Guarded, that was it. She seemed on edge, with a tic flickering just above her left eye. No wonder, with all that had been going on; it was surprising that she hadn't packed in the holiday and gone home.

They took her name, Natalie Thomson, and her address, 14 Church Street, Solihull, and her age, thirty. Macdonald saw Campbell raise his eyebrows fractionally at this, and he'd have thought she was older himself. Older, but well preserved, though he didn't think she'd thank him for that.

'Here on holiday?' he asked, and she nodded.

'Hope this hasn't ruined it completely.'

Elena gave a small, tight smile. 'It hasn't exactly improved it. But at least it's a break – and the weather hasn't been too bad. I've had lots of long walks.'

'What do you do?'

Campbell's blunt question seemed to take her by surprise, and Macdonald saw her eyes flicker. She fiddled with one of the bracelets she was wearing, intricately engraved silver cuffs.

'I'm . . . I'm in the fashion business,' she said, and moved on rapidly. 'Anyway, I expect you want to know about last night.'

'If you don't mind.'

She didn't invite them to sit down, as if to make sure the interview was kept short. 'I'd gone to bed quite early. The sirens woke me and I came through here to see what was happening. The whole sky was lit up – I didn't put on the light or anything, just went over to the window.'

'A good viewpoint,' Macdonald said. 'Did you notice anyone moving about?'

'The fire engines had just arrived and there was a crowd gathering. I watched for a while, but I knew I wouldn't get back to sleep so I flung on some clothes and went down. Just about everyone in the village must have been there, I'd guess.

'Once we heard everyone was safe and they took the woman off in an ambulance, we all drifted away. That's all, I'm afraid. How is she?'

'The statement from the hospital is that she's making a good recovery and should be discharged shortly,' Macdonald said. 'Just a couple more questions. Were you in the village earlier yesterday evening?'

'No. You perhaps know I had an unfortunate encounter with a stag earlier this week and it's left me a bit nervous about going out at night.'

Macdonald nodded sympathetically. 'I can imagine. So – nothing suspicious that you've seen? Nothing out of the ordinary that might relate to this?'

Elena's dark-blue eyes met his squarely. 'Nothing. Sorry. Except . . . well, it's probably irrelevant . . .'

'Yes?' he prompted.

'It was just . . . last night, when I got back after the fire, it sounded as if they were having a party in the chalet along the road, and I thought it was a funny thing to do just then.'

Macdonald and Campbell exchanged glances. 'Did you see who it was?' Macdonald asked.

'They came past the window – the man who seems to be living there and two other men, one of them quite a bit older, I'd say.'

Macdonald nodded. 'Sorley and the Donaldsons that'd be. Thanks, that's very helpful. Nothing else? Well, if anything occurs to you, however trivial, don't hesitate to get in touch.'

'Of course.' She went towards the door to show them out.

'Andrew Smith,' Campbell said.

She stopped as he spoke, then reached into her pocket and took out her mobile phone. 'Sorry,' she said. 'Just a moment.' She checked it, then turned round saying, 'Sorry again. I've been expecting a message. What did you say – Andrew Smith?'

When Campbell didn't speak, Macdonald said, 'Do you know anyone called that?'

Elena looked politely puzzled. 'Not that I can think of, but it's a common enough name. Is it someone in the village?'

'Just routine. Thanks for your time, Ms Thomson.'

Walking back to the car, Macdonald said, 'Didn't hear the phone ring, did you? On vibrate, I suppose.'

'Poor lady,' Campbell said unexpectedly.

Macdonald stared at him. 'Why?'

'Cuffs,' he said. 'Elaborate, with what she's wearing?'

Macdonald looked blank. 'Were they? I don't know what's fashionable.'

'Covers the wounds. She'd old scars right up her arm. Silvery marks – saw them when her sleeve slid up.'

'I'm sorry, Tam, but that's the edict,' Fleming said into the phone, bracing herself for MacNee's response. To her surprise, it wasn't as violent as she had feared.

'It's maybe just as well,' he said. 'It'll give me time to get things sorted out. You did tell the press I've been taken off duty for two or three days?'

'Yes – yes, of course.' She was a little puzzled by his tone, but she went on, 'Anyway, how's Bunty taken it?'

MacNee's voice warmed. 'She's great! You know the way she is when they bring in a stray dog? Well, she just took over – got the clothes off him, dumped him straight into a bath. He's sitting by the fire now, looking a bit confused, right enough, but he's supping some broth. I've given him a wee dram to keep him quiet.'

Fleming laughed. 'Bunty's something else! But Tam, I have to warn you – the press coverage won't be good. We did our best for you, but—'

'Och, I just won't read them and I'll see Bunty doesn't either. It'll blow over.'

'That's the way to take it. I'll call you when Bailey's forgotten about it.'

Fleming rang off feeling bemused. Tam philosophical about this – cheerful, even? She frowned. Oh well, maybe it was just that he was relieved to have got his father back and needed the time to make arrangements, as he had said.

Or maybe not.

MacNee gave a little smile as he put the phone down. No duties, no supervision. A free agent, eh? That would do nicely. Brodie wouldn't know what hit him.

Knocking on the door had produced no response at Derek Sorley's much scruffier chalet. Campbell crossed the rough, weedy patch in front of it and peered in the picture window.

'Not in.'

'He's avoiding us – the Donaldsons certainly are. As the wife was telling us they were away for the day looking at stock I could almost see her nose growing. I'd like to bring all three of them in, but we haven't a scrap of evidence to justify it. Sorley may be quite innocently at work.'

'Has to come home eventually.'

'So do we. There's no overtime on this one. We'd better get back and report to Big Marge – not that we've much to report on.'

'Not much,' Campbell said.

Macdonald gave him a sharp look, then he reddened. He said abruptly, 'Nothing to signify. And we've nothing on Andrew Smith either, and the uniforms knocking doors only got blank looks all round.

'I wonder if Georgia knows where Sorley works? We could call in on the way back.'

'Reckon she'd do us another sandwich?'

'Don't even ask. That was a favour. Bag of crisps, if you must.'

Georgia, though happy to supply the crisps, could only tell them that Sorley drove a delivery van for a stationery firm in Kirkcudbright, so there wasn't much point in going the long way round to look for someone who could be anywhere across the county.

'Bit of a wasted morning, that,' Macdonald said as they drove back to headquarters. 'No progress at all. I feel a bit dispirited, to tell you the truth.'

'I feel hungry,' Campbell said. 'Hope we get back before all the bridies have gone.'

From the window where Fergie sat, listlessly observing the outside world through the gap in the slats, he saw Brodie come down to the jetty on the mainland and climb into the small boat.

His heart gave a little frightened thud as it always did when Brodie appeared. He was quivering with nerves today – when the sirens last night had wakened him, he'd thought he'd have a heart attack. Seeing the house on fire had given him a terrible nightmare afterwards, that the bothy too was ablaze. He woke, screaming, and then was afraid all over again that someone might have heard him. He hated this place. It terrified him.

If it went on, he could go mental. He was halfway there already, sleeping most of the time, though somehow he'd no energy for his workout. He got panic attacks sometimes, when he felt he couldn't breathe, and he found himself thinking weird thoughts, like there was someone lurking in the shadows so he was scared to look over his shoulder.

Going out at night, though, didn't scare Fergie the way it had at first. The deer, he realised, paid no attention to him, and he got so stiff from lack of exercise that he was desperate to stretch his legs. He didn't go far from the bothy, though, or into the woods with the noises that had spooked him. He usually went up the hill behind and over to the back of the island, passing the old graves at the top with a shudder. He'd plucked up courage to look at them once, then wished he hadn't; there was a newish one there, a small one. Sharing the island with some dead kid! He'd run all the way back after that.

Would it be so bad being in jail? He'd have company, and the worst would have happened so the gnawing fear of discovery would be over. The worst? Who was he kidding? The worst would be when Brodie found out he'd given himself up, because he'd never forgive him. Things were bound to slip out when they grilled him, and he'd no doubt Brodie's reach could stretch to any jail Fergie was likely to find himself in. It might be easier just to top himself now and get it over with.

He watched bleakly as Brodie moored the boat and he went over to unlock the door. At least it would mean new scoff – he'd finished all the fresh stuff.

It was better than that, though. As Brodie dumped a carrier bag on the floor, he said, 'I've good news for you. They're going to risk a run in the next day or two, when conditions are right. Don't know when, but they won't hang around. You'll have to be ready.'

'No problem, Sarge!' Fergie hadn't smiled since he got here, but now he was grinning from ear to ear, and when Brodie left, he went straight to pack his meagre belongings into a carrier bag. He wasn't taking any chances.

Macdonald and Campbell had given Fleming their disappointing report and she was brooding on it now. She hadn't expected an eyewitness to fire-raising at an isolated house surrounded by trees in a quiet village in the middle of the night, but it was still depressing that the only interesting information should be that Sorley and the Donaldsons seemed to have been celebrating afterwards. Which might be nasty, but was hardly a criminal offence.

She hadn't exactly expected information about Andrew Smith to emerge either, but she'd allowed herself to be hopeful. MacNee had been so certain that there must be a link with the village, and she'd come round to agreeing with him.

Had he been wrong, though? Was this something that had its roots in Smith's activities in Manchester after all? Villains, too, had been children once; perhaps, fifty years ago, there had been some kid staying in a caravan – maybe organising his own gang even then, getting his hand in with a spot of extortion and shoplifting from the Johnnie-a'-things . . .

No, she was being silly now. But what other possibility was there? Certainly the village folk were a close-mouthed lot, but surely they couldn't all be in a conspiracy to conceal any knowledge of the man?

What would Tam say? On an impulse, Fleming picked up the phone, but it was Bunty who answered. Tam was out, but when Fleming asked after Davie, she told her he was having a wee nap, poor old chap, and she'd have his tea ready for him when he woke up.

Fleming smiled as she rang off. Bunty sounded to be in her element; whether Davie liked it or not she'd have him clean and respectable. She'd have him trundling round the coffee morning circuit yet, though Fleming did wonder whether, after the life he'd led, this would be the way Davie would choose to spend his declining years.

And what was Tam doing? Maybe he was sorting things out, just as he had said. She shouldn't be so cynical.

Fleming had just started on her clogged inbox, doing her pea-shelling act with the emails, when DC Campbell appeared. Fleming was surprised to see him; it was only quarter of an hour since he and Macdonald had left.

'Ewan!' she said. 'Problem? Take a seat.' There was something about Campbell's customary economy with words that made it catching.

'Need to warn you, boss. Christie Jack – Macdonald's not sound.'

'Not *sound*?'

'She could've left Melissa Lovatt asleep on purpose. Door was bolted – obvious that no one got out before her and Lovatt. Claims she'd a flashback – didn't notice. Doesn't know what happened.'

Fleming wasn't sure she'd ever heard him utter so many consecutive sentences. 'And you don't believe her?'

'Don't believe, don't disbelieve. Point is, Andy believes her. Or says he does. Trying to shield her.'

'Right.' Fleming had seen the way Macdonald looked at Christie Jack. She'd seemed a nice enough girl, but then she'd never even spoken to her. 'You think he should be kept out of anything to do with her?'

Campbell nodded. 'And there's this.' Campbell handed her a printout. 'Louise Hepburn's interview with Mrs Lovatt.'

'Oh yes.' Fleming had made a point of noticing the young DC since MacNee's linguistic flourish. 'Oh yes, I remember she was tasked to go to the hospital. Interesting?'

He handed it to her without reply, and she speed-read it. Yes, it was interesting: Melissa Lovatt was stating that she hadn't taken sleeping pills, and was not only accusing Christie Jack of leaving her to die in the fire, but of setting it in the first place for that very purpose.

Fleming groaned. 'Oh dear. So are you saying we have to take Andy off the case?'

'Not my job.'

He was right, of course; she had no business asking him. 'Leave it with me. But when next Christie Jack's interviewed it won't be Andy who does it.'

Campbell nodded, and left.

'Don't bring me problems, bring me solutions,' was a favourite phrase of Bailey's and for once Fleming felt in sympathy with him. It seemed to be nothing but problems today – MacNee banished, Macdonald kneecapped. Whatever next?

She'd told Macdonald and Campbell to call in Sorley and the Donaldsons tomorrow for questioning; what the neighbour had said about them celebrating was justification enough. She wanted to talk to Lovatt herself, so she could speak to Christie Jack at the same time.

She glanced again at the report in her lap. It was competently presented and Hepburn seemed to have asked the questions she'd have asked herself. MacNee wasn't often complimentary about the younger detectives – *au contraire*, as he would probably start saying now, after his French lessons. There was certainly no one else she'd felt tempted to bring on to her own elite team – perhaps Hepburn deserved a chance to show her mettle.

Sorley drove back from work in a gleeful mood that afternoon, despite his lingering headache. He was willing to bet that, rough as he had felt today, Steve would be feeling worse. Driving up the track to the chalets, he glanced across at the farmhouse, now all but a ruin, with a satisfied smile. No one could live in a place like that.

Right enough, Lovatt didn't give in easily. It had been spelt out that he wasn't welcome and anyone else would have left long ago. Still, he'd have too much to think about now to care who was walking around his island, and if the stubborn bastard did decide to rebuild and carry on farming, that would be Steve's problem, not his own.

In any case, Steve would get his share. All Sorley needed was half an hour, an hour at most, up by the graves with a pickaxe and spade. Gold, the metal detector had said. Gold.

He could slip across today, even. He'd seen police around the village, but not near the island. He could see the causeway now—

Submerged. He swore under his breath. From the look of it, the tide wouldn't be low enough for hours. He couldn't go across in the dark; a light up at the graves would be visible all round the bay, and anyway, if you couldn't see where you were going you could break your leg on the causeway. He'd have to get hold of the tide tables.

With the last of the crates of prawns landed, Cal Findlay's deckhand sketched a salute to his skipper and headed thankfully for home. Cal was a moody sod at the best of times, but today he'd been downright dangerous. OK, a line had got fouled as he brought in a catch, but the way Cal had reacted he'd been afraid he was going to be chucked overboard.

He'd look for another job, if there were any. Which there weren't.

'Oooh, teacher's pet!'

Louise Hepburn's lips tightened as her colleague made the barbed remark on the way out after the briefing, but she'd learnt, with some difficulty, that it didn't pay to lose your temper. She said lightly, 'Oh, give her an apple and she'll eat out of your hand,' and walked on to the CID room, doing her best to conceal her satisfaction.

She was dark-haired, with dark eyes and olive skin like her French mother, but her features owed nothing to her Gallic ancestry: she had her late father's strong nose and a very square chin. Combative by nature, she'd learnt to stick it out at primary school in Stranraer where 'Froggie' was the least objectionable of the insults flung at her. She'd taken on her tormentors fearlessly and gained nervous respect.

Hepburn was sorry for Tam MacNee, but she was ambitious and MacNee's misfortune was her own big chance to mark her card with the boss, if she got it right. She was looking forward, a little anxiously, to the interviews next day.

She had broken her own rule and bought some wine today, and a half-bottle of good brandy too. She needed something warming, as if it could reach through to the cold centre of her being. She felt . . . hollow, that was it. As if there was nothing there any more, except the coldness.

As darkness crept in over the sea, a stealthy shade at a time until the silver-grey had deepened to charcoal and the charcoal to black, Elena Tindall sat in her chair by the window, her shoulders hunched and her slim hands cupped round a cheap wine glass to warm the brandy it held. Her hands were icy, though, and no fragrant bouquet rose from it as she swirled it round. She drank it anyway, in a gulp at first, then, with conscious restraint, a sip at a time.

The island had almost vanished into the gathering dusk. The island . . . She twisted the bracelet on her left wrist, and winced.

A beam of light scattered the darkness as a car came up the track. Elena shrank back instinctively, but it swept on. Someone going to visit weasel-face, probably. The Donaldsons? Her skin crawled at the thought.

Her mobile rang. Eddie, of course; she wasn't in the mood to speak to him tonight, but she dared not ignore it. Asking lots of questions about what he was doing had kept him happy at first but now his impatience was starting to show and his enquiries about her own activities were more probing. Tonight she hadn't the energy for a long, fencing conversation.

He wanted to know what the weather was like. Was he sitting with a weather chart in front of him, looking for clues?

'Changeable,' she said, then after a minute broke into a question about whether she'd taken the right clothes with her. 'Sorry, darling, would you mind if we didn't talk long tonight? I've got a splitting headache and I just want to take a couple of paracetamol and go to bed.'

He was all concern, as Elena had intended him to be, and rang off. She sank back into her chair with a groan. It hadn't altogether been a lie about the headache, but it wasn't going to stop her finishing the brandy in her glass. Then she'd switch to wine – less likely to leave her totally incapacitated in the morning.

It was a question of nerve. All this – she mustn't let it destroy her. She must use the cold core to freeze the questioning, freeze the fear.

She hadn't achieved that yet, though. The hairs on the back of her neck rose as she heard a stealthy sound outside, then another, and another – footsteps! She had seen nothing; whoever was there must have come up the grass on the far side of the path to the chalet. She was holding her breath when the knock came on the door – a soft, tentative tapping.

If she slipped to the floor, here in the darkened chalet, she would be invisible from the window. But it was as if she was paralysed: her limbs refused to obey her, she was having to remember to breathe—

The tapping came again. And then, a low voice, 'Are you there? Open the door.'

Fear gave way to anger, and brought her to her feet. How dare he frighten her? She opened the door.

'Cal! You scared me half to death, creeping up like that.'

'Didn't . . . didn't want people to see me, and talk,' he mumbled.

'Then for goodness' sake don't stand out there. Come in.' Elena made to put on the light, but he stopped her.

'Curtains first.'

She nodded and went to the window to shut out the night. He flicked the switch and she stared as she saw him. He was looking terrible, his dark hair wild and his eyes bloodshot. She thought he had probably been drinking, though he wasn't actually drunk.

'What's happened, then?'

'Nothing – everything.' He made a helpless gesture with his hands.

His very weakness strengthened her. 'Sit down,' she ordered him then went to the kitchen, and came back with another glass. She slopped in some brandy and set it down on the table by the window.

'Drink that,' she said.

Cal didn't sit down. He was standing twitching; he took a couple of staggering steps towards her then grabbed hold of her, burying his head in her shoulder.

'You're driving me mad,' he sobbed. 'I can't take this.'

Elena stiffened at his touch. She had accustomed herself to Eddie, but she had not been held by another man since their marriage, and even being air-kissed by a casual acquaintance was uncomfortable. Yet she overcame her revulsion, softened her rigid arms to cradle him and, her fair head against his dark, rocked him like a baby.

'Shh, shh, it's all right. It's all right.'

* * *

When the phone rang at one o'clock, Marjory Fleming was instantly awake. She'd been almost expecting something else at Innellan and she felt the familiar lurch in her stomach as she braced herself for more bad news. At her side, Bill stirred a little in his sleep, but accustomed to such interruptions didn't surface as Fleming answered the phone.

It wasn't what she expected to hear. Her face went pale as she listened, struggling to absorb the necessary details, and she had to make two attempts at ringing off.

Then she turned to her sleeping husband, shaking his shoulder. 'Bill! Bill! Wake up! It's Cat! It's terrible!'

CHAPTER SEVENTEEN

Afterwards, it came back to Marjory in flashes, in daytime nightmares: the grim drive through the darkness up to Glasgow, neither of them speaking and her own hands gripping the wheel so tightly that the knuckles shone white under the bleak lights of the motorway; the unnatural quiet of a busy hospital at night, familiar from a thousand professional visits, yet made ominous by her own terror; the confusion as neither she nor Bill could remember the directions they had been given, blundering through half-lit corridors into dead ends, shivering with cold and shock, and always the beat in their heads – 'Hurry, hurry, hurry, before it's too late.'

They found the ward at last, and a nurse showed them into the families' waiting room and said a doctor would be with them shortly. Marjory refused tea; she knew her teeth would clatter against the mug. Bill didn't seem to have heard the offer.

There was another woman there, a woman with disordered greying hair and clothes that looked to have been thrown on at random. Called out of her bed as they had been, no doubt, and from her drawn face she too was obviously under strain. Marjory managed something that was more of a rictus than a smile.

To her surprise, she encountered something close to hostility. 'Are you Catriona Fleming's parents?' the woman asked abruptly.

Frowning, Marjory said, 'Yes, we are. Who are you?'

'Ann Bradshaw. I'm supposed to be your daughter's academic adviser.'

A red flush of anger came to Bill's pale cheeks. 'Supposed to be? You mean you've failed? My daughter could die because the woman who was *supposed* to be looking out for her welfare didn't bother?' He was shouting at her, shaking with emotion, his fists bunched at his sides.

'I can understand that you're in a state of distress, Mr Fleming,' the woman said frostily, 'but shouting won't help. Perhaps if you would sit down, and let me explain—'

'Explain!' Bill exploded. '*Explain!*'

Marjory, with a growing sense of dismay, touched his arm. 'We need to know exactly what happened, Bill.'

For a second he glared at the hand on his sleeve as if he might strike it off, then took a deep, shuddering breath and allowed his wife to pull him towards a chair.

Focus, Marjory told herself. Try to block off the picture of your daughter slipping away in a room somewhere near here, the body systems closing down . . . Focus on what this woman is telling us. It would be easier if she didn't feel so cold – was there no heating in here? Trying to control the shake in her voice, Marjory said, 'What happened, Ms Bradshaw?'

'Dr Bradshaw. As they presumably told you, Catriona was brought in with an overdose. She collapsed at a nightclub. Fortunately there were other students with her who knew who she was, and contacted me. At one o'clock in the morning.' She didn't sound thrilled about that.

Bill bristled. 'My daughter doesn't take drugs,' he said flatly.

How many times had Marjory heard that from overwrought,

naive parents? She wouldn't have described herself as naive, though; she would swear she would have noticed the signs if Cat hadn't been clean until now.

'I think it may be a new development,' she said. 'Has Cat been finding it difficult to adjust to university life?'

'I wouldn't know, Mrs Fleming.' As Bill's face got redder than ever, Dr Bradshaw hurried on, 'She didn't register. I left a note saying that I needed to see her, but got no reply. She hadn't signed on for lectures, and she wasn't in on the three occasions when I went to the hall of residence looking for her, and she ignored the other notes I left, asking her to get in touch. She seems to have dropped out before she ever started.'

Bill staggered, then collapsed backwards into a chair as if he'd been punched. The angry colour drained from his face, leaving him looking so grey that for a terrified moment Marjory thought he'd had a heart attack. But he said, brokenly, 'Dropped out? But this is what she's wanted to do, all her life! She's worked so hard—'

'Will Irvine,' Marjory said suddenly. 'Her boyfriend – is he here?'

Ann Bradshaw shook her head. 'Not in the group she was with. I have to say, she doesn't keep the best company.'

Will and Cat had always been inseparable. Something had gone wrong, badly wrong . . . And then Marjory remembered: Mary Irvine – she hadn't stopped to chat the other day. She'd thought it was strange at the time, but if Will had dumped Cat, that would explain it.

What a time to choose, when Cat would be feeling insecure and vulnerable anyway! Her dreams of university had all been of being there with Will, studying together and moving on to happy-ever-after. Hot rage grew in Marjory's heart at his callousness. If Cat died—

She mustn't let herself think that. Cat wasn't going to die. Every weekend, in hospitals up and down the country, kids were brought in with overdoses – Marjory had seen plenty, and the medics were brilliant at saving them from the results of their folly.

Not all of them, though. Marjory felt a huge, hard lump in her throat, felt the back of her eyes prickle – but she wasn't going to cry in front of this unfriendly, judgemental woman.

'I appreciate that you've been dragged out in the middle of the night, Dr Bradshaw,' she said coldly, 'and I should think you get tired of dealing with students who take drugs. But you are so obviously unsympathetic that I'm finding it very difficult to be in the same room with you. I'm sure you would rather be back in bed.'

Dr Bradshaw got up, running a hand over her face. Her eyes, Marjory noticed, were red-rimmed with tiredness. 'Indeed I would,' she said. 'I'm concerned for Catriona, of course I am. I apologise for sounding abrupt. But I'd never met her, and I spent most of last night here with one of my students who developed leukaemia last term. He died early this morning.

'So, yes, I'm finding it hard to drum up sympathy for someone risking her healthy life for the sake of what she no doubt saw as a good time. I hope you have better news shortly.' She went out.

Marjory hung her head. She would have said she couldn't feel any lower, but now she did. Bill, still slumped in his chair, was weeping quietly, and she couldn't stop herself. Tears were rolling down her cheeks when the door opened.

The registrar was young, and he looked tired as well. 'Mr and Mrs Fleming? Your daughter will be fine. We'll keep her in for another hour or two, but then you can take her home.'

The relief was overwhelming, but his tone was cool too, and Marjory remembered wretchedly how often she had felt impatient when it came to these self-inflicted disasters. How different it all looked from the other side! And now, for the first time in her life, she understood how it felt to dread the power of the law.

'Thank you, Doctor. We're truly, truly grateful. But will this . . . does this mean a report to the police?'

'Not this time.' His tone implied that there might well be a next, and worse time. 'It was mephedrone – they call it bubbles, or miaow-miaow. A so-called legal high, though it'll be classified very shortly. You can see her now, if you like.'

Marjory said awkwardly, 'I'm very sorry, Doctor. I know every parent says this, but she really hasn't been someone involved in the drugs scene.'

He smiled, briefly. 'To be fair, from the effect it had and the amount she had taken, I don't think she was habituated. Perhaps this will have given her enough of a fright to stop her trying it again.'

'We'll see to that.' Bill was on his feet and his colour had returned.

Marjory wanted to believe him, but her confidence was shaken. Cat's reaction to her splintered dreams was unpredictable. She could turn her back on everything and look again for the solution she had chosen as a way of escape.

Cat was dozing when they reached the ward, her face leaden and tear-stained, and Marjory stood looking down at her precious daughter with both pity and fear in her heart.

DS Tam MacNee was tired. He gave a yawn which threatened to dislocate his jaw, but there were hours still ahead before he could abandon his self-imposed vigil. He'd tuned the car radio to a sports chat station, but eventually even he felt it was telling him more than he wanted to know about football, and resorted to his own thoughts for company.

How often, he wondered, had Rabbie himself mounted this sort of coastline watch when he was an exciseman? Maybe there had been a path right along here even then, at the end of the track past the chalets and caravans, where MacNee had parked. It would be colder, if you'd only a horse instead of a modern car, but Rabbie had certainly taken quite a bit of satisfaction in the arrests. Maybe it was a wee bit at odds with the image he'd liked to present, but MacNee wasn't going to attribute hypocrisy, that most despised of Scottish vices, to his idol. He'd prefer to think of Rabbie having been a sort of eighteenth-century detective, doing the job MacNee was doing now and passing the hours of boredom in thought.

He wasn't sure the boss had believed him, but he had, indeed, done a bit of sorting out of his personal problem this afternoon. He'd had a chat with the doctor, who'd given him advice about a clinic and also about the level of topping-up needed meantime to keep Davie on an even keel. But the doctor had also warned him that Davie had to want to cooperate for rehab to be effective, and that was something MacNee didn't want to think about.

The other thing he'd done was to drop in on the excise boys at Stranraer. They were more than interested in what MacNee had to tell them, and happy to have a cutter on standby, ready to be called in at speed over these next few nights when there was no moonlight and a forecast of cloud cover – smugglers' weather.

If MacNee was right in his analysis, Brodie would be desperate to get a shipment in while the police had other things on hand and MacNee was apparently tied up dealing with his father. He'd be under pressure because he'd have known it wouldn't be long before MacNee was back on his case. So – tonight, tomorrow night?

At one stage he had thought he caught a flicker of movement on the island, but it was so dark that even with his powerful binoculars it was impossible to see clearly on land. It could well have been one of the deer anyway, and though he watched for a while he didn't see it again. It was a boat he was looking for, which would be clear enough against the paler sea, but none had appeared.

So not tonight, then. The red streaks of dawn were appearing, and with another enormous yawn MacNee turned the car and bumped off down the track again.

With his mind totally taken up with the prospect of revenge, it was only as he drove back, seeing the burnt-out wing of the farmhouse below, that he spared it a thought. He had just driven past Sorley's chalet, and he had little difficulty in attributing blame. What could be easier? A quick trip down with – what, petrol, paraffin? Then straight back up again before anyone knew what was going on. But it was one thing to see how it could be done, and another to be able to prove that it had been.

'Sorry, love,' Georgia Stanley said, 'Matt's not here. Round the farm, maybe, or over at the house.'

'Right,' DC Hepburn said. 'I'll go and have a look for him.'

She had been cast down at first about Fleming's absence this morning, but thinking quickly, she'd made her pitch with Sergeant Naismith to do the interviews herself before she could be allocated elsewhere. Naismith, looking frayed round the edges this morning, had nodded it through.

Her plan had been to interview Lovatt first and Christie Jack after that, but she changed her mind.

'Christie Jack – is she around?'

The woman looked at her doubtfully. 'Well, she is, yes, but she's not herself – terribly shaken, poor lamb. They interviewed her yesterday and that upset her. Do you really have to put her through it again today?'

Once you can fake sincerity, someone had once told her, you've got it made. Helped by soft brown eyes, Hepburn had made the skill her own.

'Sorry,' she said, sounding genuinely regretful. 'Afraid I do.'

Georgia sighed. 'Oh, I know you've got a difficult job. Through here, then. I'll bring you a cup of coffee. And maybe you could get her to eat a biscuit, if I brought some.'

Her response was non-committal, and her mind was elsewhere as she followed Georgia through to the back of the house. Psychology had been one of the subjects she'd studied at uni, and she knew the characteristic profile for an arsonist: disturbed background, insecure, impulsive; often a loner, lacking love and support; suffering deep frustration; looking for revenge, perhaps, as some sort of remedy for emotional distress.

Melissa Lovatt had been eloquent about Christie, and what she had said squared with most of that. When you pitched in an element of post-traumatic stress, the girl was almost a textbook case.

Though it was a mild, sunny morning, Christie was sitting forlornly by the fire, her hands held out to it as if she were cold. Her eyes were blank and she had huge dark circles underneath them.

'DC Hepburn.' She showed her card.

'Another one,' Christie said dully. 'I told them everything I could remember yesterday.'

'I know. Sorry to have to bother you again, when you must be feeling pretty rubbish. Terrible experience.' She had a very easy manner; she sat down on the chair on the other side of the fire and leant towards Christie, those sympathetic eyes fixed on her face.

She gave a little shudder, but she responded to the tone. 'Yes – yes, it was. Terrible.'

'Don't worry. I'm here to have a background chat, not to give you the third degree. Just to get a clearer picture, OK?' She smiled, got a wan smile in return and went on, 'It's tough this should happen just when you were starting to get over your war experiences.'

'*Was.*' Christie sounded bitter. 'They probably told you I had a flashback after I got Matt out of the fire.'

Hepburn nodded, but she wasn't interested in flashbacks at the moment. 'Sort of thing you're trained to do for a comrade, I suppose,' she prompted.

'Yes,' Christie agreed, a bit too eagerly. 'That's exactly right. And of course I tried to rouse Lissa first, but I didn't know I was expected to go in and take her by the shoulders and shake her in case she'd doped herself.' Christie couldn't keep the antagonism out of her voice.

Georgia came in with the coffee, just as if Hepburn had orchestrated a little pause so that her next question could sound more like conversation than interrogation.

'Have a biscuit,' she said, then as Christie shook her head, added, 'Oh, come on. Georgia's going to blame me if you don't.'

'Certainly am,' Georgia said heartily, and Christie obediently put one on her plate, earning an encouraging smile from Georgia as she left.

'I'm getting the impression Lissa wasn't an easy person,' Hepburn said. 'Difficult, even.'

Christie looked at her for a long moment, unconsciously crumbling the biscuit on to her plate. Then she burst out, as if unable to help herself, 'She's an absolute cow! Poor Matt – if ever there was a decent, honourable man, it's him. You can see that all the constant whingeing really gets to him, but he's so patient with her! And what does he get in return? She goes off and has an affair with Kerr Brodie, and flaunts it, right in front of him.

289

'Mind you, I get the impression he won't take it for ever. He's been quite short with her lately when she's been drooping around in that pathetic, poor-me way she has.'

Hepburn was quite taken aback by the success of her chatty approach. There was real venom there, exposing the sort of hatred that might well prompt you, if not to kill, exactly, then perhaps not to strive too officiously to keep alive.

'Did she give you a hard time as well?' It sounded a casual question.

'Oh God, yes! Little sniping remarks all the time, then foul hints about me having a crush on Matt. Really stupid.'

Christie's face, Hepburn saw, had taken on a flush of colour. She went on, 'Of course I admire him! He just about saved my life, with this offer of somewhere I could go to try to get my head together. He didn't have to; he's just a good person. And he gave Kerr a job too, when he'd probably have been on the scrap heap otherwise – so he goes screwing Matt's wife. But there isn't anything going on between me and Matt. I wish there was!'

It was all there, wasn't it? Smoothly, Hepburn went on to slotting in the other elements of the profile. 'Have you family to go back to now, if the house is uninhabitable?'

'Family?' Christie laughed. 'Went into care when I was about ten.'

Disturbed childhood – tick. 'That's rough. So now . . . ?'

'Oh, they say we might be able to camp in the main house in a day or two, so I'll hope to do that – if Lissa doesn't kick me out for deliberately trying to leave her in a burning house. She's getting out of hospital today.'

It was time to up the pace. Hepburn's voice grew a little harder.

'Do you have access to a car?'

Christie looked taken aback at the change of subject. 'Yes, I

290

can always borrow one if I want to go into town or something.'

'Have you been in town lately?'

'Not for the last few days – a week, maybe? Why?' She had tensed up, sitting straighter in her chair.

'Did you fill the car up?'

'Fill the car up? Oh God, you're asking about petrol, aren't you? You think I set the house on fire?'

'I don't, Christie. It's just there has been an accusation that you might have.'

Christie swore. 'It's Lissa, isn't it? Oh, you don't have to answer, I know it is. She'd tell any lie to destroy me. And you were nice to me so you could fit me up – what a bitch!' Her face was crimson with anger; she was shouting now.

Impulsive – tick. Frustrated – tick. Looking for revenge – double tick.

'Get out! Don't come back, unless you've got proof – which you won't have, because I didn't do it. And I didn't try to leave Lissa to burn. Pity she didn't, though.'

Georgia came hurrying through. 'What on earth's going on? Christie, are you all right?'

'I'm just going,' Hepburn said hastily. 'I'm sorry to have upset you, Christie.' Georgia was looking at her in no very friendly way and she didn't linger.

As she had thought, right at the start – a textbook profile. On the other hand, if Christie was guilty, her naivety had been extraordinary. It was never straightforward. That was what she loved about police work.

Hugh Donaldson, DS Macdonald thought, was a peculiarly repellent person: watery fish-eyes, a loose mouth and false teeth that clicked sometimes when he spoke.

He hadn't been rattled by the formal surroundings of the

interview room, or by the aggressive tone of Macdonald's questions. Yes, he had been in the village but only long after the fire engines had arrived at Lovatt's farmhouse. He had been asleep in his bed until then. No, he hadn't any idea if anyone had seen him leave his house. Yes, he had gone to Sorley's house afterwards. Yes, they had been drinking and laughing.

'Celebrating?' DC Campbell suggested.

Donaldson sucked his teeth. 'Call it what you like. I've no love for Matt Lovatt – served him right. He did the dirty on us over the lease for the farm and there's probably others he's cheated as well.'

Macdonald's frustration was beginning to show. 'Not clever, Donaldson. That's an admission that puts you right up there on the list of suspects.'

The man's glassy eyes met his, unblinking. 'You lot have me there anyway. You thought we let the stag out too.'

'And you deny it?'

'What's the point?' He gave a contemptuous snort. 'You won't believe me, but yes, if you like.'

'You're lying!' Macdonald raised his voice.

A sneering smile came over Donaldson's face and he said nothing.

The detective's lips tightened. They were getting nowhere; they might as well terminate the interview. 'One more thing. Andrew Smith – does the name mean anything to you?'

For the first time since he had walked in, Hugh Donaldson's reaction seemed genuine. He frowned, puzzled. 'You mean the butcher in Kirkcudbright? What's he got to do with this?'

They let him go. Macdonald leant back in his seat taking a deep breath. 'I'd better get my blood pressure down before we call in Donaldson Junior. If he's anything like his old man, I might have a seizure.'

Steve Donaldson wasn't. He was, Macdonald noted with pleasure, sweating when he came in, though the room wasn't warm. Fear was always a useful weapon in interrogation.

Steve came in blustering. 'You've no right to call me in like this. Intimidation, that's what it is.'

'Seems to be working,' Campbell said acidly.

'Surely you're not reluctant to assist the police?' Macdonald sounded sweetly reasonable. 'We tried to get hold of you yesterday. Sudden decision, was it – to go to the stock sales?'

Looking hunted, Steve mumbled, 'Aye, well – maybe it was. So?'

'And what were you looking for?'

Steve gaped, then mumbled, 'Nothing much.'

'Really? That's interesting, because your father said it had all been planned, last week, to look for some blackface tups. For your croft.'

'Well . . . could have been.'

'Just that you didn't notice?' Macdonald was enjoying this interview much more than the last. His voice hardened. 'Come on, Steve, I get angry when people treat me like a fool. You thought it would be better to lie low for a bit, didn't you?'

'Er . . .'

'*Didn't you?*'

Steve jumped at the raised voice. 'I-I . . .'

'Spit it out,' Campbell said helpfully.

'Oh – all right, maybe we did. But you can't blame us,' he whined. 'We knew you'd go picking on us. Folk like Lovatt always get the law on their side against poor buggers like us.'

'Now, that's where you're wrong,' Macdonald said. 'We're just on the side of the people who tell us the truth, and so far you haven't. Bad start. Bad, bad start. Did you set the fire the night before last?'

'No!' It was a howl of protest.

'Did your father? Did Derek Sorley?'

'No! No!'

'Don't believe you.' That was Campbell.

'He's not very good at this lying business, is he?' Macdonald agreed. 'You'd be better to tell the truth, Steve. Let's go back to the start. What did you do that night?'

'Nothing.' Steve wiped sweat off his upper lip with the back of his hand. 'I didn't do anything! I was in my bed till the stushie started.'

'And your wife will confirm that?'

'Aye, she will.'

He seemed to be on firmer ground there, and since Mrs Donaldson had treated the police like a bad smell yesterday it was unlikely that she would have anything approaching scruples about lying to them.

'And if someone says they saw you around the farmhouse earlier?'

Panic showed on Steve's face. 'They didn't! They're – they're lying! They're just saying that to get us in trouble. Lovatt – was it him said that?'

'We're not able to disclose any source of information.' Macdonald's reply was disingenuous. 'And what about letting the stag loose?'

'We never – we never,' Steve stumbled over the words. 'That's – that's another lie.'

It wasn't what you could call a convincing denial. Changing his tactics, Macdonald said kindly, 'Look, Steve, your dad's a powerful kind of guy, isn't he?'

'Aye.' That was heartfelt.

'And it would be pretty hard to stand out against him, wouldn't it?'

294

Steve began to look wary. 'Maybe.'

'You could end up taking the rap for him, you know. And you don't need to. If it was his idea, or Sorley's, you could get clear of all this just by telling us the truth.' Macdonald held his breath.

But he was disappointed. 'He said you'd do that,' Steve said. 'Try to set us against each other. Well, you won't.'

Swearing inwardly, Macdonald tried a bit more pressure, but Steve remained stubbornly unhelpful. At last, having checked that he too knew nothing of Andrew Smith, they dismissed him.

'What did you make of that?' Macdonald asked. 'Guilt, sure, but guilt about what?'

'Hard to say.'

Macdonald gave Campbell an exasperated look, then went on, 'The old man obviously primed him, and probably Sorley too.' He sighed. 'Well – better get the next one in, I suppose.'

He immediately took against Derek Sorley, with his ratty face, his greasy ponytail, his belligerent swagger.

'I can't imagine what this is about,' Sorley got his word in first. 'Why am I here?'

'I'm sorry, sir. We didn't manage to contact you yesterday and as you can imagine we are under a lot of time pressure. It's just a chat – we're not recording this. Thank you for cooperating.'

'As long as it is clearly understood that I am here by invitation and can leave at a time of my choosing.' Sorley sat down at the table.

'You're not under arrest,' Macdonald confirmed.

'I should hope not! I am cooperating as a concerned citizen and I wish I could give you information that would lead to the person who did this, though sadly I have none to give. It was absolutely shocking! They could have been murdered in their beds.'

'Indeed. If you could just give us an account of your movements—'

'I can do better than that. For the sake of efficiency, I have written out a detailed timetable.'

He handed it over and Macdonald glanced at it. It was a simple list of times and places, entirely innocuous. 'Very useful. However, there are a few questions I need to ask you—'

Sorley held up his hand. 'I wish further to state that I saw nothing suspicious that night, and to formally deny that I had any part in any wrongdoing. I have nothing to add to that statement.' He got up.

'Sit down,' Macdonald said sharply. 'I've a lot more to ask you—'

'But I don't have a lot more to say. Oh, I'm quite aware of the attitude the police have taken towards myself and the Donaldsons.' He sounded bitter. 'Your colleagues who interviewed us before made their position quite plain. I have no intention of playing along with your power games, Sergeant, and unless you're going to produce evidence rather than speculation, I'm leaving now.'

He walked to the door, still with that cocky swagger, but Macdonald noticed that his hands were shaking. For all his infuriating bravado, Sorley was scared.

Marjory Fleming was at a loose end. She had cleaned out the hens and had tried to find some housework to do, but she couldn't improve on Karolina's standards.

For something to do, she made herself another mug of coffee and perched herself on the end of the kitchen table, too restless to sit down. She looked at her watch, as she had done every five minutes since she got up this morning. Half past eleven. She'd called to say she'd be late in today.

Marjory was feeling dreadful: light-headed and gritty-eyed from lack of sleep, and her stomach churning with anxiety. She'd checked on the sleeping Cat a couple of times, of course, and she knew Bill had done the same when he came in for his break. He looked as if he'd aged ten years overnight – and probably she did too.

They'd left a note for Cammie last night in case he woke and found them gone, but he hadn't, and they'd had to tell him this morning; he'd gone off to school for a rugby match looking shell-shocked. Marjory hadn't told her mother. She couldn't bear the thought of Janet's distress – not yet, at least. Once they had things sorted out, she would need to know, of course, but perhaps they could just say that Cat hadn't liked the course and had decided to take a gap year while she sorted herself out.

She and Bill hadn't talked about it today. There was nothing to say that wasn't just hand-wringing, and there would be time for that later when there wasn't the risk that Cat might open the kitchen door on to a sudden silence and know they'd been discussing her. So they made banal small talk about the shopping list, the blocked drain in the yard, and Meg the collie's recent encounter with a hedgehog, specifically the likelihood that she had picked up fleas – anything, really, except that their hearts were breaking.

God forgive them, she and Bill had felt quite smug about the way their children were turning out: Cat with the place at vet school she had worked so hard for, with her nice boyfriend; Cammie at last doing the work necessary to get into a degree course in agriculture. Now their plans for Cat were in ruins.

'I blame myself,' Marjory had said to Bill when they had got Cat to bed last night. He'd told her brusquely not to agonise, that Cat was quite old enough to be responsible, but if she'd been Bill she'd have been wondering if a less career-orientated mother might have produced a more secure child. Blame, fault, guilt – the words repeated themselves, one after another, in her tired mind.

Perhaps she had to rethink. Cat was going to need her. She had to be there, ready to listen and support. Her salary was what kept the farm going in these difficult times, but perhaps she could request a transfer to a less demanding job. It gave her a pang even to think of it, but if that was what Cat needed, she'd have to do it.

Marjory looked at her watch again. It was torment, sitting here with nothing to do, and her mind slid back to all that was waiting in her office. She might need to apply for compassionate leave, however little she relished explaining to Bailey what had happened.

It was almost quarter to twelve now, but at last there was the sound of shuffling feet in the corridor and Cat came in, wearing a pair of ancient panda slippers and a dressing gown that was too short for her, the despised remnants of her childhood which were all she had left at home. Her eyelids were swollen and her usually fresh complexion was muddy.

Marjory sprang to her feet. 'Cat! How are you feeling?' She moved towards her daughter but Cat did a neat sidestep.

'Fine. Is the kettle on?' Her tone was bright and brittle and Marjory's heart sank.

'Yes, of course. I'll make you some breakfast. What do you want? There's bacon, and eggs, of course.'

Suddenly nervous, Marjory had said that without thinking, and clearly it wasn't tactful. Cat went paler than ever. 'Just coffee'll do. I'll make it myself.'

Rebuffed again, Marjory went back to her perch and picked up her mug.

'Anyway, what are you doing here at this time of day?' Cat demanded.

Playing games had never appealed to Marjory. 'Cat, you nearly died last night. I'm here because I think you need looking after and cherishing.'

Cat turned and looked at her with a cruel little laugh. 'Oh, really? It's a bit late for that now, don't you think? Haven't you a crisis at work you could put ahead of me in the queue?'

Marjory opened her mouth to protest, but she couldn't quite think what she was going to say in her own defence.

Cat was merciless. 'If you thought we were going to have a nice little mother-and-daughter heart-to-heart, forget it. I'm going to take my coffee back to bed. I'm a bit tired, for some reason. So you might as well go back to work instead of hanging around here.'

'You know how much that hurts, don't you?' Marjory said quietly.

'Then perhaps you understand how we've felt every time you rejected us in favour of the sodding job. Fine – that's what you wanted, that's what you've got. I expect the place is falling apart without you right now. You'd better go. They probably need you. I don't.'

CHAPTER EIGHTEEN

The stags were bellowing in fine style this morning, but DC Hepburn had almost stopped hearing them after wandering to and fro for twenty minutes, looking for Matt Lovatt. She was on the point of giving up her quest when she at last spotted him, walking down a sloping field towards the coastal path. A small herd of deer was grazing there, untroubled by his presence and also, more remarkably, by the presence of the huge dog that was roaming around nearby. It was ignoring them, but from the look of the beast Hepburn thought that in their position she would be feeling edgy, at the very least.

She saw Lovatt register her own waiting presence and at a sharp word from his master the dog came to heel. As the pair came nearer, Hepburn noticed first the man's disfigurement and then the exhaustion and drawn misery in his face. Poor bugger! Some people had it tough.

'Are you looking for me?' Lovatt called as he approached, and Hepburn produced her warrant card.

'DC Hepburn. Just wanted a word, if you've got a moment.'

Reaching her, Lovatt sighed. 'Yes, I thought someone might.' He looked around, a little uncertainly. 'I don't know where I can take you. The house is still too smoky to stay in for any length of time. I managed to get in to pick up some clothes, but that was all I could manage – and I apologise for the stink.' He was wearing an old army jersey and combat trousers, and there was indeed a strong smell of smoke.

Hepburn glanced around her. It was wet underfoot, but the early rain had cleared and a silver patch in the clouds showed where the sun was trying to break through. 'Why don't we just talk as we walk?' she suggested. 'Your dog looks as if it needs a lot of exercise.' She clicked her fingers encouragingly, but the dog paid no attention, keeping its cold amber gaze fixed steadily on this stranger.

'What kind is it?' she asked, feeling faintly unnerved by the unblinking stare. 'Beautiful animal.'

'Hard to say, really.' Lovatt fell into step beside her as they headed out along the path, with a gesture which allowed the dog to bound ahead. 'I got him as a pup when I was out in Bosnia.'

'Oh yes, you were with the army, of course. What regiment?' Hepburn said with the easy friendliness which usually encouraged people to talk.

It didn't work this time. 'KOSB,' Lovatt said, then lapsed into silence.

To business, then. 'The fire – have you a theory about who may be behind it?'

Just as she spoke, Lovatt's mobile rang, and miming apology he answered it, made a brief, brusque reply to the caller, then rang off.

'Sorry, what were you saying? Oh yes – the fire. Unfortunately, Constable, I have enemies in the village. I've said all this to your people already. There's a farmer, whose son wanted a new lease to farm my property, and another man who fancied digging up the Norse graves on Lovatt Island without permission. Ever since we arrived there's been harassment. It started with graffiti and vandalism, then they released one of my stags, and now this. I'm just very afraid of what they may try next, if your lot can't stop them.'

'Mmm. So you don't subscribe to your wife's opinion that the person who started the fire was Christie Jack? And that her plan was to murder your wife and leave the field clear for her with you?'

Visibly taken aback by the sudden ruthlessness of the question, Lovatt protested. 'For God's sake! That's absolute bollocks. Lissa – well, she's obviously still very upset. She had a terrible experience. She's not thinking clearly.'

'You mean, she's unreliable? Or maybe simply jealous, if you and Christie have a thing going?'

Lovatt stopped and turned to confront Hepburn. 'I swear to you, there's nothing between me and Christie. She's a child – and a damaged child at that, after her experiences in Afghanistan.'

Hepburn was relentless. 'And you don't think, perhaps, that those experiences might have, let's say, destabilised her? That she might not see things in quite the same light as normal people such as you or I might?'

Lovatt gave a snort of mirthless laughter. 'Who are you calling normal? With the life I'm having to lead at the moment I'm feeling anything but. Maybe I should give up, pack it all in and move away, let Steve Donaldson have the lease . . .'

He moved off, still talking, and picked up a stick to throw for the dog. Hepburn listened with interest. She had caught the flicker of unease on the man's face at her suggestion, and had no hesitation in attributing this sudden volubility to an attempt to dodge the question.

Time to move on. 'You inherited the farm from your grandmother, right?'

'Yes, that's right.'

'Is your father dead?'

Her bluntness was calculated, and Lovatt turned his head sharply. 'I wouldn't know,' he said stiffly. 'I haven't heard from him since I was nine years old, after he walked out on my mother and me.'

'I see.'

They had reached a little bay. The dog had brought back the stick then raced off again as Lovatt threw it down on to the beach. Hepburn followed the dog, the fine sand powdery under her feet. The sun was starting to break through the clouds, flicking the wave tops with tiny shafts of light. She bent down to pick up a smooth stone and sent it skipping over the water.

'What about the bairn's part?' she asked casually, over her shoulder.

'The . . . the bairn's part?'

'Oh, you know. The lawyer must have explained it to you. In Scots law, the deceased's offspring have a right to a third of the moveable property. Was that paid out to your father at the time you inherited?'

Hepburn spoke with the easy authority of one who had been totally ignorant until the question arose with the death of her own father last year. Lovatt, she was fairly sure, would have heard of it in the same way.

'Oh – oh yes,' Lovatt said vaguely. 'I don't know – the lawyers looked after all that. There was no claim made, as far as I know.'

'So your father may be dead?'

'He may be. Like I said, I really wouldn't know. I can tell you that my mother died some time ago. Look, Constable, I can't quite see the relevance of all this, and as you can imagine I've got a hell of a lot to do. Do you mind if I go and do it?'

'Of course not,' Hepburn agreed smoothly. 'Thanks for

your patience. Just one last thing – do you know anyone called Andrew Smith?'

The dog, waving the stick, was prancing in front of Lovatt, but he didn't seem to notice. The side of his face that was towards Hepburn was the side which could not register emotion of any kind, but the man stood stock-still for a second. Then he bent to pick up the stick and throw it again.

'Andrew Smith? There was a squaddie of that name in my regiment – oh, and I think Smith the butcher in Kirkcudbright is called Andrew. Is that who you mean?'

'Are they both still alive?'

This time Lovatt's puzzlement was clear. 'Yes, of course – at least as far as I know.'

'Then neither of them is the Andrew Smith who died in the cave on your island.'

'Wh-what?' Lovatt's face, already pale, went white on the good side.

'I think you heard. The skeleton in the cave. Made a connection?'

But the man was a soldier, trained to deal with sudden emergencies and the dog was a useful prop. 'There you are, Mika,' Lovatt said as he threw the stick again. His voice was controlled as he said, 'No, I'm afraid not. It's just that it seems so much more personal when you have a name to attach to that particular horror. Have you been able to find out anything else about him?'

It wasn't hard evidence, Hepburn thought as she drove back to Kirkluce, but she knew what she'd seen.

Swish! The automatic doors at the entrance to the hospital opened for the umpteenth time, admitting a blast of cold air. Melissa Lovatt, sitting on one of the upholstered benches in the reception area, gave it a resentful look and shivered.

She didn't have a coat. Matt, of course, hadn't thought to bring one yesterday. At least he'd brought her mobile, along with a bundle of what looked like charity shop reject clothes but had apparently been lent by Georgia, since her own were still in the house. She wouldn't want to wear them anyway, all saturated with smoke; they'd have to be laundered or, better still, thrown away. Matt would have to take her to Kirkcudbright to get replacements today, however busy he might claim to be.

Everything was far too big, of course. The sandals Georgia had sent were flapping on her feet, the bulky sweater swamped her slight frame and she'd had to roll up the legs of the trousers. It was lucky Georgia had thought to send a belt, but even with it fastened in the last hole Lissa still had to clutch them when she was walking to prevent them slipping down. They certainly weren't thick enough to keep her warm.

But Lissa was feeling a chill which had nothing to do with the draughty hall. She had almost died, and no one – no one at all – seemed to care.

When the ward sister arrived to tell Lissa that she was being discharged immediately, she had been quite abrupt. No professional concern there: she'd almost hustled her now former patient into her clothes and they had even begun stripping the bed before she was out of the room.

And then Lissa had phoned Kerr. She'd only done it because the romantic hero Matt whom Kerr had described wasn't the Matt who had arrived at her bedside yesterday, icily polite in the face of her emotional appeal and interested only in forcing her to say that she'd been so doped that she hadn't heard his little friend Christie's warning.

She wasn't going to admit it, though. In any case, she'd always slept so lightly that even after a sleeping pill she wouldn't have slept through someone banging on the door – of course she wouldn't! But you couldn't expect everyone to understand that, and if they were sceptical, Christie would literally get away with murder – well, attempted murder, anyway.

The nice young policewoman who came to talk to her had been very sympathetic, but even she had gone on about needing more proof, although it would seem to Lissa that the bolted door made it obvious Christie knew she hadn't left the house and had abandoned her to the flames, which ought to be proof enough. And this was the woman her husband was trying to protect!

So to call Kerr to come and fetch her had been Lissa's first thought today, even if he hadn't come to see her or even phoned since she was admitted. That should have warned her, but it hadn't. She was totally unprepared for the shock of his reaction.

'For God's sake, Lissa!' he had said. 'Can't you take a hint? It's over! Leave me alone!'

She gasped with pain. 'But Kerr, we love each other—'

'Oh, you think! You were up for a wee fling and so was I. God knows, I've tried to let you down gradually, but you just can't seem to get it.'

Her pride spoke. 'I don't accept that, Kerr. It was more, much more.'

'Do I have to take a sledgehammer to get it into your empty little head? It's over. Finished.' He rang off.

Had that been a threat? Tears of fear – or perhaps just humiliation – had welled up. They had talked of love – or perhaps only she had? Lissa felt confused, betrayed.

And what was she to do? She couldn't sit in the hospital for ever. She had to get home – though of course she had no home to go to now. She had no friends, no family – apart from a cold and indifferent husband and a little grave on a bleak Scottish island.

More tears had come, but eventually she had dried her eyes and blown her nose fiercely. She'd have to phone Matt; there was nothing else she could do. But he too had been brusque, totally unsympathetic.

'Got someone with me,' he'd said. 'I'll come when I can.'

There was nothing Lissa could do except wait, and shiver. The receptionists, she was aware, had been watching her and one came over to ask if she was all right. She'd had to say her husband had been delayed. That had felt humiliating too.

But eventually the swish of the doors heralded Matt's arrival. He went towards the desk, then spotted her and came over.

'Oh, there you are, Lissa. Come on, then.'

He was wearing old army fatigues and she could smell stale smoke. He didn't apologise for keeping her waiting, and he didn't look pleased to see her. He was wearing what she always called his 'black' look, his brow furrowed and his eyes stormy.

'You took your time,' Lissa said acidly.

'Not from choice,' Matt snapped, swinging round to head for the door.

She was a little in awe of his temper. She trotted behind him without responding, clutching at her slipping trousers.

'Where are you taking me?' she ventured as they reached the car.

'Georgia put up Christie and me at the Smugglers Inn last night. She's only got two bedrooms, but I can move out and let you stay—'

'Stay under the same roof as that murderous little bitch?' Lissa demanded shrilly. 'Oh, ideal – that way she can have another go.'

'That's a bloody silly thing to say! And don't dare repeat it to anyone else – it's manifest nonsense.' With his lips folded tight, as if he didn't trust himself, Matt drove off.

After a few minutes he said curtly, 'If that's your attitude, I'll take up the offer I had to use one of the caravans and you can stay there.'

'Fine. And you can take me via the dress shop in Kirkcudbright high street.'

'I got out some of your things.' Matt jerked his thumb at the back seat.

Lissa gave them a disdainful glance. 'I refuse to go round smelling like an ashtray. I have to have something warm to wear until they can be washed, and these things are falling off me.' She did, however, reach back to grab a pair of trainers; she wrinkled her nose, but at least they fitted.

Matt sighed, deeply. 'Oh, all right, as long as you don't take too long – there's a million things waiting for me. And for God's sake don't fling money around. I still don't know what compensation we'll get and we're running on empty at the moment.'

The set of his jaw, she noticed, was very grim. Lissa had always felt entitled to her feelings of hurt but her first thought – to say, 'Do you grudge me the very clothes for my back?' – suddenly seemed unwise. What was emanating from her husband was not just the smell of the disaster that had struck them. It was the smell of hatred.

And from Kerr, hatred. And from Christie – oh yes, from Christie, hatred. It frightened her. Too many people hated her. Where Christie was concerned, she hadn't thought it mattered. But it had – oh yes, it had.

'She won't be pleased,' DS Macdonald said. 'This whole investigation has ground to a halt and you could tell yesterday she was relying on a kick-start from the interviews today. And this hasn't come up with anything either.'

He gestured at the computer screen in front of him, where the SOCO's preliminary report on the Lovatts' farmhouse fire was displayed. He and DC Campbell were alone in the CID room, discussing their unsatisfactory encounters with the Donaldsons and Sorley. At least, Macdonald was discussing them, while Campbell grunted, mostly.

'There's nothing to say, except that Steve Donaldson is the weakest link and we failed to crack him. The best we can offer is that it shows there's a deliberate cover-up going on.'

'What of?'

Macdonald looked at Campbell impatiently. 'Now, let me think, what could it be? Oh, I remember. Setting the farmhouse on fire. Slipped my mind for a moment.'

Campbell, provokingly, shrugged.

'Look, it's obvious. Those guys are clearly obstructing the investigation. They've a history of vandalism—'

'Alleged.'

'OK, alleged, if you insist. But who else could have a motive for doing it?'

Campbell only gave him a level look, and Macdonald's face flushed with anger. 'If you're trying to suggest it was Christie, you're barking. Apart from anything else, she's not dumb enough to think you can splash petrol about and start a fire, then reckon on getting back into the house to save the person you want and leave the other to fry. And if her defence was going to be that she thought Melissa Lovatt had got out already, she wouldn't have left the door bolted. I can't imagine how you can claim she did it.'

'Didn't.'

'As good as. You're just weaselling now.' He eyed his colleague with dislike, the old Macdonald saying, 'Never trust a Campbell,' coming forcibly to mind.

'Didn't,' Campbell said again.

'Oh great! Going back to the nursery, are we?' Macdonald's voice had risen. 'Perhaps, if you could spare more than a monosyllable or two, we could have something approaching an adult discussion—'

'What's all this about?'

Macdonald spun round. He hadn't noticed DI Fleming come into the room. She was looking distinctly raddled this morning, and she didn't sound very cheerful either.

'Oh, nothing, boss,' he said hastily. 'We were just talking about the interviews.'

'And . . . ?'

He'd been right. All the signals were there: Big Marge was definitely not in a mood for bad news. He swallowed nervously. 'They were stonewalling, basically. They'd agreed a cover story between themselves and we couldn't shake them.'

'I see.' Fleming glanced at the screen they had been looking at. 'Is that the SOCO's report?'

Macdonald nodded. 'Preliminary. But . . .' He stopped. There wasn't anything cheering to say about it, and she could read the bad news for herself.

She scrolled down, the disappointment showing in her face as she reached the end.

'So – where does that leave us?'

The words 'flatter on our bottoms' sprang to his mind but in the current situation seemed impolitic, however accurate they might be. 'Sifting through the reports, more interviews,' he offered feebly.

'In line with the striking success we've had by these methods before?' Fleming said with considerable acerbity. 'Oh come on, Andy, can't you do better than that? We're simply plodding determinedly down a street marked Dead End, aren't we? What about some lateral thinking?'

She paused, looking from one to the other, but when both steadfastly refused to meet her eye, went on, 'I'm going to go down there myself this afternoon to have a go at Matt Lovatt. I said I'd take Louise Hepburn with me. Do you know where she is?'

The two detectives exchanged an uneasy glance. 'Er – I think she went down to do that herself this morning,' Macdonald said.

'She *what*?'

Solidarity demanded some sort of defence for a colleague not there to defend herself. 'I think she thought that was what you would have wanted her to do. She didn't know when you'd be back.'

None of them had known, and Big Marge in her present mood didn't seem inclined to explain her absence.

'Oh, she did, did she?' Her tone was ominous. 'I want to see her whenever she appears.'

Fleming swung out of the room and Macdonald watched her go with his lips pursed in a soundless whistle. 'Who's stolen her scone? I tell you something – I'm glad I'm not—'

His mobile ringing interrupted him. Smiling as he recognised the voice at the other end, he said, 'Hi Georgia. What can I do for you?'

His expression changed as he listened to her furious tirade. 'What a cow!' he said, when at last he got the chance. 'Don't worry, Georgia. I'm going to drop her in it so deep that she won't come up for air for a month.'

Having an investigation stall was hardly a new experience for DI Fleming. What was different this time was the feeling of utter hopelessness – about that, and about herself. She was a selfish failure who couldn't do either her job as a mother or her job as a police officer successfully. Her success as a wife – if she could claim that – was entirely due to Bill's stalwart loyalty. He'd have had a better home life with someone more in the traditional mould. Another failure, really.

She'd had plenty of mistakes to acknowledge over the years, but *failure* – that hurt in one of the most sensitive areas of her psyche, her pride. Hug the pain, someone had said to her once.

Take it into yourself, use it to grow. Sound advice, probably, when it came to her personal life.

In her job, though, it was different. If she failed, someone else could die, and right at the moment she had no idea how to prevent it. Fleming brought her fists down on the desk in an agony of frustration.

She had to do something. Her eyes itched from lack of sleep, her head felt stuffed with cotton wool and she felt no enthusiasm as she turned to her computer screen. She'd have to pan through the silt of reports from the uniforms, hoping for a glint of gold somewhere. It was unlikely, though – anything that even faintly resembled progress would have been brought to her long ago.

Somehow, she had to snap out of it, lift her professional mood. Fleming knew she'd been unfair to Macdonald and Campbell in demanding lateral thinking. Ewan had a good analytical mind and Andy was a thoughtful and efficient officer, but neither of them went in for inspiration. That was her job – hers and Tam's.

His father had been a gratuitous complication. The tabloids had, indeed, been hostile and Bailey had harrumphed a bit, but once old Davie was in the bosom of his family there wasn't really anywhere for the story to go. Another couple of days at the most – maybe even a day, if everything was still quiet – and she'd have him back on the strength. In fact, she could give him a call now; he'd have had plenty of thinking time and MacNee's ideas were always worth listening to. She reached for the phone.

'Bunty? It's Marjory. Could I have a word with Tam, if he's around?'

'Oh! Marjory! Er . . . sorry, I'll have to get him to call you back.'

To Fleming's surprise, Bunty was sounding uncomfortable, almost shifty. 'He's out, is he?' she asked. Perhaps she was imagining it.

'Well – sort of, not exactly.'

No, she wasn't. For some reason, Bunty was being evasive, and she wasn't good at it. Tam had to be behind this, with something he'd wanted his wife to cover up, but Bunty was the soul of truth and Fleming knew she would never tell a direct lie.

Taking base advantage of that, she said, 'Come on, Bunty, Tam's up to something, isn't he? Where is he?'

'Oh dear, I told him I couldn't . . .' Bunty was fluttering. 'He's – he's not doing anything. He's just asleep.'

'Asleep? At this time of day? Is he ill?'

'No, no, he's fine. Look, I'll get him to phone you when he wakes up. I really can't say anything else.'

Taking pity on her victim, Fleming rang off. But what on earth had MacNee been up to during the hours of darkness that meant he was asleep now? She could only hope that whatever it was wouldn't draw undesirable attention again and bring Bailey's wrath down on her already bludgeoned head.

Maybe he was on to something, some change of direction. That was what they needed at the moment. They were allowing themselves to get bogged down in the inquiry about the fire-raising, and the original crime, sadistic murder, was in danger of being sidelined.

Where the fire-raising was concerned, she might just have to accept that even though the Donaldsons and Sorley were prime suspects – there was a good fit with their previous activities and they had the classic means, motive and opportunity – the lack of direct proof could mean there'd be no prosecution. A crime that consumed all the evidence was close to the perfect crime.

What had emerged, though, was that both Macdonald and Campbell believed that they genuinely didn't know Andrew Smith. So . . . ?

So perhaps they were looking in the wrong direction, drawing a blank with all those interviews in the village. If the Manchester force would just come through with some more information on Andrew Smith, it would help – she'd requested interviews with known associates but of course they felt no sense of urgency about another force's years-old murder.

So where were the gaps in her own investigation? Matt Lovatt was the target of all the recent problems. What had caused this dramatic escalation, after years of petty nastinesses? It was hard to see how discovering Andrew Smith's body could have provoked it; it made no sort of sense. It simply didn't feel right, and over the years Fleming had come to trust that sort of gut feeling. It often indicated a subconscious observation that hadn't yet surfaced in the conscious mind.

Lovatt, though, was an enigmatic figure, which made her even more angry with the jumped-up constable who had denied her the opportunity of a killer interview. Maybe the man hadn't been there at the time of the murder, but his grandmother certainly had been. Fleming wanted to know more about his grandmother, at the edge of the picture so far.

Fleming could still go and question him herself, of course, but Hepburn had almost certainly sprung the Andrew Smith question, as they had all been instructed to do. If she asked Lovatt again, he would have had time, if necessary, to armour himself against it. She'd wanted to see his reaction for herself. Oh, she had a word or two to say to young Hepburn, when she appeared.

What alarmed Fleming most was the sense she had of – what? She struggled to define it. That it wasn't over – that was it. That something was happening, but to a quite terrifying degree, she couldn't say what – or where, or why, or who was doing it. All Fleming's professional instincts were signalling danger, but she had no idea which direction it was coming from.

Sitting panicking wasn't going to help. She went back to her sifting, unrewarding as it might be. She had reached the stage where she reckoned she would scream if she read one more report reading, 'I proceeded to 23 High Street' – did no one in the police force just go places any more? There was a knock on the door and DS Macdonald appeared, a little ahead of her 'Come!' He was clearly in a state of barely suppressed rage.

'Sorry to interrupt you, boss, but I've had a complaint of harassment from Georgia Stanley at the Smugglers Inn. About DC Hepburn.'

Obviously Hepburn made friends everywhere she went. She was startled, nonetheless. 'She's been harassing *Georgia*?'

Macdonald hesitated. 'Well, not Georgia. She was complaining on behalf of Christie Jack. It was outrageous—'

'Ah,' Fleming said. 'I think you need to sit down, Andy.'

She could almost see him deflating as he obeyed her, and she went on, 'Right, let's start at the beginning. I saw for myself that you're interested in Christie Jack. No, don't interrupt me,' as he made a move to speak. 'You must not have anything more to do with her, in the context of this investigation. You are not to contact her, directly or indirectly. That's an order.

'I shall speak to Georgia myself, but if you think you can present the complaint she made in a professional way, I'll listen to you.'

Fleming could see him struggling. He was a decent, uncomplicated young man, Andy, and for some reason he had fallen with a crash you could hear across in Ireland for Christie, who was taking him well out of his emotional depth. From all reports, Matt Lovatt was the big thing in the girl's life and that would be hard for Andy to accept, especially since it put Christie on the suspect list.

'Georgia says Hepburn was all chummy with Christie, then suddenly accused her of setting the fire to murder Melissa Lovatt. We'd taken her over all that before, and the tone she took sent Christie hysterical. I've advised Georgia to take it up with the super.'

'You've done *what*?' If looks could kill, he would have been a small, fizzing patch on the floor.

That got through to him. 'Well, she said she'd like to speak to you first,' he conceded.

'I've got a big problem with this, Sergeant. I thought I could deal with your attitude to Christie, who is obviously a suspect—'

Macdonald opened his mouth to protest and Fleming snarled, 'Oh, don't be ridiculous, of course she is – Melissa Lovatt's accused her. I thought I could just see to it that other people dealt with her. But I'm beginning to wonder whether I can keep you on this case at all.

'No, I don't want a discussion. I'm going to think it over, and I'll let you know of my decision.'

When he left, Fleming put her head in her hands. Just when you thought it couldn't get worse, it did. MacNee off pursuing some – probably maverick – idea of his own. Macdonald, with his brain totally in thrall to his hormones. Which left her with Campbell, who hoarded his words as if they were bawbees and many a mickle could make a muckle.

And Hepburn, who was, as far as she could see, the pick of the bunch among the other detectives, and whom she was planning to blow out of the water pretty much as she stepped over the threshold of her office.

Doggedly, she went back to the reports. And then, at last, something caught her eye. Trivial, probably, but it was something that had been missed. How often had a serial killer been free to carry on because of a box that hadn't been ticked? She was clutching at straws here, perhaps, but it wasn't as if there were convenient logs floating by.

CHAPTER NINETEEN

It was late afternoon by the time the Lovatts returned to Innellan and the sun was dropping low in the sky, hinting at the onset of the long, dark northern winter. Matt dropped Lissa outside the caravan with a key and a carrier bag of basic supplies. She had flatly refused to take any of her clothes.

'They would stink the place out. I don't feel up to washing them. Maybe your little friend Christie could do that in her spare time,' she had said unwisely, then flinched at the anger in her husband's face.

He had been angry anyway, when he'd demanded to see the credit card slip from the dress shop, and admittedly Lissa had gone a bit over the top. She'd been feeling both angry and defiant – she hadn't bought clothes for years and that was just what decent jeans and a good coat cost these days. He hadn't said anything, but he had crumpled the slip in his hand and there was a white line around his lips. He'd been annoyed, too, when she'd refused to go to the Smugglers for meals, and made him stop to let her buy groceries.

Now Matt had dumped her here, and just driven off as if he couldn't bear to be a moment longer in her company.

The caravan wasn't one of the big, smart family ones with huge windows. It was old-fashioned, small and shabby, with skimpy curtains drawn across the meagre windows, a bolt-hole for the owner of a picturesque home down on the shore during the profitable holiday rental season. It was huddled sideways into the hill behind to give shelter when the wind blew but tonight, with the shadows lengthening, it looked dark and unwelcoming.

There was a real autumn chill in the air, and even huddled into the expensive coat, Lissa was cold – and tired too, and her throat was still raw from the after-effects of the smoke. She needed warmth, a cup of tea, a rest. Her hands were icy and it took her a moment or two of fumbling to work the awkward lock.

The door opened on a dim, shadowy cavern, with a stale, unaired smell. She stepped inside uncertainly, leaving the door open, and could make out a galley of sorts, and a bed with a thin mattress, covered by a worn candlewick bedspread in an ugly shade of orange. She felt for a light switch, but couldn't find one. Surely, on a permanent site like this, it must be connected up to electricity, and plumbing, too? But there was a large empty water container on the floor in the galley; her heart sank when she turned the tap above the chipped enamel sink and no water came out, and sank further when she opened a little door at the back and found a cramped chemical toilet. As she looked around despairingly, she noticed a big camping gas light sitting on a table at the back. No plumbing, no electricity – and even the two burners in the galley were Calor gas. She hadn't thought to get matches.

She sat down on the tatty bedcover and burst into tears. It wasn't fair! It wasn't fair! But that brought an echo of what her mother had always said, coldly, when she complained: 'Whoever told you life was going to be fair? It certainly wasn't me. And you should know that by now.'

Lissa knew it, all right, but a sense of grievance had haunted her all her life except for that brief, early time with Matt when she had thought that with all he had been through he would understand, would make everything right for her. Now she felt, as she had sometimes felt in the past, that she was quivering on the brink of total disintegration, with everyone in the world against her.

Kerr had rescued her before, but she didn't want to think about him now. He had done his best to humiliate her, and she still had her pride. The very next time she saw him she would make it icily plain that she loathed and despised him. That seemed to be what he wanted, so she wasn't afraid of his silly threat.

So that left only Matt, who was so angry with her that he hadn't looked directly at her once today. Christie seemed to have turned him into Lissa's enemy now, and for the first time she wondered if they could have been acting together – Christie's daring rescue a sham, done with Matt's cooperation? Surely not – he wouldn't burn down his own house!

Yet the ugly thoughts kept going round and round inside her head, and it was a refinement of cruelty that she didn't even have the most basic comforts in this disgusting, sordid place.

Restless in her misery, she got up and went to let in such light as there was, drawing back the curtain on the window opposite the bed. Across the bay she could see the island, starting to grow shadowy in the fading light – the island, where what remained of her fractured heart was buried with her son.

She could go and sit by his grave, talk to him. She didn't think of him as the small, still thing he had been – in her mind he grew steadily and she saw him as the toddler he would be now, a sturdy little dark-haired boy, with blue eyes like her own, trotting around laughing. He never cried, of course, and was starting to babble baby talk that would make her laugh. He would never betray her, never grow away from her. Never learn to hate her. He was all she had left. Lissa needed to be there, with him.

She'd have to find Matt, though, to get the key to the boat. He and Christie were probably sitting, snug and warm in the bar, laughing together and grateful that Lissa was out of the way for the moment at least – if not permanently. She wasn't sure she felt strong enough to face them.

Lissa pressed her face against the glass to cool her cheeks, hot now with tears. Below on the shore the tide was on its way out and she saw that the causeway was almost clear. She could walk across that way and satisfy her yearning without ever going near Matt. It would be passable for hours now and perhaps when she got back she would feel heartened enough to ask someone for matches and find a standpipe to fill the water bottle.

Just for tonight. She could cope with one night, but no more. Tomorrow things would have to be different. In her expensive coat, cream-coloured and impractical, she set off on the track past the chalets and down to the village.

Louise Hepburn's jaunty step as she came back into the CID room reflected her satisfaction. For the first time since she joined she'd had the chance to conduct a major interview, and she reckoned she'd made some sort of breakthrough. Admittedly, she hadn't got an admission out of Lovatt and he obviously hadn't known who the skeleton was, but she had no doubt that the 'Andrew Smith' he'd first thought of wasn't either the butcher in Kirkcudbright or his brother-in-arms. What was more, she'd an idea that she wanted to chase up that just might produce a line to follow.

She was totally taken aback when DS Macdonald, who seemed to be lying in wait for her, launched into a tirade about bullying and harassment that called into question her judgement, her competence, her professionalism, her ethics – indeed, everything, only just stopping short of her personal freshness.

The sergeant had always seemed kind of a laid-back guy who never stood on his dignity. 'Hey, Sarge,' Hepburn protested, 'what's this about? Give me a break!'

Mistakenly. Macdonald's fury changed to icy rage. 'Don't be impertinent, Constable. I want to know why you reduced a very vulnerable woman to a state of hysteria.'

Feeling the first prickle of nervous sweat, Hepburn's hand went up to rub the back of her neck. 'If you mean Christie Jack, all I did was put to her the allegation that Melissa Lovatt had made.'

'We'd covered that yesterday, which you knew. Georgia Stanley told you. She says that you began by trying to lure Christie into making some sort of admission, then when she didn't produce what you wanted, you started bullying her.'

Hepburn opened her mouth to protest, but Macdonald swept on, 'In any case, an official complaint has been made and DI Fleming wants to see you ASAP. And I have to tell you that she's not very pleased that you sneaked in to interview Lovatt before she did, either.'

There was malice in his smile as he said that. Hepburn left the room, feeling faintly sick. She'd better go straight there and get it over with; Big Marge's reputation was that she didn't do a lot of barking, but when she bit she went straight for the jugular.

That image was to haunt her when she heard the news the following day.

The knock on DI Fleming's door was a very tentative one, and she had no problem guessing who it was. 'Come!' she said, and DC Hepburn inserted herself into the room.

Fleming's sense of the ridiculous had always been a handicap to the expression of righteous wrath. Hepburn was perhaps twenty-four, twenty-five, but she looked exactly like a schoolgirl summoned to the head teacher.

'You'd better sit down, Hepburn,' she said. 'You're in trouble.'

'Yes, ma'am. Sorry, ma'am.'

She sat down, but Fleming had made a practice of studying body language, and when Hepburn came in she'd been – yes, more scared than she was now. If she'd been sharp enough to pick up on Fleming's faint amusement, she could be valuable.

Not that she was letting her off the hook. 'As someone will probably have told you – DS Macdonald, perhaps? – an official complaint has been made about your handling of the interview with Christie Jack this morning. I've been told you were bullying her. This is your window of opportunity to put your side of the story.'

It was interesting to watch her reaction. Two ways to go – deny it, or accept it and apologise. It was even more interesting that she found a middle way.

'I don't see it like that. I asked her if she had started the fire because Melissa Lovatt had said that she did. Yes, I tried to put pressure on her to see if she would admit it, after getting her confidence first, but I stopped when she became distressed and I didn't mislead her at any stage. It was a routine interview.'

'You should know enough to understand that our job is to collect admissible evidence. Supposing you had broken her down – supposing she had admitted that she had set fire to the house? No corroboration – no case to answer.'

She saw her swallow, saw her run her hand through her untidy mop of hair to massage the back of her neck in a sort of helpless gesture. This was a crucial one: would she bluster, or . . .

'I'm sorry. I hadn't thought of that.'

Another smart response. Fleming hadn't finished, though, by any means. 'No, it's fairly obvious you hadn't. Which is why we don't send inexperienced officers out to do major interviews on their own.'

Hepburn took that like a sword thrust. 'Lovatt,' she said, her voice flat.

'Lovatt.'

She swallowed. 'Look, we'd arranged that would happen. They told me you wouldn't be in, and I thought you were anxious to have it done anyway . . .'

'Did you?'

'I-I . . . Oh well, all right. I was just pissed off – sorry, ma'am, disappointed, that it wasn't going ahead. I'd read all the background stuff, and it seemed to me he was the most interesting assignment going. None of the stuff that has been done had led anywhere, and Lovatt—' She stopped.

Fleming's interest quickened. 'And . . . ?'

Hepburn hesitated. 'There's stuff that I want to check on first—'

Her patience snapped. 'Look, Hepburn, I think you have an interesting approach. I have a strong feeling that you're keen to impress me. But if you think that the clever way to do it is by assembling your case and then laying your cards on the table and saying 'Gin', let me disabuse you. Gin rummy is one thing, a police investigation is quite another. What – did – Lovatt – say?'

Hepburn didn't seem intimidated. 'Just didn't want to waste your time, ma'am. There was nothing that would stand up in court. But there were two things – I don't think he's totally confident that Christie Jack hadn't set the house on fire – whatever DS Macdonald may think about it.'

'We'll let that one pass. The other?'

'When I said "Andrew Smith" he definitely reacted. I'd

be prepared to swear the name meant something to him. He managed to cover it up, playing with the dog – scary animal! I wasn't sure it was a dog at all, it looked more like a wolf. He really looked shocked when I told him why we were asking – I'd be surprised if that was faked. I think we could definitely get results if we lean on him. If that's not going to turn out to be bullying.'

It was a cheeky remark, but Fleming chose to ignore it. 'It sounds as if you may have got somewhere – I'll give you credit for that. Christie Jack – well, I think given the profound apologies I will make on your behalf, it doesn't need to go further.

'I'm prepared to add you to the team on this case and see how you get on. The first rule is, you don't go out on your own – we work together.'

Hepburn was beaming. 'Thanks, ma'am. I do understand.'

'So, Louise – where do we go from here?'

'You tell me, ma'am.'

The submissive reply made her laugh. 'Fair enough. I'll get you all in tomorrow, and you can make your peace with Andy Macdonald.'

She was a bit cocky, Fleming thought as Hepburn took her leave – but that wasn't altogether a serious fault, if it meant she was full of ideas. She'd her wits about her too, clever enough to make the right noises when challenged. But why did Fleming suspect that there was something she wasn't being told?

It had to be tonight. Tomorrow's forecast was for clearing skies and dropping temperatures, and though the new moon would only be a thumbnail, starlight in a frosty sky could be too bright for deeds of darkness.

The clouds were heavy tonight, though. At eleven o'clock, just as the street lights went out in Innellan, Tam MacNee drove up the track into the position he had taken the previous night. When he switched off the headlights, the darkness seemed to swoop round him, thick as fog; when he put down his window, there was a silence below the sounds of water and light wind that seemed almost physically oppressive. A stag roared, another answered; there was a sudden waft of voices and laughter from a house somewhere, but after the noises died it seemed stiller than ever.

MacNee shifted uneasily. The countryside at night always spooked him. Maybe he'd a hieland granny no one had told him about, but he kept finding himself looking around and over his shoulder, even though he knew that it was only his own imagination that peopled the shadows.

He'd planned to keep the car window open tonight to get the earliest possible warning of anyone stirring, but for one reason and another he was shivering. He'd see movement soon enough and he'd touched base with the excise lads earlier and they were on full alert. He put it up again.

Nothing to do now but wait. Stay alert, stay calm. Stifle the impatience to see Brodie pay at last that had filled his mind to the exclusion of everything else.

Caring for his father had rekindled the anger that had smouldered for more than twenty years. The poor, sad old man, bewildered and ill at ease in his clean clothes and cosy surroundings, begging for a drink whenever he saw the son who was the keeper of happiness in the form of a whisky bottle, wrung Tam's heart – a good man, a good father, reduced to a shambling wreck. He was missing the streets, too, missing his pals and what he called freedom. That Tam had been forced to become in some sense his jailer was another charge to add to Brodie's slate.

Was that a movement on the island, cutting the skyline? MacNee snatched up his binoculars but it was a brief glimpse only, and it was too dark to see anything against the bulk of the island. He'd thought he'd seen something last night, around the same time, probably, but again it could have been just a deer.

That small excitement over, he settled back to his watch.

Fergie Crawford couldn't sleep. He'd tried earlier, but his head was buzzing. He'd not got much kip the night before either – supposing he never heard the summons? He was sleeping fully dressed these days, not to keep Brodie waiting.

Maybe the boat to take him off was on its way right now. If he knew that, he could be ready watching for Brodie to come across and not get tore into for being slow. He could slip out, up to the ridge in the middle of the island, and take a wee look over along the Solway Firth. It would pass the time anyway.

It was pitch-dark outside, but he'd kind of got used to that now. He let himself out of the cottage and went round the back, skirting the trees, keeping low so if Brodie looked across from the farm he wouldn't spot him and go mental. Supposing the boat didn't come tonight? Fergie wasn't wanting to be locked in again.

The ruins on the top of the rise – more just a pile of stones, really – gave him cover as he lay down and cautiously peered over. Black sky, lighter sea; Fergie could see the white lines of the wave crests – hear, too, the wash as they broke on the rocks below. But no sign of a ship, no steady throb of an engine.

He was used to disappointment by now. He sat up again, then his eye caught something pale, in among the rickety headstones just below the church. His heart thumped uncomfortably. It was near where that baby . . . It freaked him out, that . . .

Probably just a plastic feed sack Brodie or his boss had left. Of course it was. But if he didn't check he'd start thinking daft things. He stood up, careless now, and walked down to it.

It wasn't a sack. With a groaning gasp, Fergie shrank away, gagging, then fled down towards the trees, and round the back of the cottage. He stopped to be violently sick before he dashed inside and up the stairs, locking the door against . . . he didn't know what.

MacNee's eyes were feeling heavy, and he was starting to yawn. He looked at his watch and groaned. It was after two – what if he'd been wrong in his reckoning? What if he hadn't read Brodie's mind as well as he thought?

The mobile in his pocket buzzed. He grabbed it, listened and a slow smile spread across his face. 'Hold on,' he said.

He got out of the car and walked over to the edge of the track. The rush of cool air revived him, and as he looked down over the village he saw someone come out along the main street, a familiar figure with a limping gait, hurrying down towards the jetty.

'Yup!' he said into the phone. 'We're in business.'

'For God's sake, Crawford!' It was Kerr Brodie yelling, beating on the door of Fergie's room. 'Are you dead, or what?'

Fergie came out of the deepest part of his sleep with his heart pounding. He was on his feet, staggering across to open the door while he was still half asleep, trying to work out where he was, what was happening. Brodie grabbed his arm, propelling him down the stairs.

'My bag,' he stammered, then wished he hadn't as Brodie, giving him a vicious push that had him tripping down the last three steps on to his knees, told him exactly what he could do with his bag.

'Out!' Brodie snarled, and Fergie scrambled to his feet, following the other man at a staggering run down to the jetty.

He was still not fully awake as they took off, but the sea air was bracing and before they rounded the end of the island it had come back to him in a sickening rush. The woman . . .

He choked, and Brodie's head flipped round. 'You're not going to puke, are you?'

'No, no,' Fergie managed, though he wasn't entirely sure – the woman, lying there covered in blood with her eyes wide open and her throat ripped out by . . . something. A dog, most likely the wolf-dog he had seen around with Brodie's boss. And still roaming on the island, maybe.

When he'd reached the safety of the bothy, Fergie had locked himself in, then, cold with terror, had climbed into bed to try to warm himself up. He had listened with painful anxiety for a time, but at last in the silence had dropped into an exhausted sleep, not long before Brodie banged on the door.

If this didn't work, Fergie wasn't going back there, not for anything. He'd sooner turn himself in. But it had to work – it *had* to!

Brodie was edgy, though, he could see that. He was looking all around him as they headed towards a trawler which was gliding up the firth with no lights showing. Fergie caught his unease and started swivelling his head too, until Brodie in a savage undertone told him to sit still. He contented himself with willing the little boat across the water, faster and faster – and then they were there, and a man above them was catching the rope Brodie had thrown and securing it, then dropping a rope ladder over the side. Fergie stood up, ready to grasp it—

The roar of a powerful engine seemed to come from nowhere. A high-wattage spotlight dazzled them and a megaphone boomed out a warning, then the revenue cutter, speeding out from the shelter of Ardwall Island, was alongside.

The trawler made no attempt to flee, but the deck became

frantic with activity, and a package dropped down into the sea beside them as Brodie, swearing violently, gunned his engine. But the rope to the trawler held. They were trapped.

Fergie Crawford's escape was at an end.

MacNee was grinning as he trained his binoculars on Brodie, setting off in his boat to sail into the trap MacNee had laid. The diversion across to the bothy on Lovatt Island puzzled him at first, until he made out another figure moving in the darkness beside Brodie and hurrying to the boat. Who could that be? It would explain the movements he'd caught these last two nights – and, he remembered suddenly, the provisions he had spotted in the bothy room. A pal of Brodie's in the drug business, maybe, with a reason for lying low?

His work here was done, and he could go home now to his bed, but he'd slept half the afternoon and felt disinclined to walk away from the excitement. Maybe the bothy would repay investigation – and now he noticed that the causeway below was uncovered. He could walk across, avoiding the need for a boat – and maybe even catch some of the action from the top of the island.

MacNee backed up the car and drove down to the shore, took his torch and his binoculars and set off. The causeway didn't seem quite such an easy option, now he was close. He didn't know much about the tides, but the sea, pitch-black in the darkness, was slapping at its stones now, and every so often a skittish wave would come higher than the others and break over the top. It would be wiser to turn back, maybe, but he wasn't going to miss seeing the trap sprung. He'd just have to be quick. It wasn't that far.

Iron poles had been stuck in, indicating the best line to take, but even so, in the light of the powerful torch he could see jagged rocks slippery with seaweed and pitted with rock pools. Hurrying was a good prescription for a broken ankle, but impatience made him careless after a bit. An injudicious step sent him sliding into wet seaweed and he emerged soaking, with a bleeding gash on his ankle stinging with the salt water. Swearing, he rubbed at it, then looked for the torch which had gone flying. He was in a right mess if he couldn't find it.

Mercifully, it was sturdy and shock resistant and the light shining through the bladderwrack revealed its position. His hands were shaking as he groped among the slimy tendrils for it.

The sea was covering the rocks behind him already. He couldn't turn back now, and at least the causeway rose as it reached the island. He just had to keep moving faster than the tide rose. He tried to put out of his mind the local belief that the Solway tide came in faster than a horse could gallop. It was probably just an old wives' tale, but his trainers, wet already from their immersion, were getting soaked again by the bolder waves. They were aggressive now, not playful.

Don't panic. Watch your footing. Think about something else. Think about Brodie, think about payback time. It could still go wrong, of course. It was all about timing: if Brodie got warning, he could speed off, deny everything . . .

The excise lads who had spotted the trawler coming up the firth were experienced, he told himself – they wouldn't get it wrong. And the causeway, thank God, was rising steeply now. MacNee slipped a couple of times, but just ahead there was rough grass growing down to the rocks. He had just reached it when he heard the sound of the revenue cutter coming into action, and sprinted up towards the seaward side of the island, where he got a grandstand view of it all.

If revenge is a dish best eaten cold, MacNee's was chilled to perfection. All it needed was a tot of whisky to go alongside, so he could drink to Brodie's damnation, and he'd get that later. Admittedly, it was a pity they'd take the boat into Stranraer and he wouldn't be there to look the bastard in the face as they brought him ashore in handcuffs, but he'd make sure Brodie would know who he had to thank.

MacNee was grinning as he turned away. He'd check out the bothy, then call in for someone to take him off. Even he would struggle to get seasick in the journey across from this side of the island.

It would be an hour or two before the first real signs of dawn, but the darkness was lifting a little, and he switched off the torch. He didn't need it now to see his footing and the ruined chapel against the skyline gave him direction. He was just short of it when something lighter, something patchy, on the ground caught his eye. In the semi-dark, he couldn't make out what it was and he snapped on the torch again and went to investigate.

The patches of white were the parts of the woman's coat not totally saturated with blood. And her neck . . .

An animal, that was MacNee's first thought. An animal, that had gone straight for her throat. Something like the wolf-dog he had seen at Matt Lovatt's heels.

His second thought: where was it now?

CHAPTER TWENTY

Once again, Innellan was roused in the night by sirens. Georgia Stanley came out of sleep with a sickening lurch.

It was early morning, really, though the sun hadn't risen. She grabbed her dressing gown and slippers. Oh, what now? More trouble for Matt and Christie? The girl was falling apart; Georgia didn't think she could take much more, and Matt was looking ill with the stress.

Christie was out on the landing. She was very pale, but seemed almost unnaturally calm. 'It's the police, Georgia. I saw from my window. What's going on?'

She looked at the girl uneasily. 'Come on downstairs and I'll put on the kettle, then we'll see what's happening outside.'

'Matt—' Christie said, hanging back and glancing towards his closed bedroom door.

'If he can sleep through that din, he must be shattered. Plenty of time for him to hear about it in the morning,' Georgia said, drawing Christie towards the stairs. 'If he wakes up, we'll have a cup of tea ready for him.'

Christie went down ahead of her into the kitchen. The room was luridly lit by the orange flashing lights of a police car parked outside, and then there was heavy knocking at the front door. It felt as if Georgia's own heart was thumping in time as she unlocked it.

Two unsmiling uniformed officers stood there. 'Matthew Lovatt,' one said. 'I understand he's staying here.'

'Yes,' Georgia admitted. 'Do . . . do you want to come in?'

As they stepped inside, Christie appeared. 'What do you want with him? Has something happened?'

'We're needing to speak to Mr Lovatt, that's all. If you'd just go back to bed, miss—'

'I'd rather wait, until you tell us.' Christie's chin was jutting defiantly.

Georgia took her arm. 'They're not going to tell us, Christie. We'll find out later. We can wait through here, at the back.' She turned to the officers. 'I'll just go and wake him.'

As she propelled a reluctant Christie into the lounge and shut the door, she heard one saying to the other, 'Deaf, is he, then, sleeping through all this?' As she ran upstairs and knocked on the door of Matt's room, she already had misgivings, and when she opened it, the room was empty and the bed hadn't been slept in.

MacNee sat on the camp bed in the bothy loft. He'd heard the sirens and now, between the slats on the windows, he could see the lights of three police cars. What he didn't know was how long it would take to get a trained handler and a marksman down here. There was no way a police officer could set foot on the island until these were in place, and he certainly wasn't going to step outside this room, even though he'd seen nothing moving except the deer coming out to browse in the early morning light. He'd never in his life been more scared than he'd been in the short time it had taken him to run from where the poor woman's body lay to the safety of the bothy.

He'd recognised her: Lissa Lovatt. Had the dog, roaming free on the island, turned rogue? Both he and Fleming were quite sure the animal wasn't far from its wolf ancestry, but even so, wolves, as far as he knew, weren't in the habit of attacking humans unless from hunger. There were deer all over the island for the taking, and this hadn't been a prey kill – thank God for that, at least.

Had her husband gone mad and set the dog on to her to kill her? And, in the final, hideous detail, there right on the grave of their dead child? MacNee had his reservations about Lovatt, but *this* . . .

There was something deeply evil lurking in this innocent-looking, pretty island. He had been so absorbed in his own revenge on Brodie that he hadn't given much thought to what had been going on: local politics, with the Donaldsons and Sorley, had been his casual assumption about the recent events. As for the murder, so many years before – there would be time enough to sift through whatever evidence remained about Andrew Smith when Manchester did the follow-up on known associates.

MacNee didn't believe that now. Lovatt's local enemies releasing a stag – certainly. Burning the house down – possibly. But you couldn't assume that about a second hideous murder on the island.

He could be stuck here for hours. He'd phoned in to see if there was any word of the specialist team, though he should have known better: as usual, no one had a scoobie. He'd checked out the loft, hoping for drug evidence, but all he'd found was a carrier bag containing a pathetic bundle of scruffy T-shirts and underwear, and what looked like army issue shoes with a number inside. If this was one of Brodie's drug dealer chums, you had to think he wasn't much good at his job.

MacNee paced irritably to and fro, and then his eye lit on the stock of tins. He was hungry, he realised, and it wouldn't be the first time he'd eaten cold baked beans out of a tin. He looked doubtfully at the spoon lying on the table, then shrugged, pulled back the ring on the tin and settled down to wait.

Matt Lovatt woke up, coughing. He could feel smoke in his throat and with the sound of the sirens starting to penetrate the sleep of exhaustion he thought the house was on fire again and sprang up in panic from the sofa cushions on the floor of the farmhouse sitting room.

There were two men in yellow jackets and police caps standing by the window which had been left wide open to freshen the air. 'Matthew Lovatt?' one said. He was tall and broad with greying hair, and his voice was cold.

'Yes,' Lovatt stammered. He had slept in a T-shirt and jeans but the early morning air was chilly. As he struggled to orientate himself, he pulled a blanket off the makeshift bed to wrap round him.

'We were informed you were staying at the Smugglers Inn.'

'Yes, I was, but . . .' How could he explain that Georgia Stanley's kindly fussing, and his own guilt about the effect on Christie, had made the smoke-laden atmosphere in the farmhouse seem less oppressive?

He didn't try. 'I just felt I should be here.' It sounded lame.

'Where's your dog?' The question almost burst from the other officer. He was very young, slightly-built, and definitely nervous.

'My dog?' Lovatt looked blank. 'In his kennel.' He had a confused thought that this was some kind of check-up, something to do with the Dangerous Dogs Act, but at this time in the morning? With sirens?

'Are you sure?' the older man asked.

'Of course—' Then he stopped. Oh God, they couldn't have

let Mika out, tried to find an excuse to have him destroyed – he couldn't bear it, to lose Mika!

'There's a padlock . . . if they've tampered with it . . .'

Not waiting to go to the front door, he climbed out of the window and barefooted ran across the yard to the dog's enclosure, followed more slowly by the officers.

Mika was there, prancing in welcome at the sight of his master, and a huge flood of relief swept over Lovatt.

'There he is, see? Safe in his cage. So what's the fuss about?'

Mika had gone very still, his slanted amber eyes fixed on the men. The senior officer stepped forward, eying the dog warily as he shook the padlock. Then he turned to Lovatt.

'You're saying the padlock hasn't been tampered with?'

'See for yourself. One of my stags was released before by locals with a grudge, and now we have the sort of padlocks that would need wire cutters to open.'

They should be backing off now, apologising for disturbing him. So why weren't they? Lovatt felt the first stirrings of fear.

'So you can confirm that only you could let the dog out?'

Lovatt nodded.

'And it couldn't have been loose on the island?'

'Certainly not.' He was puzzled, but on firm ground there, at least.

'Could it have got there on its own?'

What *was* this? Lovatt was beginning to get impatient. 'Look, he's a big, powerful dog. He's locked up here in the kennel unless he's with me. I never let him run loose.'

'I see. Well trained, is he?'

'Yes, of course.' He turned to the dog with a gesture. 'Mika – down.' The dog dropped immediately to a lying position, looking up at his master.

'So – you could make it do anything you like?' the officer persisted.

336

'I suppose so – within reason.'

'Like – say, attacking someone?'

Suddenly, Lovatt felt very, very cold and it had nothing to do with his bare feet. 'Someone has been attacked?'

His question was ignored. 'You are denying that you or your dog were present on Lovatt Island yesterday?'

'Most certainly I am.'

'Matthew Lovatt, I am arresting you on suspicion of murder. You are not obliged to say anything, but anything you do say will be noted and may be used in evidence.'

The younger policeman had a notebook out, ready.

With a sense of unreality, Lovatt said, 'Who am I supposed to have murdered, for God's sake?'

Again, he got no reply. 'This way.' The senior officer took his arm, urging him towards the house. 'You'd better put some shoes on and get a coat.'

Lovatt hung back. 'What about the dog?' he demanded.

The younger policeman said, 'Oh, someone's on their way to take care of *him*.' And from his emphasis it was clear that no one was talking about a comfortable basket and a nice juicy bone.

It was a considerable relief to MacNee to get the phone call telling him that the dog was safely locked up on the mainland, and the pathologist and the photographer were even now in Innellan, waiting to come across. He left his refuge and went down to the jetty to meet them.

There had been a ground frost in the early morning, and the blades of grass were etched with silver, crisp underfoot. The sun was just coming up, and it promised to be a glorious autumn day. In the wood behind the bothy, the leaves were turning and with the drop in temperature brilliant reds and yellows had started to appear.

The pathologist sniffed the clear, cold air as he landed. 'Aaah! Beautiful day,' he said cheerfully, looking around. 'Bonny place, too. We should be taking a boat out fishing today, instead of tramping about looking at remains. A few mackerel for supper – eh?'

'Up there, Doc, by the ruins,' MacNee said shortly. Right enough, if you'd a grim job like looking at corpses you couldn't afford to let it get you down, but sometimes you could be a bit too cheerful. And talking about supper as you went up to inspect the body – well, MacNee was beginning to regret the baked beans just at the thought.

The photographer was lugging his kit out of the boat, and MacNee turned back to help him take it up the hill. 'Wait,' he said to the man who had been driving the boat. 'You can take me back in a minute.'

Keeping his eyes carefully averted as he approached, MacNee said, 'The SIO is on her way, they tell me. I'll be getting back.'

The pathologist was opening his case. 'Fine. Nasty one, this.' He spoke almost with relish, and MacNee gave a little shudder as he returned to the jetty. He'd go straight home, snatch a spot of kip and then go in to the station in the afternoon. With all the fuss about this no one would be interested in his own triumph.

The boatman was a local, an elderly fisherman, roused from his bed and gagging with curiosity. 'Someone's dead, right?' he asked, before MacNee had even sat down.

'Right.'

'And Lovatt's been arrested and they're taking that dog to be destroyed. Was it his missus?'

'Hasn't been formally identified.'

The old man cackled. 'That's a yes, then. Thought it must be. Och well, they caused nothing but trouble from the day they arrived – incomers!'

Revolted, MacNee said, 'So it's all right for someone to be killed as long as it isn't one of the locals?'

He was unmoved. 'Wouldn't have happened if they'd cleared off. They knew they weren't wanted.'

Fortunately it was a short crossing. MacNee clambered out 'Thanks, Mr . . . ?'

'Rafferty.'

'Rafferty – really? A fine Irish name, Rafferty. So if someone wipes you out because you're a miserable old bastard, we just say, "Och well, he was an incomer," and leave it at that, eh? Fine by me.'

MacNee walked off before the indignant splutterings could organise themselves into speech.

Fleming had ordered a driver to take her down to Innellan. She hated being driven but she didn't trust herself. After virtually no sleep the previous night she'd been roused at three this morning, after lying awake with her troubled thoughts till one.

It was an FCA driver, and she sat in the back with her eyes closed, as if she were trying to pay off her sleep deficit, but her mind was churning as they took the now familiar road to Innellan.

This had come as a shock, but not a surprise. She had been tense, waiting for disaster; they were floundering, still with no idea where the threat was coming from, or who was threatened, and this death had been the result.

And what a hideous, bizarre way to die! Bizarre – as the death of the man in the cave had been bizarre. There was a strange echo there. But how could you arrange that a dog would rip someone's throat out?

Fleming knew about dogs. She'd lived with them all her life and she'd seen dangerous dogs – so-called handgun dogs – on far too many occasions. Despite the cliché 'no bad dogs, only bad owners', it wasn't true – some dogs were by nature aggressive, just as some people were.

As a murder weapon, though? Lovatt could have trained his dog to attack on command, of course he could. Dogs had no innate morality and savage wardogs had gone into battle beside their masters for hundreds of years. And Lovatt had been in Bosnia; could it have done that there?

She'd met his dog, though, and it wasn't some slavering beast that had to be restrained from attacking any passing stranger. It had accepted their arrival without reaction, or indeed interest – and of course, it would be familiar with Lissa. Admittedly, pets sometimes attacked family members, but the problem usually was lack of discipline. Lovatt's dog was extremely well trained. This didn't add up.

No, if it had killed her, it had been acting under instruction. Lovatt would have needed to give the order, and have trained it to understand that order, one which went counter to the behaviour demanded in normal circumstances. A complicated message to get across to an animal, however intelligent it might be.

Perhaps Lovatt thought he could blame it on the dog acting alone, reverting to its wild ancestry, but from what Fleming had seen of his affection for the animal, she didn't believe he would. So he should be confessing any minute now, in the Kirkluce headquarters where they were taking him – she'd opened her eyes at the sound of a siren and seen a badged car travelling at speed towards Kirkluce a while ago.

If you wanted to murder your wife, why choose a method that pointed inexorably to you? Unless you had your own sad and probably sick reasons – and then you'd simply confess. That was the second time she had come to that conclusion.

So – was Matt Lovatt going to admit his guilt? Fleming realised that she would be absolutely astonished if he did any such thing.

* * *

'But he couldn't have done anything!' Christie protested. She was pacing around Georgia's small sitting room as if she couldn't sit still, and Georgia had to move quickly to prevent a small side table going flying. 'He was here all night.'

Georgia sighed. 'I'm afraid he wasn't, love. His bed wasn't slept in.'

'Maybe . . . maybe he couldn't sleep, and just went out for a walk, or something. Anyway, why won't they say what he's supposed to have done?'

Georgia gave a non-committal shrug. 'I tell you what – I really fancy a cuppa. Want one?' She got up.

Christie blocked her way. 'You know something, don't you? Did you speak to someone while I was waiting in here?'

'I didn't want to tell you, love. It's probably just nonsense – you know what they're like round here—'

'*What are they saying?*'

The broken, sobbing girl, who had worried Georgia so much yesterday, had disappeared. Her fierceness now was positively alarming.

'Someone said Lissa had been attacked by his dog. Her throat . . . she's dead.'

Christie stood very still. 'Dead,' she said.

'It might not be true,' Georgia bleated.

'So they're going to say he killed her. The dog never went anywhere without him.'

The horror of Lissa's end had left Georgia shaken, but it didn't seem to have affected Christie that way – or perhaps, when you'd been through what she had in Afghanistan you didn't see things the same way as other people.

'They'd found her before they came here.' It sounded as if she was thinking out loud. 'So she would be dead by . . .' she looked at her watch '. . . say, two o'clock. And of course, before

341

Matt went out for his walk, just to get some fresh air, we were together.'

Georgia gaped at her. 'Together?'

'Yes. I was . . . comforting him. In the fullest sense of the word. Then I went back to my own room, and I was still awake when I heard the sirens. And he was here with us all evening – you can testify to that. So it couldn't possibly have been anything to do with Matt, could it? It was probably Steve Donaldson's sheepdog – collies can be very vicious.' She gave the other woman a bright, false smile.

Shocked, Georgia said, 'Christie, that's not true! Don't do this – leave it to the police. They'll find out the truth.'

'The police?' Christie laughed. 'They're the ones who came to complain to Matt about Rudolf being out, but weren't interested in who had done it. And I haven't heard that they've arrested anyone for setting the house on fire. We've got to stand by Matt – we've got to.'

'I'll tell them what I know, and I'll be glad if that proves Matt's innocent,' Georgia said slowly, but unlike Christie, it was poor Lissa she was thinking about. If this was anything other than some dreadful accident, she wanted whoever killed her brought to justice, whether Matt or anyone else.

'Fergus Crawford?' the excise officer said, looking at some notes in front of him. 'That your name?'

Fergie had been engaged in his usual practice of trying to make himself look smaller – insignificant, if he had known the word.

'Fergie,' he said.

'OK, Fergie.' He looked at the boy. He'd seen it so many times: troubled background, inadequate, not very bright, totally vulnerable to the sods ready to use him. He'd had a pal like

342

that himself at school. He hadn't been a bad kid, but he'd got a punitive sentence, while the guys who ran the operation sat back enjoying the big houses in Glasgow's Thorntonhall.

'Look, Fergie. It's serious stuff you've got yourself caught up in. There're some big guys involved, not just in this country. But if you told us everything you knew—'

'They'd get me,' Fergie said.

'We can look after that.' He knew it wasn't true: the drug networks had contacts in every prison, ready to carry out whatever dirty work needed to be done. 'You do well by us, Fergie, and we'll do well by you.'

'It's the monkeys.'

'*Monkeys?*'

The lad was looking at him as if he were a penny short. 'Monkeys. Redcaps. The military police.'

Then it dawned. 'Military police – you're a deserter?'

Fergie shrank back, as if he'd hit him.

'Right. I see.' Drugs in the military – good evidence would be pure gold. The courts would come down hard; this wasn't ton-of-bricks stuff, this was an avalanche. Come to Daddy, sunshine!

He leant forward. 'Like a cup of tea, Fergie?'

Fergie looked at him suspiciously. 'S'pose so.'

'Course you would! If I pulled strings, we could even send out for a bacon butty. Now look, I'll be straight with you. If there was someone who was using you to get drugs circulating in the military, if you give us all the stuff we need – all of it, mind you, and with you standing in court to testify – I reckon I can get the – what did you call them? – monkeys, off your back, and have you put on a witness protection programme. We'll give you another identity, and the money to start out again, on a whole new life. How does that sound?'

343

He looked at the lad anxiously, and saw a gradual smile spread over his pinched face.

'Pure dead brilliant!' said Fergie.

'What's happened to my dog? What's the problem with him?'

You tell him his wife's been murdered – though not how – and his first reaction's to ask about his dog? What was with this guy?

DC Hepburn looked at Matthew Lovatt sitting opposite her and DC Campbell in the interview room. He was shaking with what looked like anger rather than fear, and Hepburn set her feet more firmly on the ground, ready to react if the man lost it completely. She noticed that Campbell was doing the same as she glanced at him to see if he was going to answer.

When Campbell said nothing, Hepburn went on, 'I'm afraid I can't tell you. We're here to talk to you about what you did, not what the dog did.'

'I – didn't – do – anything. And neither did my dog.' The words came out through gritted teeth.

'That's what they all say.' Campbell seemed to have decided to provoke him.

Maybe Hepburn was meant to play nice cop. 'Let's take where you were yesterday, Matt,' she said soothingly. 'Why don't you talk us through it?'

Lovatt controlled himself with an obvious effort. 'Right. Where do you want me to start?'

'Last time you saw your wife,' Campbell said.

'I picked her up from the hospital – she was suffering from smoke inhalation and they kept her in for a couple of nights. I drove her back to Innellan and dropped her at a caravan someone said I could use while the house was out of action.'

'Why wasn't she staying with you at the Smugglers Inn?'

Hepburn asked, and saw faint colour come into the undamaged side of Lovatt's face at the question.

'She had developed a . . . a prejudice against Christie Jack—'

'Not surprising, if you were having a carry-on.'

Campbell's needling remark got to him. Lovatt's voice rose. 'I was *not* having "a carry-on" with her. I told your colleague—'

Hepburn interrupted. 'We have information that she has made a statement claiming you were sleeping together last night. Are you saying she's lying?'

Lovatt's dismay was evident. He gave a great groan, then said, 'Of course she's lying. Stupid little fool – she must be trying to protect me, I suppose. I wasn't even in the Smugglers last night. I went along to spend the night at the farmhouse after she and Georgia went to sleep.'

'Time?' Campbell asked.

'I couldn't be exact – around eleven, maybe? It wasn't late – we were all tired.'

'So you didn't get into your cosy bed at the Smugglers, but decided to go along and sleep in a house that was still dangerously contaminated by smoke?' Hepburn wasn't cut out for nice cop.

'I was . . . finding it claustrophobic, I suppose. The rooms are small, I had a lot on my mind, I couldn't move about without disturbing the others . . .'

'Very thoughtful, I'm sure. So from, say, half past eleven you were on your own at the farmhouse – except for the dog, of course.'

Hepburn saw Lovatt flinch, as she had intended, but before she could follow up with more pressure, Campbell said, 'The afternoon.'

'The afternoon? What do you mean?' Lovatt asked.

'Dropped your wife at the caravan. Anyone see you? Or her?'

'No, I don't think so.'

'Then?'

Lovatt shifted uneasily in his seat. 'I . . . I took Mika for a run.'

'Where?'

'Just up the hill with the deer. I wanted to check on them anyway – I've got a farm to manage, you know, despite people trying to stop me. I don't suppose anyone saw me there either.' There was a hard, defensive edge to his voice now.

'Not on the island? You might have wanted to check the deer there.' Hepburn had realised Campbell's line: that Lissa Lovatt was unlikely to have been wandering round the island in the middle of the night.

'Might have. I didn't. I put Mika back in his kennel, then went to the Smugglers Inn.'

'You didn't see a boat going over to the island? Or notice that one had gone?'

'No.'

'But Mrs Lovatt must have got across somehow. You didn't take her over?' Lovatt shook his head. 'Or give her a key for a boat?'

'No, but there's a causeway – I didn't notice whether it was uncovered. You'd have to check the tides. At low tide she or anyone else could have got across.'

Hepburn glanced at Campbell, but he didn't say anything, and she went on, 'So – to sum up. You say that you dropped your wife at the caravan, but you've no proof. You say you walked the dog, but no one saw you. You say you didn't go to the island. Do you also say you didn't use your dog to murder your wife?'

Lovatt stared at her in total horror. 'Use my *dog*! For God's sake, will one of you tell me exactly what happened?'

Sparing no detail, Hepburn told him.

It was as if somehow, under the attack of their questioning, he had shut out the knowledge that his wife was dead. This struck him like a physical blow: he rocked in his chair, then collapsed forward on to the table. 'Oh no! Oh no! It can't be – how – how vile! Poor, poor Lissa!' He began to cry, great, shuddering, painful sobs.

Either Lovatt was a great actor, or that news had come as a shock. Hepburn glanced uneasily at Campbell, whose face gave nothing away, but she was prepared to bet that both of them were thinking the same thing – which wasn't that Lovatt was a great actor.

The boatman who took Fleming across to Lovatt Island was surly, but that suited her very well. It had been bad enough fending off Tony Drummond, hopping from foot to foot with anxiety to get out the story before the big boys got here.

'Come on, Marjory, give me a break!'

'Like the break you gave Tam MacNee? No comment.' It might not be considered wise to make an enemy in the local press but considering what he did when he was meant to be a friend, it probably wouldn't make much difference.

The journey across was less than five minutes. Fleming shaded her eyes against the sun, as they powered across the calm blue water. It was a perfect morning and it looked idyllic: the neat little island, crowned with a picturesque ruin, the trees flaunting their autumn colours and the lush green grass with a couple of pretty fallow deer browsing on some low vegetation, a distance away from the activity up the hill. Ah yes, the activity.

She climbed ashore with the sick feeling in the pit of her stomach that this duty always gave her – and this one was likely to be more stomach-churning than most. She gave her name to the constable on duty, and plodded up the hill.

The pathologist came to meet her. 'Glad to see you. I've just finished all I can do here and I'd like to get back to the lab. I've a lot on my plate at the moment.'

Fleming was surprised. Usually it took longer; it must have been very straightforward. 'Right,' she said. 'I don't suppose there's any hint you can give us about the dog until you get to the lab – size, say?'

'Dog?' he said. 'What on earth has a dog got to do with it?'

'We-we thought . . . Tam thought . . .' she stammered, trying to collect her thoughts. 'He reported that the body had its throat ripped out in a dog attack.'

'He did?' The pathologist glanced back. 'Hadn't thought of that – I see exactly what he means. How very odd! It almost looks as if that's what it was meant to suggest. I'd been going to say to you that it was a highly unusual example of an injury of this kind. Usually it happens in a drunken fight, and it's the face takes the brunt – though of course she was knocked out first—'

'For goodness' sake, what happened, then?'

He smiled. 'Oh, you'd think a Weegie would recognise it when he saw it. Plenty of that in the Glasgow pubs when Rangers have lost a home game. Someone just broke a bottle, probably over her head, then set about her.'

CHAPTER TWENTY-ONE

Out in the bay, Cal Findlay was inspecting lobster pots, theoretically at least. He had pulled up a pot and landed the lobster inside it, but then he'd put down anchor just behind the island, making a show of working on the pot as he watched the comings and goings on the shore. He couldn't see what was going on at the other side, though; the hill was in the way.

There was nothing to stop him sailing round into the bay, except that everyone in Innellan knew he had no business there. He'd kept under the radar so far, and he meant to keep it that way.

Not knowing was just about killing him, though.

No answer. DS Macdonald knocked on the door again, but not hopefully. As he came up the path to the Findlays' door he could see Mrs Findlay in the front room of the croft house, asleep in her chair with her mouth open. There was a trickle of dribble coming from the corner and he suppressed a shudder. Her son must be out again, and the carer would probably only appear to give her lunch.

He'd had a note from Big Marge last night, pointing out that she'd noticed from the list of Innellan residents that there was a Calum Findlay who had not been interviewed, though the house had been ticked on the basis of an interview with Aileen Findlay.

He'd winced at that. He and Campbell had been so spooked by the nightmare Aileen that somehow her son had been forgotten – not good, when he was in the boss's bad books already.

Campbell and sodding Hepburn would be interviewing Lovatt right now, while here he was knocking on doors. Maybe the boss's decision was fair enough; even he wasn't sure about his self-control, when it came to the man who had seduced Christie then murdered his wife. In such an obscene way too – though how he'd hoped to get away with it was hard to imagine. Unless he was just going to sacrifice the dog, poor beast. Lovatt might even be reckoning that with luck, and a good advocate, he could get away with a dangerous dog charge.

Macdonald turned away from the door. He knew nothing about Findlay, what he did or where he might be found. Talking to him would probably be just as pointless as all the dozens of other interviews had been, but if he didn't do it he'd have Big Marge on his case.

The Findlays' house was high above the bay here, isolated, and perhaps quarter of a mile from the nearest house. No direct neighbours, then, but in Innellan you could be quite sure everyone knew everyone else's business. If they were prepared to tell you.

More knocking on doors. Macdonald got back into the car and drove down into the village. The Smugglers Inn was the obvious place to go for information, but if Fleming discovered he'd gone anywhere near Christie, his career would be toast. He wasn't planning to, anyway; she was hardly going to be in a receptive mood towards policemen just now, so he drove past the pub to park in the main street.

There were uniforms working the houses along at the further

end, but he'd stopped outside a cottage that looked more welcoming than the others, whitewashed and smartly painted, with window boxes full of geraniums; mostly Innellan didn't believe in frivolities like that. He decided to try there first.

The woman who came to the door was young and heavily pregnant, and either suspicious or frightened, Macdonald wasn't sure which. She opened it no more than a crack; a toddler peered round her legs, looking at the caller with large, solemn eyes.

Macdonald introduced himself, and she looked at him without enthusiasm. 'I've just told the police I don't know anything about all this,' she said, making to shut the door.

They obviously trained them young in this place – *omertà*, Scottish style. There was probably a word for it in the Gaelic.

'I was just wanting to ask if you knew where I would find Calum Findlay?'

'What are you wanting him for?'

'Just routine,' Macdonald said, with an ingratiating smile.

'Out in his boat, likely,' she said. 'All right?'

'Thanks so much for your help,' he said, laying it on thick. 'Is he a fisherman?'

'Yes. Prawns, lobsters, that kind of thing. Goes out from Kirkcudbright.'

She'd volunteered that, and she hadn't actually closed the door. Maybe she was starting to appreciate his elusive charm. Pushing his luck, he asked, 'Is that a family business?'

'No. Went away down to Barrow-in-Furness – got into fishing there then came back and got his own boat.'

'So his father wasn't a fisherman.'

There was a moment's hesitation, then she shrugged. 'Och, everyone knows anyway. Doesn't have a father.'

'So Mrs Findlay . . . ?'

'Miss.'

The toddler was getting impatient, and started tugging at her. Before Macdonald could say anything else, she said, 'Sorry, got to go,' and shut the door.

Macdonald turned away, not quite sure what that told him, except that he'd probably have to leave the late shift to contact Findlay, which was annoying. He'd noticed a small boat out in the bay, but there was nothing to say that it was his.

And now . . . ?

His next task was to check out the caravan Lissa Lovatt had apparently been staying in. It seemed unlikely that there would be anything to see – it was just another boring box-ticking exercise, but it had to be done and he seemed to be on the naughty step at the moment. He glanced at the directions he'd been given and took the familiar track up behind the village, past the big caravan he'd spent so many summers in himself, now shut up for the winter.

The one he was looking for was towards the end of the track. He'd wondered if it would be locked, but when he tried the door it opened. Even on this bright morning, the light was dim inside, with curtains closed on all the windows except the one looking out to the bay. It was a squalid little box, and clearly the owner's generous impulse had consisted only of handing over the key. Even the water container stood empty.

There was no sign of a suitcase or clothes: Lissa probably literally only had what she stood up in, after the fire. There was a bag of groceries dumped on the floor but she hadn't unpacked it, so it looked as if she had spent very little time here before going to her horrible death, destitute and alone.

Macdonald grimaced as he went out again, and fetched police tape to seal the door. He was driving back down to the village when he noticed Natalie Thomson walking briskly up the hill towards him. She looked as if she had been out for a walk and her cheeks were pink with the cold air.

He stopped the car. 'Hello! I thought you'd have left yesterday with the Saturday exodus.'

She was a little out of breath. 'I'm staying on for a few more days. Has something else happened? There seem to be an awful lot of police around. Is it to do with the fire?'

'Not exactly. There's – there's been another . . . incident.'

'Incident?'

Macdonald hesitated. It would be on the midday TV news; he might as well give her the official version. 'A woman was attacked on the island last night, by a dog, we understand. I'm afraid it was fatal.'

'By a *dog*?' She looked shocked. 'How dreadful! Oh – not that dog that lives on the farm down there? It did look very dangerous. Has it been destroyed? It's not still running loose?'

'No, no,' he reassured her. 'They took it away first thing this morning.'

'That's good, I suppose – though the farmer will be very upset. I saw them out walking a couple of times and he was clearly devoted to it.'

'Mmm,' Macdonald said. He decided against telling her that Lovatt had been arrested; she'd find that out in due course. He told her, too, that the victim hadn't been formally identified, and moved on to ask about her own movements.

She had, she said, been away doing some sightseeing and then had supper in a pub afterwards. 'You know – the one overlooking the harbour in Kirkcudbright. I can't remember its name.'

'The Moorings?'

'That's right. Then I came home.'

'And you didn't see anything unusual?'

'I'm afraid not. I turned in straight away and went out like a light. All this fresh air! I've never been so healthy.'

Certainly, Macdonald thought, she was looking pretty good.

'Thanks,' he said. 'Let us know if anything occurs to you. Enjoy the rest of your holiday.'

She smiled, then looking out towards the island, hesitated. 'I . . . I suppose it depends,' she said slowly. 'You are sure the dog will be destroyed?'

It was, he thought, the first sign of nervousness Natalie had shown, and he hurried to reassure her. 'It's not for me to say, of course. But it certainly won't be running around again.'

She nodded and turned away, while he set off back down the track.

Fleming was thinking furiously as she was taken back to the mainland in sullen silence. MacNee had jumped to the wrong conclusion, but in the circumstances she would have done the same. She'd seen far too many sheep savaged by dogs out of control, and that was exactly how they attacked.

The pathologist's conclusion changed everything. They were looking now for someone who had gone for Lissa Lovatt with a bottle. It could be anyone, and the preliminary time-of-death assessment was mid afternoon to early evening.

It was something of a problem that the person who sprang to mind was the girl Andy Macdonald had set his heart on. Lissa Lovatt had insisted that Christie Jack had set the house on fire to try to kill her. If so, when that failed, would she have taken it to the next stage – a direct attack? And, now Fleming thought about it, who was in a better position to let the stag out too? It was hard to see what the motivation for that could be, but the girl was by her own admission still suffering from war trauma. Her thinking processes might well not be what anyone else would see as normal.

Getting back promptly to HQ was a priority. But if she stopped off at the Smugglers Inn she could have a word with the girl, get some impression of the situation.

They reached the jetty and she stepped out. 'I'm obliged, Mr . . . ?' she said.

'Rafferty,' the man replied ungraciously. 'If it's any of your business.'

Fleming gave a puzzled glance back at him as she walked off.

'It's horrifying,' Elena Tindall said into the phone. 'I just keep thinking, that could have been me. They don't seem to be very good at keeping their dangerous animals under control around here. I'm only thankful it was the stag that went after me, not the dog.'

She listened for a moment, then trilled a laugh. 'Don't be silly, Cal. Of course not.'

He spoke again.

'No, I'm not going to be chased away. I'll go when I'm good and ready, OK?'

Elena's slate-blue eyes were cold as she switched off the mobile. Cal was beginning to get tiresome. She was tired of Eddie too. He'd called four times yesterday, but she hadn't answered.

It was irritating, really. Just when she was feeling so much better herself.

Eddie Tindall looked round the motor showroom, frowning. He wasn't happy with this, wasn't happy at all, and it showed. Sunday was one of the busiest days in the motor trade and he'd better things to do than chase up details his manager should have noticed. Studying the deep-set lines on his boss's expressive face, the man swallowed nervously.

Tindall went over to the low table in the waiting area, and picked up a heavily thumbed, coffee-stained magazine. 'We're not selling old bangers and cut-and-shuts. This is a high-quality used-car showroom and our customers expect high-quality service. If you think you're going to get away with out-of-date, grubby magazines, you and me are going to be parting company, sonny boy.'

'One of the girls is meant to see to that,' the man bleated, and Tindall rounded on him.

'It's your job to check on her, just like it's my job to check on you. And look at that!' He gestured towards the TV in the corner. 'Who's wanting to watch 24-hour news? You've a sports channel, haven't you?'

'I can change it now,' the man said eagerly, going towards it. He had picked up the remote when there was a bark of, 'Leave it!' He turned, surprised.

Tindall was standing staring at the screen where a newscaster was saying, '. . . near Kirkcudbright, thought to have been the victim of an attack by a German Shepherd-type dog. The woman has not been identified, but a man has been arrested and is in custody at the Galloway police headquarters in Kirkluce.'

As the newscaster went on to the next topic, Tindall said, 'Something's come up. Phone Marianne and tell her I'm going away.'

Then he hurried out, leaving the other man looking from his retreating back to the television. Then he shrugged, changed the channel, picked up the pile of offending magazines and went towards his office, shouting at the receptionist to come immediately.

She pulled a face at the assistant manager, who had also been watching with interest the confrontation with Tindall.

'He'll pay it forward, I reckon. Like in that film, you know? Wish me luck!'

Georgia Stanley was feeling harassed as she opened the door to yet another police officer – DI Fleming, this time. She'd become fond of Christie, and she was worried by the girl's state of mind. Yesterday she'd been restless, unable to settle, twitching visibly; today she seemed unnaturally calm. It wasn't healthy.

She had gone out to feed the stags this morning, and when Georgia had suggested she leave Kerr to do it, she had said simply, 'Matt will be relying on me. When they realise they have to let him out, I don't want him to find things haven't been done properly. I don't trust Kerr.'

Certainly, when Christie came back she had said, triumphantly, that there had been no sign of him, and that without her the stags would have gone hungry. She'd even seemed hungry now herself; when Georgia showed Fleming through to the sitting room she'd made considerable inroads into the plate of custard creams.

As Fleming came in, Christie looked up at her, her eyes hard and bright. 'Oh, come to try to break Matt's alibi, have you? You'll never do it. I'm standing by my statement.'

Fleming showed no sign of knowing what she was talking about. She said only, 'That's fine, Christie. I actually just wanted to ask about your movements yesterday.'

Christie sighed elaborately. 'Oh, I'll go over it again, if you want. Matt and I had supper with Georgia, then we all went up to bed. After Georgia had gone into her bedroom, I slipped across to sleep with Matt – we're lovers, you know. I got back to my room shortly before I heard the sirens, and Matt seems to have decided to go back to the farmhouse then. All right?'

There was a stillness about Fleming, Georgia thought, as if she was taking her time to assess Christie with those shrewd hazel eyes. When Christie finished, she said quietly, 'Well really, Christie, I was talking about you more than Matt. If he confirms it, you have an alibi for the early hours of the morning. What did you do in the afternoon?'

Georgia saw Christie freeze, and felt her own throat constrict.

The girl had been so stressed yesterday that she couldn't keep still, and at last had gone out, muttering that she needed to walk. She'd been out for two or three hours. And clearly the police thought that was the crucial time, so Christie's gallant lie to cover for Matt was pointless.

She was looking at her with great sympathy, when Christie said, 'Oh, I was here all the time, wasn't I, Georgia?' Her blue eyes were flashing an urgent message.

Georgia felt hot colour flood her face. The hazel eyes were coolly fixed on her now too. She felt like a butterfly skewered to a board by two hatpins.

She had no choice, though. 'Christie, I know you wouldn't have killed Lissa, but I can't lie to the police, and you shouldn't either. It's their job to find out who did this terrible thing, and we have to help them in any way we can.'

'Traitor!' Christie cried. 'Traitor! I thought you were my friend.'

Georgia felt, this time, as if the hatpin had gone straight through her heart.

'I help you, Mr Tindall?' Standing in the doorway of the master bedroom of the Salford penthouse flat, Lola stood watching in puzzlement as her employer threw what looked like a random selection of clothes into a suitcase.

'No thanks, Lola. I'm just going to be away for a few days. Not sure how long. All right?'

He snapped the case shut. He seemed very tense; she didn't like to point out that though he'd packed shirts, underwear and sweaters, there seemed to be no trousers or socks. But he didn't look as if he wanted advice and she wasn't about to offer it. She wasn't taking any risks with her nice, well-paid housekeeper's job – and now with pretty much a paid holiday too.

'Going to see Mrs Tindall?' she suggested, and was surprised when he shuddered.

'I don't know. I . . . I hope not,' he said, mystifyingly, and then picked up his case and departed.

Fleming took Campbell with her to the interview room, where Lovatt was waiting for them already. He looked dreadful: eyes red-rimmed, his good cheek hollowed in, leaving the other looking oddly plump. His head was down and he didn't even look up as Campbell went through the procedures for the recording, then came back to sit beside Fleming.

'Mr Lovatt?' she began.

At last he looked up. 'Someone's trying to destroy me.' His voice was husky and strained. 'I don't know who it is, I don't know why, but bit by bit they're tearing my life apart. They tried to destroy my farming, then my house, and now my – my wife. And my dog. Has he – has he . . . ?' He broke down.

Fleming said hastily, 'Mr Lovatt, let's deal with that first. Nothing's going to happen to the dog. The whole thing was a misunderstanding. It looked as if your wife had been attacked by an animal, but further investigation has shown that this wasn't the case.'

Lovatt seemed unable to control his tears, but he looked at her with dawning hope. 'You swear? That's not just some sort of trick, is it?'

'No, of course not. That is absolutely true.'

'Oh thank you, thank you! You have no idea what that means to me.'

Campbell shifted uneasily in his seat and Fleming, too, was uncomfortable with this heartfelt gratitude.

'I have to apologise that this happened at all,' she said awkwardly.

He hardly seemed to hear her, going on, 'You see, Lissa and I . . . well, we hadn't been getting on for some time. And then, of course, she was having an affair with Kerr Brodie – not that I blamed her, after all that had happened. But recently I had the impression he was trying to end it, so there was nothing for her here, nothing. But she couldn't just leave because—' He broke off. 'You know about the baby's grave?'

Fleming nodded, reluctant to break the flow by speaking. She wondered, though, whether they had told him where his wife's body had been found; she rather thought not, from the way he spoke.

Lovatt went on again. 'At least I had the farm. I love the life, love the land. And I had Mika – such a great dog! You're sure—' He was suddenly anxious again.

'Sure,' Fleming said.

'He's been with me through so much – Bosnia, this . . .' He touched his face. 'When I was at my lowest ebb, when I thought a bullet would be the best way out, he was there, never leaving my side, watching me, reminding me that I had to stay alive, for him. He's a one-man dog – if anything happened to me, they'd have to put him down.'

Then it struck him. 'If I went to jail—'

His voice shook, and Fleming stepped in hastily. 'Matt, we're not going to charge you – certainly not at the moment. I don't know whether you killed your wife, as yet—'

'I didn't, I swear it!'

She ignored the impassioned response. 'Extensive enquiries are under way, and depending on what emerges we may bring you back here. You must stay in the area, but at the end of this interview you will be free to go and we'll return your dog.

'There's just a couple more questions. What is your relationship with Christie Jack?'

Lovatt looked unhappy. 'Lissa always said she had a crush on me. I didn't believe her, but . . . Christie thinks she's protecting me by saying we were together. We weren't, of course.'

'Could she have been hoping for that outcome if Lissa was out of the way?'

'No!' he protested. 'She couldn't – she wouldn't! She's just a child.'

'She had very dreadful experiences in Afghanistan, I understand.'

'She did, but . . .'

His voice trailed away. He was, Fleming thought, very uneasy. He didn't think it was entirely impossible, but he certainly wasn't going to say so.

'Anyway, is there anyone, anyone at all, who would have reason to, as you put it, tear your life apart? Oh, I know you've talked of local problems before and of course we are looking into these, but this, to be honest, seems just too extreme.'

He was nodding agreement. 'I know. I can't see it. I'm positive they let the stag out, I would believe they might have set fire to the house, just to try to drive me away, but this . . .'

'Who, then?' she pressed him.

'Done something bad in your past life?'

Campbell, who hadn't spoken at all, shot out the question and Fleming saw Lovatt take it like a bullet.

'N-no,' he stammered. 'Of course not. What could I have done?'

As usual, Campbell was on to something. She followed it up. 'You were in a theatre of war. Was there something happened in Bosnia?'

She realised from his face that she had asked the wrong question. 'War crimes, you mean? Certainly not.' He spoke with all the authority of a clear conscience, and a touch of arrogant anger too at his honour being impugned.

'Something else, though?' she asked, but not very hopefully. He'd had that moment to collect himself.

'Probably in the course of my life I've upset people – be surprising if I hadn't. But there isn't a living soul who would have a reason to hate me that much.'

'Anyone who might hate you anyway, reasonably or not?'

Lovatt shrugged. 'Unreasonably – how should I know?'

He had put up the barricades, and they had no legitimate reason to keep him here any longer. Fleming got up. 'I am terminating the interview here,' she said for the benefit of the recording. 'You are free to go, Mr Lovatt. But I would urge you to be very careful. For whatever reason, you seem to have become a target, and until we know who and what is behind it, you aren't safe.'

When he had gone, she turned to Campbell. 'Well?'

'Brave man,' Campbell said. 'Knows something. Rather get his throat slit than tell us.'

'Foolhardy,' Fleming corrected him. 'Oh damn! I meant to ask him about Andrew Smith, but I forgot. Doesn't matter – I doubt if we've seen the last of him. Let's go and have a chat with his little friend Christie.'

Louise Hepburn had just finished her shift and by now should be going home for Sunday lunch. But she was too caught up in the case to want to leave, high on the adrenaline of the chase.

After the interview she and Campbell had done with Lovatt, she'd ruled him out as Lissa Lovatt's killer, especially now that Tam MacNee's conclusion had proved embarrassingly wrong. Lucky the poor dog hadn't resisted arrest and been shot on the spot!

She tucked herself away in a corner of the CID room, hoping to avoid notice from other detectives who might feel unpaid overtime was letting the side down, and cosied up to a computer. There were two ideas she wanted to follow up.

The easy one was Lovatt's grandmother's will. Wills were a matter of public record, held at the General Register Office for Scotland, in Edinburgh. She got the full name from the voters' roll, then keyed it in with an approximate date and clicked 'Search'.

It wasn't easy. There was no Elspeth Lovatt in the system, apparently. Hepburn swore. No doubt it was delayed in probate, or something – lawyers were famous for dragging their heels. That would mean discovering who her solicitor was, getting hold of him and persuading him to disclose the contents, which lawyers were notoriously reluctant to do. It would certainly take time, and she was a young woman in a hurry. What Big Marge had said about teamwork hadn't stopped her wanting to be the team member who got the breakthrough.

Thwarted, she turned to her second quest. She wanted to dig up a bit of background on Lovatt's army career. That, too, was more complicated than she had thought; information about the now disbanded King's Own Scottish Borderers was held by the Army Personnel Office in Glasgow – closed on Sunday. With some inspired googling, she managed to track down the brigadier in command at the time and with liberal mentions of the CID and a murder investigation, persuaded him to disclose the names of officers serving with the regiment in Bosnia.

This time, she struck gold. She listened, gobsmacked, to the man at the other end. She asked another question. Then she thanked the man profusely, rang off, and returned to the General Register.

Lovatt's grandmother's will was there, right enough, and the first sentence, where it stated her name, was confirmation. Hepburn looked at it with widening eyes as she scrolled down the short document. There it was – under their noses all the time.

CHAPTER TWENTY-TWO

They weren't getting anywhere. Lack of sleep was catching up with Fleming – she was feeling light-headed, her bones ached and there was a constant muzzy buzz in her head. Christie Jack, attending by invitation, was answering their questions with a mixture of shrugs, denials, and silence. Her eyes looked completely dead.

'Christie,' Fleming said, making her voice warm and persuasive with a considerable effort, 'don't make things harder for yourself. You've begun by lying to us. That's a bad start. But I can think of reasons why you did that.

'The lie you told us about being with Matt Lovatt—'

'It wasn't a lie.' Her voice was flat. 'He only denied it so I wouldn't be involved.'

'We've been there already, Christie, and we're not going there again. I'll concede that you've been feeling persecuted, so perhaps in asking Georgia to lie you were only trying to get us off your back, and it's in your favour that the "alibi" you constructed involving Matt was for the wrong time.

'But I have to look at the other side. You may be quite smart enough to reckon we'd make that assumption, and you could also have thought Georgia would be too kind to drop you in it.

You have to convince us the first scenario is the right one, not the second.'

'What would make me think you would believe me?'

'Try it and see.' Fleming's patience was wearing thin.

Christie gave her a bored, sulky look that was almost adolescent, and Fleming snapped. 'Fine. It's your choice. We request that you remain at the Smugglers Inn while investigations are under way.'

She terminated the interview and when she told Christie she was free to go, the girl got up and left without a word.

Fleming rubbed her hand tiredly down her face. 'Is she just bolshie, or is she a killer?'

When Campbell only shrugged, she said crossly, 'Oh, for goodness' sake, don't you start. I want your considered opinion. And *don't shrug*!'

Campbell duly considered. 'Bolshie, probably.'

Giving him a dangerous look, Fleming went back to her office.

DS MacNee breezed into the CID room, radiating bonhomie. A phone call to customs had told him not only that Kerr Brodie had been charged with serious drugs offences, but that his companion, a lad on the run from the army, was cooperating fully. There was nothing like a spot of revenge for putting you in a good mood.

Revenge for the poor lassie he had found probably wasn't on the cards, but he was now ready to devote his full attention to achieving justice for her, at least.

There were three detectives working at computers when he came in. 'Right, lads,' he said briskly, 'what's happened? Have they brought Lovatt and the dog in?'

To his surprise, it provoked a laugh, and he frowned. 'Come on, share the joke.'

There was an exchange of glances, and then one said, 'Ah well, Tam, it's not quite like that. You've surely been in Glasgow after an Old Firm match?'

MacNee, a lifelong Rangers fan, stiffened. 'What are you on about?'

'Thought you'd have recognised a glassing when you saw it. Broken bottle. Straight in the throat.'

He gaped. The picture of her lying there, which he'd been trying, unsuccessfully, to put out of his mind, came back with sickening clarity.

'It . . . it wasn't the dog?'

'Nope.'

He could feel cold sweat prickling on his forehead. 'They haven't . . . they haven't . . . ?'

'Will we put him out of his misery, lads?' one grinning officer said. 'Och well, Tam, I'm in a good mood this morning. It's away home with Lovatt now. It wasn't amused, mind you. Gave the handler a nasty nip.'

MacNee wiped his brow. 'Thank God it's all right. Is the boss here? I daresay she's not amused either. I'd better go and see her and get it over with.'

Someone whistled the 'Dead March' as he left and he went slowly up the stairs, feeling humiliated. He'd jumped to conclusions without proper evidence, and he knew why he hadn't waited to get it – pure cowardice.

The knowledge fairly took the shine off his satisfaction.

Marianne, alerted by the aggrieved manager, dialled her boss's mobile. He was expected back for a specially scheduled meeting with an important client with a fleet of cars he replaced every year from Tindall's ex-dealer stock. He was due in half an hour and she wanted to know what to say to him, and when to make another appointment.

Eddie's tone, when he answered, was not encouraging, but Marianne was made of stern stuff.

'What the hell's going on, Eddie? Where are you?'

'Carlisle. I'm on the hands-free.'

'*Carlisle!* You've got Brian Miller going to toddle in here any minute. What am I to tell him?'

'Fix up another appointment. I'll be back in two or three days. Probably.'

He sounded strained, unnatural. What was going on? Then it dawned. Of course! That Woman.

'Going up to Scotland, are you?' She struggled to keep hostility out of her voice.

'Yes. Kirkcudbright.'

Of course. She'd clicked her fingers and he'd jumped, just like that. Well, Eddie paid her to be his secretary, not his keeper – though heaven knew the dumb bastard needed one.

'I'll cancel your appointments till then, right? We'll need to keep in touch, though. Where are you going to stay?'

'Don't know, yet.'

With a sigh, she suggested booking him into a hotel and he jumped at the offer. So he wasn't joining That Woman somewhere, then? Did she know he was on his way – or had Clive done the detecting he was being paid for and come up with something that told Eddie where his wife was, so he'd gone up to spy on her?

That didn't fit, though. The manager had said he didn't get a phone call, just saw something on the news that had sent him off. There was a TV downstairs in the showroom; Marianne couldn't resist trying to satisfy her curiosity.

There was no one in the waiting area. She switched from the sports channel to News 24, and stood frowning, waiting for some item that made a connection. And at last, there it was – a woman found dead on an island in Scotland, somewhere near Kirkcudbright.

So of course Eddie, poor sod, had decided it was her. He'd been going on about not having spoken to her the last couple of days. It probably wasn't anything to do with That Woman at all, and Marianne could only hope that he wouldn't be in such a state about it that he went off the road.

If it did happen to be her, though, Marianne wouldn't be feeling the need to lay in an extra box of tissues for herself.

There was no answer to MacNee's knock on Fleming's door, though they'd said downstairs that she was in. Maybe she was on the phone. He opened it, and glanced inside.

Fleming was asleep, her head down on her desk. She didn't move when he cleared his throat, and remembering she'd been called at three in the morning, he turned to tiptoe out. He knocked the door with his foot, though, and this time she surfaced, raising her head groggily from the desk.

'Oh – oh, for goodness' sake! Sorry, Tam.' Her voice was thick and she shook her head as if trying to clear it. 'I must have crashed out. I haven't had much sleep for the last couple of nights.'

From the look of her, he could well believe it. He said, 'Can you not maybe go away home for an hour or two and get a proper rest?'

'I'll be fine. I'll phone for coffee. Want some?' She picked up the phone and while she ordered it MacNee tried to frame his apology.

When she turned back to him, he said with some awkwardness, 'Marjory, I'm sorry. I screwed up and it's just lucky it wasn't a whole lot worse. When I thought that dog was loose on the island, I lost it completely. Broke the land speed record getting myself safe in the bothy. I'm black, burning ashamed.'

She gave a huge yawn. 'Sorry, I'll wake up in a minute. You

weren't the only one to think that, Tam. Bill had half a dozen sheep killed by stray dogs earlier this year, and they looked exactly like that. It's how dogs attack – and frankly, I wouldn't have hung around either. We've both seen Lovatt's dog, and you wouldn't stand a chance. I'm glad the poor beast didn't have to be put down, though.'

'You could say.' MacNee's agreement was heartfelt. 'Took a bit of a nibble out of one of the handlers apparently. Couldn't blame him.'

'Lucky he stopped there. If something happened to the dog with Lovatt in his present mood I'd be seeking a warrant to confiscate his shotgun.

'Ah, here's the coffee! Thanks – I'm needing this. And biscuits – just realised I haven't eaten all day.' Fleming smiled at the FCA as she set down the tray.

MacNee watched her load her black coffee with sugar and set about a jaffa cake. 'You'll just get a sugar rush with that,' he said disapprovingly. 'You should go to the canteen and get some proper food.'

'Never thought I'd live to see the day when Tam MacNee was lecturing me about junk food. Anyway, I'm fine after my power nap.'

'Oh, that's what it was, is it?' he said sardonically.

'Absolutely. Anyway, back to business. We've both agreed it appeared to be a dog attack. And I'll tell you what the pathologist said: "It almost looks as if that was what it was meant to suggest."'

'Did he?' MacNee was struck by the idea. 'Right enough, I've seen plenty broken-bottle attacks, but I've never seen one where they went straight for the throat. Mostly it's right in the face, and her face . . .' He stopped, recalling the spattered blood. 'Well, it hadn't been mutilated, anyway.'

'Did someone just think that the dog would be blamed and we wouldn't look elsewhere? Or . . .'

They both spoke together. 'Someone wanted the dog to be blamed.'

Fleming went on, 'Wanted the dog put down. Something else to damage Lovatt. He says someone's trying to tear his life apart, and maybe he's right.'

'Brodie,' MacNee said, with sudden certainty. 'He's been on the spot each time. And he'd even a cat's paw – a lad he was hiding from the military police on the island. He could have been involved as well.'

Fleming considered that. 'He's been having an affair with Lissa, admittedly. But according to Lovatt, he'd cooled on the idea and was trying to end it.'

'Managed, then, didn't he? It's Brodie, I tell you,' MacNee said. He was visibly gloating. 'They're holding him at Stranraer. I'll get down there and—'

'Tam.'

'What?' His tone was belligerent, but he knew what she was going to say.

'It's possible. It's not a certainty. We've seen already where jumping to conclusions gets us.'

The 'us' was generous. 'Fair enough,' he said gruffly.

Fleming was tapping her front teeth with a fingernail. He waited, then she said slowly, 'I just don't see why the persecution should have started suddenly. Brodie's been living here for three years. He's had a nice little number going with the drugs – why do something like this, that was bound to have us all over them like a rash?'

'Maybe Lovatt realised and was threatening to turn him in,' MacNee was arguing, when there was a knock on the door and DC Hepburn bounced into the room, holding some papers.

'I think we've got it right here, ma'am,' she said.

* * *

A police officer, silent and, Matt Lovatt felt, shamefaced, drove him back to Lovatt's Farm in a dog van with Mika whining unhappily in the back. Staying at the Smugglers Inn wasn't going to work any more – the situation with Christie was too fraught, and he would rather sleep on the floor in his own home. The air would be a bit cleaner tonight, at least.

When they arrived, he got out without thanking the driver, just stood beside him as the man nervously opened the door to let the dog out, then scuttled back into his van.

Lovatt watched him drive off, then dropped to his knees to stroke the dog, burying his face for a moment in its ruff to hide the tears of relief and sheer exhaustion. Mika, unsettled by the strangeness of this, fidgeted uneasily, and once released pranced a few steps, looking back over his shoulder to invite a walk. At a gesture from Lovatt he raced off along the shore path, Lovatt following slowly.

Every bone in his body ached. Perhaps it was the result of his makeshift bed last night, but it felt as if the pain was a deeper malaise, the pain of the past. He was scared, too. He had lied to the police, and he intended to lie again. He was too afraid to tell the truth. A soldier, and a coward.

The series of shocks he had suffered over the last few days had affected him like increasingly powerful physical blows. He felt like a boxer in the ring, punch-drunk, unable to predict his invisible opponent's next attack. Sooner or later, it would be a knockout, and by now he wasn't sure he even cared. God knew he was living on borrowed, or perhaps stolen, time already.

He had told the police the truth when he said that he couldn't think who could now hate him so much. Lovatt racked his brains as he walked, but he could only come back to the tired old theory of the Donaldsons and Sorley, and even he didn't believe that any longer.

There was someone unseen, unknown, someone who, for reasons he could not understand, hated him so intensely that merely killing him wasn't enough: he must be destroyed in agony first. His flesh was starting to creep and he found himself scanning the hill slopes and the shore as if there might be cruel and hostile eyes watching him even now.

Elena Tindall went to pick up her handbag from the ledge by the chalet's big window. She was on her way to Kirkcudbright; she fancied a little browse round the shops, a visit to the deli to get something for supper, perhaps with a bottle of wine.

She was feeling so much better: her head felt light and airy, purged of all the dark thoughts of years, like an attic that had been swept clear of all the dust and spiders and the worse things that she'd never chosen to recognise, that lived in the secret, dirty corners. So free in her mind, so relaxed in her body. Everything was so straight and simple now.

A movement down below caught her eye: a van, drawing up outside the Lovatts' farmhouse. Then a man was getting out; a tiny frown creased her smooth brow. Another man, releasing a dog from the back.

Her frown deepened. Elena picked up the binoculars that lay on the ledge and watched as the van drove away, and man and dog walked out along the shore path. Her mouth took an ugly turn and her eyes narrowed.

She watched until they were out of sight. She put down the binoculars with unnecessary force. Then she took a deep, deep breath and put her hand up to her forehead to smooth out the frown, noticing as her sleeve fell back that the wounds on her wrist were healing nicely. She hadn't cut herself for days now.

That was progress, and she wasn't going to let this little setback spoil her mood. She was smiling again as she locked up the chalet and got into the car.

* * *

'It's there, see.' DC Hepburn pointed to the document, 'Last Will and Testament of Elspeth Smith or Lovatt.'

'It's the wrong way round,' MacNee said instantly. 'Should be Lovatt *or* Smith.'

Hepburn smiled. 'In Scotland, you record a married woman like she has an alias, with her married name first, right? So if she's formally Smith or Lovatt—'

'She was married to a man called Smith,' Fleming was stunned. 'She just used her maiden name—'

'But maybe her son didn't.' Hepburn, with bright, excited colour in her cheeks, cut across her superior. 'And there was no Major Lovatt in the KOSB. There *was* a Major Matthew Smith.'

'So – Lovatt Island, Lovatt Farm. It was her family.' Fleming spelt it out.

'Yes, she must have changed her name officially – presumably her husband did too. And her grandson was only going to inherit – look,' Hepburn shuffled on to the next page, 'provided he changed his name to Lovatt.'

'So he was lying blind when he said he didn't know who Andrew Smith was,' Fleming said. 'Could he even have killed him?'

'And all this is revenge for that?' For some reason, MacNee's mind was running on revenge.

She considered it. 'He said he'd never been here before he came into the property, and from what the locals say that seems to be true. He told us the family had been estranged from his grandmother – which might well be true too, if the son refused to call himself Lovatt. And it would explain why he wasn't to inherit.'

'Lovatt could have sneaked up when he was on leave,' MacNee pointed out. 'If you were planning on abandoning your old man to die a lingering death in a sea cave, you wouldn't take out an advert in the *Galloway Globe*, would you?'

'We've been asking the locals the wrong question,' Fleming said. 'What a bloody waste of time! We've been assuming they were deliberately obstructive, but maybe they'd never heard Elspeth's son called Smith.

'Right. Let's get the show on the road. I'll get authorisation for more overtime. Tam, call in uniforms. Get Campbell and Macdonald back here for a meeting in, say, three-quarters of an hour. Pick up Lovatt again – I want to see him before the evening briefing.'

She went to the door, then paused. 'Well done, Louise – good work. I want you there too.'

Hepburn, who had been holding her breath, glowed. Mission accomplished.

Eddie Tindall was tired. It had been a long drive, and he'd been flashed by a speed camera on the way up, which hadn't improved his mood. Still, at least the hotel Marianne had booked was on the Kirkcudbright high street, easy to find, and it looked all right.

He ordered tea in the lounge on his way up to his room, and paused there only to dump his suitcase. He'd listened to *Five Live* all the way, but none of the news bulletins had any more information about the murdered woman, though he knew now she'd been found on Lovatt Island, near some village called Innellan, wherever that might be. He was counting on a chatty waitress to fill in some of the details.

The girl who brought the tray was quite ready to discuss what was clearly a hot topic in the town and Eddie discovered, with inexpressible relief, that the murdered woman was a local and that her husband's dog had killed her. He winced at the thought, but it wasn't his Elena and he settled down to enjoy the scones. He'd missed his lunch, after all, and he supposed he'd made a bit of a fool of himself. Still, the manager didn't matter and Marianne was used to him – she'd have gone home when the meeting with Brian Mitchell was cancelled but he could phone her there and say he'd be back tomorrow.

As he sipped his tea, though, his mind slipped into its default setting – Elena. Clive had ferreted out that she was somewhere near here; maybe, if he hung around for a bit, drove round the area and asked a few questions, he might get some idea of where she was.

And who she was with. The fear had been haunting him, awake and in his dreams. She'd never been away for so long, never failed to return his calls. Of course, he reminded himself, she'd said that she'd been feeling stressed, that she was on a retreat . . .

When the girl came back for his tray, he asked about places that hosted retreats, but she only looked blank. Nothing to be gained there, then. He'd had a look at the map too and it was a huge area, with hundreds of back roads – she could be anywhere. His spirits sank. Maybe he should just go with Plan A and drive back to Salford tomorrow.

The evening yawned ahead. It wasn't four o'clock yet and the hotel didn't serve an evening meal until seven. If Eddie started in on the whisky now, he'd be in no state to leave early tomorrow morning; a speeding fine was one thing but losing his licence was another altogether.

He might as well take a stroll, have a look around the town. Marianne had said it was a holiday destination and it was a nice autumn afternoon. There was a chill in the air when he went out but it was a pretty enough place, with a kind of castle thingy and a small harbour. He watched someone stacking lobster creels for a bit, then wandered along past the shops.

He was nearly back at the hotel. He'd put in half an hour, though, so if he went up to his room and grabbed a spot of shut-eye, he could—

Eddie stopped short. There she was, his Elena. She was coming out of a food shop with a carrier bag, wearing a sort of weatherproof jacket over jeans and a T-shirt. No jewellery, no make-up. For a moment he'd hardly recognised her.

'Elena!' The word rose to his lips as she set off in the opposite direction, but he stifled it. What would he say? How would he explain what he was doing here? She would know immediately that he had tracked her down. He remembered, all too clearly, her anger when he'd questioned her about her escapes, early on in their marriage. If she discovered he'd used a detective to find her . . . Eddie felt cold at the thought.

He'd come all the way up here, fearing she was dead. He could go back home tomorrow secure in the knowledge that she wasn't; she was alive and looking fine. Plan A.

He stood watching her walk away to – to where? Where was she going – and who to? If she was looking so unlike herself, was it because she was with some man who liked a woman to look natural, not highly finished as his own beautiful Elena always was? The snake of jealousy uncoiled, and began writhing inside him.

With sudden decision, he ran into the hotel car park and jumped into his car. She wouldn't recognise it; he'd been driving one of the sales force vehicles when he'd seen the news. But he mustn't draw attention to himself and he mustn't lose her, either. When he drove out she had vanished.

His heart in his mouth, he accelerated to the corner, then turned along to his left. And – oh lucky, lucky Eddie – there she was, getting into a small car. It was a hire car, not her own BMW coupé and it was facing towards him; he drove past, then when he reached a side road backed into it, and sat waiting till the car moved away.

Then very, very discreetly, he drove off in pursuit.

* * *

DI Fleming's mind was fizzing as she got back to her office to wait for the team to gather. She was still feeling light-headed, but with that had come a strange sort of clarity, as if everything was in sharper focus, as if her nerve endings were nearer the surface than usual.

Bailey had authorised whatever overtime it took. Indeed, given that this had become a headline news story, he was ready to blow the budget totally.

Fleming sat down at her desk, ignoring the waiting messages. She wanted to crystallise her thoughts before her team arrived. She wanted their input – and young Hepburn seemed promising, very promising indeed – but to be properly effective discussions needed clear direction.

And at last they had a clear direction to go in. Perhaps now they would get ahead of the shadowy figure she became more and more convinced was behind it all – please God! – before the action moved on to the next deadly phase. If Lovatt was right that someone was trying to destroy him bit by bit, there was only one obvious conclusion.

The sense of urgency possessed her, making it hard for her to sit still – or perhaps that was just lack of sleep. She got up and walked over to the window that looked out to the plane trees and down to the humdrum normality of the Kirkluce street below, but she wasn't seeing it.

They needed to establish how the recent events were related. From the time of the discovery of the body, these had escalated in seriousness from what could be described as petty vandalism to murder – and murder so cold-blooded that it looked as if it might have been staged so that a dog would be destroyed to punish its owner.

Was there someone who cared about Andrew Smith – someone, perhaps, who had not known he was dead until the body was discovered? Someone who knew, or thought, that Matt

Lovatt had killed him and was taking appropriate revenge?

Perhaps he had, but Fleming was convinced that when it came to his wife's death, at least, Lovatt was blameless. And the more she thought about it, the surer she was that the cold brutality of the two deaths was the sort of signature murderers left on their crimes, as distinctive as the scribble of an artist at the foot of a painting.

That felt right. She let her mind run on those lines. Why, if you had killed Andrew Smith, would you choose the discovery of his body to embark on a high-profile series of crimes which would focus police attention on the present day rather than the past?

She had no immediate answer. She could get the team thinking about that, see if anything emerged. And they'd all need to focus too on which of the lines of enquiry this had opened up should take priority.

And if they got that wrong? Though the sun was streaming through the window on this sunny autumn afternoon, Fleming felt suddenly cold.

Bill Fleming checked his phone, just in case he'd missed a call, and sighed. Oh well, he knew what was going on at the moment, and he should be used to it by now.

CHAPTER TWENTY-THREE

There was a car outside the Findlays' house when DS Macdonald went back at four o'clock. This was putting him under time pressure, but he'd been on his way to Innellan again when he got MacNee's call about the meeting, briefing him on the most recent developments which included Hepburn being added to the team.

It had been hard not to let his private fury show. The woman was a total bitch, but now, with a lucky guess, she'd got promoted to being Big Marge's new best friend. So Macdonald had a choice – he could sulk in the corner of the playground, or try to play himself back into the game. Checking out Findlay meant that at least he would get first crack at putting the Andrew Smith/Lovatt question, and maybe that would bust the whole case wide open and he'd be flavour of the month. A man can dream.

He rang the bell but there was no answer. Macdonald swore. There was the car, so had the man seen him arrive and taken cover? Possible, certainly, but he'd no proof. Findlay could just have come home from work, then gone out for a wee walk, or to see someone. Kicking in doors without solid reason could seriously damage your professional health.

He looked nervously at his watch. He couldn't afford to be late with Fleming already set, in her much-mocked phrase, to have his guts for garters. In some frustration, he walked to the fence by the edge of the bluff and peered over without much hope.

It was high tide and the causeway was submerged, but there was a man on the promontory leading to it, a hunched figure sitting on the rocks, staring out across the bay towards the island. Findlay? Not necessarily, but it was worth a shot.

There was a sort of rough path further along and Macdonald scrambled down it to the foreshore. He could see there was activity on the island, where a line of stooped uniforms seemed to be doing a back-breaking fingertip search. There were definite advantages to being CID.

There was no reaction from the man, though he thought it unlikely that he hadn't heard him coming up. Certainly, he wasn't startled when Macdonald said, 'Calum Findlay?'

He turned his head, and Macdonald scented blood. This wasn't someone who had gone out on a sunny afternoon to admire the undoubted beauty of the seascape. This man looked numb with misery, hollow-cheeked, and with black rings under his eyes. At the sight of the warrant card he visibly quivered.

'What do you want?'

'Just a wee chat,' Macdonald said. He sat down on the rocks just slightly too close and noticed with sardonic amusement the other man's instinctive recoil.

'What . . . what can I do for you?' Findlay said, with a pathetic attempt at jauntiness, while his hand went to his mouth and he began gnawing at a nail which was bitten to the quick already.

'Andrew Lovatt.'

The shock registered. Findlay's mouth fell open as he gasped. 'Wh-what about him?'

'You knew him?'

'Yeah, well, yeah, of course.' He was stuttering, looking out to sea to avoid his questioner's eyes. 'He . . . he grew up here – old Mrs Lovatt's son. Drew Lovatt. Course I knew him. Everyone did.'

'Did you know him as Andrew Smith?'

There was a chill breeze, but Macdonald could see Findlay had started to sweat. He could smell the fear as the pause lengthened. Weighing up the odds, Macdonald reckoned. What did the police know? If he denied it, would he be caught out?

A verbal nudge might help things along. 'You knew him as Andrew Smith, didn't you?'

'Yeah, well, yes, I suppose so,' Findlay muttered at last.

Macdonald didn't say anything, only raised his eyebrows.

At last, Findlay went on, 'You see, there was a big bust-up with him and his mum, and his granddad had a trawler down in Barrow. His dad was dead so he went to take it on. I wanted to be a fisherman so I got a job off him, worked down there to get a bit of money then came back here. That's all.' His story had the ring of truth, and he was clinging to it like a lifeline.

Macdonald moved on. 'So he called himself Smith down there?' Findlay nodded, and he went on, 'And when it was announced it was his body in the cave, you didn't tell us you knew him?'

'You never asked me. Common enough name.'

Damn! That was true enough, and he could hear himself blustering as he said, 'And you didn't think, since we'd been interviewing everyone in the village, you might have come to speak to us?'

'I don't listen to local gossip.'

Again, Macdonald was baulked. He tried another tack. 'So – when did you decide to come back here, then?'

'Didn't decide, really. He had to give up the boat.'

'Give it up?'

There was another long, long pause. Macdonald knew enough not to break it; he could almost hear the words whirling round in the man's head as he made his calculations. What have they found out already? If I tell them, will it be better or worse?

Findlay said, 'He was a gambler, Drew. He'd a good business, could have done really well. Couldn't stop himself, though. That's how he fell out with his mother. She wouldn't pay any more.'

'So he left, changed his name . . . ?'

'Then threw away his grandfather's business too.'

There was useful bitterness there. Macdonald homed in on it.

'You didn't get what he'd offered you when you followed him down to Barrow?'

'You could say. Came home, took a mortgage on a boat, thought I could make it on my own, but you know what they've done to the fishing. And now I'm stuck with her.' He jerked his head up, towards the house. 'Can't afford to get out.'

Poor bastard, Macdonald thought, but poor woman, too. Those cries of 'Help me! Help me!' had totally spooked Campbell, and he'd thought of them since himself, too. Even so, poor bastard. Still, he had a job to do.

'So you came back here, when?'

'Can't remember. Twenty-seven, twenty-eight years ago. Something like that.'

Findlay had regained quite a lot of control as he related what Macdonald was prepared to believe was the truth. He needed shaking out of it.

'So you were here when it happened?' he said.

'What happened?' Findlay's face had gone blank, but one hand crept towards his mouth again and he bit at his thumbnail.

'When Andrew Smith, Lovatt, whatever you like, was murdered? Ten, twelve years ago, or thereabouts, the labs are telling us.'

Findlay took his hand down from his mouth, then grasped it with the other hand as if to restrict it from the telltale activity. 'I don't know anything about that. Whoever killed him was probably some big guy he owed money to.'

'That'll be right,' Macdonald said, taking no trouble to hide the sneer in his voice. 'Criminal gangs, they operate all the time here in Innellan.'

It was a mistake. Findlay's face set. He shrugged. 'Believe what you like. I don't know anything about it.'

'What about the murder last night, then?'

'Don't know anything about that either,' Findlay said, but he started to shiver, his teeth chattering together. Before Macdonald could say anything, he got up. 'It's getting cold. If you want to ask me anything more, you can come back to the house.'

Macdonald took another look at his watch. There were more big questions – a lot more – he planned to ask, but given what Findlay had said already, he'd be wise to have the next interview properly recorded. He didn't want to piss Big Marge off by being late either.

He climbed back up the path behind Findlay. When he said, 'I think that's all. Thanks for your help,' Findlay gave him a look of incredulous relief and retreated inside like a rabbit into its burrow.

Back in his car, Macdonald was grinning as he set off down to the village. Oh, he was looking forward to squeezing that one till the pips squeaked.

As he passed the end of the track to the chalets, he saw Natalie Thomson's car turning on to it. She was a strange one, that. Who, coming on holiday and finding the sort of mayhem that was going on here, the place infested by police officers and a murderer on the loose, not only carries on regardless, but extends the let?

A little niggle edged at his mind. In any case like this, you were always alert for the things, and the people, that somehow didn't fit. But then he reached the main street and glancing left saw the Smugglers Inn, which reminded him of Christie, Christie who, whatever troubles she had caused him – like, plenty – still had a grip on him. He couldn't understand it. He'd always seen himself as pretty grounded, and this certainly wasn't rational. In trying to work it out, without success, the little niggle disappeared from his mind.

Eddie Tindall had been trying to keep a car or two between him and his quarry but, as Elena turned on to smaller and smaller roads, that became more and more difficult. He was overtaken once by a police car, but then it overtook Elena as well so it hadn't helped. How long would it be before she glanced in the mirror and recognised him? He didn't even have a hat or sunglasses in the car.

He drew into the side and dug out a map. With some relief he realised it was a dead-end road she'd taken; she had to be heading for the place where that woman had been killed. He'd always reckoned only sick people did that. Surely she wasn't going to gawp, his elegant, fastidious wife? Perhaps the retreat she had talked about just happened to be down here.

Anyway, he could relax now so he waited for a minute or two, to be on the safe side, before heading down the road after her. When he reached the village by the side of the bay, there was no sign of her but there were plenty of police cars about the place, and he could see officers going from door to door. There seemed to be photographers and even someone filming with a camera labelled BBC, too.

You wouldn't think a dog attack would generate that kind of interest. Eddie drove on through to where the road ended, down by the shore, frowning. Unless, it suddenly struck him, the killer dog was still on the loose? He had a sudden lurch of fear at the thought of the danger to Elena – would she be wise enough not to go wandering about?

Where was she, anyway? Her car was nowhere to be seen. Perhaps the retreat wasn't actually here; perhaps it was beside the road somewhere and he hadn't noticed it. He'd certainly passed one or two big houses.

There was quite a bit of coming and going at the local pub, he noticed. He could always ask there, and just as he reached it someone drove out of the small, crowded car park. He tucked the car into the free space and went inside.

The bar was busy, and the woman serving was looking flustered. Some of her clients had cameras round their necks, and it looked as if most of the others were media too. Eddie headed for the far end of the room, where there were two or three men sitting together who looked as if they might be more likely to have local knowledge.

'Busy today,' he said cheerfully.

The only response to his greeting was a brief nod, and the man nearest to him half-turned his shoulder. Not what you'd call a chatty lot.

It was a few minutes before the woman came to take his order, and she didn't look inclined to chat either – understandable with someone else calling another order to her already. However, as he fumbled deliberately with change he said, 'I was wondering if you'd seen a friend of mine that's holidaying around here – Elena Tindall.'

The woman shook her head. 'No, sorry.'

Eddie looked at the change in his hand then said, 'Oh, dear, I'll have to give you a note.' He dug in his hip pocket. 'She's very slim, pretty, blonde . . .'

The woman frowned. 'Sounds like the lady that got chased by a stag. She was staying up in the chalets there but the papers said her name was Natalie Thomson. Thank you, sir.'

She took the note he held out, then turned to fetch change. He didn't wait to get it, or to finish the whisky in front of him.

'I've come to confess,' Derek Sorley said.

The young constable, detailed to deal with this random punter who had wandered in off the street and demanded to speak to DI Fleming, stared at him. She'd taken his full name and address and now the word 'Innellan' on the form in front of her seemed to stand out in huge letters. 'Con-confess?' she squeaked.

'Yes. So I need to speak to a *senior* officer.' Sorley withered her with a look. 'Find one, will you? Preferably Inspector Fleming.'

'Wait here,' she said and hurried out as he gave her a patronising smirk.

When she returned, along with a uniformed sergeant, his face fell. 'What's this? A senior officer, I said.'

'Yes sir,' he said stolidly. 'I'm a senior officer. I understand you wish to confess to murder, and I'm here to escort you to an interview room.'

'*Murder*? I'm not here to confess to murder!' Sorley's face, crumpling into dismay, was comical. 'I'm here to explain to DI Fleming that though my friends and I were responsible for releasing a stag from its pen last week – just a foolish prank, you understand – we had absolutely nothing to do with any subsequent event. I felt it was my duty as a citizen to make this clear, since it may be confusing the investigation into these dreadful crimes.'

'I see, sir. Well, I'm sure DI Fleming will be very grateful, but she's a bit tied up at the moment. However, I'm fully competent to take your statement confessing to the deliberate release of a dangerous animal – look, my constable's been writing it down already. And I'm sure you're wise, sir. An early confession plays very well in the courts. Now, let's take it right from the start.'

'Nice work, Andy.' Fleming had listened to Macdonald's report with considerable interest, not only for the quality of the information. He seemed fully engaged now, not obsessing over Christie Jack; with Hepburn on the team, he'd clearly reckoned he had something to prove. She'd always believed in teamwork, but a spot of rivalry might be just the kick up the backside Macdonald needed.

He'd always been hard-working, extremely competent, completely reliable. Not imaginative, though, not a risk-taker. Yet today he'd taken a punt on an idea and chanced annoying the hell out of her by being late. Fleming couldn't remember the last time he'd been late for a team meeting.

He'd burst in, full of apologies, and he'd had to sit on the table at the back since she only kept three chairs in her office. When there were four in the team, it was instructive to see who chose to perch on the table; it was usually a signal of disengagement.

Macdonald, though, dominated the meeting from his perch. He was possibly unconscious of the triumphant glance he had shot at Hepburn as he finished his report. Fortunately, Hepburn didn't seem to have noticed it either.

'It's beginning to come together,' Fleming said. 'Get off a request to Cumbria Police Authority for anything they can dig up on Andrew Smith, Andy. We need an immediate follow-up on

Calum Findlay – you and Ewan can get yourselves down there after we finish. Door to doors are going to bring in a lot more stuff, now we know who we're talking about. And I've been passed a note through saying that Derek Sorley has confessed that he and his nasty little pals let the stag out but denies with some passion that he'd anything to do with the rest. Where do we start?'

'It's an *embarras de richesses*,' MacNee said with a sly grin at Hepburn. Everyone looked taken aback, including Hepburn; the accent really was atrocious.

'We still have to start somewhere,' Fleming said hastily. 'Drew Lovatt's bust-up with his mother over the gambling debts; let's take it from there. What happened in the years between leaving here and being returned to die?'

'Went on gambling,' MacNee said. 'Got himself arrested in bad company. Debts got worse. They always do.'

'We're coming round to organised crime again, aren't we?' Fleming said. 'And you could make a case – he'd talked about where he came from, they thought it would be a good place to leave him undiscovered.'

'Not a lot to say about a boring hole in a cliff,' MacNee argued. 'Wasn't the sort of cave boys could have fun with. Anyway, them sitting having a blether down the casino, swapping childhood memories? Don't see it.'

'Haven't noticed a lot of gangsters around lately,' Campbell said dryly.

Macdonald frowned. 'Finding the body set it all off, right? Say that once it was discovered, the Lovatts presented some sort of threat to the murderer, or murderers – could have taken more than one to deal with Smith. So they had to neutralise the threat . . .'

'I think there's a problem with that.' Hepburn had been

very quiet as befitted the new girl; she glanced at Fleming as she spoke, and received an encouraging nod. 'If they came from Manchester, they'd have to hear about it first, then get themselves into position to deal with the Lovatts. It would be pretty quick work, and strangers are kind of obvious in a place like this. I think the problem is we're assuming *post hoc ergo propter hoc*.'

There was a stunned silence, and Hepburn turned bright pink. 'Sorry,' she said. 'Law was part of my general degree. Just means, because something happened after another thing, it happened because of it.'

'You could try just saying that, then.' Macdonald's tone was unfriendly, and Fleming gave him a sharp look.

'Go on, Louise,' she said.

'Sorley and his pals didn't choose to cause trouble for Lovatt because those kids, by chance, had found the body – they'd their own reasons. So it might be more constructive to consider that whoever set the house on fire and killed Melissa Lovatt might have had their own reasons too. Stop looking for a connection. Change the emphasis.'

Fleming saw her point, saw too that Macdonald had stiffened. It was obvious where Hepburn's reasoning was going to lead; if he pitched in now to defend Christie, she'd have to drop him from the case immediately. He didn't, but she could see the effort it took in his clenched jaw.

Hepburn was going on, 'Lissa Lovatt was convinced that Christie Jack was behind the fire, that this is all about some relationship she had, or wanted to have, with Lovatt. We've had unreliable statements from her – we definitely need to take that one further.'

'On the other hand,' MacNee said, 'what's the first thing you do when a woman's murdered? Check out the guy she's involved with, right? That was Kerr Brodie, and we knew he wanted shot of her. And with where he comes from, he'd not need to be told what to do with a broken bottle. He maybe held a grudge about Lovatt – he had the money, the farm . . .'

'Absolutely,' Macdonald agreed with some fervour. 'We've got a known villain on the doorstep, with his sidekick right on the island itself. Tam and I could get down to Stranraer and—'

'Yes, I'm sure we need to talk to them.' Fleming's tone was cool; Macdonald's reason for supporting MacNee was blatant. 'But they're not going anywhere, and right now I don't want any more pet theories being trotted out. I want to focus on the situation that's bubbling away in Innellan.

'Let's say that Louise is right and finding Andrew Smith wasn't the trigger. But Innellan's a sleepy little place – or it was. Then something happened, something that changed it completely. If it wasn't discovering his remains, what was it? *What changed*?'

She looked round the circle of faces, frowning in concentration, then at her watch. 'Think about it,' she said. 'I've got to get ready for the briefing.'

As they got up and filed out, she said, 'Tam – give me a minute.'

MacNee sat down again and looked at her enquiringly. After a moment, she said, 'I know I'm spaced out for lack of sleep, so maybe I'm overreacting.

'OK, given all the information that's coming in now, I can believe that we'll crack it, possibly even in the next few days, but I can't shake the feeling that if we can't work out what the *something* is that happened—'

MacNee supplied the ending, 'You think Lovatt could end up dead?'

'It would have a hideous logic. Working up to it – his house, his wife, his dog. Him. If Brodie's really behind it, he's safe. If not . . .'

MacNee's reluctance to give up his favoured theory showed, but he conceded, 'You're maybe right. So . . . ?'

'I said I wanted Lovatt brought in for questioning, but I want to go down there instead. Get him to stop buggering us about, then tell him to stay at the inn and we'll put a guard on the door. Buy a bit of time that way.

'And once Andy and Ewan have interrogated Findlay, I think quite a lot will be clearer. He could be key to the whole thing.'

'What about Louise?'

'Louise? I want to leave her here, thinking,' Fleming said. 'I've a feeling it's something she's good at.'

MacNee left, and Fleming began gathering her papers and her thoughts for the evening briefing. Her tired mind, though, churned to and fro. The quiet village. What changed? The inhabitants didn't.

They did, of course. It was a holiday place, where in the summer the population more or less doubled in size. There wouldn't be many people around now, but you could rent a chalet or a caravan any time. Strangers there would be just part of the normal landscape – even Campbell's gangsters would pass unnoticed. That would be easy enough to check, right now.

Fleming clicked on to the list of interviews, then sighed. No gangsters – just a couple of families and the single woman who'd been attacked by the stag. She hadn't really thought it would be that straightforward.

Eddie Tindall jumped into his car, feeling shaken. Maybe he should have drunk the whisky after all. He felt he needed it. What was all this about?

And what was he going to do now? Up at the chalets, the

woman had said, and he craned his neck to look out of the car window. The ground rose steeply on the other side of the road, and he could just glimpse some buildings set into the hillside above.

He could drive up, but cars made a lot of noise. Whatever this was about, he didn't want Elena to discover that he had been, well, spying on her – he didn't like the word, but it fitted the facts.

The only way he could get close was on foot. Even then he could be spotted, but Eddie needed to find out what she was up to. He got out, locked his car and set off along the road until he reached the track leading up the side of the hill.

He couldn't remember the last time he'd walked further than the width of a garage forecourt and the steep gradient had him panting for breath. The gates, too, bothered him; you couldn't open them quietly, and anyone nearby would hear the clanking of the bolts and be warned someone was coming. His heart was in his mouth as he reached the first chalet, then another, but there were no cars outside and one even had the curtains drawn. It was out of season, of course.

As the next chalet came into view, set up a little from the track, he saw her car parked beside it. So was this where she had been staying all this time? Why? What was there here for her?

The vista must be the big selling point. He turned to scan it, shading his eyes against the setting sun. His eye was caught by what looked like a farmhouse where there had been a big fire, but the scenery was certainly pretty – no, beautiful, on a clear day, with an almost cloudless sky: green grass, trees in their autumn colour, dark-blue sea, waves with tiny white frills like old-fashioned waitresses' caps. And the island, that looked the way an island would look if a child drew it, a neat shape, with the low cliffs and trees at one end.

Maybe it was just knowing what had happened there that made him feel uneasy about it, but he wouldn't have chosen to sit looking out at that for days on end. What could Elena be doing here, without spas and shops?

And why was she using the name Natalie Thomson, the name of a prostitute whose murder, Eddie had always thought, had been the reason why Elena had agreed to marry him at last?

CHAPTER TWENTY-FOUR

Even now, after a day with windows and door standing open, Matt Lovatt still choked a little as he came back into the farmhouse sitting room. The carpet, the upholstery, the curtains, even the cracks and crannies of the woodwork, had all been saturated with the smoke and every flat surface had a greasy film of soot. When he picked up the cushions he had slept on, another tainted whiff arose from them, and he returned them to the sofa hastily, without shaking them.

The room was icy cold. There had been warmth in the sun earlier, but now it was going down and as dusk fell the chill gave warning of another frosty night to come. Lovatt slumped on to a chair and looked around him with hopeless eyes. He ought to do something, at least, to clear up, but the scope of the task put it beyond him. It would cost thousands to get this sorted out, and it hardly seemed worth it now his life was falling apart.

The deer needed attention he hadn't the strength to give them at the moment. If he wanted calves next year, the stags should be put with the hinds any time now; their bellowing was getting desperate, poor beasts. But he'd need Brodie, who was nowhere to be found. He'd checked the penned stags and found they'd been fed and watered, but he suspected Christie had done that.

Wearily, he dug his phone out of his pocket and keyed in Brodie's number again. Still no answer, and there wasn't any point in leaving a message; he'd left two already. So he'd just disappeared, had he? Lovatt's mouth twisted in a bitter smile. With a rat like Brodie deserting, the ship couldn't be far from the rocks.

His hands, he realised, were growing stiff with the penetrating cold. It would only get worse as the night drew on; he'd have to light a fire. There was no electricity – or water, come to that – and it would have to serve as light too after dark. Assembling kindling and logs was a straightforward, mechanical thing to do, better than sitting here nursing his exhaustion and being tempted to close his eyes. He'd tried that, and what formed behind his closed lids had brought them flipping open again immediately.

It couldn't stop him thinking, though. Even as he carried the log basket through from the store off the kitchen, even as he crumpled the paper and laid on the sticks, his mind was buzzing.

Lissa. Christie, poor, sweet Christie, out of her depth and causing more trouble as she tried to help. Lissa. His father – his dead father. His mouth dried. No, no, no! Shut your mind, he told himself. You're good at that.

Kerr, then – the missing Kerr. Just how much did Kerr hate him? As much as this? Oh, he'd sensed long ago that the man's genial manner covered rancour like make-up covering bad skin. He wasn't sure why – perhaps because he was his boss, with the property and a developing business or perhaps because, though he might have a face to frighten the horses, he still had two legs. Or perhaps because Kerr owed him for giving him a haven when he'd needed it and a good job now – and as someone once said there is no more corrosive emotion than gratitude. God knew he'd tried hard to do the right thing for him and for Christie, even for Lissa, in a way, and he'd hoped to do it for others in the future. *And wreck their lives too, to salve your conscience?* a cruel inner voice mocked him.

Lovatt struck a match and the paper, with its coating of greasy smuts, flared up in a sudden burst. The kindling, dried driftwood from the shore, roared away and he fed it little by little, until the dry bark on the small logs he'd placed on top caught too and then he added more, and more, and more, until the fire in the grate was dangerously high and his face was flushing red in the heat. All but mesmerised, he went on, uncaring. Suppose the whole place burnt down. He should care?

The quiet voice behind him made him drop the log he was holding, with an oath.

'I think you've put on enough wood, Mr Lovatt. The fire brigade's hoping for a quiet night.'

He swivelled round. There was a woman standing in the doorway, the tall inspector, and the flickering firelight made her look strangely threatening. There was a much shorter man beside her.

'The door was open. I hope you don't mind us walking in,' she said. 'I don't know if you remember DS MacNee?'

What early conditioning was it that made him scramble to his feet, made him say, 'Yes, of course,' when he wanted to scream, 'No, no! For God's sake, leave me alone!'

He heard that same calm, conditioned voice saying, 'Do take a seat, but I'm afraid everything's absolutely filthy.'

Fleming moved closer to the fireplace where he was standing, her eyes glinting in the amber light. 'First things first, Mr Lovatt. Let's start by having you tell us the truth about your father.'

* * *

'He's not in, again. I'll check down on the shore, but he'd have to be mental to be out there in the freezing cold.'

Crouched in the corner behind the armchair in his bed-sitting room, Cal Findlay heard the voice of the sergeant who had questioned him earlier. He'd known they'd be back, but he hadn't thought it would be this soon.

The crunching of gravel at the front of the house seemed ridiculously loud. He was straining his ears to work out what they were doing when his mother started up on one of her moaning rants: 'Oh, the evil! The wickedness!' His face contorted with rage and he mouthed a string of swear words under his breath.

The detective had come back. 'Do you think he's inside? Better take a look in the windows.'

Findlay hunched his shoulders, contorting himself into an even smaller outline. He dared not even look, but a gentle thud on the windowpane told him that someone had bumped his head peering in.

He could hear the footsteps going on along the path round the corner of the house; they'd be on grass after that, so he couldn't hear them. It seemed a long time before he heard the voice again, saying, 'Nothing? Me neither. What do we do now?'

'Kick the door in,' a new voice suggested. Findlay's heart skipped a beat; he muffled his gasp of horror as he waited for the reply.

The sergeant's voice came. 'Big Marge is down at the farmhouse. We can drive round a bit to see he's not out on a wee walk then check in with her.'

Crunch, crunch, crunch. Then the sound of a car driving away.

In the silence, the memories came flooding back. He fought to block them, as he had done all these years. He'd learnt to live with his fear and go on as before, even if it just seemed he was putting one foot in front of the other on a pointless journey. Silence, secrecy. Until . . .

Cal had known since last week that this moment would come. He'd shirked it before, but now there was nothing else he could do. But he was sobbing as he eased his cramped limbs and stood up.

She was leaving the chalet again. As he saw the door handle turn, Eddie moved faster than he had done since he played right wing for his school football team three stones ago, to dive behind a scruffy bush beside the track. He grazed his knee, and he felt a right berk peering through the leaves, but being caught there would be worse.

Elena got into the car and drove off down the track. There was a sharp branch digging into him, but he didn't move until he heard the clanking of the bolts on the top gate, then he trotted across to peer over the drop on the further side.

That was the sound of the lower gate now, and then the car came into view as she drove round the curve down on to the main road. If she was going off somewhere, there was no way he could follow her – not without his car.

She stopped at the road, and then turned not right, towards the road out, but left into the village. That was a relief: he wasn't going to lose her. Maybe she was just popping down to the pub – but from his vantage point, Eddie could see she was driving past the Smugglers Inn. A pint of milk at the local store, then? But now he thought about it, he hadn't noticed a local store, and come to that he'd never known his wife drink milk.

She was going to meet someone. Jealousy, lulled by the isolated setting, woke again to active life. There was a man in this, somewhere. His gut cramped at the thought.

If he chose a chalet that looked unoccupied, he could park up there and not be noticed. Then he'd be ready to follow her next time, wherever she was going.

DC Hepburn was standing outside, shoulders hunched against the cold as she stood round the back of the Kirkluce HQ, in close proximity to the dustbins. She was smoking a Gitane, a habit acquired on visits to her mother's native France. She needed to think, and as Sartre or Camus could tell you, the greatest ideas come with a cigarette between your yellow-stained fingers.

She was feeling depressed. Maybe she'd got it wrong at the meeting? Maybe she shouldn't have opened her big mouth, when Macdonald had spelt it out already that he wasn't much taken with the Christie Jack theory. Something going on there? Personally, she thought the woman was a crazy, but sometimes men went for that.

There'd been a sense at the meeting that things were coming to a head. She was good at picking up vibes, and Big Marge was vibrating like a Rampant Rabbit. With so much quality info coming in now, you'd have thought she could relax a bit and just settle down to the steady, routine investigation. Instead, she was so tense you could twang her. She was expecting fireworks.

Being left at this end had been a bummer. She'd bust a gut to get on the team, brought in the best stuff, and she hadn't done that to play stay-at-home while everyone else went on the Seal Team 6 job. She might have a problem with Big Marge: women were notoriously the worst kind of sexist bosses.

On the other hand, she'd kind of liked being tasked with thinking. A novel idea, in the force. It didn't happen a lot: routine, yes, action, yes, thinking, not so much.

So she'd better get on with the thinking bit. Hepburn took

another deep draw on her cigarette, but still nothing seemed to come. Sartre's sort of idea, anyway, wasn't really the kind to go down well at Kirkluce HQ.

Hepburn was almost ready to stub it out and go back into the warmth of the station when one of the catering staff appeared round the side of the building with her own packet of fags, a middle-aged woman with menopause-blonde hair. She had a duffel coat huddled over her overall and she greeted Hepburn morosely.

'Not right, this – driving us out in weather like this. Uncivilised, that's what it is. And set to get worse tomorrow – the forecast's shocking.'

Hepburn shrugged. 'Maybe they're wrong. They usually are.'

'Aye, you're right there.' Her gravelly voice suggested that gin as well as cigarettes might feature in her life. 'It'll probably be worse.'

The characteristic Scottish pessimism made Hepburn laugh, and after a moment her companion joined in.

'Och well, that's what I always say – you have to laugh, eh?' Then she looked at her more closely. 'Here – you're one of thae detectives, aren't you?'

'That's right.' It still gave her a little thrill to say that.

'Terrible thing, that, down at Innellan. Nice wee place, too – you'd never think something like that could happen there.'

'You know it?' Hepburn said hopefully. Maybe the woman came from Innellan, knew everyone concerned, had some vital piece of knowledge . . .

She didn't. 'Never been there. Saw it on the news a wee while ago, something about some fella with a farm down there giving a break to wounded soldiers.'

Hepburn hadn't really thought she would. She stubbed out her cigarette.

'Better get back to work. See you again.' She bent to pick up the butt and put it in one of the bins.

Hepburn was walking along to the CID room when the thought came to her. She remembered the broadcast, because she'd been in the canteen at the time and there had been jokey remarks about Innellan being on the map now.

Suppose that was exactly right. Suppose the programme had broadcast to the nation that this was where Matt Smith/Lovatt was to be found, and someone had come looking?

Maybe it had nothing to do with the case, but you couldn't deny it was an original thought. Maybe the Sartre method wasn't so crap after all.

Hugh Donaldson opened the door reluctantly. His son would walk in, and friends who might drop by wouldn't wait once they'd knocked. He knew exactly who it would be – the effing polis.

He was totally pissed off. Fair enough, if Sorley wanted to confess he could go and say anything he liked to the buggers, but it was way out of order to dump him and Steve in it too. Now they were making a big deal out of nudging a bolt on a gate that should have had a padlock anyway. There were plenty gallus lads about; all they'd done was expose the weaknesses in the system, like they always said in the newspapers. Still, it would be two against one saying Sorley had done it on his own; Steve would back him up. It was just that there might be one or two problems, and he wasn't wanting to have to deal with them now.

Hugh's face was set in surly lines as he opened the door. When he saw who stood there, though, it relaxed into a leer which showed his broken and discoloured teeth.

'Well, my dear, and what can I do for you?'

The slim, pretty blonde whom he had seen in the pub didn't

smile, but held out her hand to him, a hand with skin that looked curiously smooth and shiny. 'You don't recognise me, do you?'

'Course I do. You were at the pub the other night. How could I forget?' he said, with a nauseating attempt at gallantry.

'Not then. Before that. Long, long, before that,' she said, as he moved forward to shake her hand.

She was holding something. As he keeled over, five seconds later, something flickered in his mind, but before he could fix on it, the darkness came in.

'So when one of our officers said the name Andrew Smith to you, you must have realised that your father had died, in a peculiarly unpleasant way?'

Lovatt's face, physically immobile on one side, and deliberately immobile on the other, gave nothing away. 'Yes, I knew. Yes, I lied to the young woman. But since I had nothing at all to do with it, I thought it wouldn't help to send you off on a wild goose chase.'

'I am constantly touched by the consideration of people who can't bear the thought that police investigation might somehow be hampered by being given information. Especially when it happens to be the truth. For God's sake, Matt, what the hell is this about?'

Fleming's voice was savage. Lovatt squared his shoulders, as if to withstand the force of a gale as she went on, 'You discovered your father was dead. So, like any loyal son, you reacted with – total indifference?'

The biting sarcasm stung him. 'Loyalty, in my book, has to be earned. This was a man I hadn't seen since I was nine years old. He wrecked the business he'd inherited from my Smith grandfather and if my Lovatt grandmother had let him take charge of the farm here, he'd have wrecked that too.'

'Gambling?' It was the sergeant who put the question.

How the hell did they know these things? How long would it take them to discover . . . ?

'All right,' Lovatt said. 'He gambled the money away. Then he walked out and left my mother and me to struggle along as best we could. We never heard from him again. No address. No maintenance. She got a job in a supermarket and we lived on that. She died of cancer just before I got an army scholarship. She didn't know that I would be all right. She died worrying.' His voice had risen. 'So you see, that's my view of my father – a bastard who didn't let my mother die in peace, because the support that should have protected me till I could look after myself wasn't there.'

Lovatt could feel spittle forming at the rigid end of his mouth and he wiped it away. 'You can hardly be surprised that I didn't burst into tears of grief when the constable told me. Clearly he'd screwed someone else just like he screwed my mother and me, and they'd taken their revenge. The throw of the dice was always more important to him than anything else except the turn of a card.

'And before you decide that you're going to elevate me to prime suspect, can I just say that within the time frame you seem to be talking about for his murder, I was serving with the army in Bosnia, and then having treatment in a German military hospital. I didn't have a home so I never took home leave. Once I got the dog I stayed with friends in Europe so I didn't have to bring him into Britain. You can check my passport, if you like. Oh no, silly me, I forgot. Someone burnt down half my house, and probably the passport with it. Still, I'm sure you can check it out somehow.'

The question was, had he given them enough information to stop them going to search for it? If they did, it would put him

403

again through the sort of hell he had spent most of his life trying to avoid.

The inspector's eyes were cold. It had been a moving story, and yet she hadn't been moved. 'I see,' was all she said, then, 'For the moment at least, I want you where we can keep an eye on you, for your own safety. I understand you were staying at the Smugglers Inn at one stage. I want you back there, and I've arranged for police protection.

'We are confident that everything will become clearer over the next few days, but while we are concerned about your safety, we would ask you to stay there.'

Lovatt's heart sank. Georgia's fussing concern, the tiny room, and above all Christie – Christie whom, somehow or other, he had destroyed.

'Of course,' he said as convincingly as he could. 'I'll just wait for the fire to die down then go across. Wouldn't want the house to catch fire or anything!'

The feeble joke fell flat. The sergeant, whose name he couldn't remember, said, 'Och, I think I can see to it that it's safe enough,' and seizing the poker prodded and separated the logs so that the flame dwindled into glowing ash.

'Right, we'll take you across,' the sergeant said, with a smile which somehow made Lovatt feel uncomfortable. 'Just to see you get there all right, ken?'

He didn't actually touch Lovatt's arm, but it still felt like being frogmarched out of the building.

Bill Fleming came back to the farmhouse feeling tired and depressed. His wife's car wasn't in the yard; he hadn't expected it would be, but seeing it there would have cheered him up after a day spent trying to save a sick stirk, with nothing to show for the effort except a sizeable vet's bill. He'd been daft to bother;

he'd been pretty sure from the start that he'd lose it, but looking after the beasts was his job, even when it went past the point of common sense. Just the same way as Marjory did her job.

Cat was in the kitchen, wrapped around a mug of coffee and staring into space, looking tragic. At least she was dressed; he'd been a little terse when he found her still in her dressing gown at lunchtime, and the last thing he felt inclined to do after a hard day's work was tiptoe respectfully round his daughter's feelings.

'How are you doing?' His hearty tone was forced.

'Oh *fine*,' she said with heavy sarcasm. 'As you see.'

Biting his tongue, he went to the fridge for the casserole Karolina had left to be heated in the Aga.

'I take it Mum won't be gracing us with her presence at supper again tonight?'

The sneer in his daughter's voice flicked him on the raw. He put the dish carefully in the oven and then shut the door while he counted to ten. Then twenty. After twenty, he realised he was still angry – bloody angry.

'No,' he said. 'I don't think she will be. She's working, you see. She must be absolutely exhausted by now, after two almost sleepless nights, but she's still working. It's what grown-ups do.

'The farm made a loss last year – did you know that? And the year before. On the odd good year, I break even. So the childish idea you seem to have that your mother ought to have stayed at home to do nothing but nanny a demanding and, I now think, thoroughly overindulged daughter, would have meant we lost the farm.

'It's your mother's earnings that keep us afloat. Those jeans you bought for uni, the designer ones you were so pleased with – it was her job that paid for them, and for your overseas trips with the school and all the other luxuries you take for granted.

'You're not a child, Cat, you're a young woman. You made irresponsible, silly decisions and made a mess of things, but you're not a tragic heroine. You're just wallowing in self-pity.'

Cat was gasping with shock. 'Dad! I thought *you* were my friend, at least!' Her eyes filled, then spilt over. She wiped them away with the back of her hand.

The childish gesture went to Bill's heart. His every instinct was to reach out to comfort his little girl, but he steeled himself. 'A friend is someone who tells you the truth, Cat. You're not going to sort yourself out by wrapping yourself in a great wet blanket of misery.

'I'm sorry about Will. I thought he was a nice lad, but what he did was rotten, dumping you when you were so vulnerable. But go on the way you're doing, and you could let him ruin your life. He's not worth it.'

'I know that. But I was just totally thrown at the time. Didn't know what to do.'

'You could have phoned home,' Bill began, then catching sight of her face, went on, 'but of course you were angry with your mum, weren't you? Was part of this a sort of "That'll teach her"?'

Cat didn't meet his eyes.

'You did a good job of it. She's in pieces over this. But cutting off your nose to spite your face isn't cosmetic surgery, is it?'

Cat mumbled something that could have been 'Suppose not.'

'Right, lecture over. Next thing – what happens now?'

Cat looked up, her face tragic again. 'I don't know!' she wailed.

'I'll tell you. Before supper, you're going to get paper and a pen and write down everything you can think of that might help to set things straight, and I'll think too.'

'Well . . . I could try,' Cat said doubtfully. 'I know *you* want to help.'

Bill stopped on the way to the door with an exasperated sigh.

'Lassie, your mother has put up with a lot more from you than I ever would have. I can tell you, she'll have been worrying herself sick about you all day, even while she's doing one of the most important jobs there could be.'

Having seen Matt Lovatt safely into the Smugglers Inn, and ordered a uniform patrol for later, DI Fleming and DS MacNee got back into the car. The media presence had thinned out considerably and she discouraged the stragglers with a curt, 'No comment.'

'What now?' MacNee said. 'There's quite a lot of the lads detailed for the night shift – back to Kirkluce? You look as if you could do with getting home.'

'Getting home!' Amid the stresses of the day, Fleming realised she had hardly given a thought to the situation at home. 'Oh yes,' she said glumly, 'I suppose I ought to, really. Cat . . . well, she's got a bit of a problem.'

MacNee looked encouraging, but she didn't want to talk about it. And, now she thought about it, she had neither the strength nor the inclination to go back and let her daughter use her as a punchbag all over again. Cat had made it clear she didn't care what her mother did – well, fine. There were better things to do than worry herself sick about her daughter's attitude.

'No, I've decided,' Fleming said. 'I'll just phone Bill and tell him I don't know when I'll be back. Let's get along to the incident room now. I'm too edgy about the whole situation to leave at the moment.'

'You've set a watch to see no one has another go at Lovatt,'

MacNee argued. 'Nothing's going to happen to him tonight.'

'I know, I know. But Tam, suppose we're looking in the wrong direction? Has the business with the stag distracted us? It could be Lissa who was the target, not Matt at all. It's possible. We know absolutely nothing about her, so we haven't an idea what is in the killer's mind. Anything could happen—'

MacNee interrupted her. 'That's paranoia. It's lack of sleep talking. There's plenty of cover – in fact, there's Andy and Ewan now.'

Their car was coming towards them down the little street. As they drew level, Macdonald put down his window.

'I was looking for you, boss. A query—'

'Go along to the incident room. I'll see you there.'

Cal Findlay's foot had gone to sleep; he staggered slightly and had to grab at the chair he'd been crouching behind to stop himself from falling.

He didn't have much time. They would be back before long, and in a way that was a good thing. He'd spent far too much time already agonising over what he had to do; he knew what it was, and he knew that he should have done it before, long before.

It was dark now, but he didn't switch on the lights. He couldn't be sure both men had left and he wasn't going to advertise his presence. Anyway, he could have found his way around the familiar house with his eyes closed. The hall, the passageway, the kitchen door, four steps to the drawer beside the sink. The right-hand side of the drawer.

His hand found the kitchen knife and tested the blade. That would do – yes, that would do. He picked it up, then went back into the hall to pick up a concealing coat from the hallstand.

'Help me! Help me! The wickedness . . .'

For a moment he paused, hatred filling his heart. It was her fault, all her fault. Her life for the life she had taken from him?

Yet he knew he couldn't. When it came to the moment, disabling memories would rise: a birthday cake, a story – kiss, even. His throat prickled. No, he couldn't.

The other death, though – that was different.

CHAPTER TWENTY-FIVE

'Bill?' Marjory Fleming said. 'Just to warn you – I've no idea when I might get back. It's all a bit tense.' She was standing in the street outside the incident room beside the throbbing generator truck as she made her call.

Her husband sighed. 'You're going to keel over if you're not careful. Still, I've learnt enough to know there's no point in arguing.'

Fleming laughed. 'I know. I'm sorry. Anyway—'

'I'd a good chat with Cat this afternoon.'

'Did you?' Fleming didn't mean her voice to sound cold, but she couldn't help it.

Bill obviously picked it up. 'She'll be fine, you know, given time. Do you want to speak to her?'

'No, I don't think I do, actually. I'd better go.'

She heard her husband groan, 'Oh, for God's sake! *Women*!' as she switched off the phone.

Not driving his own Mercedes had meant that he had been able to follow Elena unnoticed, but now, as he shifted from one buttock to the other and stretched his legs across to the passenger side to ease his cramped position, Eddie Tindall thought longingly of the legroom and deeply padded leather seats in the Merc.

He'd only just got himself into position outside the empty chalet two down from the one Elena was staying in when he heard the bolts on a gate being drawn. He ducked down below the dashboard – not the easiest of manoeuvres in this confined space – and waited till he heard a car go by before he looked out.

Yes, it was hers. So she was back – it had obviously been some minor errand. If she'd gone to meet a man she'd hardly have returned so soon. Perhaps she really was just having a quiet holiday, like she said. He could go back and have his dinner at the hotel – he was starting to feel ravenous, despite the scones – and drive back quietly to Salford after a good night's sleep. She would never have to know.

Or perhaps, argued the suspicious inner voice he had come to hate, she had gone to leave a note to arrange a meeting? Perhaps he should wait just a bit, to be sure.

'Dad?' Steve Donaldson called as he opened the door of his father's house. 'Are you not wanting your tea?'

The hall was dark; he stepped forward to grope for the switch and his foot touched something on the floor, something soft. He was already saying, 'Dad! Dad! Are you all right?' before he managed to put on the light.

Steve fell to his knees, put his hand on his father's chest looking for a heartbeat, but the glazed, wide-open eyes had told him immediately that he wouldn't find one.

He stood up shakily and went to the phone. 'Josie? It's my dad. He's had a heart attack. He's dead.' He listened for a moment to her exclamations, then said, 'No need for 999. There's dozens of the buggers down in the village. I'll away down and get someone there.'

* * *

The incident room had been set up in the disused church, as the only building both large enough and empty. Despite the space heaters that had been brought in, the grey stone walls bloomed with a sheen of damp and it had a dank, fusty smell. The old pews had been taken out and sold as smart hall furniture long ago, and with the harsh temporary lighting concentrated around the desks and tables that had been brought in, the gothic arches of the roof were hidden in gloom and the people moving about cast flickering shadows on the walls. Old churches accumulate their own particular atmosphere but once the prayers and praise have stopped the emptiness creates an ambience of its own.

Even with the rumour of sandwiches available, Campbell hesitated on the threshold, reluctant to step inside. Macdonald gave him a shove in the back.

'Hieland sensitivity's one thing, keeping me from my tea's another. If there's a ghoulie or a ghostie makes a move on you, I promise to arrest him.' Then, as Campbell gave a reluctant grin and stepped inside, he added in a sepulchral voice, *'Just stay out of the shadows, that's all.'*

Fleming was making a phone call. 'Louise? You left a message to call you.' She listened, then said, 'I agree it's reaching a bit, but at least it's a new approach. We'll kick it about a bit. Thanks.'

Macdonald stepped forward as she finished her call. 'Boss? Wanted a word about Calum Findlay. No answer, but the car's outside the house. We looked in the downstairs windows but couldn't see anything apart from the mother who's – well, you know, not all there, crying and carrying on. He could be upstairs, avoiding us. There's no sign of him around, we checked he's not at the pub and apparently he doesn't have friends in the village he's likely to be with. I think he's got important stuff to tell us – do we force an entry?'

'Hmm,' Fleming was saying, when MacNee interrupted.

'Crying and carrying on, did you say? Well, boys, it's your duty to rescue the poor old soul, isn't it?'

Macdonald grinned. 'Right enough,' he said. 'Angels of mercy, us. Come on, Ewan. Ewan!'

Campbell was at the far end of the chapel where there was an urn and a food tray; he was holding a pork pie in one hand and a bag of crisps in the other. At Macdonald's summons, he put down the crisps reluctantly and crammed the pork pie into his mouth. 'Coming,' he said indistinctly.

Before they could leave, Steve Donaldson appeared, in a condition of obvious distress. All heads turned, and a silence fell as he said, 'I'm . . . I'm needing someone up at my dad's house. He's dead.'

There was a freeze-frame moment, then Fleming was at his side. 'Sit down, Mr Donaldson. You're clearly shocked. What's happened?' She clicked her fingers and a uniform brought a chair forward.

Donaldson sat down heavily. 'Heart attack. He was just lying there, in the hall. The doctor warned him last week about forgetting to take his pills.'

There was a collective sigh of relief. Fleming said gently, 'Take your time, but we'll get someone up there with you to sort things out when you're ready. Do you want a cup of tea?'

Donaldson shook his head. 'My wife's up there with . . . with him. I better get back.' He got up again and at a nod from Fleming a female constable came forward and took his arm.

'Must have been a terrible shock,' she was saying as she led him out.

Fleming sank down on to the chair he had vacated. 'Phew! I thought we'd another one on our hands for a minute there.

'Right, you two. Go and see if you can collar Findlay. If he's

413

in the house, arrest him for obstruction – I'm not amused by people who think they're playing hide and seek.'

As Macdonald and Campbell left, she looked up at MacNee, and put a hand to her head. 'There was something I was going to discuss, but that's put it right out of my mind. What on earth was it?'

'Why don't you grab another of your "power naps"?' he suggested. 'You're not muckle use if you can't think straight.'

Fleming grimaced, then yawned. 'You could be right. Ten minutes, and I'll be fine.'

She staggered slightly as she stood up and MacNee watched, shaking his head, as she found a quiet corner and shut her eyes.

Cal Findlay stood by the front door, listening intently. Could someone still be lurking out there, reckoning he would make a move? He should wait, say, ten minutes, until he could be sure that any watcher would surely have had to move or make some small sound.

Ten minutes seemed interminable. He began to worry more about how soon they might come back, and he risked it after seven, slipping out of the house, pressing himself against the wall, holding his breath.

No sudden movement. Nothing – except the hit of the frosty air. As he breathed again, a cloud of condensation formed and there were ice sparkles on the drive under his feet. The trouble was, he had to go along the lighted main street to reach his objective. Going over the back would involve hills, fences, boggy ground – and time. The clock was running.

They might be on the lookout for him. On the other hand, apart from the officer who'd interviewed him, no one would know what he looked like, and as he reached the street he saw a man he knew walking along. That would be good cover, so he speeded up to catch him and fell into step.

'Off to the pub?' he said.

'Aye. Plenty to talk about tonight, eh? Have you heard the skeleton's Drew Lovatt? And they're saying Matt's to be arrested for it tonight – that's why there's so many polis around. You wouldn't think a man could do that to his own father.'

'No,' Findlay agreed hollowly. 'No.' He stiffened as they reached the old church, light spilling out from its leaded panes; a generator van rumbling away in the gateway to the graveyard. The car he'd seen in the afternoon was parked just outside. If they came out now . . .

The door remained shut, and when he glanced casually over his shoulder he saw only Steve Donaldson coming along, looking as if he was in a hurry. There was, though, he saw as he approached the pub, a police car in the car park with a uniformed officer inside.

He didn't seem much interested, as they walked past. On the threshold, Findlay stopped and slapped his hip pocket. 'Damn! Left my wallet behind.'

The man beside him grinned. 'Fine excuse, eh? Och well, I'll stand you a pint. You can do the honours tomorrow.'

It wasn't easy to look suitably grateful. 'Thanks for the offer,' he managed, 'but I'm owing Georgia. She was short of change last time and she put it on the slate. I'd better go back in case it turns out to be a long night.' How long it would be, his companion couldn't begin to imagine.

The man shrugged and went in to the pub. Findlay waited a moment, then turned left instead of right. Glancing back towards the church, he saw two men come out, one tall dark man, the other with hair that glinted red under the street lamps. He knew the dark one, and he knew where they were going. He hadn't left a moment too early.

There was the track up to the chalets now. He was starting to feel sick, and his knees felt shaky. He braced them as he crossed the road and started to walk up, his hands clenched into fists so that the nails bit into his palms. There was no room for weakness now. He knew what he had to do. There was no other way.

Eddie, dozing in his car, heard the sound of the bolts on the gate and came awake immediately, with a groan. He was frozen stiff; he couldn't leave the engine on for more than a few risky minutes at a time and it was deathly cold.

That was the second gate. He sank down in his seat once more, but now it was dark he risked peeping above the dashboard. There was the sound of approaching footsteps, and then someone appeared, silhouetted by the glow from the street lamps below. He was tall, slim, fit-looking and he walked as if the steep gradient was level ground.

He looked all the things Eddie wasn't. A dry sob escaped him, and he bowed his head. He'd known there must be somebody. What other explanation could there be? It was what he'd wanted to do – find out the truth. He'd wanted that, and now he'd got it. They always said you should be careful what you wish for.

Crushed with misery, Eddie tried to think. He'd always told himself he didn't care what she did, as long as she came back to him afterwards. After all, her past had never worried him, as long as he was in her present.

Right from the start, though, this time had been different. She had covered her traces so that he couldn't find her. She'd stopped speaking to him on the phone. And now he'd seen the man, he couldn't think why she would want to come back to him – fat, balding, aging Eddie.

He could go up to the chalet right now, confront them, discover the worst. But then the slim chance that Elena would return once this had played itself out, return for the money, the luxury he could give her, would be totally gone.

He could go up and just look, though, try if he could see what was happening – but being caught as a peeping Tom would finish everything.

No, Eddie simply didn't have the courage. He'd wait here a little longer until he was sure the man was staying, then he'd drive back to the hotel. At least it would be warm there, even if he did feel as if the temperature outside wasn't the worst of it.

It was a beautiful, beautiful night. Elena Tindall stood by the picture window of the chalet, looking down over the charming little bay, its curve marked by the string of street lamps. The sea was inky, mysterious, with a silvery surface sheen and above glittered the diamond points of stars and the pale, thin crescent of the new moon. The sky was a deep, soft blue-black; she'd had a silk velvet evening dress once exactly that colour.

And there was the island, no more than a dark shape, but when she looked at it she could see its details in her mind's eye as if it were clear as day. When she arrived, she'd hardly been able to look at it. Now – ah, now!

She had been right all along. She had known what she needed to do to quieten the demons that had raged inside her. She held up the glass she was holding and challenged them now. Nope! Not a sound. The voices that had tormented her, day and troubled night, for almost thirty years were silent now. As she brought the glass to her lips, her chunky silver bangle slipped back and she noticed the healing scar across her wrist. She wouldn't need to resort to the little silver knife in future. She was – invincible, that was the word.

Elena sipped at the vintage Cristal, frowning a little at the contrast between the cheap glass and the delicate golden sophistication of the champagne. It tasted good, though – or perhaps that had something to do with her own exultant mood.

The bottle had come from Eddie's cellar, for her private celebration afterwards. It was perhaps a little premature to open it, when there was still one more little thing to do, but she wanted to sip it slowly over the evening, savour it. And anyway, what she still had to do would be a sort of treat in the middle, before she came back and finished the bottle.

She'd been a good girl, doing the bread-and-butter stuff first. What was left to do would be like eating not just the cake, but the big, delicious cherry sitting right on the top. Elena gave a little giggle as she thought of it.

It was amazing what you could see from this vantage point. For instance, she had seen Matt Lovatt being escorted back from his fire-wrecked house and into the pub, and then the badged car, clearly there to protect him, station itself in the car park. It was disappointing: she'd had it all worked out for tonight before that, and it would be annoying to have to wait. She'd been looking forward to the champagne.

But then, from her invaluable window, Elena had seen what the watcher in the car park could not: a shadowy figure coming out from the back of the pub, keeping to the cover of bracken and gorse along the edge of the shore path and heading for the farmhouse. She knew who that was, and it was once he had disappeared inside that she opened the champagne.

Everything was ready now. She tipped her glass in salute to the capacious handbag sitting ready by the door. Her limited luggage was in the car already, and once she stepped into it and drove off Natalie Thomson would vanish without a trace – the invisible woman. The only person who had her real name was an adenoidal assistant in a car-hire firm in Salford.

And Eddie would be there, waiting impatiently for her return.

She felt a surge of warmth towards him, the only man who had ever cared about making her happy. It would be good to get back to that easy, luxurious life now, with the demon voices silent.

Light flickering behind the drawn curtains of one of the rooms on this side of the farmhouse caught her eye. He must have lit a fire. Risky, in case his bodyguard spotted it and fetched him back, but it was so cold tonight he'd probably reckoned he'd be dead of hypothermia by morning if he didn't, which was a bit of a joke. Anyway, she was glad it wouldn't all happen in darkness. She wanted to be able to see his face as she confronted him, at last, at long last, with his crime. Then it would be debt paid, the ledger squared.

There were still lots of people moving about. Police officers, locals going along for the gossip fest at the pub. And now, even an ambulance; not in a hurry, though, just proceeding along the main street.

That would be for Hugh Donaldson. Elena laughed aloud, raised her glass to it. 'May you rot in hell, you perverted bastard!'

At the sound of footsteps on the drive outside, her face changed. The police, again? Her heart beating faster, she shoved the champagne bottle down beside her chair. She didn't want questions about what she was celebrating, or why she was sitting alone drinking ridiculously expensive champagne.

When the knock on the door came, she waited a moment before opening it with a suitably surprised expression arranged on her face. It crumpled into anger when she saw Cal Findlay standing there.

'For God's sake, Cal, what's the matter now?'

'Can I come in?' He edged his way past her, and she had to shut the door with him on the inside, which was definitely her second preference.

'Look, we have to talk.' He went over to the window and

flung himself into the chair opposite the one with the glass beside it. 'This has got to stop.'

Elena went back to her place. 'What has, Cal? I don't know what you're talking about.'

'What you're doing. You've got to leave. Tonight. Before you do anything more.'

'I don't know what you mean. I haven't done anything – except the fire, and you know you helped me. You splashed the petrol around while I . . . did other things.'

'You blackmailed me,' he said fiercely. 'And anyway, what did you want with that metal bin? That's haunted me.'

She gave him a dancing look. 'You do worry about the oddest things! It was just a silly thought I had – didn't mean anything. And you agreed with me that Matt shouldn't have it all his own way. It would punish him – and you know he ought to be punished . . .'.

Cal's head went down. 'Yes, I know.'

'He'd lose a lot of money putting things right. That was justice, like paying a fine in court. There wasn't meant to be real danger to anyone. They'd have smoke detectors – I knew they'd wake up.'

'Thank God for that, at least.'

'That's all I wanted – to punish him a bit. And of course I had nothing to do with what happened yesterday – I told you that.'

Cal looked up, meeting her gaze squarely. 'And I didn't believe you. For God's sake, I've seen your idea of justice before.'

Elena's eyes were cold blue steel. 'I couldn't have done it alone. You owed me, and you helped me. You paid your debt. You're free and clear.

'Tomorrow, I'll be gone. You won't ever hear from me again. It's over. You don't know anything. Say that three times every day, keep your mouth shut and the waters will close over all this.'

'Why not now?' Cal's hands went together in an unconscious

position of entreaty. 'Why not go now? I know why – because there's something else you're going to do before you go, and I can't let you.'

'I don't know what you think you mean.' Elena's tone was haughty. How dare he? She was invincible.

He was sweating now. 'The thing is, you're my sister, and I owe you, too. But you're mad, and I can't let the killing go on. For the last time, will you walk out to the car now, and drive away?'

'Half-sister.' Her lip curled. 'And for the last time no, I won't.'

'I'm sorry,' Cal said. 'God knows how sorry I am.'

And from under his coat he brought out the knife, the knife with the razor edge his father had taught him how to produce when they were gutting fish together.

Fleming woke with a start. She hadn't really managed any more than the lightest of dozes, the sort where you were entirely aware of everything going on round about you, and where your subconscious was busy with the problems your conscious mind had set them.

The TV programme. DC Hepburn had suggested that they should look for any new arrivals after that had been transmitted, try to trace whether they could make some connection on the basis of what they'd been able to establish about the situation in Innellan.

Fleming stretched, yawned. God, she felt rubbish! Her back was agony as she straightened her neck. Could it be that the only reason she did this job was that she'd become addicted to pain?

MacNee was sitting at a nearby desk, frowning over some papers. Trying not to say 'Oof!' – so elderly! – she stood up.

'I've remembered what I was thinking about before, Tam. Louise suggested that the TV programme about Lovatt, with his injured soldiers, might have called in all this. I happen to know that the only person around who arrived after that and

421

who's still here now is Natalie Thomson, up in one of the chalets. When Andy and Ewan get back, I'll get them to go up and have a chat with her, find out why she wanted to come, see if she has any connection with the area.'

'What's that you've got there?'

'To be honest, not a scoobie.' On the desk in front of MacNee was a pile of transparent plastic document folders, and the one he was looking at had held a few sheets of handwritten paper.

'Found among the debris after the fire at the farmhouse. From the looks of it, could have come from a cupboard or a filing cabinet or something. Oh, Lovatt's passport's here too, incidentally – confirms what he said. Some of it's a bit charred-looking, but it's all legible.

'See this stuff, though – it's seriously weird.'

Fleming took the papers he held out.

I think I'll go mad if I can't confess my guilt. But whenever I've tried to speak about it, the terrible pain from the acid that rises in my throat takes away the breath to form the words. My hand's cramping now just thinking about writing it down, but for my sanity I have to try, one agonising page at a time. If I'm only writing it for me, not to show to anyone, perhaps I can do it – but even so I'm scared, knowing what it'll cost me to live through it again. I've got to get it out of my head, tip it out into written words. Then burn the paper, destroy the memory? I wish – oh, I wish! But could it give me any relief, when there's no chance of forgiveness? I can only try . . .

Fleming read on, through the other pages of raw agony.

'You see what I mean?' MacNee said, then stopped. She wasn't listening to him.

'Weird, certainly,' she said at last. 'The person writing this has the sort of problems that could cause any amount of destruction. She's talking about "recompense" – is that a more acceptable way of saying revenge? And dark, wavy hair . . .'

'That's Lissa, isn't it? Of course – she's the twin of the girl who was abducted and murdered! There'll be a record of that – we can get it tomorrow. So someone here's involved, she's found out who did it, she's stirred up trouble, and they've killed her.'

'It's possible,' Fleming acknowledged, but absently. 'I'm uneasy with that. Lissa lived here for three years and hadn't stirred up any trouble at all. She almost died in the fire, but the only person she could think of who might attempt to kill her was Christie Jack, who fancied her husband. You'd think by that stage she'd have been happy to tell us who else might have had a grudge against her. There's something—'

Macdonald and Campbell were coming across towards them, looking glum. 'Nothing in the house, boss. Findlay wasn't there, and the social services weren't much impressed when we told them the old lady is alone in a house with the door kicked in. They're sending someone out to look after her but they'll be making a complaint.'

'Never mind that,' Fleming said. 'I want you up at the chalets to talk to Ms Natalie Thomson. I want you to find out just exactly what she's doing here, and how come she's been having such a good time in this little backwater that she can't tear herself away. OK?'

'OK, boss,' Macdonald said, but as they went out he said to Campbell, 'Why do I think there's something she knows that we don't?'

'There always is,' Campbell said darkly.

Cal Findlay didn't even see the heavy bottle in Elena's hand as he stepped towards her and struck at her. It caught him on the temple and everything went black.

She got up and looked down at him with anger and contempt. She should take the knife and finish him off, but she wasn't keen. She'd prepared for Lissa, with a change of clothing ready in a carrier bag with the wine bottle, after she'd seen her pass and followed her across the causeway to the island, but even so she'd needed a long soak in the tub with her Dior Poison bath gel to remove the last traces of blood, even as the useful carrier bag, its contents weighted down with a handy stone, settled into the seabed off the island's cliffs.

The blow to Cal's temple was bleeding, and as she watched a little trickle of blood came out of his mouth. Good! But Elena's brow clouded as she looked at the pool of champagne round about him. Interfering fool – this wasn't meant to happen. She'd have to be careful that nothing went wrong with the rest of her meticulous plan.

She went to the handbag that stood waiting for her by the door. She opened it, took out a pair of transparent surgical gloves and slipped them on. She switched off the lights, shut the door and locked it.

She hadn't put on a coat but the cold, somehow, was exhilarating. The cold, and the wheeling stars and planets above her head. She was part of this passionless, powerful universe, far removed from the pathetic mortals who were the playthings of fate. She had suffered, yes, but she had been strong enough to come through, to create her own destiny: peace of mind, with every debt paid back in full.

CHAPTER TWENTY-SIX

He was completely taken by surprise. If Elena had turned her head as she passed she would have seen Eddie sitting there, behind the wheel, his shoulders hunched and his arms huddled round him. He hadn't heard her footsteps.

He'd been on the point of giving up, defeated by the cold. He could almost feel the blood in his veins slowing, thickening, which wasn't exactly smart for a man of his age and physique. He wasn't even sure what he was doing here. He wasn't going to confront Elena and her lover, so he might as well give up, return home and steel himself for the agonising wait to find out whether she was coming back to him or not. There was nothing else he could do.

Then she'd appeared, walking along in the starlit dark as if she was floating, swinging her bag in her hand like a child coming home from school. He could see that she was smiling, and she looked happier, more carefree, than he had ever seen her look before. Eddie hardly recognised her as the cool, contained woman he knew.

The shaft of pain was like a spear thrust. He desperately loved her; had he been making her so wretched over all these years? Blinded by tears, he bowed his head, defeated. This man, whoever he was, had made her happy.

If Elena did come back to him, it could only be for the money. He'd bought her company long ago, but he'd believed then that he was rescuing her; he wouldn't do that again, if buying his own happiness would be at the expense of her misery. He would have to offer to set her free, with a settlement that would be his thank you for what had been for him the most wonderful years of his life. If they had been unhappy for her, she could take it as compensation.

Still, Eddie hadn't lost all curiosity. Where could she be off to at this time of night, leaving her lover in the chalet? The only thing he could think of was that she might be going down to the pub for a bottle of wine. Surely the bloke would have brought one, though, or at least, gone to fetch it himself?

Groaning with stiffness he levered himself out of the car, grabbing at the door frame. It was sticky with frost and his fingers stung as he prised them away. He hobbled across to the farther side of the track and looked over the edge.

Elena hadn't come into view yet. That was the sound of her opening the second gate, and it would take her a few more minutes to appear on the road below. He shivered as he stood waiting.

On the still air, he could hear the sound of laughter and talk from the pub below. From further away, there came a burst of animal sound – the deer, maybe, that he'd seen in the fields.

There was Elena now, crossing the main street. She didn't go towards the pub, though. She went round the side of what looked like a house that was attached to it, through a little garden, then disappeared round the back. A moment later, he saw her again, heading out along a path round the curve of the bay. She was little more than a dim shape now as she went beyond the range

426

of the street lights but he could see that she was still almost dancing along.

A walk in romantic starlight? Eddie frowned – surely he, the lover, should be with her for that?

Elena had changed direction. She had turned off on to a drive leading to the farmhouse that had been damaged by fire, and now Eddie realised there was a light behind a curtained window. She must be going to see someone there.

Why? And why had the lover been left behind? Perhaps he'd got it all wrong. Perhaps the man in the chalet wasn't a lover – perhaps just someone bringing a message from someone else? Elena hadn't spent long with him, after all, before she had set off like . . . like, Eddie realised, someone going to a tryst.

He couldn't check out the chalet without the real risk of being spotted. But there, at the farmhouse which she had reached now, which she had entered without waiting to be admitted, he could look around unseen, perhaps even find a chink in the curtain of that lighted room.

There was no point in leaving his car here. He wouldn't be coming back; once he'd found out what was going on – or, more likely, established that he couldn't find out – he'd have no alternative but to drive back to the hotel. He could park somewhere, then follow the path she had taken.

Eddie hurried back to his car and drove down to the village. He was just parking it in the main street, a little along from the pub, when a car with two men in it passed him. He didn't see them turn off up the track.

'Not having much luck tonight, are we?' Macdonald said. 'Car outside, no one at home.'

They had parked beside Spindrift, but the chalet was in darkness and there was no answer to their knock.

'Could be inside, dodging us. And Big Marge seems really keen to see her,' Campbell said hopefully.

'You'd better watch your enthusiasm for kicking in doors doesn't become an addiction. Don't be daft. She's probably down the pub. Come on, we'd better get down there and check it out.'

Macdonald turned away, but Campbell had wandered off round to the front of the chalet and was shading his eyes, peering in the big window.

Macdonald had the car door open. 'Come on, Ewan, it's cold standing here.'

Campbell turned slowly. 'Lucky I've got my door-kicking shoes on,' he said as he came back. 'There's a body in there.'

Fleming was reading the document through for the third time. Respecting her concentration, MacNee was filtering through the rest of the documents – the usual stuff: tax forms, receipts, insurances, bank statements. His eyebrows rose when he saw the size of Lovatt's overdraft and he pursed his mouth in a silent whistle.

'You see, Tam, I'll tell you what I'm unhappy about,' Fleming said suddenly. 'Going by what it says here, Lissa would have been the person looking for revenge. She's lived here for three years and nothing's happened, but suddenly there are two attempts on her life.

'Is Hepburn right that somehow the TV programme advertised that she was here – that someone came to find her, as the only person who knew the full story, who must be eliminated in case at last she told what she knew – even the final secret that she talks about, that she somehow couldn't even admit to herself?

'Anyway, I need to talk to Lovatt, right now. Confront him with this.' She stood up, then stopped. 'Hang on – there's an obvious point. Though what that would say about—'

The mobile in her bag on the desk rang. She set down the papers she was holding and dug it out, squinting at the caller.

'Yes, Andy?'

Her face went white as she listened. 'Oh God!' she said. 'On my way.'

The warmth was making Matt Lovatt drowsy. Provided he sat close enough to the fire, the temperature was bearable and he'd placed a sofa and a heavy old armchair so that they blocked the worst of the icy draught from the window he had reluctantly left open. The sergeant had read him a lecture on the danger of the toxic fumes that persisted days after a fire.

Perhaps tonight he might manage to sleep, even on a bed of cushions. He was certainly weary enough; his head felt as if it was floating, but when he tried lying down his eyes shot open automatically, like one of those dollies whose eyelids closed when laid flat, only in reverse. It was a curious aspect of human design that meant if you were too tired, you were entirely unable to sleep.

He sat up, piled the fire with logs as high as he dared. If he wasn't going to sleep he might as well take the time to work out what he was going to do. The house, the farm – there would have to be practical decisions in the next day or two, at the most. Practical decisions were good, or better at least than the thoughts he was using them to suppress.

At the sound of a footstep in the hall, he turned his head, then sank it forward on to his knees with a moan of utter weariness. The police, no doubt, having discovered that he had escaped from the claustrophobic atmosphere at the pub, ready to march him back to Christie's white, reproachful face, asking for what he could not give her . . .

It wasn't the police. He recognised the woman who had

opened the door, but for a moment he couldn't place her. He struggled to his feet.

'Hello, Matt,' she said. She was smiling.

'I'm sorry, I didn't hear you knock. Can I help you?' He spoke stiffly, remembering now who she was – the woman who had been so rude to him after the stag attacked her. Natalie something.

She seemed to be finding something amusing. As she came across the room towards him, her eyes seemed to be dancing with merriment.

'Oh, I didn't feel I needed to knock, Matt.'

Was there something wrong with her? The way she was behaving wasn't normal – and she kept using his name as if she knew him. Perhaps she'd decided she was entitled to damages and had come looking for money.

'I'm sorry, Natalie—'

That made her laugh out loud. She was definitely unbalanced. He tried to make his voice soothing as he went on, 'If you've come to look for compensation, I'm afraid you'd have to see my lawyer. I'll give you the address . . .'

The smile disappeared from her face. 'Oh yes,' she said, and he could see in the flickering firelight that her eyes had gone hard and blank. Dead eyes. 'Oh yes, compensation, but we're not going to bring a lawyer into it.

'Sit down, Matt.'

Her voice cracked like a whiplash and to his surprise he found himself sitting down on a cushionless chair. She sat down on the sofa beside it, a little too close to him for comfort. She was carrying one of these fashionably large handbags; she set it down at her feet.

'That's cosy.' She was smiling again, but this time she wasn't amused. 'You mentioned compensation – it's as good a place as any to start.'

'Look, I haven't money here, not even a chequebook,' he said, though the hairs rising on the nape of his neck told him it wasn't about money and chequebooks. There was something badly wrong, something dangerous that he didn't understand.

'You don't recognise me, do you?' She was looking at him intently now.

'You're Natalie—'

'Don't be bloody stupid.' There was the edge to the voice again. 'Look at me.'

He studied her. Blonde hair, neat little nose, eyes that might be grey or dark blue – it was hard to tell in the firelight. It didn't mean anything to him – or did it? There was something, some faint echo of a resemblance, but . . .

'No,' he said. 'I don't.'

'And you don't remember what you did to me? I expect you've carefully managed to forget, after all these years. Funny how people do. I don't think Hugh Donaldson remembered me either.'

Matt was bewildered. 'Hugh Donaldson, the farmer?'

'Never mind him,' she instructed. 'Look at me again.'

'What on earth is all this about?' he burst out. 'You walk into my house unannounced, you start issuing orders, you say I did something to you but you don't tell me what it was supposed to have been. I'm sorry, but—'

'Look at me again,' she repeated, as if he hadn't spoken.

Again, he obeyed her. This time a faint frown came to his face. 'I suppose you do remind me faintly of someone, but I can't think who . . .'

She glanced round the room. On one wall, an old-fashioned mirror hung in a heavy wooden frame.

'Go and look in that,' she said.

* * *

431

'There's another ambulance on its way,' Macdonald said. 'Mercifully no one else has chosen to have an emergency tonight, because the only other one's on its way to Dumfries mortuary with Hugh Donaldson's body.'

'Doesn't look good, to be honest,' MacNee said, looking down at Cal Findlay's inert body. 'Bad sign – blood coming from his mouth, look.'

'I'd rather not,' Campbell said. He was reading the label of the champagne bottle lying on the floor beside it. 'Cristal. That good?'

'Expensive, anyway,' Macdonald said.

Fleming was feeling as if the bottle might have come down on her own head. This new blow, on top of the sort of light-headedness that came from exhaustion and, she suddenly realised, lack of food – what an idiot! – was making it difficult for her to think clearly. She saw MacNee give her an anxious look, and she pulled herself together with a supreme effort.

'The knife on the floor by his hand suggests this was self-defence. But I'm not happy. You'd have expected her to call us in, if she'd been attacked, and she hasn't fled in the car either. Where is she? And more importantly, what's she doing now?'

'It's all right,' MacNee said quickly. 'If this guy tried to kill her, she's not in danger now. We've lads all over the place tonight and Matt Lovatt's safely under guard in the pub.'

Fleming gave him a weak smile. 'Didn't stop this happening, did it? I won't feel easy until we have her sitting in a chair in front of us, telling us what's been going on.

'Anyway, we'd better get down there and take Lovatt apart. Right now this minute. Andy, get a uniform on duty here, circulate a description of Thomson and have everyone out on the street looking.'

At least that was decisive, though she was aware of having

stumbled a little over a couple of words. As she passed Campbell on the way to the door he pressed something into her hand.

'Thought you might need this.'

She looked down. It was a bar of Cadbury's Fruit and Nut, a little warm from his pocket and with a corner of the foil worn away, but she thanked him with real gratitude. By the time she got down to the pub, the sugar rush had kicked in.

Matt Lovatt peered into the mirror. The old glass was foxed and pitted, and it hung in deep shadow, with only the wavering light from the fire behind giving glimpses of his face. He knew what he would see, anyway: dark, curly hair, strong nose – Granny Lovatt's nose, not the best inheritance – slate-blue eyes. And then, of course, his cheek.

He turned back to his visitor. 'I don't know what this is about.'

She gave an angry little sigh. 'Oh, for God's sake. I'm Helen.'

'Helen who?' He was genuinely baffled.

'When you forget, you do a good job, don't you? Helen, your twin.'

'*My twin*?' Now he was angry – very, very angry. 'This is the sickest thing I ever heard. If you think you're going to get money out of this, somehow – a fraudulent claim on my grandmother's estate, then you're seriously out of luck. My twin, I would have you know, is dead, long ago.'

Her mouth twisted. 'Is that what they told you?'

'No, they didn't. I saw her body for myself. If that's what it will take to stop this disgusting charade, I'll tell you: her coffin was there, on the table in our dining room. There were candles and white flowers, and she was lying with her hands crossed on her chest and her eyes wide open.' His voice faltered. 'I've never forgotten it, and it's haunted me all my life. So perhaps you could

433

just forget your nasty, sordid little scam and get yourself out of here.'

'What happened to Nellie, my elephant, after I was gone?'

'*Nellie*!' He choked. 'How – how could you know about—'

'Because I'm Helen!' she shouted suddenly. 'Oh, for God's sake – an open coffin, just left lying on our dining room table, flowers and candles – are you mad? No one would do that. It's out of some Victorian novelette! You must have dreamt it.'

'I—' Matt was ready to protest, and then he stopped. So much of his memory of that terrible time had a dreamlike quality; could he be absolutely sure that she wasn't right? Then he looked at her again, and his resolve strengthened.

'Really? Then could I just point out that my sister and I were very much alike. Dark curly hair – oh, and Granny's nose. My mother always used to say that it would be all right for a man, but it wouldn't do Helen any favours.'

'But nothing a nose job couldn't fix – do you remember she always used to finish by saying that? And hair . . .' She shrugged. 'A good colourist and hair straighteners. But let's talk about the eyes. That's something you can't change – the colour of the eyes, and the line of the brow.'

Struck dumb, he looked at her yet again. There it was – the resemblance he had failed to pin down had been to himself. He felt dizzy with the shock.

'Yes, Matt, I'm Helen – *was* Helen,' she corrected herself. 'I call myself Elena now.' She was smiling again, the slate-blue eyes bright as she patted the sofa beside her. 'Come and sit down. We've a lot to talk about.'

The pub had been very busy but at least it was nearly closing time, Georgia Stanley consoled herself as she pulled the umpteenth pint. The media types had drifted off, after the brief excitement of the ambulance coming for Hugh Donaldson, but one of them had got into conversation earlier, said he was desperate to get out of the rat race and with a little pub in a glorious place like this she must be living the dream. She'd said she was thinking of retiring, and he'd actually kissed her across the bar. He was coming tomorrow to have a proper look around. It was the thought of a neat little house in Kirkcudbright that was keeping her going – that and getting to her bed.

It was with no enthusiasm at all that she saw Inspector Fleming and Sergeant MacNee elbowing their way through the drinkers.

'We need to speak to Matt Lovatt urgently,' Fleming said.

'Right.' She looked round a little helplessly. 'If you can wait a couple of minutes, I've just called time—'

'Now,' Fleming said. 'Just tell us where he is.'

'Fine. Through that door, along past the kitchen, up the stairs and it's the second door on the right.'

They had gone before she'd finished speaking.

Eddie wasn't moving very fast. It was even colder outside than it had been in the car and the light coat that was all he'd had with him was doing no sort of job at all. And it was treacherous underfoot; it was so dark he hadn't seen an icy puddle until he slipped on it and fell heavily. He had a sore hip to contend with now as well as stiffness, and as he limped on towards the farmhouse, the unwisdom of what he was doing struck him more forcibly.

What if Elena came out, to go back to the man in the chalet? He was on the drive now; there was no cover until you reached the trees at the back of the house. There was a dog, too, in a pen; a big dog, pacing to and fro as it watched him with glowing eyes. What if it started barking? It hadn't barked at Elena, but then perhaps she was a regular visitor. He eyed it distrustfully as he neared the house.

He could see that the front door was standing open, then he heard voices coming from round the side of the house. They must be in the curtained room he had noticed earlier, where a flickering reddish glow suggested firelight. And the window was open.

With exaggerated caution, Eddie tiptoed along the flagstone path and pressed himself against the wall beside the window.

'I . . . I owe you an apology,' Lovatt said awkwardly. 'I was very rude to you just now.'

'Oh? I think you owe me rather more than that,' Elena said.

His stomach lurched. She didn't know – he'd always believed – or hoped, perhaps, that she couldn't have known. And it was all so long ago.

'Of course,' he said. 'You're entitled to half the property . . .'

She ignored that. 'Aren't you going to ask me where I've been all these years? What I've been doing?'

'Well, of course.' Matt swallowed. 'You're looking very . . . well, elegant, I suppose.'

His sister made a face, pulling at the long-sleeved Primark T-shirt she was wearing. 'Elegant? I think you just probably mean expensively groomed. You see, I'm married to a wealthy man – a lovely, kind man who adores me.'

'That's . . . that's nice.' He knew that wasn't the right reply, but he was stalling, playing for time, putting off what he dreaded that she would say.

'Nice? It should be, but it isn't. Do you know why? He loves me, but I can't love him, because I can't love anyone. I'm an emotional cripple, you see. Because of what went before.'

'Before?' Matt wanted to put his hands over his ears, wanted

436

to blot out what she was going to say. The words were already forming in his head before she said them.

'What do you think would happen to a nine-year-old girl once she was abducted? Shall I tell you? Men, that's what happens. A paedophile ring. Years and years of pain and terror and torture; I would tell you in minute by minute detail, but . . .'

For the first time he saw a loss of control. She was shaking, and her hand went to her slim throat as if it were constricting. She took a shuddering breath before she went on, '. . . I-I can't. I can't go there myself. I don't allow it to destroy me. Just imagine the worst things you can think of, and they happened.'

He was feeling numb and sick as she took up the story again. 'It was such a relief when I got too old, and could just go on the game. Oh, you get beaten up sometimes – but that wasn't anything new. When you're a prostitute you get paid, and I hadn't a drug habit so I could steer clear of pimps. I could take a day off, or say no to someone I didn't like the look of – that was a real luxury! Of course I'd have liked to be a call girl – easy life, posh place to live, good clothes. But you see, I wasn't the type. Skinny. Scared. And . . .' she gave a harsh laugh '. . . with Granny's nose, no beauty.

'God knows what Eddie saw in me. He's the only good man I've ever met. But for years and years I've lived with the rage bottled up inside me, and it was starting to destroy me. I was cutting myself in pieces, literally. I have a special little silver knife to do it with, you know.' She was wearing broad silver cuffs round her wrists; she snapped one back now and showed him the network of scar tissue on her arm.

'God, I'm sorry. I-I don't know what to say,' Matt stammered.

'There's nothing to *say*, Matt. It's way past *saying* – way, way past.'

'What can I do, then?' he said desperately. 'Anything—'

'Oh, I'll tell you in a minute. But we need to talk a little more. I'd like to have had this – this little talk years ago, when I began the process of sorting myself out. I don't suppose you'd want to hear about that either. But you were unfinished business. I didn't know where you were, you see.'

'Mother died when I – we were seventeen. Then it was the army, then here.' That sounded almost like a normal conversation, filling in the gaps between separated siblings. 'And hospital, after I was wounded in Bosnia.' Matt touched his cheek.

Elena looked at him with withering scorn. 'Looking for sympathy? Don't make me laugh. I couldn't care less what you did with your rotten life. Finding out where you were was the final piece in the jigsaw I thought I'd never manage to complete. Do you remember the one we worked on for ages that turned out to have a piece missing?' She laughed.

The little, homely detail was the sort of thing anyone might produce, finding a long-lost brother, but Matt was under no illusion. 'Oh yes,' he said grimly. 'Go on. Say what you're going to say.'

A sudden hiss and flare-up from a knot of resin in a log sent the flames dancing, and in the shadow-play her face, with those bright, hard eyes, looked almost demonic.

'You were awake,' she said. 'You saw him take me. And you didn't scream, Matt – you could have saved me. You didn't. You condemned me to a life of destruction and pain. You. You. You!

'So now I'm destroying you, taking you apart bit by bit, the way I was destroyed, and I'm feeling better all the time. All the things you cared for: your home, your wife, your dog – though the brute's still here, I see. And you did it. Nothing that's happened is my fault, Matt. It's yours. *Yours!*'

Matt's head was bent, as if bludgeoned by her rising voice. 'Yes,' he said. 'Mine.'

CHAPTER TWENTY-SEVEN

Eddie leant against the wall, afraid that his legs wouldn't hold him unaided. The past ten minutes had been a dizzying series of highs and lows, from swelling joy at the way Elena described him – 'a lovely, kind man' – to pity at her sad incapacity to feel love, to bewilderment at her attitude to the brother she had just found, whom she seemed to be blaming for all that had happened to her, when he could have been no more than a child.

And then to blank horror as he realised what she had done, and what she was going to do now. His heart ached for her: she had never allowed him close enough to share her corroding anger, never let him help to talk out her pain. She had let it not only destroy her, but make her an agent of destruction.

There was no way back, no way he could make it right for her, but he had to stop her doing this last, terrible thing. His eyes streaming with tears, he blundered round the house to the front door.

'He's not here! He's not bloody here!' Fleming was beside herself with rage as she came downstairs again, with MacNee at her heels, after a fruitless visit to Matt Lovatt's bedroom, and, as an afterthought, to Christie's as well, just in case the girl's story had been true. But Christie was innocently asleep, her face childishly pillowed on her hand, and Fleming shut the door again quietly so as not to wake her.

'Does that uniform think he's being paid to kip in his car?' she demanded as she stormed through the bar without so much as a nod to the astonished Georgia, while the last drinkers moved swiftly out of the way. As the door shut behind her, a swell of conversation rose, and Tony Drummond, seeing his moment, made his way across in her wake and wrenched it open again.

'Don't think so.' MacNee was standing immediately outside. 'Back, Drummond.'

'Oh, come on, Tam,' he pleaded. 'What's going on?'

MacNee's eyes were cold. 'A murder inquiry's going on, that's what. And the officer in the car there – the one that's getting a bollocking right at this moment – will have orders to arrest you if you step outside.'

'Arrest a member of the press? You're joking!'

'For operational reasons,' MacNee said. 'He'll be telling the others to stay where they are as well.'

'Operational reasons?' With the scent of an exclusive in his nostrils, Drummond was getting desperate. 'Look, Tam, I'm sorry about the business with your father. It wasn't personal. It's just the job.'

'This isn't personal either,' MacNee said, smiling sweetly. 'In fact, this is so far from being personal that when we're able to give out details, we'll be making it general, very general. All the media at the same time. Now, inside, like I said.'

The constable, looking dazed after the hairdryer treatment, was standing awkwardly beside his car.

'Get in there, tell them they're to stay inside and see that they do,' MacNee said, and followed Fleming towards the coast path.

The street lamps switched off just as they reached it.

'Yes, I woke up. I saw him take you, and I didn't scream. Look, Helen, I was nine years old! I was terrified – you can't blame a child of nine for not having the courage to give the alarm.'

Matt was blustering now and her smile was almost pitying. 'No. Perhaps not at the time. But there was more to it than that, wasn't there?'

She knew. Now he was going to have to face the truth he had tried to hide from himself all these years. He moistened dry lips.

'*Wasn't there?*' Elena's voice rose.

'Helen, I was half-asleep. I didn't believe it was real. I thought it was some kind of bad dream.' Matt was pleading with her now, scanning her face for some sign of understanding, but it was coldly implacable.

'Bad dream?' she mocked him. 'But you didn't mention your "bad dream" to anyone, did you?'

He bent his head. 'I couldn't believe – couldn't understand . . .' He felt his throat closing on the words.

'Say it!' she screamed suddenly. 'Say it! That my own father abducted me from my bedroom – *and you let him do it.*'

Matt opened his mouth, formed his lips to say the words, but no sound would come.

'It's hard to believe anyone could be stupid enough to take themselves out of police protection after all that's happened. But at least we know where he is,' Fleming said grimly, pointing towards the flickering glow in the farmhouse window as they made what speed they could with only the pale stars for light, on the slippery, uneven ground. MacNee was out of breath, trying to keep up with his superior's longer strides. She was feeling more and more uneasy about the mystery woman, who had struck that ruthless blow and then just . . . vanished.

'I still can't get a hold on this. It certainly started after Natalie Thomson came here, and it looks like Lovatt's been the target. The twin could be him – those papers were with his stuff, after all. But if so, who's she?'

'Sssh!' MacNee stopped suddenly. 'I can hear voices coming from the house. And look – I think that's someone moving round the side.'

Straining her eyes, Fleming could see a shadowy figure. 'What do you think – is that her?' she murmured. She'd feel happier if the person inside talking to Lovatt wasn't Natalie Thomson.

MacNee shook his head. 'Nuh. Think it's a male. But look – the window's open.'

'We'll make for that, then. I'll just give warning that we may need backup.'

Who was the man? And who was Lovatt talking to? With a sick feeling of apprehension Fleming spoke softly into her phone as MacNee headed towards the house.

The man was round at the front now. He seemed unaware of their approach and as she watched he disappeared inside.

He still hadn't said it. Matt had tried to make the admission she wanted, but he was swallowing bile. Elena looked with contempt at his contorted face.

'You can't face up to it, even now, can you? If you'd just told Mum, even afterwards – I was weeks in solitary confinement, weeks! Would you like to try to imagine what that could do to a little girl? Mum must have known what he was, that nothing meant anything except gambling. That was all I was, you know – another gambling chip to let him go on playing with the big guys. She'd have believed you.'

'But-but . . .' Lovatt stammered. 'I know what I thought I saw – but how could it be him? He was there next day.'

'Cal was waiting outside ready to whisk me away. He'd roped him in to bring me here – his other son.'

'Cal? Cal Findlay? But I know him, he never said—'

'He wouldn't, would he? Oh, he wasn't all bad. I even wish the poor fool hadn't got in my way tonight. He didn't know what was going on at the time – he'd been given some story about a custody problem because there was going to be a divorce so . . .' Her lips framed the word 'Dad' but she too couldn't bring herself to utter it. '*He* could marry Cal's mother. All lies, of course. But they were willing to act as jailers for me, across there,' she jerked her head over her shoulder, 'there on the island. I was imprisoned in that bothy, until the hunt died down. Alone. Until . . . *he* came to fetch me.'

'I'm sorry. I'm so sorry.' Matt was weeping now. Then he looked up. 'Did . . . did he—'

He stopped, but she understood. 'Haven't even got the guts to ask, have you?' Her voice was contemptuous. 'No, he never touched me. I was sellable goods, you see. He did do a favour for an old friend here first, though. Presumably owed him money as well.'

Elena paused to allow Matt to say something, but he was beyond speech. 'I still have this nightmare—' She shuddered. 'But it's all right. I've squared it with him. I'm nearly there. Just one last detail.'

She picked up her bag from the floor beside her.

The door creaked as it opened. The twins, so deeply engaged, both jumped and Elena gave a little startled scream.

The fire was dying back and as Eddie stepped into the room he was in deep shadow and for a second she didn't recognise him. Then she gave a cry of dismay.

'Eddie! Oh no, no!'

'Elena, it's all right, pet,' he said, coming across towards them.

'You've had a cruel, cruel time. I know how you've suffered, why you've done these things. But you mustn't go on like this. I'll sort everything out. Come away with me now.' He held out his hand encouragingly, as if to a child.

'Oh, Eddie,' she wailed. 'You're making it so difficult for me. Just go out and leave me for five minutes – three! Then I'll come. And we can drive back home and forget any of this happened. It'll be all right, you'll see.

'Don't spoil it, darling – I promise we'll go back to our lovely life, and I'll be so relaxed and cheerful – so loving, you won't know me.'

His wife, the wife he adored, was a monster. She was sick – she was completely insane. No wonder, with all that had happened to her. His heart wrung with pity, he said, 'No, Elena, I can't leave you. I'm going to make you come with me—'

'No.' Her movement was so quick that before he reached her, she had taken something out of her bag and jumped to her feet.

Eddie paused, warily. She seemed to be holding some sort of large dart, and the skin on her hands looked oddly shiny – gloves, of course. 'What's . . . what's that?' he said uncertainly.

'Go away, Eddie.'

Matt sat, frozen. 'Do as she says, Eddie. There's nothing you can do. It's a tranquilliser for animals – fatal in minutes. Not a bad way to go, really. The drug of choice for suicidal vets.'

He turned to his twin. 'Yes, I owe you. And I don't care any more. Carry on. I'm sorry for everything.' He held out his hands, waiting.

'You can't, Elena!' Eddie cried. 'I won't let you do this.'

He lunged towards her.

'Police! Get away from her! Stand back!' MacNee yelled, launching himself through the window. The curtains caught; it was a second before he had a clear view. He could hear Fleming at his shoulder, shouting into her phone.

444

It was as if he had invaded a tableau. No one moved. A man he'd never seen before, a stout, balding, middle-aged man, was standing looking at his hand with a puzzled expression. Matt Lovatt was gaping from his position on the sofa and a blonde woman was standing holding what looked like some sort of dart.

MacNee grabbed her from behind. The dart fell from her hand and she crumpled to her knees. 'Eddie! Oh Eddie, no!'

Eddie dropped, a crumpled heap on the floor. Matt put his head in his hands and moaned. Elena was weeping as Fleming came in through the window.

MacNee, still holding Elena, jerked his head at the dart on the floor. 'Some sort of poison,' he said. 'Don't touch it.'

Matt Lovatt looked up. 'Not "some sort of poison",' he said. 'Immobilon – you need the antidote within five minutes.'

'There should be an ambulance up the hill . . .' Fleming was tapping a number on her phone, but Matt shook his head.

'They won't have it. It's vet medicine – I had the antidote in my medicine cabinet, but they took that away after the fire.' He looked at his twin, still in the policeman's restraining grasp as she yearned towards her unconscious husband.

'Dad finished us both,' he said, the word coming to his lips for the first time in almost thirty years. 'You, crippled by what happened to you, me crippled by guilt. Did you kill him? Did you chain him to a rock, and let him die? If I'd known, I'd have been right there with you.'

Elena was on her knees. She looked up at him with contempt. 'You could have told the truth any time. You've lied with every breath you've taken for thirty years. And you've killed Eddie – the only decent man I've ever known.'

Fleming had never watched a murdered man die. As long as she lived, she would never forget it.

CHAPTER TWENTY-EIGHT

They took Matt Lovatt to the Smugglers Inn. Georgia Stanley was waiting, watching the comings and goings at the farmhouse from the window of her little sitting room.

'Matt!' she exclaimed in distress. 'Are you all right? What's happened?'

He looked terrible, stooped and shaky as if in the last few hours he had become an old, old man. The police officers bringing him in, DI Fleming and DS MacNee, who'd gossiped with her across the bar, suddenly seemed remote, official, the embodiments of the law.

'May we borrow the sitting room?' Fleming said.

'Of course, of course.' She went to the door.

Lovatt spoke. 'In answer to your question, Georgia, I seem to have been responsible for the deaths of my father, my wife, my half-brother and a thoroughly decent man I'd never seen before.'

Georgia gave a squeal of distress, but at a look from DS MacNee she scuttled out.

Lovatt collapsed into a chair, convulsively clasping and unclasping his hands. Haltingly, and with long pauses, he repeated what his sister had told him while Fleming and MacNee listened in silence.

He bowed his head when he had finished, then looked up again. 'I sort of knew it was him, I suppose. But sort of not. He was there at breakfast.'

No one spoke, and he went on, 'I don't think you understand: *He was there at breakfast.* I was nine years old, and my father was sitting there, reassuring my mother: Helen had just got up early, gone out without telling anyone. Then they found a ladder and everyone believed it was a break-in. How could I say what I'd seen – or what I'd thought I'd seen?

'I'd wakened up, you see, presumably because I heard him coming through the window of our bedroom. We had a house that looked out to sea. I was half-asleep, and I always sort of thought he came out of it.' He shuddered. 'In my dreams, he always did. He was standing beside my sister's bed, all in black, with a stocking mask over his face and his hand across her mouth. I-I saw her look at me, begging me to do something.

'I still thought I was dreaming—' He broke off. 'No, that's a lie. It's a lie I've told myself so often that I've come almost to believe it. I knew I was awake. At first, though, I didn't know who he was. But as he carried her out, kicking at him, trying to bite him – Helen was always brave, unlike me—'

'You were a soldier,' MacNee said.

'A soldier! Comrades, training, support . . . That's easy, in an odd way. You do what you have to do because you're trained, conditioned. My—' He choked. 'The man said to me, "It will be you, the next night, or the next." I was afraid, and the only way I could deal with it was by believing it hadn't happened, that I'd dreamt it.

'The dreams I believed were the wrong ones. I utterly believed that Helen was dead. I set out to try to make restitution for the evil I'd done, by helping people who'd suffered, like Christie—'

He stopped, then with an obvious effort, carried on, 'It was the only thing I came up with that I was in a position to do. If I'd known Helen was alive, what she had suffered . . .'

His eyes were full of tears as he went on. 'I only wish she had killed me. Her husband – he was a good man. I'm rubbish.'

Fleming fixed him with a steady gaze. 'Mr Lovatt, don't blame your nine-year-old self. It was an intolerable situation, and you have suffered too.

'But let's talk about more recent events. You're not a fool. You know that if you'd been open with us from the start, it's possible that the other deaths could have been prevented. I daresay you feel, right at the moment, that getting yourself a handful of pills would somehow pay for that.

'I'm not in the business of handing down justice and nor are you. We can only look for truth, and to achieve justice under the law we have to rely on proof. You said you wanted to make restitution to your sister. The way you can do that now is to be there to explain how it happened, whatever it may cost you.'

Lovatt looked up. 'Yes,' he said, his voice infinitely weary. 'Of course I must. But you've no idea, no idea at all, how terribly, terribly tired of it all I am.'

He was near breaking point. Hastily, Fleming said, 'One last thing. Do you know anything about your father's murder?'

'She couldn't . . . couldn't have done it herself.' He was starting to slur his speech. 'She . . . she sort of told me she did it, though, and implied that Cal Findlay helped her. Once she'd had her revenge on us all, she would be . . . all right, she thought. An eye for an eye . . .

'She was always so much stronger than me, so much cleverer . . . My mother said at the time it should have been me that was taken. She wished it had been me. And afterwards she . . . she never hugged me again.'

As he wept, he was rocking to and fro with his arms wrapped round himself, as if hoping to find the comfort the child had been denied.

As Fleming dragged herself up the stairs back at the Kirkluce headquarters, she felt deathly tired herself. But there was work to do . . .

The door to her office was standing open and MacNee was lying in wait.

'Away to your bed,' he said.

Fleming had got past the point of tiredness. 'It's all right,' she said. 'I've got my second wind.'

'You only think you have. I heard you tripping twice coming up the stairs.'

She glared at him. 'I just stumbled, all right?'

'And now you're getting belligerent. That's another sign. There's a driver waiting for you.'

'Ever think of a job as a nanny? I hear it pays better than police work, these days.' But it was a feeble protest. Fleming knew perfectly well she needed to be on top of the job before she started trying to clear up the aftermath, and at the moment she most certainly was not.

'I'll be back at six,' she said.

She was asleep before the driver reached the farmhouse. She woke up when the car stopped, sparing him the embarrassment of having to wake her.

'Thanks,' she said, a little thickly as she got out, trying to stay half asleep until she could get up the stairs and into bed. The light in the kitchen was on; Bill must have left it so that she wouldn't have to come home to darkness. She was feeling a surge of affection as she opened the kitchen door.

Her daughter was sitting at the kitchen table, cradling a mug.

Meg the collie, in her basket by the Aga, opened an eye and ruffled her tail a fraction but didn't raise her head.

Cat looked as startled as she felt. 'Mum! I didn't realise you were still out.'

Marjory looked at her without enthusiasm. 'Yes. I'm just on my way to bed. What are you doing up at this hour?'

'Couldn't sleep. I can't make up my mind what to do. Mum, do you think if I—'

Marjory cut her short. 'I'm sorry, Cat. I've just watched a good, decent man die, and I want to get some sleep before I start wondering whether it was my fault. Everyone else certainly will be. I'll be up again about six, so unless you're still awake then, I probably won't see you at breakfast.'

The wall of his bedroom seemed to be a sort of bluish-grey, which was odd because it had always had wallpaper in dreary brown and orange flowers. Strange. His head hurt too, and his mouth was painfully dry. Cal Findlay licked his lips; there was a metallic taste from caked blood round the rim, and when he explored with his tongue, there was a hole where one of his molars had been. He groaned.

A woman in green overalls was standing at the foot of his bed, writing something on a clipboard. A nurse. Hospital. Of course. He'd been taken there last night, he vaguely remembered.

His head was sore, and his cheek. Accident? Must have hit his head. He felt it, encountering a plaster, and pleased with the success of his reasoning struggled to sit up.

'Waking up, are you?' the nurse said. She came to help him, moving the pillows behind him. 'All right?'

His tongue felt thick. 'Water,' he croaked.

She poured him some from a carafe on the table beside him. It was warm and tasted tinny, but he drank it eagerly. He put his hand to the bandage again. It was painful, but his mind was beginning to clear. 'Did I hit my head?' he asked.

'As I understand it, somebody hit it for you. You're lucky – just a bit of concussion and a lost tooth.'

He registered that her tone seemed brusque, but then of course, the ministering-angel style had gone out long ago. 'What happened?' he asked.

'I don't know. But we were told to inform you when you woke up properly that the police want to speak to you whenever you're ready.'

Recollection hit him like the freak wave that had almost capsized his boat last year. For a moment, he couldn't get his breath and the woman looked at him in alarm.

'Here – are you all right?'

He managed to nod. 'Just . . . just shocked. Give me a moment.'

'I wouldn't have said, only the doctor cleared it and they're saying it's urgent.' She sounded defensive. 'You can say you're not well enough.'

'No point. They'll not go away, will they?'

The nurse didn't respond.

'I'll speak to them,' Cal said. The nausea and dizziness still lingered, but now that the moment had come he realised that it was almost a relief. It was his chance to tell his story at last, to explain how he had been a victim too.

DC Hepburn had come in to work, buoyed up by the boss's positive response last night to her idea about the TV programme being the catalyst for all that had happened, and was crushed to discover that events had overtaken her success.

At the morning briefing, Fleming looked as if she had been chewed up and spat out, and she seemed to have forgotten

Hepburn's contribution; she didn't so much as mention her when it came to the follow-up.

Hepburn felt sick as she listened to the details. Like every modern child she'd been endlessly warned about paedophiles; it had given her recurring nightmares, but none even came close to the horrors Elena Tindall had suffered.

She felt seething anger at the men who had done this to a little girl, not only her evil father and his perverted friends, but the men who by their silence had allowed it all to happen. The sins of omission, she seemed to remember from her Catholic girlhood, could be mortal sins too.

She wanted to be in there, fighting for Elena, not tasked with some mundane job. They hadn't charged her, just arrested her on suspicion of murder; Fleming, of course, would be doing the interview once Elena's brief arrived from Glasgow, and Macdonald and Campbell were recording a formal statement from Matt Lovatt. MacNee was off to have what was described as a preliminary chat with Cal Findlay to glean as much information as possible, now that he'd be entitled to a lawyer whenever he was under arrest. It was a blow that Hepburn didn't seem to be part of the inner circle any longer.

Hepburn slipped out of the briefing room before Sergeant Naismith could nobble her. All she could do for Elena was dig up everything the records had to offer about the Helen Smith case for a plea in mitigation. That wasn't a job for the police, but she was going to do it anyway. She'd just sneak out for a smoke first. It had worked last time.

When DS MacNee appeared round the corner of the dustbins, saying, 'Thought you'd be here,' she had to repress an urge to hide her cigarette behind her back as if she'd been caught round the back of the bike sheds. She inhaled defiantly.

A mistake. When he said, 'Want to come with me to chat to Cal Findlay?' she choked.

He laughed, the bastard. 'Sook, dinnae blaw!' he said, and Hepburn couldn't recall feeling so humiliated since the time the sexy history master at her school had caught her smoking and drawled, 'It's only cool if you're a thirties' movie star. And believe me, Lauren Bacall you're not.'

Lovatt was looking drained and ill this morning, but he sounded emotionless as he repeated all that his sister had told him, along with his own recollections, for the benefit of the recording device they had placed in front of him on Georgia's coffee table.

Letting him talk, Macdonald silently vowed to be professional, but if he even put aside his own feelings about Christie, it was hard not to view him with disgust and contempt. People had died because of Lovatt's lies.

'Thank you, sir,' he said, when Lovatt reached the end of his recital. 'Now tell me about Cal Findlay.'

'I didn't know about him, except as a local fisherman. Maybe he worked for my father?' Lovatt said. 'There was quite a little fleet of trawlers in Barrow, before they were gambled away. My mother was bitter about that, as she was about most things.'

He stopped. Neither Macdonald nor Campbell spoke and after a moment he went on, 'I thought I'd seen Helen dead, but of course when she mocked the open coffin on the dining-table . . . It was obvious, I'd dreamt it. Why didn't I see that? I could have looked up what had happened, but . . . it was buried deep by then. Somehow, even thinking about it hurt too much.' The pain showed on his face.

Macdonald's resolution to be professional had been meant to stop him being prejudiced against Lovatt. Now he was actually beginning to feel sorry for the poor sod. Professional! Come on!

'Let's leave that there,' he said. 'You were told that someone called Andrew Smith had been sadistically murdered in a cave on your island. You told us you had never heard of him.'

Lovatt became more animated. 'Could we rewind, please? Can I have that moment back, with all the advantage of 20/20 hindsight? I had nothing at all to do with my father's death. I knew if I told you he was my father and that I had inherited all of the estate because he had not made any claim to it, you would make it your business to go after me. To be honest, I stopped buying into the middle-class idea that the police are our friends quite a long time ago.'

'So you thought lying to us was the answer?' Macdonald's response was immediate and fierce. 'Given the proper information, we would have discovered that your twin was alive. We had information on your father already which might have let us trace her, before there were two more deaths, and nearly one more—'

'Cal.' Lovatt spoke heavily. 'I beg you to believe I didn't know he was my half-brother. I guess he was waiting below when my father constructed his little scenario with the ladder, happy to carry Helen off, to be a jailer – here I'm using Helen's exact words – on the island, until the fuss died down.

'May I suggest that you talk to him about what happened? I think he knows a great deal more than I can tell you.'

As they walked back to the car, Macdonald said to Campbell, 'The boss is worried about him, but I don't think he's a suicide risk. He's making excuses for himself already. He's just weak, that's his problem. But you do find yourself wondering what you'd have done, put in a situation like that with your own father.'

Campbell looked at him in surprise. 'Shopped the bugger, of course. Would have saved a lot of trouble.'

Macdonald gave a crack of laughter, but as he was opening the car door he saw a figure striding out along the coast path, walking away from him, buckets in her hands to feed the bellowing stags.

Loyal to the last, Christie was. Loyal, and decent – and lost to him.

The pain he felt was a real, physical pain, somewhere in the region of his heart, as if something vital had been torn away. He couldn't kid himself that there was any way back, after all that had happened. He could only hope that one day the woman he still couldn't help loving would find someone worthy of her and that, please God, it wouldn't be Lovatt.

Fleming had spent some time preparing carefully for the crucial interview with Elena Tindall. The Supreme Court in London had forced a recent change in policy, in line with English law, which meant that a lawyer had to be present at all questioning after arrest. It was a change which had raised a lot of hackles – after all, Scotland's relaxed policy on questioning was coupled with a rigid requirement for corroboration that had prevented the forced confession scandals the English system had suffered.

Having to second-guess what the accused's brief would take exception to was an art Fleming was only beginning to acquire. As she walked to the interview room, taking Campbell when he got back from the Lovatt interview, she said, 'I thought we'd start straight in with Eddie Tindall. Elena can claim accident, of course, but that's her most vulnerable point. Might give us an in to the questions about her intention to murder Lovatt.'

She glanced at Campbell, but he didn't seem impressed. She raised her eyebrows. 'No?'

'Won't say anything.'

Campbell's instinct was her reason for asking him along, rather than the more senior Macdonald. 'She was coming apart last night,' she said, a little doubtfully now.

'Won't be, this morning. Saw her into the van last night afterwards. Cool as the proverbial.'

Fleming's heart sank. 'Oh well,' she said, as they reached the door of the interview room. 'Over the top.'

The woman who had last night been sobbing, incoherent and on the verge of disintegration, was sitting calmly beside her brief, a small, terrier-like man whom Fleming knew as one of the most successful criminal defence lawyers in Glasgow. Elena's control was awesome: she didn't look like someone who had spent the previous night in a police cell, with her shining blonde hair smooth and her jeans and white T-shirt looking somehow pristine. She wasn't wearing make-up, but with skin that good, Fleming thought with just a tinge of envy, who needed it?

The formalities completed, Fleming said, 'Eddie Tindall. I wanted to ask you—'

'My client has asked me to state that she deeply regrets the accident that caused her husband's death. She is, of course, in deep grief and too distressed to answer you herself. I ask you to respect that.'

Elena Tindall's dark-blue eyes – so like her brother's – met Fleming's impassively.

She didn't offer condolences. 'This wasn't an accident that couldn't have been avoided. Mrs Tindall, how did you come to have the darts in your possession?'

There was no answer. She tried again. 'Mrs Tindall, you killed your husband. I accept that it was unintentional, but I need to know what you did intend to do with them.'

'My client has no further comment to make.'

Fleming looked directly at Elena. 'Look, we are aware of the background. We know what you have suffered. There is evidence in mitigation that we are more than happy to promote, but we need your full cooperation. You killed your father—'

'No comment,' the lawyer said again.

'Let's talk about Melissa Lovatt, then,' Fleming suggested. Elena looked back at her with cold eyes.

'Melissa Lovatt?' Fleming put more pressure on the name.

'You asked that question already,' her lawyer said. 'My client does not wish to answer.'

'The forensic teams are at this moment taking your chalet apart, and I can assure you that evidence will be found.'

Silence.

'All right, let's talk about the fire at your brother's farmhouse. Mrs Tindall?'

Silence.

'Perhaps you might have something to say about the death of Hugh Donaldson?'

Fleming saw the name register in a widening of the dark-blue eyes and a tiny shiver. The lawyer was clearly taken by surprise, and he turned towards his client, looking a question.

Elena shrugged her slim shoulders, and he said, 'My client has nothing to say.'

'All right. The bottle attack,' she stressed the words, 'on Calum Findlay? You may remember that a bottle was used to murder Melissa Lovatt.'

'My client wishes me to state that this was self-defence.'

'Does your client,' Fleming said, struggling to match Elena's coolness with her own, 'have anything at all she conceivably might wish to say about any of the charges we are about to raise against her? You know that an early guilty plea can mean a considerable reduction in sentence.'

Elena looked at her contemptuously. 'There isn't a jury in the land who wouldn't be on my side.' She glanced at her lawyer. 'I assume you can find someone who can make it clear what I went through?'

'Well, of course. Am I right that you have nothing else you wish to say?'

The incline of her head was positively regal.

CHAPTER TWENTY-NINE

Cal Findlay didn't like the look of Detective Sergeant MacNee. Small, cocky, and smiling in a way that made you feel it would be much more reassuring if he didn't.

'Just a wee chat,' he'd said, sitting down on the chair beside the bed. There was a girl with him who didn't say anything, just sat down in another chair in the corner. She looked too young to be in the polis.

'I'll explain. We've a few things we need to clear up. You're not under arrest, and this isn't formal questioning – yet. But maybe if we can sort something out between us now, it won't come to that, eh?'

There was the unsettling smile again. Findlay sat up straighter on his pillows.

'OK if I record this – just so DC Hepburn here doesn't get writer's cramp scribbling?'

Findlay shrugged. MacNee set a small tape recorder down between them and began.

'We've evidence you were involved in Andrew Smith's murder, and of course your fingerprints were on the knife in Elena Tindall's chalet. Have to say it's not looking good, Cal.

So maybe you need to think about getting out your side of the story?'

Findlay gulped. That chimed with his own idea, but now the moment had come, he wasn't sure. His head had begun to pound and there were stabs of pain from his aching jaw.

'Tell me about the knife, Cal, just for a start,' MacNee prompted.

'I know what it looks like, but it wasn't like that,' Findlay began. 'I knew what she'd done, and I knew what she was going to do.'

'Why didn't you shop her, then?'

To his astonishment, it was the girl who interrupted, and it was a very aggressive question.

'Look, miss, you don't understand—'

'Don't think either of us do,' MacNee said. 'We're asking you to tell us.'

Findlay began to sweat. 'I was just trying to . . . to prevent her killing her brother.'

'That's "prevent" as in "kill" is it?' the girl sneered.

Outraged, he looked at MacNee, hoping he'd pull her into line, but he was smiling faintly. 'Go on,' he said.

'It wasn't my fault!' Findlay cried. 'I—'

Then he stopped. He didn't see MacNee hold up his hand to his constable in a warning gesture, or even notice the silence that followed; he was trying to focus, trying to stop his thoughts jiggling round along with the waves of pain.

'She's told you her side, hasn't she? I don't suppose she mentioned blackmail and coercion,' Findlay said savagely. He tried to gauge their reaction, but both faces were impassive and he said it again, 'Blackmail and coercion – do you understand?'

'Oh, we understand what you're saying,' MacNee said, with a hint of stress on the last word.

They didn't understand. No one understood. No one ever had. The years and years of pretence, and silence and fear; years of a devil's pact with the mother whose misguided love for a villain had brought him into being, then denied him a life. The thought overwhelmed him.

'You don't know what it's like,' he burst out, 'waiting for the knock on the door. I just want it finished with now. It eats into you, you know. Eats through to your very bones.'

'Guilt?' the girl suggested.

He turned on her. 'Guilt? Not guilt, no. I'm angry that I let myself feel guilt for something that wasn't my fault, because she made use of that. They both used me – first him, then her. It's the fear that's destroyed me – fear.

'When she came back just now – that was it. I knew then – finished. Couldn't control her. Somewhere in it all, she'd gone crazy – calm, quiet, crazy.'

'So your calm, sensible decision was to kill her?' The bitch wasn't letting up.

Findlay ignored her, turning to MacNee. 'I'm maybe guilty under the law for what we did to Drew, but you've got to see it was what she demanded as justice, to make up for what had happened to her. OK, I helped Drew grab his daughter and brought her back here. He was going to marry my mother – like he should have when she fell pregnant and he wouldn't even acknowledge me,' he said in a bitter aside. 'Told us if he got a divorce he'd lose his daughter.'

'*What* a shame!' the gadfly in the corner murmured.

She was really getting to him. 'Don't believe me, then,' he said angrily. 'But you'd have believed him, if he'd told you. Charm, you know? Oh God, yes, charm.' His face twisted. 'And maybe Helen was a victim, but so was I. And my mum too. She's off her head, you know? And that's his fault, too.'

'You and your mother, of course, were blamelessly locking up a little girl in solitary confinement, while a search was going on all over the country, with appeals on TV from her weeping mother, no doubt. Watch them, did you, then settled down to congratulate yourselves on doing the right thing?'

Findlay gaped at her. The detective's eyes were blazing with anger, and it was as if she'd punched him in the stomach, winding him. He had never been faced with the stark reality before. Even when Elena had confronted him with the truth, she'd had her own reasons for wanting to channel blame in one direction only. He'd been protected by a cocoon of self-pity; now it had been stripped off and he was left naked and squirming as any grub. He stumbled on – what else could he do? – but what he said was beginning to sound hollow even to him.

'I-I swear I-I never knew. I swear it.' Sweat was dripping into his eyes and he put up a hand to wipe his brow. 'Didn't recognise her when she turned up at the front door those years later – well, she was grown-up, skinny and kind of slutty-looking.'

Findlay broke off. He saw Hepburn open her mouth; saw too the silencing gesture from MacNee once more. At last he said, 'You'll know what she told us. My mum went mental – never really recovered.

'She called herself Elena now, not Helen, she said. And she gave me my orders. She didn't have to spell it out. It was blackmail – blackmail and coercion, like I said.'

He was making his strongest argument, but even he could hear it sounded weak. He had to do better, let the anger and bitterness he felt come through.

'Look, she forced me to agree – I wouldn't have done it otherwise, I swear it. Not like that. Though God knows he deserved it for what he did to us – and to her, of course,' he added hastily. 'But it was all her idea – said it had to be slow.

"He's got to know, he's got to suffer at my hands like I did at his. An eye for an eye: evil for evil." That's what she said. Word for word.'

He stopped again.

'Nearly there,' MacNee said softly. 'Your turn to tell us what happened – she's getting hers.'

'Oh God!' He closed his eyes for a moment. He knew how she could turn things, twist things, how ruthless she was. Truth would be better than the lies she would tell.

'All right. She'd tracked him down in Manchester. I was to bump into him, take him for a drink. She gave me stuff to put in it. He wasn't exactly pleased to see me, but he couldn't refuse a chat in a pub. I asked him about Helen, you know. Working in London, that's what he told me.' He gave a short laugh. 'When he started feeling groggy I offered him a lift home. Simple.

'I picked her up, drove up here. I'd the prawn boat by then and it wasn't hard to land him there. I'd the staples in the cave ready. She hammered them in herself. He came round before we left, and . . . well . . .' His voice trailed away.

Findlay took another sip of water. 'She wanted to go back, you know, so he'd think we'd been bluffing, and then leave him again, but I wouldn't go. That was too much. She was angry, but I still refused.'

He ignored the chippy little cow's, 'You're all heart,' comment. 'Then – well after that I had just to put it behind me, forget about it as best I could.'

'You're a good forgetter,' Hepburn said. 'A-star, I'd say.'

MacNee frowned at her. 'Just carry on, Cal,' he said.

If he'd been asked to stop, he wasn't sure he could, now. The words were bubbling up; he was feeling better that now, at last, he was able to tell his story.

'She'd had stuff done when she came back this time. Didn't

462

recognise her. Then I couldn't believe the timing – just after his body had turned up. And she knew about what had happened but she still came here, wouldn't change her plans. I argued with her that it was crazy but she wouldn't listen – she was hell-bent on revenge.

'Then she'd just vanish. Great! *I* couldn't, of course: it would probably dump me right in it.' He could feel conviction surging back into his voice now; he was unconsciously clenching his fists in rage at the injustice of it all. 'I told her that, begged her to get out, come back later once the fuss had died down, if she had to—'

'At which point, of course, you'd have called us in and told us all about it?' the girl needled.

It was as if she'd slapped him. 'You going to let her go on like this?' Findlay demanded, addressing MacNee.

'She's just training to be a DI one day,' MacNee said, and now his voice too was harsh and unfriendly. 'Give us an idea, Cal – what are you going to put your hand up to? Fire-raising? Killing Andrew Smith? Attempted murder of Elena Tindall?'

'She made me do it – the fire.'

'Made you? A great big man like you, and her half your size—'

Findlay had stopped listening to her. 'It was killing his wife, killing her like that – That was wrong, you see. Drew was different. He deserved what happened to him. I'm not saying it was nice but it was justice.

'But Lissa Lovatt – well, she hadn't done anything. And I knew Elena was going to kill her brother for something he did when he was a little kid. That wasn't right either.

'Look, I didn't want to kill her – she was my sister, for God's sake, but she was beyond reason. If she got away with that, she wouldn't stop, and—'

463

He only realised what he'd said when he saw the look on MacNee's face. 'You knew that you'd be next, right? And you couldn't afford to turn her in because she'd have taken you with her. I'm afraid my ideas on justice are a wee bitty different from yours.

'Calum Findlay, I am arresting you on suspicion of murder and attempted murder. You are not obliged to say anything but anything you do say will be written down and may be used in evidence. Do you understand the caution?'

Findlay nodded numbly. He had failed to make them see that he'd been a helpless victim, and now he wasn't even sure he could see it himself.

MacNee gave Hepburn an amused look as she drove him away. 'Right little tiger, you are,' he said.

Hepburn's cheeks were still flushed. 'I was just so angry. That great lump of self-pity, projecting all the guilt he should be feeling on to Elena and his father – not that I'm saying Andrew Smith was anything other than scum and if you're talking rough justice he probably got what he deserved. But for all he said, Findlay wasn't talking justice, he was talking self-interest. He knew from the start that what he was doing was wrong. There's a limit to what Andrew Smith can be blamed for.'

MacNee looked at her quizzically. 'And doesn't that go for Elena Tindall as well? She'd choices too.'

She turned her head to glance at him. 'Elena was fighting with monsters. You know – Nietzsche.'

'Bless you,' he said politely.

Hepburn made a face at him. 'Very funny. German philosopher: he warned about fighting with monsters, in case you became one. And then there was the part about an abyss – "If you gaze for long into the abyss, the abyss gazes also into

464

you." It swallowed her up – the abyss. That's where she is now.'

MacNee was more prosaic. 'Aye, she's in a mess right enough. Strong woman, though. Runs in the family – strong women, weak men. Her granny was a right old battleaxe, apparently. Wouldn't even let her poor wee henpecked husband keep his own name. According to the locals, he was so happy at getting away, he died with a smile on his face. Matt and Cal obviously favour their father's side.'

'Funny to think of them as brothers,' Hepburn said. 'Certainly deal with their problems the same way – don't look at them hard enough, and maybe they'll go away. Do you think they realise what damage their feeble cowardice has caused?'

'Prefer Elena's more robust approach, do you?' MacNee said sardonically. 'Tough cookie. I wonder how the boss has got on with her?'

As they walked back along the corridor after the abortive interview with Elena Tindall, Fleming said bitterly to Campbell, 'She's terrifying, that woman. We'd better hope that forensics can find something in the chalet to tie her to Melissa Lovatt's murder. If not, all we've really got against the woman for Andrew Smith at the moment is the evidence from Lovatt of the oblique confession she made, and the fact that she had the lethal dart for the attempt on her brother – fortunately we can testify to that too. I can tell you, with the sob story she's got to tell, her brief just could get an acquittal – and then where are we?'

Campbell grinned. 'Corroboration'll be out the window by the time this calls in court.'

'What?'

'The new rules. It'll just be about credibility – and a disfigured soldier's about the best witness you could get.'

'You've got a nasty habit of being right, Ewan,' Fleming

conceded. But she still regretted that one person's word against another, instead of one person's word backed up by evidence, could put someone behind bars.

And she'd always thought, anyway, that if you could talk to someone accused of a crime, without a lawyer telling them that if they didn't say anything they might get off with it, it delivered something closer to justice for victims.

But then she would think that, wouldn't she?

'Oh, for God's sake! Stop the car!' DS MacNee erupted suddenly.

They were nearing Kirkluce. Giving him a startled glance, Hepburn pulled in to the side and MacNee, swearing, was out of the car before the wheels stopped rolling. The rain was coming on; he plunged across the road, dodging the oncoming traffic.

Hepburn watched, puzzled. He had gone up to an elderly man, well-dressed but with, she thought, a drinker's complexion, who was walking along by the verge on the other side, hitch-hiking.

MacNee had grabbed his arm, and was shaking it. He was shouting, and she lowered the window to hear what he was saying.

'What the hell do you think you're doing? You'll get yourself killed, walking along here. If you want to go somewhere, tell Bunty and she'll take you.'

'Aye – to one of her bloody coffee mornings,' the old man said sourly. 'Och Tam, for any favour, leave me alone.'

MacNee ignored him, watching for a gap in the traffic. Still keeping tight hold on his arm, he steered him across the road and held open the back passenger door. 'Get in,' he said, and muttering under his breath the man complied.

MacNee got back in. 'My father Davie, Louise. Do us a favour – drop him off at home, will you?'

'Sure.' Hepburn drove off, suppressing a smile. MacNee's colourful father had been the subject of quite a bit of station gossip.

MacNee was still raging. 'What did you think you were doing, Dad?'

'Getting back to Glasgow. Might have made it too if you'd not come along.' He sounded like a Colditz prisoner recaptured by the Gestapo.

MacNee turned in his seat, hurt. 'Dad, you were on the streets in Glasgow! You were killing yourself with the drink. A chest infection could have finished you off—'

'Aye, well, maybe it'd be better than dying of boredom. I'm not taking it, Tam. You're maybe my son but you're not my keeper.'

'Can't you see you're better now?' MacNee demanded. 'You're healthier, your drinking's well-controlled—'

'It is that,' Davie said with feeling. 'Och, I've no doubt you mean well, you and Bunty, but unless you lock me up I'll be away back to my pals.'

As the car drew up outside his house, MacNee sighed deeply. 'OK, Dad, I'll talk to you later when I get in, all right? And don't do anything daft meantime.'

Davie got out. 'All right,' he said. 'As long's you don't think you'll talk me out of it.'

As they drove away, MacNee said, 'Sorry about that.'

'No problem.' Hepburn hesitated, then said, 'What are you going to do?'

'He's going to do it for me, isn't he? I knew he was getting kinna fed up. It's the drink, though – he'll kill himself if he goes back to it.'

'You can't stop him, though, can you? Like he said, he's all grown up. Is there nowhere he could go where they'd keep an eye – a hostel, say . . .'

MacNee shook his head. 'They can't monitor the inmates one-to-one – there's too many of them. They just make rules, and he'll break them and be back on the streets. Unless—' He broke off, thinking.

'There's one of our old neighbours, a decent wifie, who takes in lodgers. She still sends us a Christmas card, and she'd always a soft spot for my father. I could see if she'd maybe take him on, and I could tell him that if I don't get a good report from her I'll fetch him back.'

'And make him go to coffee mornings,' Hepburn suggested.

'That'd do it. Given the choice, I'd rather be on the streets myself.'

From his chalet above the bay, Derek Sorley looked out through the sheets of driving rain towards the island. Tascadan – treasure, in the Gaelic. He hadn't done much homework for his classes the last few days; it looked as if he might not be needing to tap into the growing market for publicly funded Gaelic speakers, after all. The police had finished their investigations there and the place was deserted. It certainly looked as if Lovatt would have more on his mind than people taking an innocent walk across his property. Even with a metal detector.

Another ten minutes, and he'd be able to walk across the causeway, so he might as well set off now. He'd only to pick up the machine, and a spade, and he'd be there.

Sorley was in an unusually cheerful frame of mind anyway. He'd suggested to Steve that if anyone pursued them – which they maybe wouldn't, with all that was going on – he'd retract his confession and say that it was Hugh who let the stag out. He'd said to Steve, 'It's what Hugh would have wanted,' and though Steve had looked a bit doubtful, he'd agreed.

The rain was teeming down, coming in on a northwester, and

he huddled into his cagoule as he left the chalet. Further down the track a large van was parked and figures in white hooded overalls were going to and fro from Spindrift, but they paid no attention as he walked past them and down to the shore. Even in the bay, the sea was being whipped up into a froth of whitecaps and the spume stung his face as he went down to the causeway. It should be clear by now, but there were rogue waves still breaking across it.

He couldn't bear to wait any longer. What was a little water when the gold was there, so near, almost within reach? He hardly noticed that he was soaked, or even when he slipped and landed painfully on a jagged rock. He'd have bruises to show for it tomorrow, but that hardly mattered.

It wasn't easy, either, to keep his feet on the slippery turf when he reached the island. He lost count of the number of times he fell forward, but making prostration to the gods seemed somehow appropriate.

There were the graves now, grey in the fog of mist and spray. He remembered perfectly where he had been, the moment when the machine signalled 'Gold', the moment just before the wolf-dog had appeared. He went back there now and switched it on, with a murmured prayer. What if, in his alarm, he'd been mistaken?

But no, there it was, the clicking that proved to him that dreams, after all, really did come true. He set it down and began to dig.

A tinfoil package came up first, just a couple of inches below the surface. It seemed to have some mouldy bones – chicken, they looked like to him, probably from some picnicker who'd buried the debris rather than carrying it home. He chucked it impatiently aside, and dug on, dug and dug and dug.

He was soaked through and wind-battered, but he was

sweating with the effort he was making, getting increasingly frantic. Perhaps he'd got the angle slightly wrong? He stood up and picked up the machine again, swung it over his excavations.

Nothing. Silence. He checked that it was on properly, swung again wildly in his impatience. As the metal detector swung across the discarded package, the clicking he had been so desperate to hear sounded again.

It felt as if his stomach had fallen into his boots. In disbelief, he looked at what it was telling him. There it was – gold!

He'd got the machine second-hand, without a book of instructions. Now, an uneasy flicker of a half-forgotten something he'd heard once crept into his mind: something about metal detectors having the same response to tinfoil as to gold.

No riches, no glorious future. The rain was trickling down the back of his neck, his shoes were waterlogged and he had a blister on his muddy hand. He looked down at the yawning hole in front of him and saw the grave of all his dreams.

They were sitting having supper in the farmhouse kitchen when Marjory got home, light-headed with exhaustion. After the horror and intensity of the past hours, there was something almost surreal about the familiar, peaceful domestic scene.

Bill jumped up as she came in. 'Marjory! That's good. Didn't think we'd see you till much later.'

She rubbed a tired hand across her face. 'Wasn't doing any good there. Too tired to concentrate. Food then bed, I think – though not necessarily in that order.'

Her husband laughed as she slumped into her chair. 'Fortunately Cammie hasn't got round to seconds yet. There's still some supper in the oven.'

The savoury smell wafted across and she realised she was ravenously hungry. Bill put down a plate of something chickeny in front of her, along with a glass of white wine. 'You look as if you need that.'

'You could say.' The hot food, the cold wine – she might feel almost human shortly.

'Got them all banged up, have you, Mum?' Cammie asked with cheerful insensitivity.

Trying not to wince, she said, 'Not exactly. How are you all – had a good day?'

Cat, who, Marjory noticed, had ostentatiously moved nearer to her father's end of the table, said nothing. Cammie said, 'Fine,' and Bill said, 'Just the usual. Got quite a good price for some stirks at Kelso.'

Cammie looked at him, then shifted in his seat. 'Dad, have you ever thought of switching to arable farming?'

Marjory, who had been fighting to keep her eyes open long enough to finish her food, stretched them wide in astonishment, and Bill stared at his son.

'Arable on a hill farm? Laddie, have you gone daft?'

Cam's face, marked with acne, flushed a deep, adolescent red and he knocked over his empty water glass. He was growing so fast that he never knew where his extremities were and was a danger to any small object not firmly fixed in place. 'I-I just thought . . .' he mumbled.

His sister said sarcastically, 'You see, Cam, the up-and-down bits – we call them "hills" – make ploughing just a bit difficult.'

'It's just – well, it's not very nice to kill things for a living,' Cam blurted out.

Bill seemed lost for words. Marjory, seeing her son's tortured expression, suddenly understood: this was all about the power of a pair of big brown eyes.

'You know it's not quite like that, Cammie,' she said mildly. 'There's all the caring and nurturing as well—'

'And then you kill them.' His jaw stuck out, in an almost comic imitation of his father's 'stubborn' face.

'Enjoy your chicken?' Cat put in unhelpfully.

Bill recovered his voice. 'For heaven's sake, Cammie, you've lived on a farm all your life. You know how we look after the beasts, how we give them a good life. And yes, of course they go for slaughter in the end, but people eat meat. We're carnivores.'

Marjory could hear the hurt in his voice, but Cammie wasn't listening.

'Yes, but we don't have to be,' he argued. 'We could all be vegetarian. Animals wouldn't have to die and it would be better for us. Better for the planet, too, you know. We can't go on like this.'

Cat looked at him mockingly. 'Well, well, this from the guy who likes six slices of bacon on his butty! Who have you been talking to, then?'

Bill sank back in his chair. 'That girl – what's-her-name. It's her, isn't it?'

Cammie jumped up. 'She's not "that girl". She's Zoë, and what she says makes total sense. I hoped I'd be able to find a way round it, but if there isn't one, that's it. I'm sorry, Dad, I know the whole idea was that I should go into farming with you, but I've got my own life to lead. I've made my decision and I'm not going to let you coerce me. I don't want to be a farmer. OK?'

He left the kitchen, slamming the door and leaving a stunned silence behind him. Bill looked devastated, and Marjory said urgently, 'Cat, can you go after your brother and try to talk some sense into him?'

Her daughter looked at her coolly. 'Not sure I can, really. He's realised that he's not just your puppet, that he's entitled to make up his own mind. Maybe if I'd realised when I was his age I wouldn't be in the mess I'm in now.'

She walked out too, leaving her parents staring at each other across the table in dismay. Marjory was the first to find her voice.

'It's so bloody unjust! I've never wanted Cat to be a vet – I couldn't care less! She's said that was all she wanted ever since the first time the yard cat had kittens.'

Bill was scowling. 'So I've been pressuring Cammie, have I? Funny that I've never been able to keep him away from the farm. It's just some stupid fad, because of that girl. I'm furious with the boy.'

This was the last thing Marjory needed on top of everything else. 'This is all so stupid and unnecessary,' she said wearily. 'Last night I had to watch a man die, Bill, and there was nothing I could do.'

'Want to talk about it?'

'Not really. I'd prefer not to think about it, if I could.' She finished her wine, then picked up her empty plate and glass and took them across to the dishwasher.

'I'll stack it, if you like,' Bill said, clearing the table. 'How's the rest of it going?'

Marjory sighed. 'Oh well, Elena Tindall and Cal Findlay have been charged so now we'll be under judges' rules and the media will have to lay off, which is always something. He's made a formal confession now. She certainly won't, but they've got fingerprint evidence from the staples in the cave, so if they match we're in business anyway. And the SOCOs have found blood in the trap below the drain from the bath and again, if it's Melissa Lovatt's we've got her on that too.'

'Won't they go for whatever it is you call it when someone's got mental problems?'

'Diminished responsibility? Almost certainly, I should think.' Marjory scrubbed out the casserole and set it upside down on the draining board.

'And she'll get a sympathetic jury, after all that happened to her,' Bill said.

'Ye-es.' Marjory wasn't entirely sure. 'If she'd just killed her father, and hadn't killed Melissa Lovatt as well, probably. But with the level of sadism, and the planning for thirty years for her revenge on her terrified nine-year-old twin, I'm not sure how indulgent they'll feel.'

'Do you think she was just so damaged that she can't be held responsible?'

'To some degree, of course I do. It was psychopathic behaviour, and what happened to her meant she'd had to learn to deaden her feelings, just to survive. But did she realise how terrible her crimes were? I think she did. I think she was quite coldly and clinically aware. The only thing that makes me think "psychopath" doesn't apply was her utter devastation when she accidentally killed her husband. So perhaps there was human emotion in there somewhere, even if she was cold and ruthless in every other direction.'

Bill started the dishwasher. 'Was she capable of choosing not to do those hideous things? That's what I'd want to know if I was on a jury.'

Considering it, Fleming dried the casserole and put it into the cupboard. 'I simply don't know. The amount of choice any of us have is debatable, and there could be a genetic angle there. According to Tam, her grandmother victimised her husband, and Andrew Smith's decision to sell his daughter to pay gambling debts was sick beyond belief. Perhaps it's the usual mixture of what you are and what situation you find yourself in.'

She gave an enormous yawn. 'I must get to bed. I'm out on my feet. Tomorrow's going to be stressful at work and at home. Cat's barely speaking to me, and now Cammie probably won't be speaking to you.' She paused. 'Could make for some interesting mealtimes.'

The funny side of it suddenly struck her, and she began to laugh, weakly at first, then with a sort of hysteria. After a moment he joined in.

Wiping her eyes, Marjory said, 'Oh dear! If the kids hear us, they'll think we don't care.'

'Good,' Bill said firmly. 'We need to keep a calm sough, as your mother would say. If we get drawn into their dramas it's only going to make things worse. Of course they've got their own lives to lead, but if we back off they won't make stupid decisions just to annoy their parents. If Cammie decides he's a veggie, that's his choice and I'll keep my mouth shut.'

'Of course,' Marjory agreed. 'But maybe – sausages for breakfast, do you think?' That set them off again.

'Right,' she said. 'I'm off. Can you lock up?'

'Of course, love. I'll try not to wake you when I come up.' He kissed her. 'Sleep well.'

At the door she turned. 'Don't forget to take the sausages out of the freezer,' she said, and went upstairs. From Cammie's bedroom, she could hear the low hum of voices – no doubt their parents' ears should be burning.

Perhaps, even if they chose to enact dramas when the last thing you needed was more stress, having a family was therapeutic. It gave you something else to think about, blotted out the hideous images from the day job.

But those put the family stuff into context too. Cat and Cammie, loved, treasured and fundamentally happy children, would be all right, one way or another. Even as Marjory climbed gratefully into bed, she was haunted by the thought of that poor little girl, alone on that strange island, wailing her terror out across the dark waters, the little girl who had vanished, to be replaced by Elena Tindall, cold-blooded killer. Helen Smith had been murdered by her father, as surely as if he had held a knife to her throat.

Tomorrow, though, it would be all about routine: further investigations, more reports, more statements, piles of paper as she did her duty, compiling the strongest possible evidence of the case against Elena Tindall for the procurator fiscal to present to the attorney general. As Marjory Fleming drifted into sleep, she breathed a prayer of gratitude that the decision on how to proceed wasn't hers to make.

Marianne Price scowled at herself in the mirror in the staff toilet. Black had never been her colour, and accessorised with eyes rimmed with crimson that clashed with her ginger hair wasn't a good look. She'd cried ever since she got the news about poor bloody Eddie – a good man wasted on that evil bitch. How often had he choked her off when she had tried to warn him the woman was poison? Even if she hadn't meant it literally at the time, she wasn't surprised. If he'd only listened . . .

Well, he hadn't, and that was that. She took out her make-up bag and set to with the Touche Éclat. Eddie's son was due this morning to take his place at his father's desk, running Tindall's. There'd been no love lost between Eddie and his son these last ten years, thanks to That Woman, and if Marianne was to keep her job, she had to look like she was professional, not going sogging around the place. Jobs were hard to come by these days.

With a final blow of her nose and a dusting of powder, she went through to Eddie's office to empty his desk. Mercifully, the firm should be all right, even if That Woman got off; at least Eddie hadn't been so blind to his family duties that he'd left it all to his wife.

Her photograph, a glamour shot in soft focus, was sitting on Eddie's desk, where he would see it every time he glanced up. In a sudden passion of rage, Marianne threw it to the floor and stamped on it with her stiletto heel, smashing the glass and gouging into the serene, superior face.

Then she picked it up and put it into the bin, feeling at least a little better. Rubbish where it belonged.

As suddenly as the police presence had arrived in Innellan, it departed. The church was locked up and abandoned again; all the deer had gone and Lovatt's farm was on the market. The first of the winter storms came whipping in up the Solway Firth, taking down branches and one big tree, while the villagers huddled in their houses, listening to the shutters rattle.

By the morning, it had passed over, like many another storm before it. There was damage, but nothing that couldn't be repaired and then forgotten about. Innellan was good at forgetting.

In the troubled dawn, under a purple and orange sky, the island seemed a brooding presence out there in the bay, with angry waves lashing its shores. But once the sky cleared with the day and the roar of the sea sank to a mutter, it would be ethereal in the sunlight, a symphony of greens and greys.

A prison, a grave, an idyll, a dream. All of these – or none at all, merely the stage where human tragedy had been enacted. A passing show, nothing more, set against the eternal rocks and the sea and the ever-changing sky.

ACKNOWLEDGEMENTS

My most grateful thanks go to Dr John Fletcher of Fletchers of Auchtermuchty, the first deer farm in Europe; to Major Anna Fraser, RLC; to Captain Jamie Fraser, Royal Welsh; and to Dr Nick Goldfinch, Royal (Dick) Veterinary College, Edinburgh. They were very generous in sharing their expert knowledge and such mistakes as there may be are mine alone.

LOOK OUT FOR THE NEXT GRIPPING NOVEL IN
THE DI MARJORY FLEMING SERIES . . .

BAD BLOOD

It can be hard beating your brain to dredge up something
you've forgotten. But how would it be if you couldn't
forget anything – ever? Except, of course, the one thing you
desperately want to know: why, at the age of eleven, you had
been found alone in an isolated cottage, with a head injury
and your mother gone? And why had the police investigation
been so strangely low-key?

Twenty years later, Marnie, a victim of hyperthymesia, is
asking questions, hoping that the answers may break the loop
that runs constantly in her mind of that last day before her
life fell apart. And she's looking for a woman who was a
young police officer then who might be able to tell her what
she needs to know . . .